Red Rain

Red Rain

BRUCE MURKOFF

ALFRED A. KNOPF · NEW YORK
2010

THIS IS A BORZOI BOOK
PUBLISHED BY ALFRED A. KNOPF

Copyright © 2010 by Bruce Murkoff
All rights reserved. Published in the United States by Alfred A. Knopf,
a division of Random House, Inc., New York, and in Canada
by Random House of Canada Limited, Toronto.
www.aaknopf.com

Knopf, Borzoi Books, and the colophon are
registered trademarks of Random House, Inc.

Library of Congress Cataloging-in-Publication Data
Murkoff, Bruce, date.
Red rain / Bruce Murkoff. — 1st ed.
p. cm
ISBN 978-0-307-27207-2
1. City and town life—Hudson River Valley (N.Y. and N.J.)—Fiction.
2. Hudson River Valley (N.Y. and N.J.)—Fiction.
3. New York (State)—History—Civil War,
1861–1865—Social aspects—Fiction. I. Title.
PS3613.U695R43 2010
813'.6—dc22   2009041692

Manufactured in the United States of America
First Edition

For Suzanne

The lepidopterous insects in general, soon after they emerge from the pupa state, and commonly during their first flight, discharge some drops of red-colored fluid, more or less intense in different species, which, in some instances, where their numbers have been considerable, have produced the appearance of a "shower of blood," as this natural phenomenon is sometimes called.

Showers of blood have been recorded by historians and poets as preternatural—have been considered in the light of prodigies, and regarded, where they have happened, as fearful prognostics of impending evil.

—Frank Cowan, *Curious Facts in the History of Insects*

The world is a bad dog. It will bite you if you give it a chance.

—Joseph Conrad, *Victory*

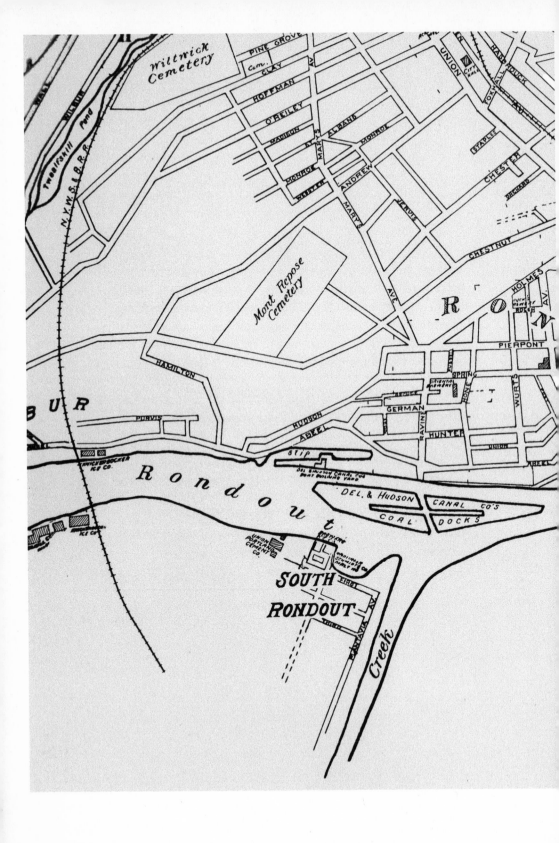

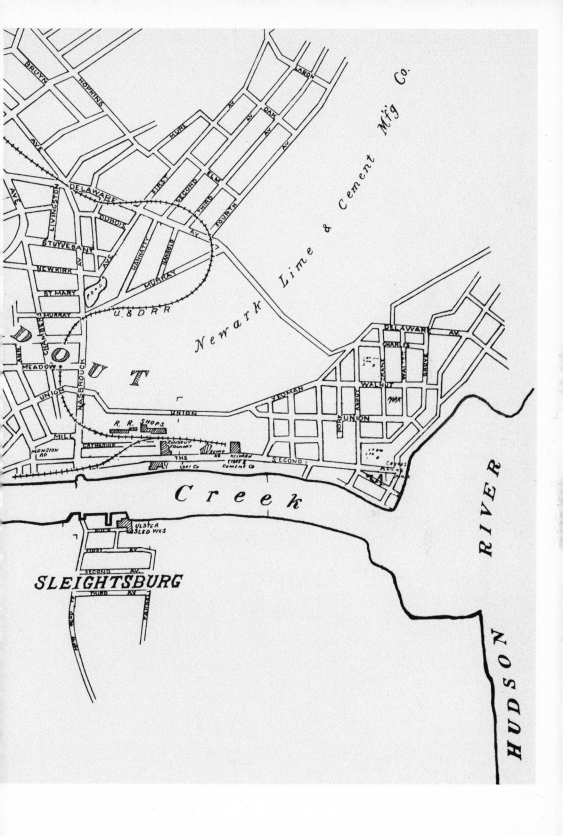

June 1864

WILL HARP stood at the bow of the *Ella May* and drank deeply from the medicine bottle he held in his hand, tilting his head back to enjoy the sudden warmth blossoming behind his eyes, swallowing greedily as a fledgling, not at all interested in the artificial health benefits of the syrup. He cared only about immediate results, letting the alcohol numb pain, thought and his too-quick senses.

He'd been awake and on deck for hours, ever since the sloop passed Breakneck Ridge just north of Cold Spring. The midnight air had been clear and crisp, and beyond the town of Beacon the hills unfurled like a crimped back ribbon against a taut sheet of starry sky. The Hudson was wide and flat here, the riffles upriver cut into a million refracted pieces that swooned across its surface. Now, as the sky began to lighten, the stars faded away and the moon moved eastward. Standing alone at the bow, he listened to the passengers below, the soft notes of their snores and moans, the muffled babble of their contented sleep.

Earlier that evening, a bearded man had introduced himself as Alexander Lowe, manufacturer of the nation's greatest herbal remedy. He was sailing north with his brother and two investors, who'd already boarded the *Ella May* when Will arrived at the pier on Christopher Street. He'd previously booked passage on the steamboat *Chauncey Vibbard*, but at the Forty-second Street dock a long line of wounded Union soldiers was waiting to board, limbless or in litters, on crutches or with chests and heads bandaged. They were going home, and there was solace in that, those who could climbing the ramp of the steamboat as if in a solemn procession entering church. Not eager to travel with such stoic, soul-bitten men, Will walked south on Tenth Avenue and bought a ticket on the *Ella May* instead.

The medicine drummers were sitting on crates of Lowe's tonic and drinking beer poured from the keg a cabin boy had rolled over from a Barrow Street saloon, and they asked Will to join them. Although he wasn't looking for company, he sat in the shade and drank their beer, already warm and foamy and tasting like it had been brewed with old coins.

Lowe handed him an advertising card—*Lowe's American Tonic: three drops a day for the good of body and mind*—and a small amber bottle from the open crate at his feet. "I guarantee a daily dose," he boasted, "will bring an end to imperfect sleep, physical pain and debilities both general and specific."

Will examined the bottle, whose label featured three healthy-looking women in clinging wet dresses, holding hands and dancing barefoot through silver puddles. The banner below them proclaimed AS NATURAL AS RAIN. The back label listed the many ailments this tonic cured, including headaches, earaches, toothaches, moodiness, thoughts of irresponsibility and quinsy.

At Lowe's urging, Will removed the cork and sniffed the concoction, the heady vapors releasing a punch of cloves and bitter orange.

He laughed. "It's not an inhalant, Mr. Harp. You must savor it."

Will took a sip. The liquid was lighter than syrup but painted his tongue with a greasy slip that almost gagged him. When he swallowed, the alcohol preserving the herbal ingredients burned a path down to his belly and filled his eyes with tears.

Through the blur he noticed the one other passenger on board, a young Negro woman sitting on a plank near the stern. She looked close to seventeen and was just about to grow out of her tight brown dress, likely starched and ironed for special occasions and worn fifty-two Sundays a year for as long as the coarse fabric would allow, the seams restitched as flesh and bone demanded. From the burlap sack on her lap she pulled out broken pieces of bread or cake, which she nibbled on much like some men chewed tobacco. She sat alone and watched the white men with suspicion, letting the crumbs fall from her mouth, where they gathered on her lap and around her feet like a whittler's shavings.

Will blinked, then washed away the bitter taste of the medicine with beer as the merchant paced in front of him.

"I stand by it, sir," Lowe continued. "I've used it myself for the last five years, and I haven't suffered a single cough or sniffle. My baby boy was suckled on diluted droplets from the day he first opened his mouth to cry, and now he's the most cheerful, stoutest lad in all of Gramercy Park. My own wife, as skeptical as Plato himself, ignored the curative powers of my tonic for years, until she entered a spell of female nervousness. And after only three weeks of daily consumption, her footsteps were no longer feeble, her cheeks shone pink with well-being and she was freed from the ignominies of her more delicate sex."

A large man, Lowe flailed his arms as he spoke, each oversized gesture threatening to shoot off one of the buttons that fastened his tight black coat. The top of his head was bald, all follicular energy contained in the wild nest of dark sideburns that ran down his cheek. His voice was loud and assured, more bullying than true, but he was a salesman and truth was hardly what he was after.

"We've been quite successful with our remedy, Mr. Harp," he continued. "P. T. Barnum himself allowed us to advertise on the great curtain at the American Museum when General Tom Thumb and his wife were onstage to entertain the Prince of Wales. Isn't that right, James?"

Lowe turned to his brother, whose face was cheery with drink. Until that moment he had seemed content in a fuzzy doze, but when Lowe called his name, it was like a cue from the wings and he sprang upright as a marionette.

"Yes, yes, yes, as right as the sun in your eyes," James declared in a voice just as loud and robust. "Mr. Barnum himself, dapper soul and gentleman. As true a prince as the one from Wales." He waved a finger in front of his own face while taking great slurps from his glass of beer. "No, sir, a king!" He wiped his lips and fixed his eyes on Will's high boots. "May I ask you, Mr. Harp, where you acquired those excellent boots?"

"From a bootmaker in San Antonio," Will replied.

"Texas?"

"That's right."

"A man of the West!" Lowe's brother exclaimed, almost falling off the crate he was perched on.

IT WAS STILL dark when he walked naked past Duck Pond and started out across the meadow, following the deerworn path to the water and keeping clear of the prickly rose and raspberry thorns. The wild rice was as high as his knees and left damp slashes across his legs. He'd left his clothes behind the brickyard and now was cold, so he picked up his pace through the marsh grass and flinched only when a flock of plover spun from their mating beds and burst like scattershot above him.

He could see the outline of the schooner along the far bank of the river, just south of the bend leading to Kipp Cove. The *Pinetop*'s skipper, Jacob Rust, had left the Rondout wharf at midnight, buoyed by the land breezes off the Catskills, and anchored off the cove to wait for daybreak and high water. The small boat, no more than sixty-five feet long, carried a light on her bow, and in the penumbral haze Mickey Blessing could see early-season hay piled high across her deck and hear the bleating of the twenty sheep that rubbed together in the small pen near the wheel. Rust had rerigged this old schooner with the help of his brother-in-law, Joseph Ripley, a shipbuilder in Low Point, who'd trimmed her white-oak plankings and timbers when she was first launched from the same yard in 1842. Battered and graceless now, with bagging canvas sails he couldn't afford to replace, she still rode fat and sturdy, running twice a month from Rondout to the Manhattan harbor.

Mickey stepped into the river and watched the black ridges of water push away from his ankles. The river was cold, fed by snowdriven rivulets that ran through the Catskill gorges, past Peekamoose and Table Mountain, past Hemlock and Panther Mountain, forming the named and unnamed streams that dribbled through the high blue peaks and gathered strength before flowing thick and strong and icy into the Hudson.

It seemed to Mickey that he was always standing in water. Although he remembered little of his Irish childhood, he'd cobbled the story of his young life together from his mother's idyllic sketches and the vagaries of family lore. About the meager farm on the outskirts of Newtownbarry, where he'd pretend to swim in the green waters of the stone trough while thirsty calves bleated and stamped their cloven hooves, where he'd stand waist-deep in the River Slaney while his father fished for sea trout, where he'd disappear out of the corner of his mother's eye to scamper about in the muddy ravines that creased the foothills of the Blackstairs Mountains, or escape his sister's lazy care to float on his back in a seasonal pond never more than three feet deep. He was quicker than a dowsing stick at finding water and quicker still to jump in, and when he came home soaked and shivering, his matted hair the color of wet leaves, his mother would laugh and take him in her arms to dry his frozen bones. Those were the good days, before misery and famine reached their village and blackened land and spirit, days he didn't choose to recall at all, instead living carefree and innocent in the stories he'd heard long ago. But he still remembered the constabulary coming to take his father to Cat's Fort prison for stealing a horse and feeding it to his children, fighting and crying until a block of wood was brought down upon his skull. And he remembered visiting his mother as she lay down in sickness in the women's ward at Beaumont Hospital, her fingers shaking and splayed, a victim of poverty and fever. And being packed onto a crowded oxcart by his uncle Joe Devlin, three boiled eggs in one hand and his older sister, Jane's, gripping the other, and the great push of people as he and Jane clung to their uncle and boarded the big stinkboat *Virginus* at the Dublin quay. Those were things he'd never forget.

He silently walked forward until the water cupped his testicles, then pushed out and let his body glide across the surface. When fully extended, he thrust out his arms and began to swim, keeping his head up and his eyes focused on the *Pinetop*. Halfway across the river, he could already see Jinks pacing back and forth at the stern, his movements jerky and impatient, and knew the little man was no longer drunk, all that rum and beer having been pissed over the side after Jacob Rust left the Rondout dock five hours before. The cocky nerve he'd shown all afternoon was gone, leaving him just anxious and scared.

They'd spent that entire day drinking together at Natterjack's saloon on Division Street, Mickey allowing himself only two glasses of ale and paying for whatever Jinks wanted with the money he'd been given for that very purpose.

Jinks had come to Rondout the year before, migrating from Little Falls, in Herkimer County, where he'd lived his whole life and worked at the Cheney hammer factory on the Mohawk River, running a belt-driven lathe that turned hard planks of white cedar into handles as smooth as ivory. He drank then, too, most evenings and every Sunday, but not enough to interfere with his job or an existence defined by pennies saved and pennies spent. Knowing he was weak, he married a woman even weaker, and they lived in a one-room shack on the road to Top Notch, their side yard rich with chickenshit and decay. She died at sixteen when giving birth to their only son, Tommy, who, when he turned sixteen, ran away, unwilling to claim this grievous inheritance, and joined the Ninety-seventh Volunteer Infantry at Camp Schuyler. Four weeks later, in early August 1862, fighting with Pope's army at Cedar Mountain, Virginia, he died in his first afternoon of warfare, stomped to death by a gutshot horse as Union troops battled Jackson's foot cavalry on the Culpepper road.

Jinks then took to drinking even more, and after he lost his job with

Cheney's, and the paper mills and starch factory refused to hire him, he drifted along the Erie and Delaware canals, working just hard enough to make whiskey money, a friend to tavernkeepers from Ilion to Eddyville, now working for Jacob Rust for the past six months, long enough for Mickey to know that he was the one.

At noon they'd left Natterjack's and walked across Division Street, the wide expanse of dirt road permanently etched by the constant flow of immigrant labor and agrarian trade that came to the docks of Rondout Creek. Mickey slowed down for Jinks and watched six wagons come up from the wharves, their beds piled high with stiff cowhides from faraway ports like Puerto Descado and Belém, the skins carried up the Atlantic coast from South America on magnificent vessels with names like *Comodoro Rivadavia* and *Padre Paulo*, heading back to the tanneries in Prattsville and Shandaken, where they'd be sweated and pounded and turned into boot soles for the Union army. When he was younger, Mickey had worked for the Simpson tannery in Phoenicia, years of hard labor reeking of peeled bark and thick smoke and putrid hides that he remembered fondly. They ended when he turned eighteen and took a shovel to the foreman for back wages never received. For six months he hid in deserted camps and berry pickers' cabins in the hills above the Stoney Clove Road, but when fall came, he was captured digging potatoes out of the cold ground behind the Curtis farm and sent to prison. That was five years ago, when he was just a boy and not the workingman he was now, a citizen of this fractured world.

He kept an eye on Jinks and listened to people's accents as they passed, the Irish and German immigrants who inhabited the stick-and-brick buildings of Rondout's slum. They stopped first at Tom Leonard's so Jinks could have his seventh glass of ale, and when they got to the bottom of the hill, they stopped for another at Pat Carley's, a dismal shack of oily wood that was always crowded with bargemen and drifters. Carley said there were more Irishmen drinking here than in the small tavern he once owned by Nimmo's Pier in Galway, and he was glad for it.

Mickey knew that Jinks was stalling, but he let him have a second glass of rum. Sitting at a small table by the door, he went over the simple plan once more while the little man's eyes were still shiny. "You just take your orders from Jacob Rust and be on deck in the morning."

"I won't have to do no more?"

"That's right."

"Just do what I do for old Jacob, and you'll do the rest?"

"I'll do everything, Jinks." Mickey smiled to ease the man's wariness. All he had to do was drop the rope and sound the alarm, and in the end he'd be cheered for his quickness and bravery, the talk of the town. "You won't have to buy a drink for a month."

At this lovely thought, Jinks smiled and finished his rum.

He'd been swimming this river for the past fifteen years, from freeze to thaw, and knew the rhythm of its tides and all its peculiarities as well as any captain between Troy and the Brooklyn boatyard. He was familiar with its muddy warmth and could tell when a storm was coming by surface tremors and wind-driven pops on the water, as obvious as the prickling of his own skin. When arriving in America with his sister and his uncle, they'd endured six years in the slums of Manhattan, the children raising chickens outside their pine shack on Dutch Hill while Joe labored in the stone quarries off First Avenue. Mickey first swam through the marshy waters of Turtle Bay, floating on his back with his eyes closed, letting the stench of dying reeds fill his nostrils, as thick and moist as the aroma of warm bread his empty belly ached for. It was the river that made him feel at home, the river that saved him.

Mickey cut long, silent strokes around both sides of the boat, making sure nobody but Jinks was topside. He could hear the sheep moving on deck, their hooves slipping on the unfamiliar planking, their tremulous bleating sharp in the morning air. Rust always anchored away from the harbor so his small crew wouldn't be lured by the saloons and prostitutes that made Rondout so popular. He would wait here for the morning tide to lift and carry the *Pinetop* south toward the Highlands, the first leg of his trip. Almost seventy, he'd been shipping produce and livestock out of Rondout for fifty years, a stern captain, neither timid nor foolhardy, who knew when to wait out the west wind in the hellish narrows of Martyr's Reach, and when to ride the turbulent ridge-backed water into the broad silvery flange of Newburgh Bay, never once losing a crock of honey or a bale of hay in the harrowing storms that sometimes blew down the Hudson at summer's end. He demanded much from his crew but paid good wages, and although never popular, he was always admired. Mickey often saw him walking to St. Mary's with his wife, both of them stiff-backed and dour, he rail-thin and she bloated at the waist. Childless, they gave money for civic causes and the upkeep of the Franciscan Brothers' school next door, where the bored offspring of Irish laborers often gathered in the weedy churchyard, just waiting for the chance to singsong "Fat and lean, fat and lean, she's so big and he's so mean" as the Rusts smiled back at them in near-deaf oblivion.

Mickey saw the hemp rope dangling off the stern and grabbed it, then pulled himself up hand over hand, careful not to let his feet bounce off the transom. The early-morning air chilled his body like a rasp being drawn quickly across his skin. He swung up to the sternpost and landed on the deck, six feet behind Jinks, who turned and stumbled backward against the rail. This was the response that Mickey wanted, to be standing there naked and dripping, his body sparkling in the white light of the lantern while the old boy was shocked into silence and cowed by his dominant stare. Mickey knew they'd have to move quickly, before Jinks was overcome by self-reproach in a rare moment of clarity when liquor forfeited its chummy appeal. The sheep in the forward pen milled around in a tight pack, humped together and sliding in their own thin dribbles of waste, alert to movement on deck. Men were snoring in the forward cabin, and he could hear the soft slap of river water along the stern. He picked up the dry bundle of straw that Jinks had tied together but refused to carry, held it up to the lantern flame until it ignited, then ran it along the bottom of the mainsail and waited for the canvas to explode.

The fire roared up the old sail so fast that he barely had enough time to turn away before the skin along his right side felt like it was being peeled from the bone. He watched Jinks push through the terrified sheep and grab hold of the wheel, then pitch his body forward into the open cabin door and yell, "Fire! Fire!"

He turned to Mickey and tried to smile, but his lips were curled in uncertainty and his eyes still as unclear as the smoke rising from the stacks of hay. Mickey knew that if he'd kindly and firmly called "Come!" then Jinks would've run up behind him as submissive as a puppy and followed him right over the rail, but there was no time for second thoughts. So he dragged him to the stern and carried him overboard instead, holding him in his arms and taking a deep breath as they hit the water, making his body slim as a dagger and allowing the two of them to slide quickly into the black depths of the river, Jinks struggling more fervently the deeper they went, Mickey merely tightening his embrace and waiting for him to die.

He swam easily to shore, resting on the Rondout Meadow. The schooner was ablaze from foremast to stern, and he could hear the splash of men and sheep and the cries of distress above the crackling wood. The brightness on the water was stunning in the gray morning, and he watched until the burning boat broke in two and the bowsprit stood straight up in the air, wrapped in a cloak of flame. He stood to examine the long scratches from Jinks's ragged fingernails, from rib cage to pelvis, and wiped away the pinkish blood that trickled into his pubic hair, then walked quickly through the open meadow before the sun rose and sleepy eyes would open to the wonders of his deed.

She was waiting in the buckboard where she had said she'd be, at the side of the plank road, and he didn't try to cover himself as he grabbed the bundle of clothes she'd placed behind the seat. She refused to look at him and kept her eyes straight ahead, holding the reins tight in her hand and keeping the two horses still as they sniffed the wisps of smoke wafting off the water. The air had dried him, but he had to dab a stitch of blood with the tail of his shirt before putting it on. He dressed slowly, enjoying the slight erection that seemed to flourish in the crisp air before he buttoned up his pants, then climbed onto the wagon and looked up at the white line of daylight over the peaks to his west.

She turned and slapped him hard across the face, which he accepted because she was his sister, Jane, and also his partner.

～◎～

WILL HARP had left Los Angeles nearly twelve weeks before, traveling by horseback along a southerly route to avoid late-spring snows in the mountains, following the Gila River through the New Mexico Territory to its headwaters in the highlands west of Valverde, riding north past Fort Craig and keeping the Rio Grande in sight as he made his way into Santa Fe. He followed one whiskey with another at La Fonda and strolled through the portals of the Palace of the Governors, where less than two years before Sibley's men had run up the Confederate flag, only to see Canby's Regulars yank it down just a few weeks later when they took back the town and chased the rebels south toward Albuquerque, where they scattered like rabbits into the vapors of the Chihuahuan Desert.

He rode out of Santa Fe after a few days, picking up the old Cimarron Cutoff on the other side of the Mora River, and over the next week he watched out for roving bands of Kiowas and stayed clear of the army supply wagons running between Forts Fillmore and Bliss, deep in Apache country. He rode mostly at night, never lighting a fire, looking for any dust storms that might indicate movement in the far-flung valleys, and if he spotted one, he'd hold up until the sky was clear again before continuing his nighttime journey, accompanied only by his moonstruck shadow. He heard the crinkling of leatherweed and creosote as his horse's hooves found the hard earth, and the whoosh of pronghorn antelope prancing away in the darkness; he saw the silhouettes of cactus wren and killdeer flicker across the black sky and, when morning came, the bronzing horizon as the sun slowly rose through bands of red and orange and gold in the paintbox sky.

During the day he rested, either under a protective ledge in the canyonlands or in the sparse juniper forests at the verge of the shortgrass prairie that rolled out almost as far as the Arkansas River. Sometimes he read his shabby copy of Paley's *Natural Theology*, its idealistic, benevolent version of God's creation still intriguing him as much as Darwin's more rationalist account of a violent universe. Or he might take out his notebook and sketch the tumbledown canyons around him, or the fearsome pose of the short-horned lizards that basked in the sun and hunted for ants in patches of bunchgrass, drinking all the while from a flask until it was time to ride again, when the sky turned gray and the world around him was dull and safe.

He traveled on like this, warily, until he met up with a small wagon train just south of the Smoky Hill River. There were five men and three wagons coming out of Boggsville, Colorado, heading east to trade two dozen Mexican cows for sacks of sugar and flour, good-natured cattlemen who'd made peace with the Cheyenne and married their women. They were vigilant and quick to laugh, and Will fell in easily with them, slowing his pace to travel along as far as the City of Kansas, where he left them at the river crossing and rode across Missouri to St. Louis.

Will had first seen the city in 1851, when he left New York to join Captain Sitgreaves on his western expedition to California. Coming over the flattened hills on the Illinois border, he'd seen a creeping layer of black smoke in the sky and was certain the distant city was ablaze. It wasn't until he got to the top of the last rise and gazed across the Mississippi that he realized the foul air was caused by the dozens of steamboats on the great river, their coal stacks trailing fumes like blown-out candles. Even then he was surprised by the city's size, the bustling market houses that lined the docks, so soot-grimed they looked as though they'd been constructed of burnt wood, and beyond them the elegant brick houses on wide tree-lined streets.

Will took a room at the Planter's House Hotel, where he'd stayed thirteen years before, and bathed indoors for the first time in over a month. He treated himself to a generous supper in the dining room downstairs: a small carp prepared "in the German style," wrapped in slices of larding pork and baked with onions, followed by breast of prairie chicken with currant jelly and bread sauce, and a dish of asparagus tips princesse. The European conceit that gave the menu its pedigree amused him, and he finished his dinner with a plate of "fancy cheese," which went down nicely with the strong Madeira that accompanied it. Despite its worldly pretensions, it was a good meal and a welcome departure from the dried beef and occasional rabbit he'd been living on since parting company with the cattlemen and following the Missouri east.

When he finally stood up from the table and settled his bill, it was full dark. He left the hotel and walked toward the river, where steamboats still crowded the docks as tightly as horses tied to a corral. Even at this hour the waterfront was chaotic, and he stayed close to the buildings as mule-drawn wagons fought for space on the cobblestones, their wooden frames bulging with pig iron and hay bales and boxes of musket cartridges from the local arsenàl. The wagons passed one another wheel-to-wheel, and the mule teams pulling them were lathered and frenzy-eyed as drivers stood on their seats and snapped whips like charioteers. All along the levee, foremen shouted orders and were answered by the immigrant curses of the men working for them, this trumpeting of voices competing with braying mules and ringing bells as provisions were wheeled up gangplanks into steamboats bobbing three abreast in the heaving river. Will walked to the wharf at the foot of Locust Street, where a boat was being loaded with Confederate prisoners headed upriver to the military prison in Alton. As he watched the motley procession, a Union soldier kicked a shackled man off the wharf into the river. Will saw him go under, his arms spinning in the dark water, his face coming up twice before the weight of his irons drowned him. The commotion on the docks was so great that the cries for help and the booming laughter of the soldiers floated up from the Mississippi with the stink of coal and dead fish. Will's head ached with it, and he turned away and walked back to his hotel.

The next morning he took the ferry across the river and caught the early train from Illinoistown to Cincinnati, the prairie speeding by in a golden blur. The clouds overhead were long and slender, like fingers grasping from east and west. Outside of Vandalia, as they crossed the steel bridge over the Kalkaska River, he saw a trio of flatboats floating downriver, packed tight with black-and-white cattle that were calm as gentlemen. A boy jumped up on the lead animals, balancing on their backs like he was riding a logjam, and waved furiously at the passing train. The engineer blew his whistle and the boy did a little jig, turning with the train as it flew by, dancing until the flatboat disappeared under the bridge.

When the train finally pulled into Cincinnati, it was a day later. The station where he switched connections to Pittsburgh had as many spurs as the back of his hand had veins. This train was more comfortable, the seats upholstered in velvet and the wooden cars adorned with gilded rosettes. And as they pushed through Pennsylvania, making stops at Harrisburg and Lancaster, the coaches became more crowded and single women had the temerity to board alone. The train rattled on, filling with the scent of tobacco and lavender soap, and the talk among passengers became lively and robust. Opinions were loudly proclaimed, as if the vitality of their great society gave men the confidence to rejoice. Will had forgotten about this aspect of city life, the flamboyance with which good fortune was displayed. And as the train pulled into Philadelphia, his last stop before New York, he found a strange comfort in the noise and substance of the enveloping city. It was the hum of urban life, and he suddenly realized that he'd missed it. It was so different from what he had become used to, that desert whisper of the West that begged only for passive reflection. He was back where life was outspoken and lived on the tip of the tongue.

Will was still standing at the bow of the *Ella May* when morning broke over the Hudson. He drank from another bottle of Lowe's medicine, no longer wincing with each sip, thankful for the burn of it as a stiff breeze rolled off the Catskills. He was glad when midnight had come and his traveling companions had finally gone to their bunks below, beer-drunk and thickheaded, their movements almost graceful as they walked across the deck, swaying with the toss of the waves. He stayed on deck all night, he and the young Negro woman, who sat on her stern plank and watched him like an owl, the burlap sack clutched to her lap like the queen's jewels. Earlier that evening she'd pulled boiled chicken legs and fresh tomatoes from the sack, tossing the cleaned bones overboard and wiping her hands on the towel they'd been wrapped in, then sucked on a piece of hard candy and closed her eyes. Will slept only a few hours, not deeply, aware of the sloop passing beneath the great expanse of the Palisades, which seemed to stretch forever along the eastern shore.

For the last hour he'd been standing at the rail as the river began to straighten and widen, lying before him like some colossal snake, its surface made scaly by the wind. As the sloop passed the Morse estate just south of Poughkeepsie, the landscape began to look slightly familiar, like a memory just out of reach, and near the Rondout lighthouse this thought became so discomforting that he averted his gaze from what was at once recognizable and strange.

He tossed the empty tonic bottle over the side, reached into the crate for another one and bent over to pull out the cork with his teeth. When he turned back to the approaching shoreline, he saw a ship burning just beyond the harbor, its smoldering light like a star that had fallen on the water.

⟋◎⟍

JANE WAITED in the wide hallway outside Harry Grieves's office. In a corner by the window were a chair and a table, and from here, on the fourth floor, she could see down Division Street all the way to Rondout Creek, where dust rose from the brickyards and black smoke stained the sky above the tall chimneys over the cement works, all signs of the thriving industry that helped pay for the Grieves Building and the other establishments he owned here and in the countryside. The whole town knew he had a stake in everything in sight from his office in this ornate brick and bluestone structure he'd named for himself, and if you were in business in Kingston or Rondout and didn't owe him money, then you wouldn't be in business for long.

At the other end of the hallway was his life-size portrait. Local artist Jervis McEntee was best known for his paintings of the natural world, specifically the drama of autumnal landscapes in the mountains high above the Hudson, but he'd accepted this commission to help finance a trip to explore the museums of Europe. Jane was always surprised at how well he'd captured Grieves, having positioned him in front of a tall window, with his left hand on a mahogany table, fingers arched lightly over the surface as if he had caught something there, and his right hand firmly planted on his hip to protect the money thrust deep into his pocket. Through the window was a misty view of the Catskills, the dense foliage a blur of green through which a high waterfall flowed liked molten silver, and although no such view could be had from this room, the artist would not be denied the spectacularly imagined vistas for which he was famous. In the painting, Grieves's body was twisted slightly, while he looked straight ahead. He was a healthy man in his early sixties, with a balding head and dark beard worn without mustache, and a soft spread of belly that implied a rich diet. For the portrait he sported a long black frock coat over a high notched-collar vest that had become popular a few years earlier, but his cravat was still wide and as elaborately tied as an Episcopal minister's. He posed with his head up and his eyes focused outward, looking not at the artist but above him, and that's what Jane found most remarkable about the painting: that McEntee had caught his ability to look beyond what was right before him and concentrate on whatever lay ahead. This tenacity was crucial to his many accomplishments, and his rivals could only stand aside and blink shortsightedly as he stepped into the frays they were too timid to risk.

She heard a loud voice she didn't recognize from behind the thick oak door, and then Grieves's own firmer voice rising in reply, this frenzied back-and-forth booming through the walls. Resigned to wait, she pulled a letter out of her bag and carefully opened it. The folds in the paper were so worn and fragile that some of the words written along them had faded into ghostly reminders of what had once been there but which by now were known by heart. She read the letter, as she had at least once every day since it arrived last month, to remind herself that he'd been alive not long ago, and remained so, at least in these observations he'd committed to paper.

Dear Jane,

We are deep in Virginia, marching south every day. Grant's in charge now and we're the better for it. We push on without looking back, and all along the road is the stuff of battles fought before us, old fieldworks and rusted canteens and pieces of blue cloth stuck in brush and brier. The army around me seems to stretch a mile in every direction, and Lee must feel our breath hot on his neck.

Our division is under the command of General Birney, Alabama-born but stiff as New England pudding. One of the boys says he's expressionless as Dutch cheese, and another says his beard is the color of a smokehouse ham, and we all agree he'd make a far better meal than a general. He's a small man, compact in body and wee with praise, and the best I can say for him is that he knows how to sit a horse. We content ourselves that we march for Grant and Lincoln and let Birney prance before us like a banty rooster.

We are fast at Lee's heels but just can't seem to flank him. The rebel army stays ahead of us. We march, dig trenches and raise our rifles at one another across empty fields. Sometimes the bullets seem thick enough to block out sunlight, so many rifles discharging at once that I've seen the woods behind me set afire. But I'm luckier than most. Before we left Brandy Station I made enough money playing poker to buy myself a Spencer rifle, so maybe now I'll be able to fire fast enough to save my life.

This month of May, Lee's army waits to fight us at every creek and bend. The dead lie everywhere. Inside a rebel trench the bodies were piled so high that all we could do to bury them was collapse the ramparts and say a prayer. On the banks of the Anna River I saw men and horses in a deep gorge, blue coats and gray both, the ooze and blood just one great slurry. During the battle at Haw's Shop, I heard John Plummer from Saugerties had his middle taken out by a cannonball and his arms and legs spun away like thrown sticks. I didn't witness the occurrence myself but never saw him again, either.

Last week I ripped out a map of Virginia from a Harper's Weekly I found in camp. I can pretty much tell where we are and where we are going, and I bet we chase Lee all the way to Richmond. Grant says that if we catch him, we can be done with this war by summer's end, so we fight our battles like madmen and hope his hunch is true. Because I want to be back in Rondout in September and marry you when the leaves are bright.

I'll warn you again to keep a sharp eye on Harry Grieves and a sharper one on Mickey. They are not the best of men, but we do what we can in troublesome times.

It is morning now and rained last night, and after it stopped the air stayed hot and damp and I woke up smelling like something dug out of the rotting ground. We are camped on the edge of a ruined farm outside Bethesda Church, getting ready to march again. We'll be laying down lines at Cold Harbor, but I'll get home soon.

Your Frank

It was Cold Harbor that stopped her heart. The newspapers were full of stories of Grant's defeat there, and of the thousands of soldiers who had perished on the Virginia battlefields. Although she hadn't heard from Frank again, she did believe he had survived, simply because he owed it to her to do so. This was the bittersweet bargain they'd struck before he sailed down the Hudson to join up with the Ulster Volunteers, and she'd upheld her end of it. With the help of her brother, she'd taken over Frank's job with Grieves, leaving Frank free to fight.

Like most of the Irishmen who worked on the canal boats in Rondout Creek, Frank Quinn was a splendid brawler. But unlike most of them, he could read and write, and those were the qualities that had attracted Grieves's notice. When taking Frank on almost two years ago, he had demanded that he use his wits and the more respectable methods of unspoken threat and menace to get his way—not the imprint of his celebrated knuckles. It was like cutting the long hair from Samson's head, but Frank did as he was asked. He wore clean clothes, kept his manners in check and allowed the ferocity of his reputation to sway the minds of those he approached for payment. He did it because the employment was steady, the respect a tonic and Grieves provided a small house near the Lutheran church on Spring Street. But it didn't take long for Frank to miss the sporting side of brash encounters, and his lust for a good fight led him to the Army of the Potomac. Jane loved him nonetheless, and wanted him back.

The office door swung open and Grieves stepped boldly into the hallway, followed by his assistant, Mr. Simpson, and a farmer Jane recognized as Peter Vandeman. Still angry, his cheeks blazing beneath the bristle of his beard, Vandeman leaned on a hickory cane that he stamped down every time he moved his foot. He was a short, stringy man, whose elbows poked out as he ranted, "You're offering me less than I paid that thief Bogardus!"

"I'm offering you what it's worth," Grieves replied, calm as a Sunday-school teacher.

"That land's worth more than twelve hundred dollars!"

"Not to me."

"Then I ain't selling it to you, goddammit!" Vandeman spat out harshly. "I ain't selling you a blasted acre!"

Grieves barely looked at him. "The value of land is always in flux, and prices go down more easily than they go up. It's the buyer who regulates the market. Remember that, Mr. Vandeman."

"Up and down is my life affliction, Mr. Grieves," Vandeman sputtered.

"It's a fair offer."

"Fair to your pocket, maybe, but not mine."

"It's a serious offer."

"Then how come I'm laughing?" Vandeman replied, his voice hideously shrill.

Grieves only smiled. "We'll talk again."

"Not today, goddammit!" Vandeman replied as he stalked away. "No more talk today!"

Jane rose from her chair, refolded the letter and gently put it back in her bag.

Grieves ignored the clomp of the farmer's boots and walked to the window, pulled apart the curtains and looked south toward Rondout Creek, where his wharf was crowded with sailing ships. He raised his chin and squinted in the sunlight that streamed across his face like goodness. "Mr. Simpson?"

"Yes, Mr. Grieves?"

"I want you to pay Captain Rust a visit this morning. Let him know that though his prospects are slightly less today than they were last week, I won't abandon him. I will gladly take over any contracts he has outstanding and make good on the material losses he suffered, but not on his vessel." He stepped back into the shadows but kept his eye on the wharf. "That opportunity is no longer practical."

Grieves was not a tall man, and though Simpson was inch for inch his equal, he stood there like a cowed wife. "Of course, Mr. Grieves."

"And tell Captain Rust that the same offer I made him a month ago still stands." Grieves allowed himself a smile. "The only difference is that he'll now captain one of my boats instead of his own."

Simpson waited a moment longer to make sure his boss was through with him, and barely glanced at Jane as he brushed by, close enough for her to smell the fresh sweat that dampened his skin, which always looked as if it had been carved from wax and molded by thumbs. "When I'm dead and dying," Frank once told her, "and it's my time to be taken over to the other side, I'm certain that my escort beyond the grave will look a lot like Mr. Simpson."

Jane and Grieves stood alone in the wide hallway outside his office. She could hear him breathing deeply as he looked over the town below him. "I could smell the burning wood when I awoke this morning, and I knew that Mickey must have plucked a wild hair," he said with a rush of elation. "When I walked to my window in my bare feet and gazed east to the river, the dawn was absolutely bright with his handiwork." He turned to face her for the first time, his lips hooked in a wide smile. "It's bad business we sometimes practice, but business nonetheless." He fixed her with a stare of simple pleasure. "But you know that, don't you, Miss Blessing?"

"It's why I'm here this morning, Mr. Grieves. I'd like to be paid."

He watched her with amusement. "You Blessings are quite the pair." He chuckled softly.

"We're brother and sister," Jane replied. "Hardly a pair."

"You're a pair all right. Be certain of that." Grieves reached in his pocket to retrieve an envelope and stepped toward her, his eyes never leaving her face. "Stubbornness is not always a virtue, Miss Blessing. But it holds rewards for those who know its worth."

"Are you referring to yourself, Mr. Grieves?"

"To the both of us."

When he handed her the envelope, she could feel the weight of paper money inside, then withdrew her hands, put the envelope next to the thinner one already in her woolen bag and walked away.

"Miss Blessing?"

She stopped but didn't turn around.

"Tell Mickey I'd like to see him."

⌇

COLEY HINDS pulled himself to the edge of his horsehair mattress and vomited on the floor, missing his boots by inches. He put both hands on the wooden rail of the bed and gripped it with all his might, his eyes pinched shut, the muscles in his stomach clenched in painful convolutions. Not much came up, just a few gobs of liquid heat from deep inside his guts. Looking out the corner of his bleary eye, he saw the little squirrel leap from its perch on the high shelf and skip across the room to lick at the wet shine he'd just left on the hard ground. "No, Pinch!" he shouted, and kicked at it with his bare foot. The squirrel jumped back, tail blown out in anger, and squealed through its teeth. Then it turned and zigzagged up the wall to its perch, where it sat and stared, hunchbacked and wringing its front paws like an old crone.

Coley hugged himself as the spasms subsided, catching his breath as warm sweat ran down his ribs and flanks. When the tremors eased he fell back on the bed, his body weak and weightless from the exertion.

He remembered the first time it happened, the morning almost a year ago when he'd stumbled out of his basement room beneath Shapiro's house, squinting like a kitten in the blazing sunlight. He'd made his way up Hone Street, one foot twisting in front of the other, his head spinning as if he were climbing a mountain into the clouds. At Union Street, he sat down hard on the dirt curb in front of the run-down house on the corner. Ofer Peoples was on the porch, sweeping away the feathers from a chicken she'd plucked and left dangling from the post over the side yard. She'd been watching Coley since he spun past Shapiro's stable, and the features on her soft, round face were pulled into a lopsided grin. She came down the steps and stood in front of him, her wheezy cackle cutting like a sharp knife through the gloom in his head. She was a fat woman, not as fat as her sister Pixie, but fat enough to block out the murderous sunshine, and Coley was grateful for that. Feathers were sticking to the hem of her long and dirty skirt, and the hair sprouting from around her ankles was as coarse as a man's beard.

She cackled louder when she saw his dumbstruck expression. "You look about as jacked as Bill's goat," she said.

"I'm sick," he replied, feeling as if his body had been pulled inside out.

Ofer bent down and took his chin roughly in her hands. When she saw his bloodshot eyes and smelled his breath, she let go with a jerk mighty enough to snap his neck. "Sick like hell. You're drunk!"

He hadn't believed her at first. He'd been working at Von Beck's Brewery for a month, hired to help the night man, Dickie Flanagan, clean up after closing, working six nights a week from eight o'clock until two in the morning. He started out mopping floors sticky with spilled groats and barley, and helping lug blocks of ice down to the fermentation cellar when the nights were warm. But he worked hard, harder than Dickie, so after the first week, Dickie showed him how to stir the mash vats upstairs and, after the second week, how to feed the boiler that cooked the barley. By the end of the third week, he was doing most of the work himself, and Dickie had little to do but make himself a comfortable throne from half a dozen sacks of grain and drink pint after pint of the lager he artfully tapped from the barrels waiting for delivery in the morning. In a gesture of lazy magnanimity, he taught Coley how to draw the lager out himself, taking just a bit from each barrel so the brewmaster, August Koehlers, wouldn't notice. Coley thanked him and went back to stirring the vat, checking on him every hour, waking him up only when it was time for Coley to go home and Dickie to sober up. Most nights, Dickie got him started on his chores, then drank himself into a quick and earnest stupor. He was the skinniest man Coley had ever seen, with not nearly enough meat on him to absorb all the alcohol swimming to his brain. His eyes were set so deep in his bony skull that you had to look twice to make sure you weren't staring into empty sockets. Dickie usually passed out on his mound of sacks about an hour after Coley arrived at the brewery, his scrawny arms and shins exposed and pointing in every direction, looking like a dropped sack of sticks.

It was only after Coley was done chopping wood for the boiler that he first took advantage of Dickie's tutelage. Sweaty and drained from working so close to the heat, he thirstily drank down two quick pints of the strong lager, indifferent to the bitter taste but thankful for the coolness that ran quickly into his empty stomach. That it made him light-headed didn't bother him at all. Before he left the brewery, he tapped another glass, enjoying the rare satisfaction of a full belly, and chopped extra wood just for the sudden joy it gave him.

His next recollection was waking up at Shapiro's, moaning as if he were rising from his deathbed, then caterwauling into the diamond-bright sunlight before Ofer Peoples snapped his head back and laughed in his face.

She took pity on him and dragged him inside, forcing him to take a pinch of salt under his tongue and gulp down a glass of water, then led him to the table and made him eat three runny eggs cooked in an inch of bacon fat. Coley balked, trying to shut out the sizzling aroma of day-old grease and the wretched choir singing in his head, but Ofer ignored his miserable yowls and blocked him with a thick forearm every time he tried to bolt.

"Grease is the salvation you're looking for, boy, and you'll stay until that plate is clean."

It took Coley almost an hour to eat his breakfast, and Ofer Peoples budged from his side only to stir the potato soup she was making in a black kettle over the fire. Toward the end, he had to chip the eggs out of the grease with his knife, but when he was done, he could at least raise his eyes and sit up straight. He had never been drunk before and didn't like it. He used to laugh at the men walking sideways out of Welch's liquor store and Natterjack's saloon down by the docks, singing songs in warbly voices, moving slow and unsteady, swinging their arms for balance and leaving their pockets unguarded and free for the plucking of an occasional coin. Coley wasn't much good at that feat but the other boys were, always coming up with enough to pay for the beer that Coley later took to stealing from Von Beck's whenever he got the chance, mixing it with the English gin Al Deyo pilfered from his father's store.

Eventually, Coley learned to drink without the sickness coming on, but it still happened on occasion. Now thirteen, he didn't make many mistakes.

He sat up in bed and walked to the table in the middle of his dark room, took a pinch of salt from the burlap sack on the table, put it under his tongue and had a long drink of water from the pail by the door. The squirrel came down the wall again, weaving between chair legs and racing across the hard-packed floor right back to that wet spot. This time, Coley let it clean up his mess while he drank water until the pail was dry.

He walked over to the wall where he kept the dead bat he'd found a few weeks before, tacked to a pine board with its wings extended and its little hands open. It had been dead a long time but still looked fresh, the tiny brown body plump, furry and soft as velvet. He moved in closer and stared into the evil little face that never ceased to fascinate him. It was as if God had blinked when He made this creature, allowing the devil to mark it with his own pointy ears and savage teeth.

He could hear the Shapiro women moving around the kitchen above him. He picked up the last of the griddle cakes that the daughter, Esther, had left outside his door the morning before. They were cold but not yet stale, so he slathered them with honey, stuck them together and took his first bite. He walked to the center of the low-ceilinged room and stood beneath the kitchen. Looking through the gaps in the wide boards, he could make out their shapes and shadows as they stood firmly at the long table, throwing dough for bread. He moved around until he located Esther's bare feet, smaller than her mother's and, Coley imagined, softer, too. Two years older than Coley, she was very pretty, with long black hair spilling halfway down her back and a body that moved lightly against the layers of cotton fabric that covered her, causing a friction that often left the most subtle impression of a slender leg or a small breast. Coley found it almost unbearable, but he watched anyway, and Esther knew it. Sometimes she would stand so close that he could smell the warmth of her skin, and sometimes she brushed against him as she passed by, digging her hip into his thigh. Her affection was a cat's tease, and Coley enjoyed the sweet torment. Now he stood inches from the floorboards, his head lifted into the thin slivers of sunlight that knifed into the packed dirt beneath him, and gazed up between the planted feet of Esther Shapiro, staring directly into the shadowy dusk of flesh and cloth, closing his eyes as flour drifted down and dusted him like sleep.

Then Shapiro started banging the stable door with his shovel, almost as if he'd caught the boy peeking up his daughter's dress.

Coley finished his griddle cakes and left the crumbs in the tin pan for the squirrel. As he laced up his boots, he glanced at the latest copy of the *New York Weekly*, which still lay open on the table from the night before. He loved the paper's serialized escapades of Buffalo Bill and Buckskin John, the prairie guide who was more cunning than any Indian. He loved the tales of trappers and scouts with names like Red Dick and Cinnamon Tom, and even gave careful consideration to the more romantic stories of Captain Kate, the Heroine of Deadwood Gulch. It was the lore of the West that gripped him, any whiff of adventure from Kentucky to the California coast. He kept a year's worth of the newspapers in a neat bundle under his bed and often pulled them out to revisit the tales, and to count the growing stack of paper money he'd hidden beneath his mattress. Soon he would have enough to buy his own horse from Shapiro and travel west himself to look for gold in the cold rivers north of Sacramento and explore the deep canyons beyond the already settled prairie. For now he just paused at the table and let himself be carried away by the story of Scarlet-Face, White Chief of the Shawanese, and he was halfway through the account of the Illinois chief's bloody tomahawk fight with a band of rogue Chippewa when Shapiro started banging again.

Let him beat the walls with his shovel until his hands ring with the effort of it, Coley thought as he slammed his fist on the pages and stormed across the room. When Shapiro next struck the wall, he had already hoisted himself up and out the narrow window into the back alley next to the stable, smiling as he hopped over the low wooden fence into Casper Breed's yard, and raced through the backyard maze of tenements on his way to the Rondout docks.

❧

THE NOISE THAT rolled over him was as forceful as a burst of wind, carrying with it the high whir of human voices and steam whistles and the clatter and bang of machinery. The air itself was dingy with the relentless eruptions from the smokestacks and brick kilns that rose above the river town. The wharves and company docks were packed with canal barges loaded with coal from the anthracite mines in Pennsylvania and timber from the local hills, while barges and large schooners sat low in the water, weighed down by cargo both exotic and mundane. When Will stepped off the gangplank, he paused a moment to inhale the vile stink of soot and men and animals, watching half a dozen pigs run wild across the cobblestones, chased by barefoot boys with sticks and pokers.

Standing on the dock, he remembered a trip he'd taken to Rondout with his father many years before. Rather than traveling seven hours on dark roads back to their house in the Clove, they'd spent the night at the Eagle Hotel in Kingston. Those had been fine days, having time with his father, and he'd loved staying at the hotel, where the transient lives of borders and guests fascinated him. He remembered seeing two strange men in thickly wound turbans and narrow-cut silk jackets on one of his last visits. His father told him they were Burmese princes from beyond the Indian Ocean, taking part in a hunting expedition on South Peak Mountain, where panthers still roamed the rocky cliffs. They were thin and elegant men, with smooth skin the color of burnt custard, and when they walked by, Will's eyes watered from the overwhelming perfume of foreign spices. An hour later, he stood in the open window of his room on the second floor, listening to the horses snuffling in the livery below and wagon wheels clattering up Fair Street and a man and woman arguing behind one of the darkened windows in the row house opposite the hotel. He was enthralled by these village night sounds, so different from the hush of turning leaves and the sweet rush of creek water outside their farm in the Clove. Then, early in the morning, they retrieved their horses from the hotel livery and rode to Rondout to view what his father called "that great cesspit where money is made."

They took the old Union Plank Road, wide enough to accommodate a pair of carriages, and rode easily through the pine forest that separated the genteel village of Kingston from her rowdier neighbor. Passing wagons full of tanned hides and produce from the valley farms, Will looked down at the brown ruts that scarred the road, deepened by traffic that was becoming livelier every season. In front of him the row of trees dipped and became a steady line to the east, and he knew they were getting closer to the river. When they finally started down the last hill toward Rondout, he began to hear what sounded like the banging of one hundred hammers. But it wasn't until the road straightened that he could actually look down to the working heart of the town, where the raw power of life seemed to boom up from the earth itself. As their horses moved through the crush of people on Division Street, he heard the sharp bark of German shouted from the baker's shop and the growl of black-faced Irish coal heavers and boatmen going home for a meal. It was a mongrel English they all spoke, buoyant and full of dark slang and old-world epithets. Their ramshackle neighborhoods were christened "New Dublin" and "Germantown," and the stick-built shanties they inhabited were so haphazardly constructed, they looked as if they'd been lifted and dropped back down by a raging storm. They seemed to grow on top of one another, and as Will and his father rode past, he imagined the people inside packed tight as bees in a hive.

Those had been the early days of sudden prosperity. Only ten years had passed since representatives from the Philadelphia canal company came and bought the old Van Gaasbeek farm along the north bank of Rondout Creek, now covered with all manner of maritime business and called the Strand. The town was quickly transformed into one of the busiest ports on the Hudson, and the riches found at its tidewaters were as abundant as tadpoles skippering in the mud.

They had breakfast at Felix Murray's saloon at the foot of the hill. From their table overlooking the creek, Will could see the canal boats lined up at the Strand and the conical mountains of black coal piled on Island Dock, waiting to be transferred to barges for the trip to Manhattan. Looking north, he saw a great tri-masted schooner come off the river at Columbus Point, its huge sails deflating as they lost wind, the bow pushing off a rounded swell as it slowed and entered the flat waters of the harbor. And even though the windows in the saloon muffled the outside noise, the roar of activity still seeped in and was an almost physical presence in the room, forcing men to raise their voices and compete for attention over the chiming of their forks and spoons. Prosperous city merchants stopped by their table to pay their respects to his father, who was always addressed as "Major Harp." Will sat up straight when introduced and returned a firm grip when a hand was offered, just as he'd been taught.

Those were grand mornings, topped off with his city breakfast of salted mackerel and fried eggs served with crisp onions and potatoes and thick slices of brown bread to sop up the broken yolks. Then once their plates were clean, the two of them walked the length of the Strand for their health and digestion before mounting their horses for the long ride home.

Now he was back. He stood on the end of the dock, carrying the same valise he'd left with in '51. The medicine drummers were still on the deck of the *Ella May*, yawning and stretching, their thoughts on a quick meal and future prosperity. The young Negro woman stood at the bottom of the gangplank, swaying gently and standing on her toes. She reached into her burlap bag and popped fat strawberries into her mouth one by one as she searched the crowd for a familiar face.

Will hoisted his valise, careful of his tender shoulder, and walked toward the center of town.

⌇⌇⌇

COLEY HAD JUST broken out of the damp and twisting alley behind Abeel Street when he saw the mob gathered across from the Mansion House Hotel. He slowed down when he heard men cheering, their voices raw and fresh, and changed direction as easily as a moth flitting toward light. Already winded from his flight over trampled fences and patchy backyards, he paused long enough to catch his breath before leaning forward to nudge past the rigid backs and elbows of the throng. When he finally poked his head around the imposing stomach of Danny Crow—thankfully, it contracted as he raised his hands to his mouth to shout "Cowards! Show your worth!"—he saw two dogs, big and ugly and wild-looking as wolves, dancing around each other in the dusty road. Their heads were down and their backs arched, the fur along their spines standing stiff as wire as they pawed the dirt and growled lowly at each other. Coley could tell they'd been at it for a while, their muzzles wet with slobber, their teeth stained with blood, each panting deeply as it circled the other, their ribs prominent through greasy flanks, their eyes shiny and alert. The smaller dog, black, with one ear chewed to a nub from an earlier battle, had a long gash on her side that opened at every step and widened like a grin. The other, just as black but meatier and anvil-headed, was clearly the aggressor, slowly advancing in a sideways motion, tightening the circle, his pointed ears flat to his skull and his whole body jittery, as if he were walking on sparks. Suddenly he stopped and lay flat on the ground—panting still, but more quietly—and stared at the other dog while licking his thick paw, the blood dripping freely where a nail had been pulled out in combat. It was as if the fight had been knocked out of him and he was content just to rest there in the middle of the street, not in victory or defeat, and tend to his hard-earned wounds. Coley knew this was all a feint, a bit of cleverness hidden under the hard bones of his skull, even if the other dog did not. And it didn't take long for the one-eared bitch to make the move she probably regretted the moment it occurred to her, her growl loud enough for Danny Crow to raise his arm and shout, "Oh, you good wife!" as she jumped and hurled her beaten body forward. The male stood quickly when she charged, his teeth bared and fierce, the sharp points rusty with blood, and they met again in the dust of the street, standing on their hind legs to tear at each other's necks, grappling like street brawlers. The men closed in around them, whooping encouragement, and Coley saw Henry Schenk taking bets on the outcome, his fists bulging with coins. The dogs rolled in the street, the little bitch taking the worst of it, submissive now between the forelegs of the bigger male, her chest barely moving and her tongue limp in the dirt, and Coley was sure she was done for. Then Constable Sirrine came walking up the Strand with his long-barreled Remington revolver and fired three shots into the sky. The men ducked and scattered, and in the confusion Coley saw Schenk drop his coins in the thick black water that ran along the sidewalk, and then both dogs scrambled to their feet and trotted off side by side like old pals. Coley stayed close to the immense bulk of Danny Crow as the big man hoisted his drooping trousers and ran with the rest of them. He stumbled in front of the nervous horses that pulled the Kingston stage, sidestepping the big hooves that pounded like hammer blows as the horses reared and whinnied. While the driver tried to settle his team, Coley grabbed the traces of the first horse and vaulted over the whippletree, running as fast as he could to the waterfront.

⟲❦⟳

PEARL HOUSE woke up in the back of the wagon, then sneezed hard enough to bang her head against the wooden slats where her head had been resting. Still groggy from her muddied dreams, she swatted vigorously and feebly at the blue-jay feather that shimmied above her nose, but it kept jerking away unnaturally, as if windblown. Then she heard her brother laughing.

Her eyes flew open, and she was fully awake and completely peeved. "That ain't funny," she said.

"It is from where I'm sitting," Sam replied from the buckboard seat above her, dangling the feather from a string wrapped around his finger.

Pearl tried to sit up, but her tailbone was sore and her right leg asleep. She thrust her hand into one of the bushels of blackberries that filled the back of the wagon and started firing them at her brother's head.

"That's enough, Pearl!" her father said from the seat next to Sam, as the two mules shied from the blackberries raining down around them. "And you, Sam, take hold of these reins and stop acting like some boy whose bottom I still need to wipe."

Sam turned around as Joop slapped the reins across his lap.

"Keep them straight, and don't rile 'em and fuss 'em too much."

"I'll lead them just fine. I done it before."

"They'll be more likely to prance now, so keep the reins laid down and hold 'em tight."

"I done it before," Sam repeated, trying hard to keep the irritation out of his voice. Pearl, seeing a blush as dark as a bruise cover her brother's brown neck, smiled in satisfaction. She stepped on the thick pallet of skins she'd sell to Hap Shay at his shop off the Strand and shoved her brother aside with her thighbone, squeezing him to the far edge of the seat as she sprang up next to her father. Then she smoothed out the bottom pleats of her yellow dress and straightened the sleeves, which had twisted during her long nap. It was made of lightweight cotton, ordered from a catalogue at Hanson's store in Rondout, the yellow as rich as churned butter. Her mother had reluctantly bought the material and just as reluctantly cut it according to the pattern Pearl had picked out. She shook her head and tightened her lips the morning Pearl first tried it on, knowing that the dress and its color and her daughter's obvious beauty were a dangerous combination.

She'd felt the same unease that morning when she saw that Pearl had put on the yellow dress for the trip to Rondout.

"That dress . . ." Sallie House sighed as she wrapped biscuits and ham by the warm glow of the oil lamp.

"What about it?"

"It makes you look . . ."

"It makes me look what?" Pearl inquired as she walked past her and stood at the window, watching her father and Sam load the blackberries into the wagon, their outlines etched by moonlight.

"It makes men look."

"So what?" Pearl said, mother and daughter now facing each other like two cats on a fence. "I'm not looking back."

"Then maybe you'd better take that dress off until you do."

Pearl groaned and helped her mother finish wrapping the breakfast, Sallie silently praying that Pearl would change her dress and Pearl just as silently defying her mother's wishes. They embraced in the doorway and then Pearl climbed into the back of the wagon, holding the long matronly shawl Sallie handed to her for protection against the evening chill.

She was perched on the seat as they joined the horse-drawn traffic moving down Division Street. The mules grew skittish, but Sam kept them balanced, jostling into the line of carts and wagons heading down to the wharf. Six months had passed since Pearl had been in town, and she couldn't get enough of the men and women on the sidewalks and the merchandise in the storefront windows. In her mind, Rondout was a splendid city, and she had always looked forward to these trips down from Jug Hill. Although she loved the ragged beauty of the Shawangunk Mountains, there was something otherworldly about this river town that both repelled and attracted her, much like the taste of sweet onions dug fresh from the earth. She could look past the grime that sometimes hung in the air like a fine rain, and block out the steady stream of profanities that were shouted as casually as greetings. To Pearl, in Rondout possibilities were scattered about as freely as feed to chickens, adventures were granted and every day was a holiday.

When they crossed the Strand, she looked at the schooners and steamboats that crowded the piers at Rondout Creek. As Sam pulled in behind a wagon loaded with crates full of squawking ducks—the noise of them sending the mules into frantic snorting—she reached into the back, grabbed her bundled skins and vaulted over the side onto the cobblestone street. "I'm going to meet the boat!" she yelled over her shoulder.

"You be at Sam Ridley's yard in an hour," Joop shouted back as he took his hat off and scratched his curly red hair.

"I will!"

"And don't be late!"

"I won't!" Pearl shouted back, already dashing toward the wharf. She kept her eye on the masts bobbing in front of her, gliding around a one-legged soldier propped up on a cane, the left side of his face a welt of pink scars. Keenly aware of the steady rhythm of her strong legs, she was unwilling to break the fluid pace as she sidestepped a cart of over- turned oranges and wheeled by a troop of well-dressed passengers wait- ing to board the steamboat *Manhattan* at Cornell's dock. There she caught a glimpse of a young man's admiring smile and the scent of strong gardenia perfume from the younger woman at his elbow, and in that partial second of vanity and hesitation she lost focus, coming down hard on her right foot into a collision she didn't anticipate, spin- ning into the air, a dervish in a yellow dress.

When Pearl sat up on the cobblestones, a boy was sprawled on the ground opposite her, rubbing his elbow. Too angry to speak, she quickly stood up, and was relieved to find out her dress was unscathed, except for a slight oily smudge on her hem. The pelts were an unrav- eled mess at her feet, and when she bent down to pull them together, the boy scrambled to her side and picked up a small fox skin. She snatched it away from him and gathered it to her chest. He was stunned, standing just a few inches away and staring at her. His large eyes were partially hidden behind the swatch of brown hair that hung in his face, and there were crumbs in the corner of his mouth.

"What are you looking at?" she asked.

"Your skins," he replied.

Pearl felt anger rise up from her chest and open like a tulip along her throat and around her cheeks. He was no better than the stupid boys who lived on Jug Hill, their knees and eyes and ears full of dirt.

"Fox, ain't they?" he said.

"Yes."

"You save the head?"

"What?"

"The skull, I mean. You save the skull?"

"Why would I do anything like that?"

The boy shrugged, and she was aware of the crowd steering around them. She bent down to one knee and started gathering the skins back into a bundle.

"I got a deer skull," he continued, "and a rat and a dog and a pos- sum, and even a baby bear, but I don't have a fox."

Pearl stood up and tied her thin rope around the skins.

"Think you might get yourself another one?"

"Of course I will," Pearl snapped.

"You think you might save me the skull?" He was sincere, unaffected by her rough tone. "I collect things like that, bones and all. I even got a pet squirrel."

When she looked into his earnest face, her exasperation disappeared. She finally caught a glimmer of what she'd been expecting from the beginning: the widening of his eyes as he took her in for the first time, straightening from his boyish slouch as he forgot about her skins, his gaze sharpening and dipping low, sneaking around the curves that defined her and filled out her favorite dress. He was paying attention now, and she felt much better.

"I guess I can save you a skull."

"What's your name?" he asked boldly.

"Pearl. Pearl House."

"I'm Coley, and I was—"

But Pearl was already looking past his shoulder toward the wharf. "Tally!" she yelled.

He watched her run toward the *Ella May*, which was tied to the end of the pier, and up to a dark-skinned Negro girl, who dropped a bag of strawberries as the two girls fell into a spinning embrace.

His friends had already gathered on the wharf when Coley joined them. Sitting on the back of a loaded farm wagon, its bed packed tight with the first haul of summer potatoes, the boys reclined on lopsided sacks, watching passengers disembark, hoping for busy men whose coats were carelessly unbuttoned and well-heeled women made giddy by the commotion around them. They were looking for blinks of uncertainty and hands occupied with luggage or newspapers or horse's reins, for the scarlet faces and telltale staggers of men who drank rum with their eggs and ham or drank beer simply to toast the morning. Scouting the piers for any sign of oblivion or inattention that might result in loose pockets and fallen coins was a game they played, and most times it resulted in enough extra change to pass around at the end of the week or pool together for Mary Utter, who then would keep her curtains open on Saturday night while sailors undressed her in the back room of Trainor's boardinghouse. They kept only coins for themselves and gave any wallets or papers they lifted to Mickey Blessing or Charlie O'Fay. Most of the men working on the docks knew what they were up to, and they either kept a hard eye on them or offered their own slick-fingered advice.

Coley grabbed the brake arm and jumped up, landing between Tim and Danny Magruder.

"Who's your girlfriend?" Tim asked him. He and his brother were craning their long necks, looking back at the *Ella May,* and Coley saw Pearl House and the Negro girl walking arm and arm along the docks.

"She ain't my girlfriend," he said.

"Pretty for a colored girl," Danny said.

"She ain't colored."

"Sure she is, Coley."

"She's a Jug Hill nigger," Tim chimed in. "Don't matter how many Indians her daddy fucked, or how many Dutchies fucked her momma, she's still a nigger."

"Well, she ain't my girlfriend," Coley said, swiping at Tim's hat and sitting down next to Al Deyo.

"She is pretty, though," Danny mused. "Wouldn't mind getting a peek under that yellow dress."

"Then why don't you lie down in the road and let her walk over you," Coley said.

"Might just do that." Danny smirked. "Lot easier than trying to knock her over just to see what's 'tween her knees."

Coley faked a jab, but Danny dodged and snickered.

The Magruder twins were a year older than Coley, lean and tense as whippets. Tim was tall and blond, with a face as round and clear as a porcelain plate, while Danny had a headful of tight dark curls and skin the color of spring mud. They had the same small noses and dented chins, and walked with their elbows tight to their sides and their left toes pointed inward. They looked more like distant cousins than natural twins, but together they were graceful and bold and the best pocketeers on the docks.

"How's the pickings today?" Coley asked them.

Danny poked his chin toward the *Ella May,* where a small group of well-dressed men stretched their legs while kegs of wine were rolled down the gangplank to a wagon sent from Charlie Costello's saloon. Coley could tell the men were roughed up from their night on the river, mossy-eyed from a rolling sleep and too much rum. One of them yawned without even bothering to cover up the great hole in his face, then smacked his lips like an old goat and stretched his arms as if he stood in the privacy of his own room.

"Look at him," Al sneered, "poking out his fat belly like he's the governor himself."

"He ain't got the sense that morning brings." Tim nodded, narrowing his eyes. He'll wake up and step a little lighter when I'm through with him."

"Anyone for me?" Coley asked as he scanned the pier over the bobbing heads of tradesmen and sailors. A long line of wagons hauling bluestone was backed all the way to the foot of Division Street, and on the slats Coley could see the faded names of the quarries where hard men pounded the vertical seams with wedges and hammers, then loaded the blocks of coarse-grained stone onto these sturdy wagons, each carrying eight to ten tons at a time, to be driven down a dozen miles of bad road and put onto barges destined for Manhattan, where they'd be chiseled and dressed as doorsills and lintels and Fifth Avenue sidewalks smooth enough for a pretty girl's bare feet.

Then he noticed the delegation from the Jefferson Dragoons standing in their usual spot near the steamboat landing. There were four of them this time, men too old to fight in the Union army but not too old to come out and honor those who did. They gathered on the wharf every morning, dressed in full-parade regalia, straight-backed and proud in their long blue frock coats trimmed in gold to match the tight-fitting pantaloons they wore tucked into tall Hessian riding boots. They were white-haired old Germans with pointed white beards, part of a group that had met weekly in the tavern at Metzger's Hotel for the past forty years, taking up the long table in the back to socialize and drink plum wine. Now they stood in an orderly line, holding their plumed caps in their hands, ready to meet the soldiers coming home from battle, alive or in coffins, and to offer solace and compassion to the wives and mothers who keened before them.

Al Deyo suddenly laid his arm across Coley's shoulder and sighted down the pier. "There's your man."

Following the straight line of Al's finger, Coley wasn't so sure.

◦◦◦

WILL HARP stood with his valise on his shoulder and waited for a wagon hauling cedar shakes to pass. The horse pulling it had thrown a shoe and stopped every few steps to paw the dirt with a cracked hoof, the driver cursing and whipping the animal with the reins. When Will shifted his weight, he felt fingers crawling over the button on his pocket. He clamped down on the hand resting there and felt the thin arm tense as he yanked it around and faced the little thief holding his money clip.

The boy, startled but defiant, spoke through lips squeezed tight in pain. "It was falling out, mister!"

"Was it?"

"It was halfway out your pocket already, hanging there like it was ready to drop. I was just trying to help."

"Then put it back where you found it." Will's grip didn't loosen as he guided the boy's hand back over his gaping pocket.

He slipped the money clip back where it belonged and kept his eyes locked on Will's face. His ears were tipped in red, but he didn't whimper or squirm. "You ought to thank me, mister," he said.

This audacity made Will want to laugh out loud. "Should I?"

"You ought to let me go," he added in the same even tone.

Then Will felt something bang against his other side. He pushed down on his right knee to keep his balance and spun around in time to see a dark-haired boy racing away, dodging barrels as he glanced once over his shoulder and disappeared into the crowd. Meanwhile, the boy whose wrist he was holding pulled as hard as he could and broke free. Will looked down at him as two more boys stampeded by, one of them shouting, "Run, Coley, run!"

Coley stared at him a second longer, and Will saw the smirk on his face as he dug in his toes and took off like a rabbit, joining up with his friends in a clearing on the Strand, the four of them coming together as naturally as feeder streams into a river. And then they were gone.

***

IT WAS THE day of the month Jane dreaded most, and she slept later than usual in a futile attempt to avoid it. When she awoke, she put on one of the four dresses she owned and tried to drink a cup of coffee doused with warm milk, but her stomach revolted and she could only nibble on the dry biscuits left over from the night before. She stood in the parlor and looked out the front window at the maple trees that shaded the yard, their leaves tipped by the summer sun, their trunks warped by imperfections in the glass. She picked up the bag that held Frank's letter and stepped out the door.

Her first stop was Knetch's Bakery at the top of Division Street, where Mary was behind the flour-dusted wooden counter, filling large cloth-lined baskets with fresh loaves of bread she'd begun baking long before sunrise. Customers were already jostling for position, so Jane found a place in line and caught her eye. Mary nodded delicately as she dropped a dozen rolls into the burlap sack presented to her by Mrs. Brenner, then smiled at her next customer.

Jane had known her for years. Her husband, Alfons, had joined the 120th the same day as Frank, but he'd been wounded at the battle of Mine Run before last Christmas. He'd languished in a field hospital until after the New Year, when he was finally transferred through the rail yard in Manassas and on to Washington with a bum arm and his head wrapped tighter than an Egyptian mummy's. Mary didn't learn of his injuries until February. She was told he'd been struck by three musket balls—two in the left arm and one in the left side of his face, the ball taking out his eye and exiting through the ear—but was recovering well in Seminary Hospital. By the time she was able to reach Washington in early March, Alfons was resting on prescribed opiates, and the inflammation had subsided enough for the doctors to stitch his eyelid with a lead suture. To Mary, the missing ear looked no worse than a small cabbage left to rot in the ground, and when Alfons's sideburns grew back, the hair would cover most of the mutilated skin. The only setback was a new acuteness of hearing in his other ear, which unbalanced and dizzied him; for a while he was prone to fainting fits and epileptic seizures that often brought on a "confusion of ideas," and the doctors decided to keep him in the hospital until these passed. Mary had gone to Washington weak with dread but returned to Rondout knowing she could live with Alfons's deformities, and that he'd be home soon. Meanwhile, she worked grueling hours in their bakery, and would continue to do so, long after the war was over, without bitterness or complaint, because God had spared them both the worst.

When Jane reached the counter, Mary took an envelope out of her money box and laid it down before her. It was smudged with flour, but Jane didn't bother to brush it off before putting it in her bag. It was Grieves who would handle it next, and his cuffs that would be dusted when he pulled his penknife through the seam to get at the rent money Jane collected each month, as Frank had done before her, when it was handsome Alfons handing the envelope over. The women who'd been left behind conducted this transaction without bad feelings, because most of their feelings were invested somewhere else.

"Any word from Frank?" Mary asked.

Jane shook her head. The list of dead and wounded had just started to arrive in the towns and villages north of Manhattan, but there had been little information on the fate of 120th or any other local militias at Cold Harbor. Though she didn't dwell on the news of that terrible battle, she read the daily paper and did her job and kept to herself, brave as any mother, wife or lover. In quiet moments she tried hard to trust in God, but at times it felt easier to trust in a line of stars or the predictions of the old Negro woman from Hurley who threw a handful of stones in the mud to read your fortune. She wanted to believe in mercy. She wanted even more to believe in promises made.

Mary set a floured hand on top of Jane's and squeezed. "He's a fighter. If ever one was born to come out of trouble with his head in the air, it's Frank."

Jane smiled, and in a moment, she began to laugh quietly. It was as true an image of Frank as could be imagined. Mary joined in, the helpless giddiness contagious.

Jane spent the rest of the morning going from storefront to storefront in the buildings Grieves owned along Division Street, always expected but never welcomed. She felt as if her shadow preceded her through the open doorways, growing wider, dark as a raven, falling across the purses and money boxes she had come to empty. At Mercer's Grocery and Conklin's Tobacco Shop, the owners angrily pushed the money at her as though it were dirt offered at the end of a straw broom. Jim Conklin had given her trouble when she took over Frank's route those long months ago, laughing at her nerve and refusing to pay her half a nickel. She left without a word, Frank's advice ringing louder in her ears than the laughter. "Don't let them get away with anything," he'd said. "They took the damn lease and signed the papers. They got no rights. They got no say. Don't let them rise an inch above you, Jane, not any man." That day, Jane had walked directly to Natterjack's saloon and found Mickey sitting out front with the Dooley brothers. He took a worn ax handle off the Dooleys' wagon and gladly went back with her. Without wasting breath or step, he entered the shop, where Conklin was arranging a new shipment of Mexican cigars, and whacked him across the back of the neck. Jane stood in the doorway with her arms crossed and recalled the rest of Frank's warning: "In times of trouble, blood dries fast as ink and it's just as binding. That's what Mickey's for." She watched as Mickey kicked Conklin flat and then brought him back to his feet by placing the ax handle under his chin and yanking him upright with both hands. Then he just smiled and held open his palm.

Today, Jane didn't look away from Conklin's pained eyes, knowing the shame he felt would serve her well. Her brother wasn't as subtle as Frank, but the force of his knuckles was just as effective.

At Klein's Dry Goods on Garden Street, she pushed open the heavy door, heard the old man grumble in the shadows and caught a glimpse of him scuttling toward the back room, his broad back disappearing between the fluttering rows of Persian carpets that hung from the rafters. She waited by the door as she always did, letting her eyes adjust to the gloom within. It was a dreary shop, smelling of the oilcloth that sat in great bolts on the counter and of the dust on the window shades and curtains Klein displayed from wooden poles anchored to the walls and sold by the yard. He soon returned with a stack of crisp bills tied with string, the corner of each one marked with a small finely inked *K*, the proof of payment he presented to her every month. A clever man, he smiled at Jane without resentment. "Good morning to you, Miss Blessing," he said as he handed her the money.

"Good morning, Mr. Klein," she replied, slipping the packet in her bag, now swollen with money. Relieved that her morning duties were fulfilled, she started down the hill toward the Strand, where she would make one last stop at the post office. It was how she ended every morning since Frank had left for war: anxious for news, her pulse beating steadily between hope and fear.

⎯⎯◍⎯⎯

WHILE SHAPIRO hitched one of his big Morgan geldings to a wagon out front, Coley stood in the back of the last stall and rested for a moment, leaning on the handle of the broad shovel and breathing in the sweet scent of the fresh manure he'd been ordered to clean up as punishment for being late. Shapiro had ten stalls in his stable, with two horses in each, and it would take Coley a dozen trips with the wheelbarrow to get rid of last evening's waste. He'd dumped most of it in the deep ravine that ran behind the back of the property, where it would eventually be washed away by the rain into one of the choked and fusty streams that leached into the Hudson. The rest he would smooth and dry in the sun, and it would later be added to the chickenshit that Mrs. Shapiro collected and raked into the garden, where she grew horseradish and thickets of dark greens that looked as bitter as they tasted. When the mucking out was finished, he'd have to climb into the loft to pick the thistles and burrs from the cheap hay Shapiro bought from Paul Collyer. Then it would need to be forked into the wagon below and dispersed into the wooden bins in each stall. By the time he was done feeding, his eyes would be teary and his body itchy from all the hay dust, but he wouldn't complain, because Shapiro was a better man than most.

When he was five years old, his mother died of what the newspaper reported was a "singular death." Breena was a stubborn woman, and had been for all of her twenty-four years. She'd survived youthful outbreaks of black vomit and smallpox by simply refusing to accept the possibility of her own body failing, weathering the illnesses that took her brothers and sisters, confounding doctors and neighbors who were busy burying their own. Coley had a daguerreotype that had been made of her the year she died. It was just how he remembered her: a short woman with round features and thick tawny hair that fell in a spray of curls over each shoulder. On that day, she'd worn a black high-collared dress that was tight at the waist, with thin vertical white stripes that magically trimmed her generous figure. Her head was cocked slightly to the right and, as always, she was smiling. The photographer had hand-tinted her eyes blue, though Coley remembered they'd been green, and dabbed a light flush of pinkness to her lips and cheeks.

Six months later, Breena had accidentally struck the forefinger of her left hand with a hammer. She'd been hanging new curtains and was too impatient to wait for her husband, Jimmy, to come home from the docks to help with the last one. Tired as she was, she balanced on wobbly tiptoes and took careful aim at the nail high above her head, then missed and hit her finger instead. She yelped just once, and Coley remembered coming in from the front yard to see her stomping before the hearth with the finger stuck in her mouth. When she pulled it out, there was a small blood clot under the nail, but after an hour it didn't hurt much, so she doused it with camphor and finished hanging the curtains. The next morning, when the finger began to swell, Breena took it as a sign of healing and went about her business. On the third morning, Jimmy woke up and found his wife's arm flung across his chest, and it was so bloated that he'd mistaken it for her leg. Even she agreed it would be best for Dr. Wilkie to have a look. She spent the day with Coley, and he could still picture her chasing him around the yard, both of them reeling through the dirt and laughing as she tried to tickle him with a corn husk held in her good hand. By the time the doctor arrived, it was just getting dark, and the finger looked as fat as a smoked sausage. He pleaded with her to let him remove the digit, but the most she would let him do was drain the pus. When he cut into her mottled flesh, a frothy liquid ran down her arm, and the incised blister emitted such a rotten odor that she wrapped herself in her sheet and buried her face in a pillow. On the sixth day, fever set in, and Dr. Wilkie made her as comfortable as possible, shaking his head at her intractability and treating her kindly but without pity. On the seventh day, mortification had spread past her wrist, and she allowed Coley into her room only after it was dark and the sight of her dying arm wouldn't frighten him.

This was a grievous blow, since until that day he'd spent every waking second at his mother's side, accustomed to her unwavering attention and supervision. Now he was being shunted off to neighbors who looked at him sadly and kept their distance, as if the sickness in the Hinds household was infectious and he was a carrier. Being five, he understood nothing but the unfairness of separation. In the evening his father would carry him home and put him to bed, where he slept deeply, his dreams unremembered, until the tenth day, when he dreamed his mother was in the kitchen, laughing as she chased mice across the floor with a broom. He awoke quickly, jumped out of bed and ran to his parents' room, then pushed open the door. His mother was lying flat on her back in bed, her long hair damp and spread across the pillow. Her body was trembling and her left arm hung over the side, black past her elbow, and to the boy, it looked as if she were wearing an evening glove. His father was still in his nightshirt, sitting on the bed beside her, holding her head in his arms. Coley could see he was crying, and he wondered if it was his father's tears that had dampened his mother's hair. She turned at that moment and looked at him, and though the light was still dim, Coley saw her features soften, and her cheeks, hollow and pale just a moment before, reddened as she smiled.

"Good morning, Coley," she whispered. "Bring your mother some water."

He rushed to the jug on the kitchen table, then grabbed it with both hands and walked quickly back to his parents' room, ignoring the water that splashed on his bare feet. When he got to the door, his father was already shutting it, but he caught a last glimpse of his mother still smiling in his direction, and he held it until the latch clicked shut in front of him.

She died very early that afternoon, exactly ten days after smashing her finger. In his grief, Jimmy took the hammer out into the yard and flung it as high into the air as he could, his strangled cry stunning and awful in the quiet. The hammer spun over the rooftops and smashed through Kenny Malloy's window in the next alley, but he knew better than to return it.

Coley and his father lived a simple life after Breena's death, neither hostile nor loving toward each other, each absorbing the loss in his own way. Jimmy went back to work the very next morning and took time off only for the burial service at Montrepose Cemetery. He held his son's hand during the ceremony, but Coley sensed the difference between his mother's clasp and his father's grip, between affection and responsibility. With his father back on the docks, he again stayed with neighbors, calmer now, unable to miss something that was no longer there. In the evening, Jimmy would pick him up and they would go home for supper, respectful of each other's silence and allowing it to grow. Sometimes he would hear his father moaning in the dark while he lay in his own bed, unable to sleep. It scared him, and he tried not to move until the moaning stopped. Other times he would hear his father get up and leave their small house to wander the tight maze of streets alone, and again he would remain frozen on his pallet for those long black hours, waiting for his father to return home.

When Coley turned six, Breena's younger sister, Rita, came up from Brooklyn to stay with them. She was glad to leave the gritty streets of Red Hook, where she was still living with her father in a crowded tenement and fending off the eager boys who worked in factories along Buttermilk Channel and would corner her against a brick wall to beg for kisses, and she'd squirm and squeal and fight just enough to keep them interested. Her father was happy to send her upriver, hoping that Jimmy, in his need and sadness, would relieve him of yet another daughter.

Although she was a pretty girl of seventeen, Rita lacked the ample fleshiness that made her sister so appealing. She had the same thick hair and joking smile, though, and her facial features, if small and snug, were supported by the same family bones. When she greeted Coley with a hug that might have lacked the maternal power he was used to, it was still familiar, and that was enough to win him over. Jimmy, too, had seemed glad to see her when she first arrived, but as she held his hand and looked up with the same green eyes as his wife's, it sparked an already-frayed nerve and he turned away. Rita walked softly through the fragile ruins of her dead sister's life, leaving Jimmy to mourn while she took care of the house and devoted herself to Coley.

Grateful for the attention, Coley gave her a tour of their small vegetable patch and took her to the shops where his mother had done most of her shopping. Rita took this in with blithe indifference; she didn't cook anything that couldn't be boiled, preferring the simpler recipes of meat and potatoes or barley gruel. In the mornings she played with him like a good aunt, and in the afternoon she straightened her clothes and mingled with the neighborhood women in front of the shops in Rondout, where they took a shine to this kind young woman who'd come all this way to "help poor Jimmy Hinds regain his manly nerve." Later, while their supper boiled away in a pot over the fire until the meat turned gray, she sat Coley down at the table and taught him how to read.

A quick learner, he cherished the worn copy of *The New England Primer* that Rita set before him, its woodblock illustrations frightening enough to carry the lessons into his dreams:

> The **A**sse's kick will snuff the candlewick.
> The **B**at will fly and steal a pie.
> The **C**at will play with claws that fray.
> The **D**og will bite a thief at night.
> The **E**agle's eye will watch you die.
> The idle **F**ool is whipped at school.

At first he would write out the individual letters over and over again, his small hand cramped around a pencil while Rita praised his penmanship. After a few months he was reading on his own, sputtering his first lessons out loud and then gobbling up whole sentences as they raced across the page, ravenous for the next.

For Coley, the time spent with Rita was bliss. For Rita, it was a satisfying distraction. While she loved the boy in her aunty way, her heart and soul were pinned on Jimmy Hinds. She'd always thought him an agreeable-looking man, but the solemn air of tragedy that now enveloped him had added an attractiveness she hadn't noticed before. He was still young, and coal dust still stained his rough trousers and the stubble on his chin, and she found it irresistible that he'd experienced things most young men wouldn't know for many years.

Jimmy acknowledged her presence without giving her much thought. He was grateful for her service, but only for the boy's sake. He no longer had any designs or desires and became as inward-thinking as a moral philosopher. After meals he'd leave the small house with barely a word to join his friends at John Fox's saloon or maybe Kelly's, where he would sit at the table with the men because it was something he had always done and he needed to pass his waking hours. Never a drinking man, he nursed a single pint of ale through the long night, sipping until it was flat and warm. Then he would return home and walk silently through the kitchen, past the open door where Rita slept next to Coley, unaware that she was awake and watching him. She would let him grieve because he needed to, and she would be patient. She missed Breena, too, yet, in her youth, was more concerned about what walked and talked and could give her pleasure. In a year's time she would be eighteen, and she'd wait that long for Jimmy to truly open his eyes.

For now, Rita was content to share a bed with Coley while planning her future resting place in Jimmy's arms behind the bedroom door. She kept giving the boy lessons and ingratiated herself with her neighbors in New Dublin, becoming friendly with the wives she hoped to emulate, her young, undeveloped mind already rich with feminine aptitude. And she cooked and cleaned and made the house habitable with the small amount of money Jimmy handed her each Saturday morning with few words of encouragement. Still, Rita was determined, and they lived together like a family. She treated Coley as her own and Jimmy as her better half, though without the connubial warmth she thought she deserved and believed would eventually come her way. But it didn't.

By winter's end, Jimmy was as much a ghost as her dead sister, never less than civil, never more than dutiful and polite. Whenever she tried to engage him in conversation that required him to look her in the eye or reflect on a personal issue, he sidestepped her like he would a dog sleeping on the sidewalk. But she kept the bargain she'd made with herself and stayed on through the four seasons.

Rita woke up on her 360th day in Rondout and packed her bag, waiting until Jimmy left for work before she gathered her things together, dropped Coley off at a neighbor's house and walked downtown to book steamboat passage to Manhattan. Within six months she was married to a brakeman on the Myrtle Avenue horsecar and living in an apartment on the floor beneath her father's in the even more crowded tenement on Coffey Street in Brooklyn.

Coley didn't cry when he realized she was leaving; the suddenness of it had staggered him. Seven now, he took over the chores, cleaning the house and tending the garden and chickens that scratched out back, gathering their eggs in the morning and, when he was older, wringing their necks.

When he turned eight, his father took a better job with the new fire department, as the assistant to the foreman, Dan Tibbetts, at Lackawanna Engine Company Number 1, where he managed the horses that pulled the bucket carriage and the old hand-pump wagon. In those days, fires in Rondout were nearly as frequent as lightning strikes, and he often spent four nights a week at the firehouse. Jimmy and Coley settled into this simple existence and continued to grow apart.

Although he knew every mother's eye was on him, Coley drifted freely with the other New Dublin boys who gathered at the waterfront after their chores were done. They'd watch the coal boats come up Rondout Creek, steering clear of the sour men who worked the wharves, or wander to the end of the landing to see the enormous schooners gliding in from foreign ports. If they were lucky, the sailors would toss them a few coins for running errands, or pay them with grapefruits or bags of sugar from the Virgin Islands. Other times, irritable from a bad crossing, the same sailors might cuff or curse them, and they'd still get a thrill from the brilliant screed of profanities they could later use on one another.

In the early spring they'd wander up to the rich farmland along Esopus Creek, where Indians had settled two hundred years before, and hunt for arrowheads and tomahawks in the freshly plowed earth, digging for long-buried treasures in clumps of black soil that broke apart in their filthy hands.

In the year the war started, Coley began helping his father at the firehouse. He was ten years old and big enough to take a brush and currycomb to the horses under Jimmy's care. He liked the changing smells of the horses' hides as he groomed them, how competing scents of smoke and dust and sweat were released with every swipe of the bristles, and how the texture of the hide would change from rough to smooth as he went back and forth, stopping only to shake his sore wrists. These big Morgans ignored him even as he doted on them, swinging their heads like truncheons when they turned to yank carrots from his outstretched hand. They were stupid and loyal only to the feed bucket, but he admired their gruffness and strength.

When he was done with his chores, he sat with his father in front of the wide wooden doors, nodding to the people who passed by and reading the local newspaper. The firehouse was right around the corner from Shapiro's, and the stable owner often stopped in to inquire about the health of the horses he'd sold to the engine company. Jimmy would lift the hooves of the four geldings for his inspection, while Shapiro tried to engage him in talk about horseflesh and the ragged baseball game played the Saturday before at the Eclipse Club, where the score remained tied through seven innings, until Rob Flannery bounced a hard drive off Karl Ehmer's forehead and Andy Hogan danced across home plate to win the game. Jimmy never said a word, and when Shapiro was done expounding on the small but important state of his universe, he clasped his hands behind his back and walked briskly back to his stable. Father and son then settled back in their chairs with the newspapers, Jimmy following the war news that was highlighted on the second page, while Coley went right for the sideline articles that were balanced with humorous stories and tales of local crime.

They lived like this, in a state of suspended love, until the great fire that started in Jonas Weiland's junkyard.

The weather that week had been so hot and dry that the air seemed to crackle on its own. Coley turned twelve that summer, and one of the things he always remembered about the terrible heat was the sight of once-wild dogs that had raced through the narrow streets now lying in the gutters and gasping like dying men, their thin hides drawn tight, their bones showing, their tongues hanging loose and pink in the baked dirt.

Weiland lived on the bottom floor of a dilapidated two-story house at the end of Hunter Street. The porches sagged in one direction and the roofs in the other, and the wooden posts that supported the balcony were as fragile as old bones. He owned the house and rented the top floor to the Kleidall brothers, a pair of itinerant musicians who played fairs and social halls from Troy to Newburgh. Henry, the younger of the two, had delicate features and a voice as feathery as a woman's sigh. He was a favorite among concertgoers, who leaned forward in their seats and concentrated in absolute silence so as not to miss his sorrowful tones. His brother, Charlie, accompanied him on piano or guitar, and they often performed with the Ulster Guard and other militia units that gathered at the Rondout docks to send off troops or greet the lucky ones coming home. Coley remembered hearing them in 1861, when soldiers in the Twentieth Regiment returned from their first tour of duty in the fields of Maryland. Although they'd seen no action, Colonel Pratt marched them grandly to the Academy Green, high-stepping to the boisterous marches performed by the Clinton Hall Brass Band, their cornets and alto horns held up to the sky, the rat-a-tat of notes as loud as pistol shots. There were sausages and rhubarb pies and lemonade provided by volunteers from St. Mary's Church, and every man with political ambitions mounted the podium to make a speech that was cut short by the heckling crowd. But it was the Kleidall brothers whom Coley enjoyed the most. When Henry took the stage to sing "God Bless Our Brave Young Volunteers!" not even the chipmunks stirred. He sang it an octave higher than most men could reach, holding the notes as long as Charlie could sustain them on the piano, the effort causing his cheeks to erupt in a scarlet flush. While his brother sat humped over the keys, playing the song as slowly as he could without losing the melody, Henry sang as if he were delivering the message from the pulpit, and as the last note faded into the humid air, women dabbed at their eyes with handkerchiefs and men bawled like babies.

On the night of the fire, the Kleidalls had just finished practicing in their room. That same afternoon, Weiland had completed his monthly sweep of the farms and villages below the Catskills, and his side yard was filled with the scrap he'd collected on his journey—pots and pans, old wheels and buggy beds, rusted tools and bundles of worn clothing. His mule was tied to the empty wagon, eating the wilted heads of lettuce that Weiland's daughter, Caddy, tossed through the kitchen window. Caddy was twenty-six and unmarried, pretty but prone to tantrums that left young suitors with their faces scratched and their wits addled. She loved her father, and for all her howling and connip-tions, she kept a vigilant eye on his junkyard.

She was asleep that night in the little storage room off the kitchen, where on hot summer nights she liked to curl up with the sacks of potatoes and flour because it was a corner room and had two small windows to catch what little breeze was there. She slept intermit-tently, with her nightgown bunched up and her loose brown hair stick-ing to the sweat that rolled off her neck and shoulders. Charlie Kleidall, unable to sleep in the god-awful heat, stood at the window above her, wearing only his cotton drawers, his pale chest shiny with perspiration, while his brother, Henry, slept in the bed behind him, a muslin sheet pulled up to his chin, as if there was a chill in the air. Charlie wiped his brow and reached for the pipe on the table, tamped in some fresh tobacco and, leaning out the open window, lit it with a wooden match. Once the tobacco caught and flared, he dropped the match, which landed on a pile of threadbare shirts below. Charlie turned his back to the window and cupped his hand over the bowl of his pipe as the shirts began to burn.

Caddy didn't smell the smoke as much as feel the heat coming through the open window over her head. She sat up quickly, her body awake but her mind still drowsy. Hearing the mule bawl, she ran bare-foot into the side yard, where the fire rose before her like a splendid curtain. Now fully awake, she pushed through it to untie the mule from the burning wagon, the animal braying as it sat back on its haunches and the taut rope sizzled and frayed. Then the rope snapped and the mule tumbled onto its back, legs kicking wildly over its fat stomach, and Caddy was thinking this was the funniest spectacle on earth, when her nightgown caught fire with a rush of sparks that ascended right up her body. The mule rolled onto its feet and bolted through the fence, and Caddy screamed the first alarm as she watched the fire take the skin off her arms and legs. It wasn't pain she felt, but sheer mad terror, and she inhaled through charred lips and screamed again, spinning back into the house like a human torch.

Neighbors were awake now and bells were sounding. By the time people were out in the street, the entire first floor of the Weiland house was engulfed in flames—a combustible maelstrom snorting ribbons of fire that had already ignited the porch of the Evans house next door and the roof of the McMillan house behind it.

Jimmy Hinds was with the first engine company to arrive. When he pulled his bucket carriage up to the foot of Hunter Street, five houses were burning and it seemed the whole sky was on fire. Jimmy's skin itched with the roar of it. The big Morgans pranced and balked when he snapped the reins but then inched forward, the stiff hair of their manes rising in the pulsing heat.

Neighbors began running across the road to grab the water buckets off his carriage, and they were a ragged crew—some dressed in night-shirts, their bare feet scratched and bleeding and their hair warped by sleep, others streaming up from the saloons and whorehouses down by the river. Blacksmith John Connolly seemed more wide-eyed than usual, with his eyebrows and bristly beard singed from his face as he freed chickens and goats from backyard stalls. Salesman Rudd Dyjk, suddenly sober but his every pore damp and sweet with rum, reached for a bucket with arms the color of burnt cork. Up and down the street, women were screaming out the names of children still missing, hold-ing on to the ones they'd recovered by arms and ears or the scruff of a neck. Older boys broke free to help the men on the bucket brigade, attacking the fire as it raged on, gobbling up the next house like drag-on's breath.

Jimmy Hinds kept the buckets moving until he heard the sound of Henry Kleidall's voice coming from above and looked up. Through the shimmering darkness he saw the brothers huddled together in an upstairs window, barely visible through the black smoke pouring out around them. Henry's voice carried above the crackling intensity, now with a tremolo of fear that gave it added heartbreak. As Dave Van Etten maneuvered his hook and ladder onto Hunter Street, he heard Henry scream and saw Jimmy running toward the burning house as if heeding a siren's call. He cupped his hands over his mouth and yelled, "Jimmy!" just as Hinds disappeared into the overpowering blaze.

When Coley pushed through the crowd on the corner of Ravine Street, smoke had gathered like huge black fists in the sky, pumping high above the burning ruins, and he took it all in: women being dragged away from burning houses, writhing and kicking and trying to break free, barely dressed, nightgowns ripped and smudged, their dreams turned to nightmares; slack-jawed children mesmerized by the devastation; Isaac Pardee strutting close to the wall of fire in the colonel's uniform he still wore night and day, proud of the stripes sewn on the right sleeve that was pinned above the elbow, the rest of the arm lost at the battle of Bethel Church during the early months of the war. He saw what was left of Hiram Sherry being carried across the street and dropped on a patch of dirt away from the fire, where his bloated and blackened remains let off whiffs of smoke like burned meat. And, squeezing closer, he saw his father's bucket carriage standing across from the scorched remains of the Weiland house.

He ran past men pounding down the street with shovels and pitchforks and climbed onto the carriage, hunkering low on the floorboards, out of sight, waiting for his father to come back. He raised his head high enough to watch Dave Van Etten climb to the second-story window of a house down the street, where Mrs. Crosby handed him her two little girls, the fireman placing each inside his thick coat and carrying them down the ladder to the ground. Then the flames jumped to the roof above Mrs. Crosby's head, and the shingles curled and split and flew off the roof as the fire worked its way into the eaves. He never saw Mrs. Crosby again.

Coley sat there watching for two more hours, long after the sun had risen, washed out, a hesitant hole in the sky, the soft clouds above the river now the color of bruised oranges. The fire slowly lost its passion, dying with the wind that suddenly stilled. He waited while ashes swirled around him as thick as blackflies, the heat so intense even now that he imagined the fire was burning underground.

He was still waiting when Dave Van Etten sat down next to him on the carriage, his face caked with soot, smeared and running from the sweat that poured from his matted hair. He smelled terrible. "Your father went in after those Kleidall boys because he heard them crying for help," the man told him. "He thought of nothin' but that."

Coley wondered what Henry Kleidall's cry must have sounded like at that dreadful moment. Had his father heard it as he dove through rings of fire? Had it floated upward in perfect pitch, like a lyric in the saddest song, a note sustained in the red air as the burning house collapsed around them all?

"It was pure bravery, son, and that's how he'll be remembered," Van Etten said gruffly, not truly believing it. "He was a man to stand with, Jimmy Hinds was." Then he bumped Coley's shoulder with his own before jumping off the carriage to help pull apart the cooked remains of the ten houses that had burned down that night.

Coley endured the news in such stoic silence that the fireman would remark on it for days to come. "The boy's got Jimmy's piss and spleen, but let's hope to Christ he's got more sense."

Coley felt a heaviness in his limbs and sat on the buckboard long enough to see Jonas Weiland emerge from the wreckage of Hunter Street, his exposed skin grimed with soot. Both his hands were burned, the knuckles raw and the flesh around the wounds glistening white. His steps were as light and exaggerated as a bird's as he picked through the rubble, and Coley realized he wasn't wearing any shoes. The old man stooped to retrieve a twisted pan and shrieked as his hand touched the hot metal handle, then threw the pan to the ground and spit on his fingers. He found a wooden cart amid the charred wreckage and pulled it to the street before going back into the ruined houses, his own included, emerging from the first with a barrel of vinegar and some horseshoes and a pair of boots he measured for himself. After six more trips, his cart was nearly full, and he was back in business again.

Coley flicked on the reins and drove the horses back to the fire station, led them to their stalls, put away the harnesses and hung up the tack. Then he fed them their summer hay, and while they ate, he washed them down and gave them a good brushing to erase the stink of smoke from their hides. It was almost noon when he finished, sat outside on the chair next to his father's and made himself consider the man who was no longer there. His death seemed just an ordinary fact. Jimmy Hinds was one of eight who had perished that morning, and this dreadful simplicity left the boy more stunned than heartbroken. He knew in his marrow that he'd lost his father when his mother died, that he'd merely lingered seven years before fading way.

When he looked up, Shapiro was standing in front of the firehouse, his shirt stained yellow and brown from the fire. He was staring at Coley, but when the boy met his gaze, he looked away and moved into the open doorway. With a blackened hand on his right hip, he glanced at the horses.

"The animals are good?"

"Yes."

"You feed them?"

"Yes."

"And you?"

Coley was used to Shapiro's truncated phrasing, and he liked how it circumvented pleasantries. And when he realized how hungry he was, he said so.

"Come, then."

Shapiro walked off, and Coley followed him into the house next to the stables. Mrs. Shapiro fed them fried lamb chops, brown bread sweetened with molasses and cold beets in a puddle of vinegar. Coley saw Esther for the first time when, at Mrs. Shapiro's insistence, she served him a third lamb chop, shoveling it onto his plate with a great splatter of grease. Her black hair was long and thick, the twists in her braids perfect. Her breasts were small but, to Coley's eyes, flawless. She was fourteen then, obedient to her parents and quietly respectful, but there was already a furrowing of her brow and a smirk on her lips when their backs were turned.

"Come, then," Shapiro said as he pushed away from the table, and Coley went with him and set straight to work taking care of the horses in his livery. He never left.

He was cleaning dried mud off a breast strap when the man walked into the stable. He didn't see him at first, busy as he was working his brush around the stitching that held the buckle.

"Can I help you, sir?" he heard Shapiro ask the stranger. Coley didn't even bother to look up, disgusted as he was with his boss's lack of consideration for hired help. "I'd like to buy a horse," the man replied.

"Come, then."

Coley heard them walk into the stable through the wide doors on Hone Street. Shapiro shuffled as he always did, his shoes raspy on the spilled hay, wheezing with each step, like the same straw was stuck in his throat as under his heels.

"Coley!" he called. "Show this gentleman the horses in the yard."

Coley stood and brushed the dried mud from his hands. When he looked up the man was staring at him, grinning slightly, his valise still balanced on his shoulder. Coley's first inclination was to run, but all he could do was stare back.

"Coley!" Shapiro yelled again. "Help Mr. . . ." He looked up at the customer and turned his palms upward.

"Harp," Will said. "Will Harp."

Shapiro pressed his hands together sharply. "Help Mr. Harp with his bag."

When Coley walked toward the men like a wary dog, Shapiro could barely conceal his impatience. "What's the matter with you, boy? Did you get kicked in the head?"

"No."

"Good. Don't make me kick you in the pants."

When Will handed him his valise, Coley noticed the U.S. INFANTRY insignia stitched into the side. The bag was heavy, and he could tell there were books inside as he set it down and motioned with his chin to the paddocks out back. "This way, Mr. Harp."

He followed Will around the fenced yard and watched him examine the half dozen horses. He wasn't particularly tall, but he stood very erect, and his back was wide and strong. He approached the horses with his arm extended and his hand flat, letting them breathe in his scent before running his fingers down their flanks. His long hair hung below his collar, and his wide-brimmed hat was creased like the adventurers in Coley's weeklies. But it was the boots that caught his attention.

"You from out west, mister?" he asked.

"Yes," Will replied, grabbing hold of the halter on the black gelding and walking him around the yard.

"You been to California?"

"I live there."

Coley tried not to sound too anxious as he stepped closer, the questions lining up in his head and threatening to spill out in a jumbled mess when he opened his mouth. "You seen the Rocky Mountains?"

"Yes."

"And the Texas desert?"

"Yes."

"The Pacific Ocean?"

"That, too."

"Indians?"

"Many," Will replied as he circled the gelding again.

"Apaches? Comanche?"

Will turned to him and smiled, but before he could answer, Coley's mouth was open again. "Sioux?"

"I've seen a lot of Indians."

"Were you a scout?"

"No."

"Were you in the army?"

"I was."

"Did you fight Indians?"

Will paused, and the smile froze on his face. "I did what I had to do."

"Mister, I—"

"I'll take this horse," Will said, interrupting him. "And I'll need a saddle and blankets and a bridle. Can you get those for me?"

Coley had more questions, but he knew better than to voice them. "Sure I can, Mr. Harp."

He took the lead rope out of Will's hand and led the black gelding inside. He stopped in the doorway and turned back to Will, who remained standing in the corral, watching the sparrows fly into the dark shadows under the eaves on the barn. "I'm going out west myself someday," Coley said. "As soon as this war's over, I'm going to California."

Will slowly angled his head and looked at him as if he'd forgotten the boy was even there.

"And Mr. Harp?"

"Yes?"

"On the docks?"

"Yes."

"I wasn't meaning any offense."

"I know."

"Good."

Shapiro kept a small office in an oversized stall at the front of the stable. It was a clean room, swept free of loose straw and cobwebs, where he had a desk and a large window with a clear view of the street. There was no door, so Will leaned against a post and waited to pay while Shapiro took an order from the young woman who stood before him.

"Tomorrow, then," Shapiro told her, his head down as he scribbled in a ledger. Sunlight shone on his shiny black hair, and the thin line of scalp that showed through the part looked as if it had been drawn with chalk. "Three bales of alfalfa and a bag of oats."

"Thank you, Mr. Shapiro."

He nodded and looked up at her, squinting in the sunlight. "Is there any word from Frank Quinn?"

"Frank Quinn," Will murmured. It was only when he looked up and saw the two of them staring at him that he realized he'd spoken out loud.

Jane regarded him eagerly. She laid a cool hand on his own, gripping his knuckles as hard as she could, and he felt the urgency of her touch travel up his arm. "Do you know Frank?" she asked.

Will stared at this pretty woman with long caramel-colored hair, and her blue eyes held him, unblinking.

"Do you have any word of Frank Quinn?"

Recognizing the anxiety in her voice, Will knew that whatever he said would disappoint her. "I knew a Frank Quinn," he replied, "a long time ago. He sometimes worked for my father at our farm in the Clove."

Her fingers slowly loosened, and she lowered her eyes and seemed to breathe for the first time. "Thank you."

Will stepped aside as she walked past him and out of the stable, his eyes fixed on the long braid that ran down her back.

Shapiro came around his big desk and yelled after her. "I'll have the boy deliver in the morning, Miss Blessing!"

The men watched her walk along the dirt path bordering the road until she passed out of sight.

"Is it the same Frank Quinn?" Will asked Shapiro.

"He's a Rondout man."

Will nodded. "Where is he now?"

"Cold Harbor."

Will knew about Cold Harbor. Every headline he'd seen east of St. Louis had been bold and black with the news.

⟍❦⟋

HE WATCHED from beneath the heavy black cloth, where it was safe to stare, as if within his own dreams, and studied the strong body of the man who sat naked on the divan. He focused on the penis, which lay solid and firm along the inside of his right leg, a patient extension of the much less patient man. His hands were moving, Arthur could see that, but he knew he would stop when directed, when the light was right and they could go on.

A naked woman was perched on each of his knees, which were spread wide to accommodate them. The women were young, no more than eighteen, and as similar as sisters, though Arthur knew they weren't. They'd been here many times before, sent up from Manhattan by his benefactor, who gladly paid their steamer passage because he fancied their looks. They were chubby, their plump little rolls of belly as creamy and smooth as folds of thick cream. Their hair was dark and artificially styled into ringlets, hanging loosely over their shoulders in the manner of harem nymphs, and they wore silver bracelets on both wrists and ankles. This was also done at his client's request, and he often provided extra funds for the purchase of such extravagant accoutrements as the plush drapes of maroon velvet with golden tassels that were hung behind them to suggest a Bedouin tent.

The light was almost right now, falling down from the skylight like rays of desert sunshine across the contrived tableau before him. Arthur relaxed for a moment and again turned his attention to the man. His body was hairless except for the few reddish curls that sprang across his breastbone and the bright weave of pubic hair that sent wiry sparks up to his belly button. He had a tapered waist and wide shoulders stained with coppery freckles, his whole physical being brilliantly defined by the grappling of tendon and bone. So rapt was Arthur's pleasure that he forgot the noxious scent of collodion and nitrate, a chemical fugue that rose thick and warm under the black cloth.

His senses invigorated, he scanned the details of the frame in the ground glass—the heavy drapes, the Persian rugs, the tall samovar and silver goblets—until he was satisfied with the minutiae of his Arabian Night, as finely imagined as an engraving by Gustave Doré. He was about to call his assistant when he noticed the girls were squirming, and the sublime elasticity of the moment snapped. These models were trained to sit as still as sleeping parakeets, and paid well for their ability to feign stupefaction. About to come out of hiding and raise his voice in displeasure, he then caught a fleeting glimpse of the impetus for their motion. As the girls swayed gently on the man's spread knees, their own thighs parted slightly as his fingers moved nimbly between their trembling legs, two fingers on each hand sliding up and down, slowly and with great care. The girls tried hard to maintain their poise but failed, arching their backs and relaxing their muscles, yielding to his touch. Arthur watched their breasts rise with each deep breath, and he breathed along with them, as if he were being dandled on a third knee. And the whole time, Mickey Blessing stared directly into the camera lens, in complete control.

Only when a diffused spray of light filtered down through the grimy skylight did Arthur remember to concentrate on the job at hand. He didn't raise his head from beneath the black cloth, just stamped his foot and shouted, "Thomas!"

From behind the partition, Thomas Farrow emerged in a cloud of sulfur fumes, carrying a glass plate as if it were a tablet of the Ten Commandments. He was a stocky young man, pinched into one of the double-breasted wool vests he wore through all seasons, the heavy garment stretched at every seam by pounds of soft flesh. He inserted the plate into the wooden sleeve of the camera with more force than was called for, then stood there with his round hands clasped behind his back.

Arthur heard the plate click into place and waited a few more seconds as the falling light grew brighter and Mickey's hands receded from view. The girls held still now, almost dreamy in appearance; the smaller one on the left tilted her head back and raised her heels off the floor, balancing on her bent toes and throwing an exquisitely contoured shadow across the floor. With the natural light sketching every muscle on his naked torso, Mickey kept staring right into the lens, directly at Arthur, every bit as empirical as a desert prince. The beauty of the man took his breath away.

Arthur closed his eyes for a brief second, then studied the scene before him and exposed the plate.

An hour later he was sitting at the desk in his shop. It was a large, well-used room with twelve-foot ceilings and two big windows looking out to the Strand. In the left window, in classic lettering the color of tarnished brass, bold letters announced:

ARTHUR DOWD
PHOTOGRAPHS AND FINE ART GALLERY

In the other window, in similar script, a sign read:

ALBUMS AND CARTE DE VISITES
FRAMES AND HAND COLORING

The interior walls were covered with photographs, in frames oval or round, gilded or metal. There were daguerreotypes and ambrotypes, some hand-tinted with subtle blushing, others livened with a sweep of India ink. There were photographs of children with their pets, bankers with their wives, newlyweds and fiancés, families posed behind a table decorated with flowers or in front of a painted backdrop of a forest glen, somber portraits of bearded patriarchs in tight suits, their elbows propped on pedestals or clutching family Bibles, and glamorous ones of women in summer finery, standing next to wicker carriages full of curly-headed babies swaddled in linen and lace. An entire wall was devoted to soldiers going off to or returning from war, with many fewer of the latter.

Arthur was bent over the desk, writing a letter to Isaac Stokes and agreeing to go out to Butterfields to photograph his Irish wolfhounds in an "environment more natural to their spirited posture." He was a lean and almost handsome man, his nose a shade too prominent, and in his youth had been likened to a character in a Washington Irving story. At thirty-three he was still youthful, though he didn't feel so himself.

Still writing when the front door opened, he didn't look up, but wrote more quickly, so as not to seem rude. Listening to his visitor's footsteps, he dipped his pen one last time and signed his name with an easy flourish. He then affected the smile he bestowed on all his customers, but it stalled when he saw the man standing in front of him and grew broad and genuine. "Will Harp?" he said, and stood to embrace him.

～❧～

HE SCRUTINIZED the large map, framed on the wall behind his desk, that depicted Ulster County more than sixty years ago, commissioned by his own father from an assistant to David Burr, the great cartographer who'd mapped the United States when it extended with blunt force as far west as Missouri. The earliest markings were dated March 25, 1804, the same day his father, Abraham Grieves, had stepped ashore at Columbus Point and made his first fortune by purchasing the smoldering rubble of three Rondout streets ravaged by fire that very morning. Over the next few years he continued to make good investments and fast enemies with equal speed, buying land deemed worthless until he had it cleared for an apple orchard, green-rippled pasture, sawmill or store and leased it back at a substantial profit. On Chestnut Street, he built for his wife and young son a beautiful clapboard house designed by an architect from Virginia, with a columned portico, the same large Palladian windows favored by Thomas Jefferson, and a magnificent garden, tended by slaves. It was a house to envy, and Abraham Grieves never denied the gossip of extravagant costs, sighing as though his own bold aesthetics would trump the dollar every time. He liked to display his achievements with a flourish, his actions about as confident as a thumb poked in his neighbor's eye.

Then the rumors started. It was said—always quietly and behind his back—that the Rondout fire was highly suspicious, and no one had actually seen Abraham Grieves step off the sloop that sailed into the harbor that day. Once baffled out of a good investment by the quicker maneuvering of Grieves, Ian Ballard, the veterinary surgeon, posited the notion that he'd traveled overland from the forests to the north, half-mad with grand intentions for their little port town, and started the fire of 1804 himself, only to emerge from the smoke and wreckage with his fortune assured. Grieves loved the story and did nothing to dissuade its telling.

In truth, Grieves's past was as common as sour-milk pudding. A bored and unsuccessful lawyer in Vermont when he turned thirty, he convinced his young wife to sell their home in Shelbourne and travel south with their young son to start anew in the urban wilds of Manhattan. But as their sloop came down the Hudson from Troy, he saw plumes of smoke rising above Rondout, and once the boat docked, he examined the shabby town built around the wharf. There were a couple of storefronts by the water's edge, where wooden crates of apples were piled high under a sizzle of buzzing flies. Dogs slept on the planks by their owners' feet, man and beast splayed in the noonday sun. Standing on the pebbly shore, breathing in the charred fumes, Abraham Grieves smelled opportunity.

By the time Harry was sixteen, his father had already purchased a great deal of the farmland between Kingston and Rondout. When he joined his family's business, the canal that would bring affluence to the region was already under way, and Rondout soon filled with workers and entrepreneurs who built houses and businesses on the streets that his father owned, and they grew wealthier still.

Abraham instructed his son to honor other men's dreams and aspirations, because even if they lacked ambition, their desires could prove valuable. "Act decisively," he always said. "It's easy to pull out of a lady's cunt, but it's hard to get your cock inside if another's already in there." Though seldom vulgar, he enjoyed how such language sawed through the pretense of good manners and exposed the bile that seeped through every man.

In the summer of 1831, Abraham and his wife boarded the *General Jackson*, bound for Manhattan. It was his wife's birthday, and he had planned on surprising her with dinner at Delmonico's and then a carriage ride to the Bowery Theatre to see Rossini's latest comic opera. Harry, by then in his late twenties, saw his parents off that morning, giving his mother a ribboned box that contained a brooch he'd ordered from a renowned Philadelphia silversmith. She wasn't supposed to open the box until they had champagne in their room at the Astor House before going out to dinner.

But his parents never made it to Manhattan to drink champagne, open presents and enjoy the opera. The *General Jackson* blew a boiler outside the harbor at Peekskill and sank quickly in the calm June waters. While Abraham Grieves had amassed a small fortune and outfoxed most everyone, he'd never learned to swim. He went down with the broken vessel, drifting to the bottom of the Hudson with his wife and her silver brooch.

Of all the passengers who perished that day, Abraham and Helen were the most notable, and Harry made sure their death notice was prominently displayed in newspapers from Albany to Manhattan. Then he took over the business and, as his father would have wanted, never missed a day's work.

On the map, every property and parcel he owned was marked with red ink, the marks so plentiful that it looked like the map had been sprayed with blood. Over the past thirty years, Harry had doubled the Grieves's holdings throughout the county. Whereas his father had been content to dominate the relatively small district of Kingston and Rondout, Harry viewed the world through a wider frame. Beyond the local dynasty his father had started and the thousand or so acres he owned throughout Marbletown, he was also a partner in a quarry in Palenville, a sawmill in Rochester and a gunpowder factory in Saugerties that had a substantial contract with the Army of the Potomac.

On the surface he attempted to convey a kind of commonality with his peers, joining other men of means who linked the good of the city to the heft of their own pockets. So he sat in meetings and supported plans for the Ulster railroad, investing time and money in an enterprise he was convinced would transform the region. Thousands of miles of tracks were already being laid through the West, and when the war soon ended and the destroyed southern lines were repaired, the entire country would be connected by a latticework of steel, joining the broken states like a clasping of hands.

The war was changing everything. Grieves could feel it even as he sat in his office and viewed it from a luxurious distance. In this time of trouble, commerce never stopped and profits held steady. As southern cities were decimated, their northern counterparts prospered. Everyone needed cement and bricks and bluestone to construct their buildings and pave their sidewalks, and the boats carrying these goods left the Rondout docks as quickly as they were loaded. These businesses needed manpower to help fill their orders, men needed places to live and therefore rents had to be paid—precipitating an explosion of activity where money seemed to be passed around with every handshake.

He was grateful that his own sons were still too young to volunteer. He'd never let them, of course, but they didn't know that yet. He allowed Daniel, the oldest at sixteen, to discuss the war at the supper table and boast of friends and their battlefield exploits. And Franklin, younger by two years but already taller and stronger, applauded the collapse of Lee's failing army and vowed to march into Richmond himself to sock Jefferson Davis in the eye. Grieves and his wife were as patriotic as any couple in Rondout, and though lapsed Whigs, they came to believe that the war was just and that Lincoln was a good president and a great man. Albertina rolled bandages for the Ulster Volunteers at the Eddyville Church, and Harry, a major in the National Greys and a village trustee, had also helped start the Rondout Soldiers' Benevolent Society to aid veterans returning home from the southern fray. But he would never allow his civic duty to supersede his fatherly role and would rather tie his sons to their beds or lock them in the cellar than let them walk out the door to die.

His eyes lingered on the large map, following the thick black line that was drawn tight to the western edge of the Hudson. It was the proposed route of the New York Central Railroad, and ran from Albany to Manhattan, swinging west at junctions for Syracuse and Buffalo and the interior of Pennsylvania. Other lines were being stitched together under the cold, brilliant eyes of Carnegie and Vanderbilt, providing further opportunities that would only bleed gold.

And that's what Grieves was counting on, and why he'd spent the last several years quietly buying up land along the Shawangunk Ridge, where he would build his great hotel in the wilderness. That was his grand ambition. His future.

He became aware of knocking at the door and realized that he'd been hearing it for quite some time. With the next series of taps, he lowered his eyes from the map and slowly turned.

Mickey Blessing leaned in his open doorway, arms crossed and right hip cocked outward. "Can I do anything for you, Mr. Grieves?" he asked with a grin.

Grieves looked at him and nodded. He admired the man's barefaced stance, his ability to control the space he occupied with only the shameless power of his will. There was nothing passive about Mickey Blessing. He might not have been as fixed in action or temperament as Frank Quinn, but Frank was probably dead in some Virginia cornfield, his blood and flesh and bones already mulched into the rich earth, and Grieves couldn't afford to be without a persuasive arm. And while Frank was a steadfast and reliable enforcer, there was something to be said for the corkscrew quality of Mickey's approach. Over the past year, having gotten used to Mickey's more colorful and challenging remedies to the complications of his business life, Grieves had begun to rely on him with growing trust and urgency, often just for the shocking pleasure of unpredictable results.

"You're collecting rents in the country tomorrow?" he asked.

"Yes."

"Good. I want you to deliver a letter to Isaac Stokes in the Clove. It's not out of your way."

"Wouldn't matter if it was, would it, Mr. Grieves?"

Mickey smiled, and Grieves couldn't help but smile back as he pointed to the envelope on his desk. "In the morning would be best. Make it your first stop, Mickey."

He nodded, then slipped the envelope into his jacket pocket. "Are there any other special visits you'd like me to make?"

"Not tomorrow, Mickey."

"Then I'll be off."

"Good-bye, Mickey."

He lowered his head, one eyebrow raised as if he was looking under the brim of a hat. It was a look he had practiced often. "So long, Mr. Grieves."

THEY SAT UPSTAIRS in Arthur's parlor. It was just getting dark, and as they drank brandy, a sudden rain rattled against the window like a spray of stones.

"I found your address in your father's papers. I wrote as soon as I could."

"I know. Thank you, Arthur."

"I was very fond of him. He was a good man."

"He had a good life. It was just old age. He was stubborn enough to withstand everything else."

"God, it must be more than ten years since you've been back."

"I suppose it is," Will replied. "It seems almost a lifetime."

Arthur watched his friend with a solemn smile. He was careful not to intrude unless invited to, and then he would only prod as delicately as one might check for bruises on ripe fruit. He sat up suddenly, his whole body seeming to straighten in the chair. "You're home now! And I believe the change will do you good. It will be like a freshening wind."

Will barely nodded and drank off his brandy.

"But you'll go west again. I'm sure of it," Arthur continued. "I expect it calls to you like a barking dog."

And Will imagined he could hear it, even above the tap of rain running down the windows like silver filigree: the yelping of the mutt that roamed the alley behind his small adobe house on Olivera Street, her nightly cries rising like sour notes in the thin Los Angeles air. "Yes. As soon as I take care of my father's business, I'll go back."

"Well, I'm glad you're here now, and I'll take advantage of your company for as long as I can."

Will poured himself more brandy from the decanter and offered some to Arthur, who declined with a raised palm.

"You drink too much, Will," he said.

Will replaced the glass stopper in the decanter and didn't deny it. He tipped his glass back, the brandy fumes sharp in his nose.

PUSH, PULL, PUSH, pull, push, pull was all that went through Jane's head as she sewed another triangle onto the block of her quilt, her mind numbed by the repetition of her work. She sat in the front room, on the wide chair that Frank preferred, the unfinished quilt gathered in her lap. She had the windows open to Spring Street, where she heard Adam Novak's horses clomp by as they pulled his milk wagon home after a long day of work, and when she dared to look up from the straight line she was working on, she saw Ann Feeney sitting on her porch across the street, ignoring the drizzle to take advantage of the warm night air.

Push, pull, push, pull, push, pull. The rhythm of it was steady as water dripping into a pail. It was Mary Knetch who had gotten her involved with the women at St. Mary's Church, a dozen wives and mothers who'd been making quilts for hospital beds since the war began. For the first month, Jane had sat in a circle with the women in the church basement, watching their quick fingers and taking their advice, joining in their talk of community life and local blather. They never spoke of the war that had brought them all together, partly out of deference to Alice Crown, whose husband had died at Gettysburg, and partly out of the superstition that the quilt they worked on might become the shroud for the husband or son whose safe return they prayed for every night.

Having never made a quilt before, Jane chose the easiest pattern she could find, the simple stacking of triangles that represented geese in flight. Still, she'd been working on this quilt for over eight months now, with no end in sight. She had planned to give it only an hour that afternoon, but before she knew it, three had passed and it was full dark now, and in the brief moment it had taken her to notice Ann Feeney, she realized the line she had just finished was crooked and she'd have to rip it apart and start all over again. Her fingers were cramped, her hands hurt and her eyes were sore, so she stood in frustration and let the quilt fall to the floor, stretching her back and stepping away from what had turned into her life's work.

Jane lifted up the spectacles she'd taken to wearing and rubbed the red indentations on the bridge of her nose. Over the past year she had found it increasingly difficult to read unless in bright sunshine, and when she couldn't finish Metta Victor's *The Unionist's Daughter* by the evening fire without holding the page inches from her eyes, she'd given in and gone to see the eyeglass salesman when he came through Rondout last February. She was the first in line when he set up his cases in McMann's shop, trying to avoid the wagging tongues of early-bird gossips sure to gloat over her failing eyesight. She'd bought the first pair that seemed to correct her astigmatism and shoved them deep into her pocket, where they stayed for a week. They were silver-framed, with oval lenses, and when she finally put them on, she couldn't bear to look at herself in the mirror. She wore them only in the privacy of her home, grumpily satisfied that they brightened any page she was reading and made her stitching go faster, if not more accurately.

Jane took the glasses off as she walked into the kitchen, almost stepping on the old cat that slept by the hearth. The cat had been here when Harry Grieves gave Frank the small house, and he hadn't the heart to send her off, instead making her a bed of his favorite shirt.

"She was here first," Frank said when she asked what he was doing.

"But she's so ugly."

"So's my mother, but I love her, too."

She accepted the cat's company and the cat accepted hers, and they shared the house like sisters, waiting for the return of the man who doted on them both.

At first, Jane felt uncomfortable about moving into the house, but Frank had insisted.

"What will people say?" she asked him.

"They'd have nothing to say if you'd marry me."

"I'll only marry you when this war is over."

"Then I'll join up quickly and get it done," he said with a laugh, and hugged her. She moved in the day he boarded the troopship to Manhattan.

Jane stood at the window and flexed her aching fingers. She looked out over the side yard—big enough for a two-horse stable, a modest garden and half a dozen chickens—and thought about the very first letter she had received from Frank, last July, just a week before he saw his first battle at Chester Gap.

Dear Jane,

I am near Washington now, and I imagine there are more soldiers here than in all the battlefields of Virginia. Our camp is outside the city, and as you come over the hill the hundreds of tents spread in the valley are as abundant as whitecaps on the Hudson. We are here with regiments from Pennsylvania and Connecticut and Maine, every single man anxious to ram a ball down his musket and get his knuckles bloodied. But we march and drill and march and drill and count the daisies as we wait to march and drill again. Plenty of terrible food here, and even the dogs that beg around camp spit it out and go hungry. But some of the farm boys have trapped rabbits and squirrels in the woods above camp, and we roast them over a fire to keep our strength up, and spread the grease on the hardbread they give us to make it slide more easily down our throats.

I've been to Washington a few times but have yet to meet Mister Lincoln. Perhaps he is busier with the war than we are, but it would be a pleasure to shake his hand. The city is full of pretty women, though I don't look at them much unless I need to be reminded of you. Because you are still the prettiest girl I know.

Your Frank

It was hard to believe a year had passed.

Jane put on her eyeglasses and walked back to the wide chair in the parlor, picked up the quilt and pulled it across her knees, searching for the triangle she'd last worked on. When she found it, she pulled out her scissors and began carefully to break each stitch.

The front door opened, but she didn't look up as Mickey entered the house. She heard him stop and could feel him staring at her as she lifted loose threads with her fingernails.

"Look at you," he scoffed. "Wearing spectacles and working on some fancywork like a doddering old maid. If Frank came home right now and saw you sitting like that, he'd turn in the doorway and march right back to the war."

Jane looked up over the rim of her eyeglasses and smiled. Yes, she thought, if only Frank could see me now.

∽◦⊚◦∾

ARTHUR LAY in bed and watched Will strip off his shirt and refresh himself at the basin. The rain had stopped and the moon was high and nearly full over the harbor, pinned there like a bright button holding fast the clear black night. Arthur reclined with his hands behind his head, his brain slightly foggy from all the brandy, more than he'd imbibed in years. Will had insisted they toast the major and one another long into the night, and Arthur was drunkenly content as he listened to the breeze rustle the upper boughs of the maple tree outside his window, the leaves brushing together like crinkled paper.

As Will moved over the basin, his body lit only by the moonlight, Arthur saw a scar under his right nipple. The disfigurement was raised and purple, about six inches long, running at an angle across his chest. When he turned to dry his face on the towel that hung by the mirror, Arthur noticed a similar scar on his back, smaller, but with the same hard, puckered flesh.

"You've been shot," he said.

Will shrugged dismissively as his fingers lightly traced the old wound. "Just once," he replied as he pulled back the rough blanket and climbed into bed.

The thin mattress barely moved as he lay down next to Arthur, his back turned away. Arthur sat up for a while longer. The room was filled with the clean scent of the fallen rain, and his lips were still sweet with the brandy he had enjoyed an hour ago. He closed his eyes then, slightly dizzy but as happy as he'd been in a very long time. He breathed deeply, until the rhythm of his lungs matched his friend's, and fell asleep.

MICKEY LAY ACROSS Hannah Millen's rumpled sheets and looked at her naked back as she sat on the edge of the bed in front of him. She was as blond and fair-skinned as her Swedish mother, and Mickey thought she was the finest girl he'd ever laid eyes on.

He had ridden out to the Millen farm after delivering the letter to Isaac Stokes, arriving in the early afternoon. He always saved the Millen farm for his last stop on rent day, and he looked forward to the hour or two he would spend in Hannah's company.

She was an American girl, born in New Hampshire, and had come to the Clove with her husband, Joe, five years before, leading four Guernsey cows bred from original Alderney stock. They were hardy cows that calved easily, and the Millens soon had the herd they needed, letting them roam free on the green pastures they leased from Harry Grieves. It wasn't long before Joe Millen was known from Albany to Dobbs Ferry for the quality of his butter and the sharpness of his cheddar cheese, and he was soon making a nice living and a modest profit. But like many patriots, he could not ignore the call of duty, and he proudly joined the ranks of the Ulster Volunteers when Colonel Sharpe made a demand for more recruits in '62.

Mickey was remembering his first visits to the Millen farm, when he sat in the kitchen while Joe counted out the rent money. Sometimes Hannah would sit there with them or else busy herself at the wooden counter, cutting up a chicken or folding bread to be baked, her forehead beaded with perspiration, a delicate line of sweat running straight down her back as she bent to work, her dress clinging to her skin and the stain spreading like butterfly wings. She might pause then to push back a blond lock with her forearm, or Joe would do it for her and wipe the line of flour from her cheek. Mickey couldn't help but stare, wishing it were his caress she felt. In those days she was easy to humor and never once cross with Joe, but he imagined she had a wonderful temper when pricked and he liked to think of the heat rising off her honeyed skin as it reddened with excitement.

Joe had survived the Union defeat at Fredericksburg, where three hundred Confederate cannons fired on the barren plains below Marye's Hill. He was sprawled on the ground with five thousand other soldiers as the known world exploded around them, the earth shaking more than his own frightened bones. For the next six months he was afraid to sleep and afraid to die, a victim of his wretched imagination, but he marched on until a sharpshooter's bullet shattered his skull at Gettysburg.

It was last August when Mickey saw the long list of war dead posted in the *Rondout Courier* window. He rode out the next morning to give Hannah the news, stopping along the way to pick up a neighbor woman. He didn't intend to go into the house that day. He'd never seen Hannah cry, and he didn't want to face the depth of her despair.

It wasn't until September that he touched Hannah for the first time, and though she resisted, he was stronger and deaf to her screams. When he pulled the dress down from her shoulders and laid his face against her bare skin, the heat rising off her was just as sweet as he had imagined.

He now reached out for her and pushed aside the blond hair that fell across her shoulders, ignoring the sudden cringe that tightened her body as his fingertips traced the length of her spine.

He leaned forward and gently pulled her toward him. She fell back across his arms and let him lay her down, obedient as a child. He pulled the sheet off their bodies and stretched out alongside her, admiring her breasts—rounder now with every passing month—and the magical expanse of her growing belly. He put his ear to one side of her stomach and placed his hand gently on the other side, then closed his eyes and listened. Hannah was eight months pregnant and full of Mickey's baby.

◦◦◦

THEY TRAVELED on together, taking narrow trails through deep woods he hadn't been in since he was a boy. Most of the way they rode side by side, but now Arthur was following Will's horse through a tight maze of hemlocks, glad to study his friend's straight posture as they wove through the dense growth and crossed shallow ravines trickling with clear water. He breathed in the warm air, flavored with the rich scent of pine trees lightning-struck the week before, now broken and bent-armed over the almost invisible path. He glimpsed a black squirrel springing from rock to rock, only to disappear in the thick boughs of a laurel bush that shuddered and then stilled. He watched red-tailed hawks skim through the air above the canopy of colossal oak, sometimes dipping below the branches to inspect the men passing through their hunting grounds. Will followed the contours as if he'd ridden them just the day before, and Arthur trotted behind him in perfect joy, realizing he'd been spending far too much time in the photography studio. He had surprised himself by volunteering to accompany his old friend to his farm in the Clove, and was delighted when Will accepted.

He took pleasure in their mostly quiet companionability, as if the many years that had passed between them were as inconsequential and woolly as the string of clouds above. Comfortable in their shared history, they were satisfied with the simple fact of being together again. Arthur now told him about the memorial service at the Old Dutch Church in Kingston, and the many accounts of his father's service to the community and the nation during the War of 1812. An old soldier, Sazarius Staats, who had served under Major Harp at the battle of Chippawa, traveled all the way from Delaware County, helped along by a daughter at each elbow, wearing an old uniform that looked as if it had been stolen from a scarecrow, and paid eloquent homage to the man who led their militia against the British more than fifty years before. The church was so crowded that those who were unable to find a seat stood in the aisles and lined the walls during the service, some wedged into the narrow vaulted doorway of the sacristy while others filled the choir stalls.

"I saw men who hadn't spoken a civil word to one another in over a decade clasp hands in his honor," Arthur continued. "It was fine to see, Will. He was very respected."

"Yes," Will replied.

Arthur could hear sorrow in the clarity of that one word, and his thoughts wandered back to the time they'd first met, more than twenty years ago, after the major sent Will off to Kingston Academy to further his education. For the school year, the boy moved from their farm in the Clove to live with his uncle, Hiram Harp, whose stately Greek Revival house was next door to the Dowds' more modest brick Federal on Fair Street. They were ten at the time, and Arthur could remember that September morning when he looked out his window and saw Will in his uncle's front yard. It was chilly, the sky still as dark as a velvet curtain, and Will was standing by the wrought-iron fence that separated their properties, dressed in a short woolen coat and long pants, and staring up at the night as if ready to howl.

Arthur ran from the window, pulled on his twill trousers and boots and quietly left his room, trying to soften his footfalls on the runners in the upstairs hallway. After he safely passed his parents' bedroom, he scrambled down the stairs and out the front door.

Will Harp stood perfectly still as Arthur confronted him across the iron fence. He merely glanced at him before arching his neck and turning his gaze back to the sky, his long brown hair falling away from his face and settling around his ears. A thin boy, tall and long-legged, he had his arms crossed and one knee bent, looking as serious as a scholar.

Arthur slowly moved closer to the fence and rested his hand on one of the iron picket spears, the shaft damp and cold. He quickly pulled it away and flicked the dewy droplets into the air. Will ignored him, and Arthur began to think he might have made a mistake in rushing outside, that sleep would be a far better recreation on a Saturday morning, that his ducks needed feeding, that this new boy might be as dull as a snail. In the uncomfortable quiet, he decided to give him one more chance. "What are you doing?" he asked.

Will raised his arm and pointed to the east. Arthur followed the line of his finger to an opening in the sky above the pine trees, and there he saw the full moon being shunted through a riffle of gray clouds. It was shiny and fat, playing through the drifting clouds like a silver dollar in a magician's fingers. Arthur thought it was one of the most perfect things he had ever seen. He took a deep breath and stood across the fence from Will, his neck bent back and his arms loosely crossed, staring gratefully into the beckoning sky.

Will marveled at the landscape that slowly opened up around them, as stubborn and enduring as the facts of his own history. After all the long years spent following rivers and trails across the broad back of the country, he was surprised at how strongly the eastern geography still gripped him.

They crossed the Esopus Creek east of Hurley, then took the old mine road straight through the lowland valley. This gentle swath of land was ideal for farming and had long views that stretched for miles, crested by a long ridge of razorback hills densely forested with hardwoods that would shelter generations to come. Cattle grazed freely beyond stake fences that followed the road and separated the fields. Corn and wheat were growing in the early summer heat, planted by families named Schoonmaker and Dubois and Hasbrouck, Dutch and Huguenot immigrants who'd settled the county after Stuyvesant's militia pushed inland from its Hudson landing two hundred years before.

Will reined his horse to a stop and waited for Arthur to catch up, gazing at the countryside. It was so different from the West, where the air was dry and the land drier, where empty deserts gave off shivers of heat and trees grew majestically at higher elevations, giant sequoias and pines, straight as nails driven into the hard ground. Nothing like the unruly tangle of oak and maple before him, with gnarled limbs and thick trunks, the surrounding woods dark and captivating. It seemed a good place to get lost in, but he was lost enough already, and if he needed the woods now, it wasn't for that purpose.

Arthur joined him on this high point of the road, where they rested for another minute, taking in the views while their horses snorted and shook at the loosened reins. Will heard him draw a deep breath.

"Is it good to be back, Will?" he asked.

But he couldn't answer. His feeling for this tempered wilderness had filled his head like a fever.

At midday, they stepped into the low-ceilinged room of Misner's Tavern in Stone Ridge, the thick planks above them darkened with black streaks of soot from the cook fire. The few tables were crowded with local tradesmen and hunters wearing tall boots, their dogs asleep against the stone wall, braces of wood duck slung over the backs of empty chairs, blood still dripping from their beaks.

Will recognized Bernd Misner immediately. He looked just like his father, with the same flat face and greasy weft of black hair parted over one ear and combed across the scalp to fall over the other. They'd known each other as boys, but that was long ago and Bernd was too busy to notice. They found space at the long table near the back, already occupied by two old farmers sitting across from each other, each speaking loudly to the other's deaf ear, heads canted slightly to catch every word. They ordered plates of cold chicken and biscuits, and the ale Misner was noted for. They were hungry and ate quickly, and Will had another glass of ale, as well as stewed peaches for dessert. Before they left, Will bought four bottles of whiskey at the small store Misner's brother ran next door, and they were back on their horses while the sun was still high in the sky.

They rode toward the village of High Falls, staying west of town and crossing Rondout Creek on the wooden arch bridge near Robison's gristmill. They continued south along a road that passed through farmland and the forest skirting the base of the Shawangunk Mountains. Will breathed in the scent of turned earth and the tang of early summer. They crossed a shallow stretch of the Coxing Kill and stopped long enough to let their horses drink. Looking at the white birches across the stream, Will recalled a similar stand behind his father's farm, where as a boy he'd hunted rabbits with his grandfather's ancient Springfield musket. He smiled at the memory. The rifle was smoothbore and not very accurate, and he'd blasted more chunks of bark and dung-colored leaves than rabbits.

"Are you ready?" Arthur asked as he rode up alongside.

Will looked at him. For a long time he'd considered this part of his life over, merely a period of youth that he'd enjoyed within its finite bounds. In all the years since, he had never thought he'd ride these old roads with Arthur again, and he was enjoying it. "Let's go," he replied.

They rode up a hill and came to the small cemetery at the edge of the Brodhead property. A new grave had been dug in the far corner, the mound of bronze earth still without a headstone.

Arthur nodded at it.

"Charlie Brodhead. Remember him?"

"Sure I do," Will replied.

Charles Brodhead was two years older, and when Will was fourteen, they were both in love with Sarah Davis. She lived with her family at the other end of the Clove, and Will and Charlie vied for her attention whenever they had a chance. They'd been friends long before Sarah became a fixture in their musings, and the quickening of their adolescent desires compounded their natural competitiveness. If Will helped Sarah tie up the husks of the broomcorn her father grew, then Charlie spent the afternoon picking huckleberries with her on the ridge above

Enderly's Mill. If Will brought her apples from the Harp orchard, then Charlie brought her perfect tomatoes from the Brodhead garden. It went on like this through that summer and fall, and ended in early winter, when fifteen-year-old Sarah eloped with Hugo Slater and moved over the mountain to his family's farm in Springtown.

"He died last October at Bristoe Station, Virginia. By the time the army shipped his body back, the ground here was frozen, so they put him in the icehouse and didn't get him buried until April."

Will looked down at the Brodhead farmhouse at the bottom of the hill and heard the cows bellowing to be fed—a sound that triggered faint memories he tried hard to summon up while Arthur's words droned in his ear.

"He had a wife and two sons. I took their photograph before Charlie joined the regiment. She asked me to send it to him, and I did, and it was buttoned in his shirt pocket when he came home."

They rode on for another hundred yards, and Will turned easily into a narrow path that was barely visible in a grove of trees. When he was twelve, he made a map of the nineteen Clove tracts and marked all the sites where he'd found arrowheads and fossil bones. He knew every bog and feeder creek in the valley, and his father's friends often consulted him before planting crops or running fences in the rich soil below the mountains.

He was home, and his acceptance of that fact startled him. He'd given up this sense of place years ago and taken his comfort in wandering around the West. He'd enjoyed the nomadic life, joining army expeditions through the badlands of the Dakotas and traveling with Whitney and Brewer in California. It was a life he'd made for himself, one with great satisfactions and rewards, but all that had changed last year on the banks of Bear River. He had seen the unbelievable and been forced to believe it. That life held little pleasure for him anymore.

At the top of the next ridge the land flattened out, and they came to the stone marker that separated his father's farm from Elias Depuy's. They crossed the small stream that ran down from the shale cliffs, and Will remembered coming to this spot years ago with his father when some of their cows fell ill after watering there. The creek had been free of debris until it flowed underground, but at the northernmost edge of the farm it surfaced again, forming a little pool where a fox, half-eaten by wolves, had contaminated the water. Will helped pull out the remains, and when they walked home, he asked his father if the creek had a name.

"Not that I've ever heard."

He suggested they call it Dead Fox Creek, and his father said, "We will!" and laughed out loud.

They pulled up between two massive maples that stood like twisted pillars where the forest began to thin, the wild grasses lapping down the gentle slope to the glen where the Harp farm began.

The stone house stood at the far edge of the clearing, eclipsed now in afternoon shadows, set back from the Clove road and overlooking wide pastures dissected by the Coxing Kill. There was an addition that Will had never seen, a whitewashed extension almost as long as the original house. The barn that Cornelius Jansen had helped his grandfather build with timber cut from the hardwood between their adjoining properties had a smaller barn cobbled onto the back, where a dozen sheep grazed behind a wooden fence whose rails looked newly split. And beyond that a dozen cows were walking toward the barn, herded by a man with a stick.

When they rode out from under the locust tree in front of the house, Will recognized him as one of the men from Jug Hill, where mixed-blood families had been living at the far end of the Clove for almost as long as the Harps had been living at this one. He was a strong man, maybe five years older than Will was, with skin more yellow than brown. His tightly curled hair, the color of fired bricks, was cut close to his skull.

"Dr. Harp?" he said.

Will dismounted. "That's right."

"Joop House," the man said, and they shook hands.

Will took a harder look and slowly smiled. "I remember you."

Joop smiled back. "I've been helping out here the past few years. Doing things that needed to be done when the major couldn't do them himself."

Will looked around the farm, where every fence rail was in place and the stone house looked as solid as it had when he'd left.

"Though he did more than most, I'll say that," Joop added.

Will nodded, remembering his father's determination. The year Will turned ten, while his mother, Elizabeth, was in Albany visiting a birthing sister, his father had used her absence to surprise her with a washhouse. She'd always wanted the convenience of a well close to the house, so she could fill the kettle or a bucket without having to send her son or husband or the girl from Jug Hill to the spring above the farm. So for three weeks a contingent of Clove men armed with picks and shovels followed the course the major had staked out, digging a narrow trench from the spring down to the house. At the beginning of the fourth week, only a few days before Elizabeth was to return, the major enticed the first rivulet of water into the stone-lined gullet of the trench. Will raced him and the water to the washroom, where at the turn of a spigot it ran clean and clear into the copper tub below. "Won't her face be bright because of this!" his father exclaimed, and Will remembered how true it was.

"He was strong all right," Joop was saying. "Seems like only last week he was out in the thunder and rain bringing in his own calves, so stubborn that he couldn't even wait for sunup and me to come down off the hill. And then the next sunup came and it was over. Found him in bed," he said, slapping at a mosquito on his arm. "Guess that's a good thing. Just close your eyes and let it be."

Will couldn't imagine his father allowing anything be. And most likely he would've faced God with his eyes wide open.

"I'll come by in a couple of days, see if you need anything. Though I imagine you know your way around here better than me." Joop smiled broadly. "You're home now, Dr. Harp."

◦◦◦

JANE STIRRED the big kettle that was suspended over the fire, turning the thick piece of beef that floated in the center of it. It was a nice arm roast she'd bought from Edgar Duffy that same afternoon, after standing patiently in his shop and listening to him praise the rump and flanks and shoulder chops of the steer he'd butchered for it. The best butcher in Rondout, Duffy loved his beef cows as devoutly as he did the Lord, and blubbered madly as he slit their throats, singing Protestant hymns to ease their suffering and his own. Jane had put the entire roast into the kettle, leaving on the rind of fat because it added a greasy slickness to the broth, which was already flavored with pieces of onion and cabbage that rose and were submerged again with the coaxing of her iron spoon. She swung the crane in a few inches, and the old cat leapt off her perch on the windowsill to lick the drops that had splattered on the hearthstones. Wiping the sweat from her forehead, Jane moved to the open window to find the breeze and watched the late-afternoon shadow from the church spire cast a dark rift across the street. She had just closed her eyes when a sudden loud crash came from the stable.

"Damn you!" her brother bellowed.

She turned in time to see him slap Solomon's rump. Frank's spirited saddlebred had knocked over his feed bucket, and now Mickey kicked it high in the air.

"Mickey!" Jane hissed.

"Goddamn horse!" He pulled back to slap it again, but Solomon lashed out with his back leg and Mickey almost fell over trying to get out of the way.

"Leave him be, Mickey!" she shouted.

"I'll leave him all right. Damn horse can eat dirt for supper." He snatched his coat from a hook outside the stable door and angrily punched his arms through the sleeves.

"Where are you going?" she called.

"Natterjack's," he grumbled as he stalked off.

"Supper will be ready soon."

Mickey waved her off, his cheeks red as a baby's, and she went outside to check on Solomon. He was content in his narrow stall, munching on the leftover hay in his feeder, and snuffled calmly when she ran her hand along his broad flank. He was a tall, handsome horse that Frank had bought from a Kentucky trader before the war. He'd ridden him every day, for work or for pleasure, supremely proud of this animal with the long neck and powerful gait, but for the past year Solomon's only exercise has been a weekly ride from Jane or one of the stable boys in town. Now his well-muscled chest was disguised with fat, and his haunches had grown as slack as those of a pastured mule.

Jane knew that her brother wouldn't be back for supper. He'd stay at the wharfside saloon with Charlie O'Fay and all the others, occupying the big round table in the center of the room and ordering the poor girl around, then leaving a few coins in the puddles of the beer they'd spilled, as if Natterjack's was their own private club. They would talk loudly without saying anything worth listening to, accepting free rounds from those who needed favors, and Mickey would be prince of the table, keeping the clearest head and staying until the overreaching jabber stopped making sense. Then, bored with their drunkenness, he'd visit a war widow who would take him to her bed, or go to the whorehouse on Catherine Street, where he'd spend the night in the second-floor room that Pete Hackett kept free for his pleasure.

Mickey had become the beneficiary of this arrangement more than a year ago, when the world-renowned clairvoyant "Bosco, the Pres-tidigitator" came through Kingston on his tour of the Eastern States. A portly man with long dark hair that flipped over his ears and curled wildly over his collar, he wore a white suit and maroon vest and spoke in a deep, beautiful voice, drawing out vowels that hung in the air as clear as organ notes. He performed before a large crowd at the commu-nity hall, where he began the program by calling for a volunteer to assist him in a demonstration of the "mesmeric arts." Louise Cole-man, a prominent Kingston matron whose father was once a county judge, came to the stage, encouraged by the three Temperance House ladies she was sitting with. There she took the chair she was directed to while the great Bosco paced the boards and rubbed his temple and so perfectly described the tender heart of her recently deceased husband that Mrs. Coleman fainted dead away. He later captivated the audience by correctly describing the contents of Martin Finlan's pockets, includ-ing the engagement ring he had been planning to present to his fiancée that same evening, and by deducing with perfect accuracy the age of every person in the front row. At the end of the evening he called on the war veterans, and half a dozen men came forward, including Jo-hannes Meese, who'd lost a leg at Fredericksburg. Bosco positioned them at the front of the stage and solemnly moved down the line with-out uttering a word; the only sound in the hall was the tap of his heels against the floorboards. When he finally faced the silent crowd, his eyes were closed, and when he opened them again, they were wet with tears and he was smiling. "I can tell you with certainty that this war will cease by year's end," he announced in that magnificent baritone, "and your dear ones, to a man, will be coming home."

The audience erupted in thrilled applause as two huge American flags were unfurled against the back of the stage, and the boys choir from St. John's appeared from the wings and sang "Columbia, the Gem of the Ocean." Women wept and men rose and stamped their feet as Bosco moved to center stage, raised his arms above his head and bowed.

It was after this triumphant performance that Bosco, wearing a long indigo cape over his white suit, took a carriage to Hackett's house and requested a virgin, and Pete, a witness to that evening's show, almost genuflected before him and gladly presented a young girl who'd arrived the day before from a farmhouse in western Connecticut, the shy youngster "as pure as morning dew." Of course Bosco didn't believe any such thing could actually be possible in this backwater town smelling of pigshit and burning coal, but he was a man of vast imagination and took the girl to the suite that Hackett provided. Timid and quiet, she stood still while Bosco stripped away her flimsy garments, admiring the freshness of her body, and she lay down on the bed when he asked her to, opening her legs at his command. Concerned only with the buttons on his drawers and his own urgency, he failed to notice that her knees shook and her smooth belly quivered, and when she turned away from his upright nakedness, a line of tears ran down her smooth skin. He leapt onto the bed with the agility of a dog half his age and mounted her with the same enthusiasm, going about the poor girl like a hammer to a nail.

Done quickly, he rolled over to catch his breath and ease the discomfort of the girl squirming beneath him. She had cried out once, but he ascribed that to his diligence and was surprised when she bolted out of bed and ran into the dark corner, hiding behind the high-backed chair where he'd thrown his suit. "Come back here, you," he demanded kindly, charmed by her bashfulness but unable to recall her name. Extending one hand toward her, he balanced himself on the other. Then he saw the blood that spotted the sheet and laughed out loud. Hackett had supplied him with a fresh biscuit after all.

She watched him, cowering behind the chair, and used his white suit jacket to dab between her legs.

"You stupid girl!" Bosco shouted, lunging at her. "Put that down!" When she ducked away, he grabbed a hank of her flaxen hair and pulled her backward. "Give me my coat!" As she reeled past him, he snatched the jacket from her hands and punched her straight in the nose. Her head snapped back and broke a windowpane, and she fell to the floor on the shattered glass, naked and unconscious.

Hackett, already running up the stairs when glass started falling in the street, burst through the door and saw Bosco standing over the girl. He took an uncle's pride in the women who worked for him, and in a moment of reckless anger, he forgot about the man's renown. He grabbed him by the curls and slammed his face against one knee and then the other before going at him with his booted toes. The girl regained consciousness and screamed like a siren; when she ran out of the room, Hackett looked down at the bloated, beaten body at his feet and sent for Mickey Blessing.

Mickey had already begun working for Grieves. When he got word of trouble at the whorehouse, he left his boys at Natterjack's at two in the morning and entered Hackett's through a door on the alley, taking along his most trusted ally, Charlie O'Fay. And the great Bosco was seen no more.

Rumors about this incident quickly drummed through Rondout saloons, and the telling of Bosco's rampage became as overfed and exaggerated as the entertainer himself. All morning long, men came by the house to look at the broken window, but no constable showed up to investigate the disturbance and no inquiry was ever made. That same afternoon, Mickey was seen promenading around the docks wearing a fancy maroon vest, and by evening it was known that he'd pulled off the biggest trick of all—making the great prestidigitator disappear.

Rubbing her hand along Solomon's long neck as he chewed at the dry hay in his stall, Jane thought about her brother and the man whose shoes he'd filled. She'd vowed to Frank that she would keep an eye on Mickey and not let him stray too far from the jobs to be done. She kept a room for him in the house, though he scarcely used it, and was mindful of all his activities, keeping her ear attuned to the hum in town. Jane loved Mickey as best she could, certain there was a cunning that belied his wildness; and although he pushed her as far as he could, realizing she was a presence in his life, he would always back off, saving his bravura for those who were intimidated by it.

She remembered the evening when Frank came home and told her he was going to join the regiment. He had found out that day that his friends Matt O'Hare and Ian Gillet had been killed at Chancellorsville. He had sat still, because there was little else he could do, while their mothers sat across from him and cried.

"No one should have to hear that," Frank said as he cut into the beef tenderloin she brought to the table. "Never."

"Grieves won't let you go."

"He can't stop me," Frank replied.

"He'll buy another man to take your place."

"I won't let him."

"I don't want you to go," Jane said, knowing already that he was as good as gone. She stood and reached across the table, laying her hand on his arm.

He stopped chewing, but his mind was made up. "Can't be helped, Jane," he said softly. "I should've gone long ago."

"It isn't your fight, Frank."

"It is."

"It isn't your fight unless you start it."

He laughed, because he'd told her the same thing many times, but then he put down his knife and took her hand. "It's mine to finish." When she gripped him back as hard as she could, twisting on his fingers, he only smiled. "Oh, Jane."

⌒◦⦵◦⌒

WHILE ARTHUR put up the horses, Will walked alone through the rooms of the stone house where he'd been born. It was just getting dark, and he lit a lantern in the front parlor, which had always been his mother's favorite room. Little had changed since she'd died, when Will was sixteen. The same Queen Anne furniture that had come with her down the Hudson River still graced the room, and a small oil painting of Saratoga Springs hung over the mantel. In the corner was the small cottage piano his parents had purchased on their honeymoon in London in 1824, and on the small oval table next to her chair, under the front window to catch the afternoon light, was a copy of Edgar Allan Poe's *Tales*, open to "The Murders in the Rue Morgue," the mystery story she'd been reading when she fell ill.

Will walked into his father's study and poured a glass of whiskey from the well-stocked cabinet. Though identical in dimensions to his mother's parlor, it was darker here, and the gaping stone maw of the fireplace made it darker still. Will placed the lantern on the enormous kneehole mahogany desk in the middle of the room. The far wall was taken up by the large map of the Clove he'd drawn as a gift for his father, as colorful as a flag and vast as the world. On the other side of the room was the gun cabinet, an oak breakfront that stood from the floor to the ceiling, sturdy as a bank vault. The leaded-glass panels were at eye level, and Will could see the barrels of the dozen or so rifles, from his great-grandfather's country fowler to his father's newer Whitworth benchrest rifle with a telescopic sight. There was a large brass lock on the cabinet, and Will knew his father always kept one key in his vest and a second in the desk drawer.

Will sipped whiskey and sat at the desk. Two spots on the polished mahogany had been worn smooth by the major's elbows, and the desk was bare except for a small box that held dip pens and ink boxes, a candle reflector and a silver-framed photograph of Will and his mother made by an itinerant Russian photographer who traveled through Ulster County each summer with his mule and wagon. In the photograph, Will was standing on the old carriage step, while behind him his mother was seated on Jack, her pure black gelding, a long stream of piss shooting between his legs. His father had found Jack's urgency amusing and displayed the photograph proudly.

Will put his glass down and slid the desk drawer open. He was looking for the key to the gun cabinet, but his eyes fell on a large envelope on which his father's bold cursive handwriting had spelled out his name. He looked at it, immobile, and the black shadows that fell across the room took hold of him.

When he picked up his drink, his hand was shaking. Without disturbing the envelope, he pushed the desk drawer shut and left the room.

He drank whiskey through supper and into the evening. Arthur kept his friend company, but whiskey made him regretful so he tended not to drink too much. They sat on the porch for hours, smoking the hand-rolled Turkish cigarettes Arthur had ordered monthly from a Bleecker Street tobacconist. Will's outlook became brighter, and he entertained Arthur with stories of his adventures. He said little of his time in the army, other than noting he'd fought on the Shoshone frontier, but when Arthur pressed him for details, he grew stony, as if that part of his past wasn't far enough away. He refilled his glass and changed the subject to Arthur's own life.

"Not much to tell," Arthur said. "I stayed home."

"But you traveled."

"Yes, I went to Paris to study."

"So there is something to tell."

Arthur fondly recalled the two years he'd spent in the studio of the renowned photographer Gustave Le Gray. Even then he was mostly interested in portraiture, and he arranged for sittings with street sweepers and vegetable sellers from the market on place de Clichy and blood-splattered assistants from the Montmartre abattoir on rue Rochechouart. They were wary young men, but they went with him because he was insistent and his French comical and simple enough for them to understand. They posed in Le Gray's small studio, where Arthur photographed them against a plain background, the bitten nails of their fingers rimmed with dirt, their aprons stained as yellow as their teeth. When they tried to brush their hair or smooth their wrinkled coats, he stopped them, and in their annoyance they sometimes stood with hips cocked and arms crossed. And that's exactly what Arthur wanted: the same resignation and pride they'd showed when he first encountered them on the street.

What he didn't tell Will was the other truth. While he tried to resist his attraction to those men, he lacked the self-control to mask his feelings, and some mocked him gently, without real malice, still willing to sit across from him and sip an afternoon beer, glad for the coins he offered. Sometimes these coins found other young men willing to share a meal and accompany him back to his fifth-floor rooms in Montmartre. In those days, Arthur was young and handsome, and some required no coins. He had relished these sybaritic nights, especially when Jean-Yves, a fellow student at Le Gray's studio, switched the roles and invited him to dinner and back to his apartment.

"So you enjoyed Paris?" Will asked.

Arthur looked up and smiled. "Yes, I enjoyed it very much."

Will drank too much; he knew that. But if it didn't help him sleep, at least it helped cleave those dark hours. Different thoughts came to him that first night home, rolling through his mind like the familiar rumble of an earthquake. The first one he experienced, soon after his arrival in Los Angeles, had taken place early in the morning, and he'd sat up in bed and looked out the window in time to see the dirt road rise and fall as gently as a bedsheet on a clothesline, a wavering of dust hanging in the air the only proof of what had just occurred.

Most nights during the last year had left him with the same kind of dust-addled reflections. Every time he stretched in bed or opened his eyes, a new impression would disturb his sleep, and he'd be shaken with unwanted turmoil that no amount of whiskey could dampen.

While Arthur wheezed in the next room, Will lay in bed thinking about his father. Daniel Harp had fought with Winfield Scott and the First Brigade on the Canadian border during the War of 1812, and came back to the Clove after the battle of Chippawa, somber and unscathed, having risen from second lieutenant to major during his two years of service, and not yet thirty years old. His tales of warfare complemented those of Harp men before him, and young Will often imagined him leading his Regulars across the bridge at Street's Creek, chasing the British into the pine woods and back across the Chippawa River, taking the battlefield as their own.

A treaty was signed in Belgium just a few months after the ordeal, and Daniel returned to the Clove from his service on the Niagara frontier. He stayed home for a few years, helping his father clear another ten acres on the western edge of the farm, and sailed to Europe in 1816. Under the auspices of West Point, he went to Paris to study protocol at the famous artillery school at Saint-Cyr, then spent another two years observing the military arts as practiced at academies in Vienna and Mannheim. He returned to West Point a grown man, a bachelor still, and taught civil engineering to cadets for the next five years. In 1823, he visited an old friend in Saratoga Springs, Col. James Searing, a surgeon who'd attended to the wounded during the battles they'd both endured. Daniel stayed at the San Souci Hotel in Ballston Spa, where he took in the mineral springs and fished for trout in the sparkling streams that fed Saratoga Lake. On his third evening, he attended a dinner in the hotel's courtyard and was introduced to Elizabeth Murray by Colonel Searing, her second cousin. Despite the fact that he was twice her age, they spent the evening walking together along the marble terrace, their conversation long and full. By the end of the year he traveled to Manhattan to ask for her hand. He told Elizabeth that he had already lived a full life and was ready to settle down to begin another, and they were married in the spring, at St. John's Chapel on Hudson Square. He resigned his position at West Point, and the couple moved back to the Clove, where he helped his aging father with the family property.

When his mother died of pneumonia Will was sixteen, grateful that she'd lived long enough to know that he was following in the footsteps of her own grandfather by studying medicine. And if the major was disappointed that he was going to Albany Medical College rather than to West Point, he didn't show it. Will knew his father had been supremely happy in his marriage and regretted only the short grace of it. They buried Elizabeth in the family cemetery, and he remembered how his father had looked as he heeled the shovel's blade into the soft dirt, the straightness of his back in his clean white shirt, his silver hair long as a saint's. Daniel Harp was already over sixty years old, though still as strong and independent-minded as men half his age.

Will had often come home from Albany to help on the farm; he enjoyed being back in the Clove and using muscles that had gone soft in the classroom. The men from Jug Hill came down to help when necessary, but the major took care of the daily chores himself and put off the bigger jobs until Will's seasonal visits.

A few years later, Will took his first assignment as surgical assistant with the Topographical Bureau in Washington, joining Capt. Lorenzo Sitgreaves's 1851 expedition to the Zuni territory in New Mexico.

Now twenty, he traveled by stage and rail from New York to St. Louis and then on to Santa Fe, the whole country a revelation to him. He had to wait a month in New Mexico for the expedition to get under way, and he spent the time exploring the western plains, accompanied only by a Coyotero Apache whose broken English was courtesy of a French trapper named Leroux. They rode the fringes of Navajoland, along short hills as sharp and craggy as the edges of a broken bowl, heading toward mountains that stayed distant even after days of travel. For long, happy hours Will's horse carried him through winding canyons, the narrow walls glittering yellow and red with jasper, while black eagles wheeled through the iron sky overhead.

In September, with twenty men and as many pack mules, Sitgreaves's expedition started out from the Zuni Pueblo with an army escort and followed the wisp of river westward toward the Little Colorado. Will assisted S. W. Woodhouse, the expedition's physician and naturalist, in collecting specimens for the Academy of Natural Sciences in Philadelphia and the Lyceum of Natural History in New York, the two men filling dozens of saddlebags with surprisingly abundant botanicals and wildflowers. It was a strenuous trip, with both hardships and marvels during the six-week trek to Fort Yuma on the California border. Water was often scarce, and when supplies were low, some of the men grew sick with dysentery from eating raw mule flesh. They spent time with a large band of Mohaves, the warriors standing six feet tall, with hair down to their waists, their scalps capped with dried mud to kill the vermin that lived there.

Will found fossilized oyster shells in a tributary of the Little Colorado, exposed in the stinking muck of a green lagoon like coins on a dealer's felt table, and as they pushed into the foothills of the San Francisco Mountains, herds of mule deer provided fresh game. Will watched buffalo wolves stalk dissipated antelope along the gray tablelands, observed fat porcupines in the gamma-grass prairies, went to sleep listening to the cry of panthers and awoke to the trill of mockingbirds. One evening he chased a pack of jumping rats that invaded their camp—their lively shadows making it look like an invasion—and in the morning tended to the burns of the Mexican driver who'd stumbled into the embers of the cook fire when attempting to flee from the bouncing rodents.

Then the Indians attacked. Eight miles from the Gila River, a band of Yuma warriors rushed across open ground, their bows raised, spitting arrows through the pale sky, the narrow shafts nearly invisible as they whistled overhead, the stone tips clattering harmlessly against the hard soil when they missed their mark. The Indians fought boldly, retreating only after the soldiers returned fire with rifles and musketoons, killing five. Vanishing as quickly as they had appeared, the Indians fell back and dispersed into the ravines that creased the land near the river, leaving behind only spent arrows and bloodstains after they carried off their dead.

When they reached Fort Yuma at the end of November, Will continued on to San Diego with a guide and half a dozen hired Mexicans. He settled there for the winter, exploring the grasslands and beaches along the ellipse of the bay. One afternoon, a winter squall rose quickly off the ocean, the clouds heavy and dark and rolling in like poured tar. Will hastily made camp in the lee of the dunes on Point Loma, just before the wind started howling and the sky turned apocalyptic. The rain fell in blistering sheets, and the roof of his tent popped all night with the fury of it. Finally, an hour before dawn, the rain and wind lessened. Will climbed out of the tent then, soaked to the skin, his ears still ringing from the wrath of the storm. As he walked toward the ocean, sand raced across the rippled surface of the beach and flared around the tips of his boots and stung his face and hands, and each footprint quickly filled with seawater and disappeared behind him. He stared out at the waves, breaking in sequence at a great distance, the crests nearest the shore yellow with foam, and he looked up as the sun began to rise in that thin white crack forming on the horizon, a bright pinpoint between the black ocean and the blacker sky, opening upon the earth like the eye of God.

Will turned twenty-one that morning, knowing that he had traveled across the nation and found his home.

The landscape of dreams is a wide-open country. Later that night, in his jousting sleep, Will returned to the last time he was in Rondout, his father accompanying him to the steamboat landing. They had spent the night at the Mansion House Hotel, and in the morning they ate bacon sandwiches and drank milky coffee on the covered porch, elbow-to-elbow with the merchants and canal workers who stood at the railing watching Claude Sims yank his recalcitrant sow to Gay Hiram's butcher shop at the other end of Division Street. The sow dug in her cloven hooves and fought him to a draw, both man and beast streaked with dirt and sweat and squealing back and forth over the rope that was stretched tight as a bowstring between them.

"Come on, you fat old whore!" Claude screamed as his hands slipped on the rope tied tightly around the sow's neck, his backside just inches from landing in the dirt. He shuffled his feet and managed to hold his balance, if not his wits. "You goddamn hog!"

"Hey, Claude," Johnny Coombs shouted from the porch. "That ain't no way to talk to your lady friend."

"Shut it, Johnny," Claude yelled as he pulled on the rope, the muscles in his neck thick as fingers. "Just shut it!"

"No wonder she won't have nothing to do with you," Ed McCoy piped up. "Be nice now, Claude. You got to treat all women with a kind word and a smile, no matter how prickly or ugly they are. Just close your eyes and pretend she's wearing her best bonnet."

The men on the veranda started snickering.

"Shut it, Ed, damn you! " Claude roared, the tips of his ears so red, they looked as if they were about to burst. He grabbed the long end of his rope and swatted at the pig, which got her screeching even louder as she squirmed away from the frayed ends that found her hide.

"Just trying to be helpful," Ed replied before taking a big swallow of coffee.

"Yeah," Johnny added, trying hard to keep a straight face. "You wouldn't be dragging your own missus down the street like that."

"Ain't that who it is?" Ed asked incredulously. "I don't got my spectacles on."

And the men on the porch howled, spilling coffee and spitting up bread. Even the major laughed as Claude Sims knelt in the street and started laughing himself, his hand loose on the rope. The old sow took one last pull and snorted free, mincing up Division Street, her hooves kicking up dainty clots of dirt. Will joined in the laughter and finished his sandwich as four men jumped over the railing to catch the runaway pig while Claude lay sprawled in the middle of the street with his head in his hands.

And that was what Will remembered best before leaving for St. Louis and the West: his father's hand on his shoulder and the laughter that rolled through them on the last day they shared together.

He sat up in bed and blinked, smelling his own whiskey sweat, realizing his eyes were open and had been since he put his head on the pillow many hours ago, his mind alert, fully awake.

IT WAS TWO o'clock in the morning, and Coley had finished his shift at the brewery and was heading for the coal docks to find the Magruder twins. They were visiting their father, who came back to Rondout every month from the mines in Pennsylvania, spending just the one night on the same coal barge that carried him here, long enough to give Tim and Danny enough money to cover the rent on the room he kept in Shelley's boardinghouse on Hunter Street and a few extra coins to pay for their keep. He always took them out to dinner, splurging on steak and potatoes at Kerr's Hotel, where he would nip at his bottle of gin while the boys filled their bellies. Tom was a good father despite his long absences and steady thirst, and the twins would walk him back to the barge that fourth Wednesday of every month, steadying him as he rocked back and forth between them, helping him on board and then into his bunk, sitting with him until he passed out, listening for the whistling notes he let loose through his crooked teeth before each snore. Then they would take what was left of his gin and wait on the bow for Coley and the others to join them for a drink.

Coley had just reached More's Corner when he saw three men walking under the dark canopy along the Strand. The tall man out front, Duncan Fisher, was unmistakable, with that high, naked brow, the hairline starting at the top of his skull like some Japanese emperor Coley once saw illustrated in an old *Harper's Weekly*. He always walked with a forward thrust, as if his legs struggled to keep up with the rest of him, and wore a long dark coat that hung to his ankles and concealed the hickory club he favored when he ventured into Rondout to pleat the heads of drunken Irishmen. Of course, they'd have to be drunker than Fish himself, who was very seldom sober after noon but always traveled with a small army of other Bumble Bees to make sure someone had a hand steady enough to deliver the beatings they considered their native right.

He stopped on the corner and watched Fisher and his Bumble Bees—their tight group like a giant shadow—head west, toward the coal docks. When he was sure where they were going, he turned around and ran.

❧

SHE SLEPT ON her side with one leg flung across Mickey's, her hand flat on his belly, the pinkie resting against the tip of his cock. He was wide awake and had been since he got there an hour ago and found

Gitta already in his bed. She was a big Hungarian girl about his own age, with blond hair and meaty thighs, who'd come to Hackett's five months ago from a house in Yorkville that was shut down by the Moral Reform Society. When he first took her to bed, she pushed against him as if they were wrestling, then rolled him over and held him captive in those big thighs, raising herself up and down with a smile on her face, as willing a partner as he'd ever found. She quickly became his favorite girl at the house, and it bothered Pete that he monopolized so much of her time. But Mickey didn't give a damn about Hackett, who'd frowned at him when he came into the front parlor that evening, his face a narrow wedge between his big ears. Mickey ignored him, as he always did, and headed upstairs to his room on the second floor. Hackett could only watch his back and grunt and mumble into a closed fist, wise enough not to air his displeasure, knowing that Mickey Blessing would come when he was needed and leave when he was ready.

Mickey lay there with his head cradled in his hands, looking out the open window. It was a clear night and moonlight made the sky glow like a sheet of tin. He listened to the quiet lapping of the distant river and thought about rising at daybreak, before the drunks and sailors roused themselves, and going down to the landing for a swim.

Gitta suddenly shifted at his side, still asleep, her knee moving up his leg and her hand across his belly. She murmured into his neck, her breath smelling sweetly of the peach brandy he'd paid for, and moved in closer, her nipples cold and pointed against his chest. He thought about waking her, and had just laid his hand across the hollow on the base of her back when he heard a commotion downstairs. Voices were raised and doors slammed, and he could make out the grappling of hands that slapped and pushed against skin and cloth, and then a sudden yelp that sounded like it came from Hackett's own mouth. When he heard footsteps racing up the stairs, he leaned on his elbow, already anticipating an interruption he almost welcomed, and watched as the door was thrown open by the boy from Shapiro's stable. Hackett seized him from behind, but he jammed an elbow into the soft folds of Pete's gut and skittered across the crumpled rug and grabbed the bedpost, blinking a few times before finding Mickey and the girl in the darkened room.

"It's Fish," Coley said.

He followed Mickey around the corner, watching him tuck his shirt into his trousers and pull his suspenders up over his wide shoulders. He couldn't help thinking of the naked blond woman: the beautiful breasts that rose as she woke up and yawned, and the raised knee that she pulled to herself without regard to modesty as Mickey climbed from the bed and angled himself into his pants. She sat there in the silver light like a molten statue to be admired for eternity, and Coley stared at her with all the focus his eyeballs could muster until Mickey clamped a hand on his shoulder and yanked him out of the room.

Amber light shone weakly through Natterjack's oily front window. Mickey stepped through the wide-open front door with a fluid motion that Coley tried to imitate, walking under the sign of the ugly Irish toad that gave the saloon its name. He followed him to the bar, where Tim Rooney was pouring another glass of whiskey for Charlie O'Fay. Coley saw the six or seven men inside look up as Mickey reached behind the bar and took out the long quarryman's crowbar Rooney used to pry apart chest-banging men who'd drunk too much. Charlie, stocky and bald, with a nose broken so many times that it lay limp as a dead mouse in the center of his face, smiled when he saw the pitted steel in his friend's hand.

"Let's go," Mickey said.

Charlie drank his whiskey in one swallow, his throat pleasantly numb from the half dozen that had gone down before it. When he grabbed the neck of the dark bottle that Rooney had left on the bar and got up, everyone in Natterjack's stood with him. Coley shuffled sideways as they thumped across the rippled floorboards and followed Mickey outside. Rooney, old as a grandfather, vaulted over the bar and was the last man through the door. Coley paused there, tempted by the coins left scattered about, but loitered only long enough to down the half glass of whiskey Dick Small had left behind, then chased after the men who already were halfway to the docks.

DUNCAN FISHER found what he was looking for on the first canal barge tied from bow to stern on the black creek. "As sure as rats," he muttered when he saw the prone figure sleeping on deck with his mouth open. It was an Irishman, he was certain, and if it wasn't he could hardly be blamed, because in his mind only Irishmen and wild dogs slept under the crook of the moon, and both deserved to be beaten into porridge. Not for sport—as most Bumble Bees considered these nocturnal missions, when they rose with the stars to walk through the pestilent Rondout slum wielding chair legs and fireplace tongs—but to preserve the battle-won rights of their fathers and protect the impending rights of their sons, to defend their soil from the waterborne hordes that arrived like flotsam on these shores, eager to take their jobs and ruin their women.

Duncan followed the law of their leader, Bob Baggs, who let it be known that any Irishman who wasn't fortunate enough to perish under Atlantic waves would wish he had. Baggs had come to this conclusion ten years before, when his father, who sold fire insurance for the Mutual Company, was lifted from his buggy seat by a group of Killarney rowdies who pummeled him until his left eye hung free from its socket, only because his horse had stepped on the toes of a drunk sleeping down by the wharf. The spectacle was unwitnessed and the perpetrators, identified to a man by Donald Baggs, went unpunished for lack of evidence. Bob was fourteen at the time, and he waited until he was sixteen—when the incident had faded from popular memory and the scars around his father's blind eye had healed—before venturing down to Rondout in search of Will Cooney, whose knuckles had taken his father's sight. He found him surrounded by cronies in front of Flynn's Groceries and Liquors on Division Street. Bob entered this group of strangers, innocent as Jesus among the lepers, and bumped into him with clumsy intent. Cooney, his eyes watery with cheap rum, wheeled around in a fury, but Bob stood there unapologetic, the stench of Irishmen like sulfur in his nostrils, and waited. For Cooney, the sanguine look on the boy's face was enough of a provocation, and he lifted his great fist. Bob watched the arc of the knuckles—huge and scarlet as iron bloom pulled from a furnace—then jerked the small single-shot percussion pistol from his waistband and put a bullet through Cooney's left eye—the same eye that he had taken from his father— where it was caught in the lard of his brain, giving the man only enough time to blink away a tear of blood before collapsing at Bob's feet, his spirit leaving him as soon as his head hit the ground.

Bob Baggs was hardly a man that day, and the sheriff deemed his action self-defense and escorted him back to his parents' house in Kingston. An article in the *Rondout Courier* about the unfortunate incident stated, "The bullet from young Baggs's pistol struck William Cooney as decisively as a stinger from a bee." The Kingston boys who came to the Baggs house that day to marvel at his feat vowed to defend their native ground against the Irish scum. And it was Duncan Fisher, third-generation Kingstonian and Bob's best friend, who sat in a wing chair in the parlor and first called them the Bumble Bees, a name that took as easily as Will Cooney had died.

"You luckless bastard," Fisher hissed as he looked over the barge rail at the sleeping man, letting the foulness of his own rummy breath place a spark to his dry anger. He pulled the hickory club free of the loop under his coat as his three companions moved in, hovering behind him as close as a drawn curtain. He put the pointed toe of his top boot on the burlap-covered rail, and as the boat rolled with his weight, he used the action to bring his club down on the man's head, a crack that sounded no louder than the thumping of a melon. Fisher could feel the force of the blow as it shivered along the wood and up his wrist, but the Irishman didn't make a sound or move a muscle, his brain and body in slumbering peace.

"Is he all done, Fish?" Jesse Gray asked.

"No, just resting."

"You going to clobber him again?"

Fisher shook his head. "I'd break my arm before I broke his skull. It's like they grow rocks on their shoulders."

"Then what, then?" Gray inquired, his thick eyebrows jumping into the deep welts on his forehead.

"Drop him in the soup," Fisher replied, stepping back and balancing himself on the gently rocking boat. "Let him sink or swim back to his Irish mama."

"There'll be no swimming this night, Fish."

The voice rose from the darkness behind him and Duncan Fisher quickly turned, his eyes coming to rest on Mickey Blessing and the men from Natterjack's standing on the cobblestones in the middle of the Strand. They were stretched out across the wide street, their shadows making them seem as numerous as a small army.

Jesse Gray made a noise like a trapped mink and grabbed at Fisher's arm, but he shook him off and kept his balance. Though he tried to stand tall, his thin body inclined forward as it always did, and he was no more threatening than a crow on a wire.

"You've wandered a little off your map, Fish," Mickey said, a smile slashing across his face.

"I'll wander wherever I damn please," Fisher declared.

"You risk getting lost."

"Lost!" Fisher scoffed. "I was born here, Blessing. I'm a son of this town. I have more of a right to be here than you or any man behind you, and I'll set foot where I please and when I choose and will not be challenged by the likes of you."

"Oh, you will, Fish. You certainly will," Mickey replied, his voice light and jovial. He gestured toward the prone figure splayed across the front of the barge. "What happened to Danny Short?"

"Short?" Fisher asked, before remembering the man at his feet. When he poked the man's thigh with his boot heel, he gurgled and gassed. "Short had it coming."

"Was he sleeping too soundly for you, Fish?"

"I don't give a goddamn how he sleeps!"

"Then what made you bash him?"

Fisher's eyes went left and right. "The bastard cursed my mother!" he finally sputtered.

"He did?"

"He did," Fisher repeated, liking how the lie sounded. "With language that would burn your ears!"

"You sure, Fish? The Danny Short I know would rather bite off his tongue than use a colorful figure of speech. Got a sweeter mouth than a parson."

"He cursed her, I tell you!" Fisher yelled as he jumped off the barge. The other Bumble Bees massed around him as he stood flat-footed and defiant, writing the play as it came to him. "He raised his dirty head and cursed her as I walked by. Called her a whore. My own mother! 'A goddamn whore' is what he said! I won't stand for it!"

"So you cracked his skull?" Mickey asked, his voice as easy as syrup, the same undemanding smile on his face.

"You're damn right I did. As I would rightly do to any man."

"Would you do the same to me?" Mickey asked, sauntering forward as lightly as if he were stepping into a Galway reel. "So if I told you your mother's quim fit my cock like a velvet glove and I was wearing it not more than an hour ago, would you take that piece of hickory stick to me, too?"

In the moment that passed, quiet as it was, Coley could hear the water rolling up Rondout Creek from the river, slapping against the hull of every barge tied to the coal dock. He could hear the whoosh of sparrows in nightflight, and the squeaking of mossy ropes shrinking around the slick pilings. He could hear the leaves above him caught in a breeze, rubbing together like cricket legs, and the tiny scratch of a match being lit far away. And above it all, in the exacting clarity that silence brings, he could hear Duncan Fisher's ragged breath.

"You bastard."

Coley stood to the side and watched Fisher's body rock back and forth, the anger buzzing through every vein and muscle. The Bumble Bees stood mute behind him, useless as a rotting fence.

"We'll be back," Fisher said to Mickey, his forward-leaning face carrying a nasty sneer. "When I tell Bob Baggs about this, we'll—"

Mickey neatly drew the crowbar from behind his back and whipped it across Fisher's open mouth. The force of the impact straightened him up for the first time that night, forcing him up on his toes before his knees gave way and he crumbled to the greasy stones, the hickory stick dropping from under his coat and rolling into the creek.

"You won't be telling Baggs anything for a while," Mickey said to the humped figure at his feet. Then he turned to Charlie O'Fay and Tim Rooney. "Pick up old Danny and bring him along."

Coley stood there as the men jumped onto the barge, each grabbing an arm, Danny Short hanging there between them, dragging his feet.

The boy couldn't take his eyes off Duncan Fisher on his hands and knees on the cobblestones, the bottom half of his shattered jaw hanging together by skin and tendon, the blood falling from his broken lips as ropy as dog slobber. Coley felt a hand on his shoulder and looked up into Mickey Blessing's smiling face.

"Come on, boy. Have a drink on me."

❧

IT WAS EARLY morning when Will entered the woods, following a well-trodden path that became spongy beneath his feet, covered now with a rusty carpet of pine needles from the tall trees spiraling above him. He hiked up the gentle slope to where the land flattened out and stopped before the clearing that was the Harp family burial ground. His great-grandfather, Simon Harp, had picked out this spot, as lush as Tatiana's bower, even before he sited the house that would be built on these hundred acres granted to him more than a century ago by Lieutenant Governor James DeLancey for fighting bravely with General Braddock at Monongahela during the French and Indian Wars. Though the battle was lost and Simon's arm shattered by a Mingo war club, he kept his wits about him and retreated with the fleeing army across the river, where he lay on the slick bank while Shawnee warriors on the opposite shore—their upper bodies tattooed in hideous curlicues and the tips of their scalp locks dyed red—leaned over wounded soldiers and stripped them naked and scalped them cleanly. A year later, with his young wife and new son, he moved to the tract of land granted to him in the Shawangunk Mountains for his service to the king.

Will always found it odd that his ancestor had given so much thought to this graveyard; perhaps he'd been anticipating his own death, which would come two years later at the age of forty years old, from a rattlesnake bite in his own woodshed. His coffin was the first to be swallowed up by the hillside that overlooked this perfect vale.

Will walked through the cemetery, acknowledging headstones tall and crooked, his great-grandfather's four-sided obelisk rising above the rest, with the same line of Scripture inscribed on each side of the base: *"For whoever exalts himself will be abased, and he who humbles himself will be exalted." Luke 14:11*

Next to Simon's grave was that of Oliver, Will's grandfather, whose rounded headstone sat firmly in the hard ground, straight and modest, adorned with only name and dates. He lived well into his eighty-fifth year, his body and soul intact, though his memory dimmed over time, becoming as feathery as the hairs remaining on his head. As a child, Will had been awed by this stern old man, who in suitable weather liked to sit on a hickory rocker on the front porch. Life in the house quieted whenever he entered a room, the footsteps hushing around him, though he could barely hear the creak of the floorboards anymore. Even at this age, his spine was stiff and he stood over six feet tall, his presence as commanding as if he were still a lieutenant in the Continental Army.

Like his father before him, Oliver had been adept at war. "We were a new country, and you defended her as you would a new wife," he told his grandson as he sat on the porch recounting the great battles of New York and New Jersey in 1776, when the English fleet ruled the rivers around Manhattan Island as convincingly as they did the open seas. He relived the siege of White Plains, where the English and Hessian forces marched south from Throg's Neck to face Washington's army, and he told Will how he'd stood with Capt. Alexander Hamilton on top of Chatterton's Hill, facing down the enemy forces that came up the Bronx River.

Will was his grandfather's chief companion those last years, and he absorbed his stories about the Christmas crossing of the Delaware River and the battle of Trenton as if each word were a drop of water. He was ten when the old man died, his heart stopping while he rocked on the porch. Will, thinking his grandfather was only napping, sat there for more than an hour, waiting for him to wake up and tell another story.

He continued through the graveyard, reading the familiar inscriptions, the dates and the favorite Scripture that summed up his ancestors' best intentions. Between these lines of wisdom and goodness was the real Harp family history, and Will's as well, both the artifice and truth of it.

He stopped again in front of his mother's grave, a simple stone of Vermont marble. His father was buried next to her. Will braced himself and looked down at the freshly turned earth mounded over the major's casket. He'd never really considered the possibility that his father might die during his long years out west; discounting snakebites, Harp men seemed to live forever. Although nearly eighty, Daniel Harp had never complained or mentioned any affliction. And he'd never pressed Will to come home, pleased with his accomplishments so far away. In one of the last letters, he wrote:

Your adventures will only add to your life, for I believe that fine memories help keep us alive by encouraging us to search for others. You see beyond the carrot poised in front of you, and that is what makes the hours of your days worth living. And by doing so you've made your life exceptional, and my own for allowing me to share it.

Will knew that his father was proud when he left the Whitney expedition and enlisted in the Union army the year after Lincoln declared war. He was a Harp, and Harps served their country. When he came out of the mountains and offered his services in Los Angeles, he asked to be assigned to a New York militia, but his request was denied and he didn't challenge it. He accepted the position of field surgeon with the Third Infantry, California Volunteers, joining the troop at Camp Halleck, outside of Stockton.

In 1862, he marched with Col. Patrick Connor and the California Volunteers across the Sierra Nevada into Utah, where they established Fort Douglas on a hill overlooking Salt Lake City. After helping capture a Shoshone raiding party that had killed a family of Mormon settlers in the Cache Valley, Will rose to the rank of captain and was with the soldiers a year later when they brutally confronted the Shoshone on the steep banks of the Bear River.

His father's letters kept coming to Will after that battle, but he no longer had the heart to respond. He wasn't strong enough to part with them, though, and they remained in his satchel, a dozen or so brown envelopes tied in a bundle with a rawhide cord. He knew this had worried his father, but silence was the only thing he could offer. The last letter Will wrote to him was in February the year before, when he tried to explain what had happened that January afternoon when he was left to die with a bullet in his shoulder, the blood frozen around him like a halo. He loved his father so much then, as he did now, and couldn't bear to face his disgust.

He could barely face his own.

July 1864

WHEN PEARL HEARD the strange cry, she sat bolt upright in bed, certain that one of her traps had sprung. It was still dark and she wasn't quite awake yet, so she sat there while her senses caught up with the rest of her and let her toes inch along the wood floor, trying to locate her boots. When the thing cried again, it sounded most like a raccoon, but more fragile than the mournful drone she was used to. Shifting her weight in the bed and tilting her ear to catch the last fade of the high-pitched wail, she accidentally elbowed her cousin Tally on the tip of her nose.

Tally shrieked, slapped the elbow away and sputtered, "Dammit, Pearl!"

"Ssshhh." Pearl knew from experience that Tally woke up prickly, just as likely to poke a finger in your eye as say good morning, and she put her hand over Tally's mouth to keep her quiet. "I got something."

"Some old sick thing," Tally grumbled.

"I got it trapped."

"Then it ain't going nowhere." She pulled on Pearl's nightgown and yanked her back down on the bed.

Pearl already had one foot in her boot and clenched her toes to keep it from falling off, but it spun away and banged into the wall that separated this room from her brother's. She heard Sam swear, and the creak of his bed frame when his big feet hit the floor. Pearl and Tally both jumped under the covers and lay still as the door flew open, Sam swaying in anger. Pearl knew he wouldn't cause a ruckus loud enough to wake their parents in their little room upstairs, but he might rap the top of their skulls with his bony knuckles hard enough that they'd have to fight back tears. He was naked from the waist up, lanky and strong, and the curly hair on the left side of his head had been flattened by his pillow. The girls couldn't help noticing the erection that tented the front of his cotton drawers.

"Looks like you got some company, Sam," Tally said with a smile.

He looked down in embarrassment, his anger even sharper now, and bent to scoop up the short boot that Pearl had sent sailing across the room. Both girls dove beneath the blanket as he flung it at them with all his might. Pearl blocked it with her arm, and they huddled under the blanket until they heard Sam return to his room and flop noisily back down on his own bed, breathing heavily, trying to recover whatever dream had been giving him so much pleasure.

At seventeen, two years younger than Sam and a year older than Pearl, Tally had been nurturing a crush on Sam ever since she first visited their farm on Jug Hill when she was four. The only one not blinded by the power of her affection was Sam himself, who insisted he was the master of his own reckoning, not the puppy of some forward girl from Brooklyn.

You think he's in there thinking about me right now?" Tally whispered.

"I'd say the thinking part's over," Pearl replied, and the blanket and sheets rose again with their laughter. In this family, secrets didn't exist and modesty was expected but not easily imposed. Pearl recalled seeing her own father leaving the house on occasion, awakened in the early morning by the urge to relieve himself, showing proud as he walked through the kitchen to the back door. She'd seen things she wished she hadn't and others she hoped she'd see again, and she knew for a fact that privacy ceased to exist the moment you left the womb.

When all was quiet in Sam's room, the girls pushed off the covers. Tally scratched at her ribs and sighed. "Someday I'll be sleeping on the other side of that wall, not in here."

"And then I'll have this old bed to myself again."

They saw each other only once a year, but the cousins were as close as sisters. They fell into easy companionship in the short time they had together, walking through the hamlet and talking until they were exhausted with it, then not needing to talk at all. While Tally was a big girl, her skin dark as a summer plum, Pearl's skin showed the pale pink of her Dutch ancestors. And while Tally had strong bones to frame her ample flesh and plump her cheeks, Pearl had her grandmother's fine-bridged nose and the upright posture of a Mohican maiden. The year before, when Joop took them to Sanderson's sawmill to pick up boards for a new corncrib, Sanderson looked at the girls and remarked, "You put 'em in a burlap sack and shake 'em real good, I bet what comes out is one normal-looking nigger."

. . .

It was still dark when Pearl stepped onto the front porch, but the soft-bellied clouds reflected enough moonlight to etch out the freshly plowed field in front of the cabin. She jumped down and ran through it, kicking up great clods of the loamy soil. A smell of ripe decay rose with it, a scent of life and death that produced the best buckwheat and winter rye on Jug Hill. Because it was the one fertile spot in their few stony acres of farmland set against the woods, her father tended and fed it as if it yielded gold. Jug Hill was once owned by Carl House, who'd sold off parcels of his vast property to his freed slaves, including Pearl's great-grandfather Darius. He called it "the thumb of his kingdom," and it consisted mostly of shaded slopes and boggy fields that weren't good for anything except goats and chickens and the wormy cabbage they grew to feed them. Pearl's ancestors—and those of the Minters, Smittys and other families who'd been freed after serving in the Revolutionary War—started anew on this unwanted land, raising as much grain and livestock as the thin soil would bear, living as free men and women in self-determined isolation in the rugged hills east of the Shawangunk Ridge.

Pearl followed the tight picket of corn stalks that served as a windbreak along the farm's northern border, stopping at a little clearing near the end of the line and kneeling in front of the box trap she'd set the day before. The trap was sprung but empty. Crouching to reset the box, she saw the scat of the frightened animal, a broken porcupine quill sticking out of the droppings. Pearl shook her head at the loss. It was a fisher she'd almost trapped, the only animal dumb enough to eat a porcupine, quills and all.

Pearl quickly checked two more traps at the edge of the woods, both undisturbed, then stood still in the quiet morning and listened carefully, but she heard nothing more than crows bickering in the hemlock grove that lined the field. She followed a narrow path that led through the forest to the highest point on Jug Hill, where she looked back and saw woodsmoke from the chimney of her farmhouse flattening in the warm air. She knew she should head back to let out the cows and bring in more wood, but instead she turned in the other direction and saw the turkey vultures, three of them making lazy circles above the tall oak trees a few hundred yards to the south. When they began to spiral downward, Pearl moved quickly through the woods to keep an eye on them. The birds were large, and although graceful in flight, there was something hideous about them, she always thought, with their short necks and small red heads and yellow feet. She lost sight of them as she got closer and the woods closed around her, but she knew they were on the ground someplace close, examining whatever was dead or dying.

A moment later she broke into a clearing and saw them, one on a low branch and the other two waddling like cripples over the stony ground. She scooped up some small rocks and sprayed them at the birds, and when they backed off and took flight with an awkward fury, she saw the source of their fascination: a newborn baby, loosely wrapped in coarse linen, his tiny penis redder than the rest of his pale body, the umbilical cord curled tight as a piglet's tail. He was lighter-skinned than most people on Jug Hill, even lighter than Pearl. The wisps of colorless hair on his head were as fine as lines drawn with a quill pen.

She knelt down beside the body and saw the linen cloth was spotted with the stains of his birth. She wondered where he'd come from, and who could've left him out in the deep woods. She hoped it had been a peaceful death, which she doubted because of the sorrowful cries she'd heard in the night, and wished she had come out earlier. She laid her cheek against the baby's cheek and shut her eyes, saddened that the new skin was still warm. Then she felt a puff of life from his lips, and the sudden cry that followed was so shrill that she sat back hard, clasping her hands over her ears as the little thing raised his pink fists and prepared to fill his lungs again.

❧

PETER VANDEMAN trudged through the streaming mud, his boot tips kicking apart the braided trails of filth that coursed down the old wagon ruts at the back end of his property. It hadn't rained for a week, but this sorry earth was sill swamped by the rain that had fallen steadily the week before, creating just enough summer muck to carry under his newborn calves. He hated this corner of his land, the cabbagey smell of it, the ground soft as fruit pulp, and with each step he could feel it percolating beneath his feet. He'd known this when he bought the two hundred acres seven years ago, but he'd ignored it as long as he could, as purposefully as he did his wife and the debts he owed, a man eternally trapped in the dire turns of a life abundant with bad choices and worse luck.

He remembered when Bogardus showed him the land for the first time, the two of them sitting high on big-bellied horses swollen with

June hay. They'd reined in to survey the breadth of the property from the ridge of hemlock trees on the northern boundary. To the west he could see the long crest of the Shawangunk Mountains, extending like the pitted blade of a bread knife over the valley below. To the east he saw the stone wall that marked Isaac Stokes's property, running along thirty acres planted with buckwheat and corn, and on a rise above the fields he glimpsed the large gabled house, affectedly christened Butter-fields by some long-dead Stokes when he first let loose his herd of dairy cows. To the west was Major Harp's farm, another fine plot of land that signaled prosperity. On that day, Vandeman took a deep breath and choked back an eagerness that tasted like honey in the back of his throat. He'd been ready to pay the asking price a month ago, when the two hundred acres first came up for sale, but for once in his life he'd woken up wise and insisted on riding the property from marker to marker, keeping his eagerness in check and his purse buttoned tight, even though he and his wife both knew that before the day was over Bogardus would get every dime he was asking for.

That morning seven years ago, Vandeman's mare took a sudden step sideways and almost threw him. He bit deep into his lip before squaring himself back on his saddle, and saw the cur that followed him everywhere take off between his horse's legs and lunge down the slope toward the pond, lost in the goldenrod that shivered around him. He cursed the dog and surveyed the wide expanse of wetlands that spread like spilled molasses through a few thin trees. He heard the snap of dry twigs as a pair of blackbirds rose from a low stand of alder, and watched the small dog set his head low to flush a covey of grouse from the spikerush at the edge of the black pond. The grouse took wing and the dog raced after them, dashing through water so shallow, it looked as though he were skimming on top of it.

Bogardus laughed. "Goddamn little feist, he is."

Vandeman sucked on his bloody lip and looked over the land, green as Eden, he thought, like paradise seen for the first time, and ignored the sweet scent of decay that carried in the spring air.

Bogardus stuck out a thick arm, unrolled his fingers like he was throwing dice across a table and pointed into the glen. "I shot a bear here spring past."

It was a known fact that every Bogardus from the Mohawk Valley to South Brooklyn was a liar, an inherited trait, like bad teeth, handed down from father to son. Take half of what a Bogardus said and ignore it, and you'd be wise to ignore the other half, as well. But on that bright day in June, Vandeman chided himself for such un-Christian thoughts, based on local exaggerations overheard at Matthew's tavern, the tales of Bogardus deceit growing bolder and more fantastical with every pint of beer drawn and emptied. He permitted himself to forget everything he'd ever heard, and squinted just enough to picture elk and deer in these wetlands, and flattened turkey beds in the bent blades of grass, and a black scroll of geese in the sky overhead. Vandeman imagined there was enough game here to sustain him for years, and a moment later, when Bogardus declared the swamp a meadow, he believed him because he wanted to, because he wanted this land.

Now he walked toward this dismal end of his property, resting the weight of his sore left hip on the stick he'd been leaning on since February. He'd hurt himself while chasing pigs across the frozen patches of hard snow that had drifted into the bottom stalls of the barn, going down hard on his side because his son wasn't there to do the job. He had joined the Ulster Volunteers, and they hadn't had a letter since late November, when Andy had used most of his ink and paper complaining about the rain and mud and cold, saying the leather of his boots was stiff and peeling like bark from a tree. He always kept writing until he ran out of paper, his last thoughts scribbled in air, wistful and incomplete, a fact that worried his mother more than news of the war. It was as if his life came to a sudden end on that last hiccup of a word, and she was left to contemplate his unfinished notion and the bleakness of his days. She was afraid for her only child, eighteen years old and meek as a newborn. Vandeman knew the boy was smart, but also as skittish and lazy as a banker's son. They fought often, the boy ready to jump out a window if he saw his father simply raise a hand to wipe his brow. Vandeman wondered where he got the nerve to enlist in the first place, and he hated to think it was just to get away from him.

The little dog brushed against him as he ran past, and Vandeman swiped at it with his stick. The beast was older now, more meat than muscle, but his legs still worked and he was always underfoot, chasing after whatever prey he was able to conjure up in the feeble corners of his mind. His belly was black with mud, and the brown spots on his mangy hide were faded to the color of dust. Vandeman had never bothered to name him, but Andy liked to call him Little Joe, even though the ugly mutt responded only to shouts and thrown rocks.

As Vandeman came to the top of the hill, he heard frantic howling over at Butterfields. It sounded like the cries of children being strapped, but Vandeman knew it was only the wolfhounds that terrorized the valley and played havoc with his pigs. Stokes never raised a finger against them, never scolded them for nipping children or digging up flower beds. He paid for any damage they caused and rewarded them with more affection than he bestowed on his wife. Whenever Vandeman rode over to complain about them chasing his pigs until they dropped dead in fear, Stokes just stood on his wide porch laughing, then reached for his wallet. Vandeman would've liked to shoot one of the dogs and see if Stokes laughed then, but he lacked the spit.

So he cursed Bogardus and he cursed Isaac Stokes and he cursed Harry Grieves as he navigated the stinking mud. He regretted not selling out to that bastard when he'd had the chance, and woke up with this regret every morning, his jaw aching from all the gnashing that went on in the dark hours. He should've taken the insult with the little money he was offered, keeping his lip tight as he pocketed the coins. Twelve hundred dollars might be slightly more difficult to pass than a kidney stone, but still enough to outfit him and allow him to head west to pan for gold in the rivers below Sacramento. But he'd lost his chance and knew it.

He hobbled along on his hickory stick and followed the worn wagon trail down to the bitter reaches of his land. At the beginning of March, he'd finally decided to clear the swamp of dead wood and the sharp remains of beaver-hacked birches left standing in the shallow water like a row of abandoned fence posts. Below him, the three colored men he'd hired from Jug Hill were trying to drag out a half-submerged stump with a pair of mules. The men were up to their waists in the brown water, and the mules were slipping in the mud while trying to bite and stomp the little dog barking in their faces. Vandeman cursed the dog and hurried along, slogging across the uneven ground and the boggy soil that seeped beneath him and tried to pull his boots off. Finding a few yards of momentum in his downward trek, he became sure-footed and careless, until the muck rose again and held his heel so fast he twisted his ankle.

The three men looked up as his angry cry carried through the wet air. Joop House let go of the rope he was holding and flicked the sweat from his eyes, standing in the water and watching as the old farmer limped toward them, waving his stick and high-stepping through the brush as awkwardly as a scarecrow being pushed by the wind. Joop felt like laughing but swallowed it back, then turned to the Smitty brothers, John and Earl. They were two years apart in age and still in their teens, splashing each other like kids in a washtub. Joop clapped his hands. "Smitty!" They both responded to the one name and picked up the rope that had gone slack between them.

Joop slogged ashore, and the summer air felt cool on his wet pant legs. He stood next to the mules, resting his hand on the rump of the animal his brother had given him two years ago, just before he left town in a hurry. Three years older than Joop, he'd been working in the smokehouse behind George Thompson's butcher shop at More's Corner, flirting with the butcher's chubby young daughter, Molly, whenever she came to the back door and yelled for a pork shoulder or side of beef. He allowed her to touch his biceps when he handed her the meat, and didn't stop her when she once ran her finger along his belly, then giggled and raced back into the shop with a string of sausages under her arm. Walter was vain about everything, including his long reddish curls, and couldn't resist telling his brother or anyone else he drank with about the pretty white girl who would sit in his lap, content as a kitten. When a back-alley rumor suggested that the extra weight Molly carried would soon become Walter House, Jr., he quickly figured he'd stand a better chance of surviving the treacherous waters around Cape Horn than the boots and fists that would befall him in the back of Thompson's shop, so he took a job on the *Gallivanteer, a* Portuguese schooner about to set sail from Rondout Harbor. Months went by before it was determined that the weight Molly was showing came from nothing more than sweets and pudding, and everybody soon forgot about Walter, except his brother. Walter had promised to write, but no letters ever came, and after a few years Joop was convinced the *Gallivanteer* was at the bottom of the ocean and that his brother's bones had become part of great coral reefs or were lodged in the bellies of exotic fish.

He patted the mule as Vandeman approached, the old man squinting as he followed the line of the rope into the water.

"I'm not paying you to waste time with stumps, Joop."

"Ain't a stump, Mr. Vandeman."

"Course it's a goddamn stump."

"It ain't."

Vandeman bent forward to peer into the muck. Anything between his extended hand and the horizon was woolly around the edges, and he squinted mightily, surrendering to the fact that even his eyes were betraying him. He could make out a blockish shape, brown as the swamp and the size of a wagon wheel. "What the hell did you catch there?"

"Looks to me like a big cow skull."

"You got cows that big on Jug Hill, Joop?"

Joop saw the mocking turn of Vandeman's lips and didn't answer. The cows they raised on that stony soil were so wretched and forlorn that the milk they gave was as thin as dishwater and full of lumps that floated in the pail like dumplings.

Vandeman cackled gruffly and shook his head. Joop House was as red-haired as an Irishman, but no matter how many white Dutchmen had taken companionship with his great-grandmother, he was still a Jug Hill Negro. He looked at the Smitty brothers standing in the water. In contrast to Joop, they were as black as smudged ash. He waved his stick at them. "You boys get on up here."

They did as they were told.

"I want you to tap these mules and get them moving," Vandeman said. "But don't do anything until I give the say."

The Smittys nodded and took their places alongside the mules.

Vandeman walked over to an ax resting in the grass. When he reached down for it, he saw the little dog watching him warily, his black nose up in the breeze, as if trying to catch a whiff of his master's intentions. "Come on, Joop," he said. Giving up his stick, he grabbed the tight rope for balance and waded into the water. "Grab a shovel and let's get that trash out of my swamp."

Joop watched thin lines of sweat appear like whiplashes across the back of Vandeman's shirt. He'd rather have worked the thing out of the mud himself, but it was Vandeman's dollar he'd be folding into his pocket, so he followed him into the water and nodded at the Smittys to make sure they were prepared.

Vandeman walked between the ropes tied around the object of their labor. It looked like old bone, pitted and cracked, but when he rapped it with his knuckles, it was hard as stone. He trudged farther into the swamp, where the water rose over his belt line, and leaned against it. When it started to give, he quickly looped his arms around the ropes and hung there like wet laundry. "Goddammit!"

"I already got it loose," Joop said, coming alongside. He offered Vandeman a hand, but the old man shrugged loose.

"Then let's get it the hell out of here." He ducked between the ropes and whistled at the Smitty brothers. "Wake up, boys! Get those damn mules moving."

The boys slapped the mules with flat hands but had to twist their long ears to get them to step forward. The little dog danced in front of them, barking in their faces and nipping at their lowered muzzles.

Vandeman watched the ropes pull tighter. "Get a shovel behind it, Joop."

Joop shoved the blade of his shovel deep into the water. He found a spot of leverage, gripped the shaft with both hands and let the force of his weight do the work.

Vandeman kept walking backward, his eyes fixed on the strange form as it started to emerge from the deep mud.

Joop kept his weight steady on the shovel handle, pushing down until his chin was nearly in the water. "It's coming, Mr. Vandeman. It's coming!"

The dog went on yapping in the mules' faces, his rear end sticking up in the air, and they strained against their ropes, eager to stamp his brains into the mud. Earl tried to gentle them, but the larger of the two lunged at the dog and snapped his rope. Vandeman looked up to see it curling back across the water just as the thing in the swamp canted to the left and turned sideways, now drawn by a single rope. There was a deep sucking sound, and out of the corner of his eye he saw a spear rise out of the water, shiny as bronze and smooth as barkless wood, and he knew it was a huge horn, the damndest one he'd ever seen. He held his hands out just as the sharp, ragged point ran through the soft skin of his upper thigh, just below his right testicle, dragging him upward as it twisted out of the mud. Vandeman grabbed hold of the smooth shank as he was hoisted six feet into the air, screaming in agony. His last memory was of the little dogbeast racing up the Shawangunks with that insane mule behind him, and through the crimson pain and wash of tears, he wished them both to hell.

⤜౷⤛

IN THE MOMENTS before waking, Jane saw his face in front of her, his handsome grin inches from her own, the corners of his smile lifting up his full cheeks, his eyes bright behind them. She stretched with the anticipation of his caress, as if hoping the sensation of touch could be conjured as easily as that of desire, that her desire could be realized, that he was home. But she held these thoughts in abeyance, knowing they were foolish, and kept her eyes closed so his face would linger there still, in that dark place where memory was allowed to waver and play its tricks.

Jane had first met Frank Quinn three years ago, when he offered his hand and helped her off the floor of Kelly's saloon. She had been working there for months, but that Saturday night, her twenty-first birthday, was the last time she'd ever run her gray rag over those filthy surfaces again. The front and back doors were left open the length of the day, regardless of the rain or snow that collected there and warped the floorboards, which tripped the drunks coming in or out, just because Brian Kelly wanted it that way. A thick stump of a man, he firmly believed in the curative powers of fresh air and its abilities to rid the body of the night's unfortunate ingestions. He drank beer as well as served it, draining his own kegs with the determination of a bingeing sailor. His competitors often wondered how he managed to stay in business for so long, but he never had to worry because his saloon was at the foot of Ferry Street, as close to the working docks as a wobbly man could ask for. It served many men their first drink of the day and their last of the night.

Jane had worked a ten-hour shift, and it was because of her uncle Joe that she had the job. He was a great friend to Kelly, the two of them having grown up near Leighlinbridge, County Carlow, their mothers both known to tramp the hills outside of town to feed them wild blackberries when times were fair, and nettles and brown cabbage when they were not. They were a decade apart in age and had grown up on opposite sides of the River Barrow, and they had never laid eyes on each other until the morning Joe stumbled into Kelly's Rondout saloon, but as boys they had explored the same ruined castles and eaten salmon from the same river, and in a country far away from their own, that shared past was enough.

Joe Devlin was a good uncle to Jane and Mickey, even though he was only ten years older than Jane and barely a man himself. He was not quite twenty when the three of them debarked from the *Virginus*, trailing the other Irish families that mingled on the Castle Garden pier in Manhattan. It was a blazing August morning in 1849, and there were five hundred of them clustered together like timid sheep, every man, woman and child afraid to take that first step forward into the city blooming before them. They could only stand and stare at the faraway buildings that rose through the steamy mist, trembling in the distance as surely as their own sea-weakened legs. Jane and Mickey stayed close to their uncle, their fingers tight around the coarse fabric of his pant leg. Joe swayed drunkenly alongside, keeping a squinty eye on his new friend, Kenny King. Using his hip flask as a calling card, he had introduced himself to King and his wife soon after they set sail from Dublin. He offered his flask much as another man might offer his hand, tipping and pouring his way into conversation. It eased his own shyness and the wariness of the stranger he hoped to engage, and in most cases Joe and his new chum would soon be showing each other their brown teeth and palavering like brothers. It was easy with Kenny, who was the same age, boisterous as a waltzing cock and almost a neighbor from Ballywilliam. The whiskey shrank even that distance, and they soon were careening around the deck, pausing only to spit over the railing into the gushing sea, laughing at other passengers like delinquents. Joe soon learned that Kenny had an older brother already living in Manhattan, a mason from Shannon, who'd promised him a job in the stone quarries where he worked as a foreman. Having no relations on the American continent, no prospects there and little money left in his trouser pockets, Joe hoped that Kenny might speak a good word for him, so he stuck as close to the man as his supply of cheap whiskey and Kenny's wife would allow. In the end, Kenny came through, boasting faithfully of his new pal, and the brother helped Joe find a job and a pine shack on Dutch Hill for his wards, though before long the endless, arm-numbing hours at the quarry made him wish he'd never shared his whiskey or opened his mouth.

For Jane and Mickey, the first days in America were bliss. Dutch Hill was full of children as aimless as they were, a whole gang of them reeling through the long summer hours without care or supervision. They spent their mornings sliding through the mud flats at the edge of Turtle Bay, caked to their knees with slime, letting it harden into gray boots they later danced off in the lapping waters of the East River. In the afternoons they would sleep on the shore or chase the flightless geese that escaped from Paul Delaney's yard, the birds loud and angry as they squawked down alleys and trampled the neighbors' gardens, bursting ripe tomatoes as they scavenged for fruit worms and stinkbugs. The children scampered as freely as leaves picked up by the breeze, mostly ignored by weepy-eyed mothers too unhappy with their own circumstances to deny them their brightness. Even though they were grateful to be free of the black fever that killed their friends and the bitter winters that ruined their crops, they remained good daughters of Ireland and pined for the emerald countryside of their buried mothers. And in their hand-wringing sorrow, they turned a blind eye to their wild children.

Jane reveled in these childhood pleasures, whirling into them with all her heart, eager to make up for the years when she'd gone without joy or playfulness. To the children, the tumbledown patchwork of Dutch Hill was much like the neighborhoods they'd abandoned, and the city itself was humped in the hazy distance like some belching dragon, breathing smoke and stink that had little to do with their own fevered recreation.

These halcyon days were short-lived. In early September, Tommy Gallagher and Mickey built a raft, the waterlogged scrap gathered from the weed beds of Turtle Bay, the leather straps that held it together stolen from Jack Plum's harness shop. The sorry contraption was no more stable than the bobbing junk the children grabbed hold of when they swam in the river, and the two boys had to kneel on the uneven planks and hold on tight, as if it were an ornery mule they were riding, instead of the bucking current that sucked them away from shore. It was a blustery morning when they set sail, and the wind caused the saw-toothed bow to dip into the rising tide, almost catapulting them skyward and into the frothy drink. But they held on like good pirates, their small wrinkled fingers wrapped tightly around the straps, and when the straps loosened and fell apart, they grabbed the planks, holding them as they would their own mothers' necks, giving up the ship only when what remained of it crashed down on a wave and broke apart in twenty feet of water. Mickey, tadpole that he was, swam to shore, but Tommy floundered, his arms slapping the water like a broken-winged duck, and had to be rescued from the chop by two old Negroes fishing for eels. He died two days later, his stomach bloated from all the water he had swallowed. Then, in late November, Mary Toole had the tip of her finger yanked off by one of Delaney's geese, the digit swallowed as easily as cracked corn, and she ran through the dirt streets with her bloody hand held high as a Christmas candle, her shrill screams filling every mother's ears on Dutch Hill.

That fall, Jane turned nine, and she and her best friend, Sally Roy, were hauled out of their childhoods and taught the principles of domesticity. Jane resisted, but Uncle Joe was powerless in the face of the female horde that descended on their shack, dragging the girl kicking and scratching into the world of womanly servitude. She was taught the many uses of a wash bucket and how to hand-sew a straight seam, boil a pot of water and time the oats or carrots or beef that was thrown into it, cooking them until they were so pale and tasteless that not even a pint of salt could resuscitate their flavor. The Dutch Hill women worked the two girls without pity because none had ever been bestowed on them, and after some hair pulling and face slapping, Jane and Sally soon learned the deaf-and-dumb mannerisms of the perfect wife. They did as they were told and watched husbands accept the piles of clean and folded clothes, then sit down to meals prepared for them as if they were honored guests, never acknowledging the labor of the women who served them. Afterward they would sit back with belts lowered below stuffed bellies and emit self-satisfied grunts of pleasure, the same grunts the girls knew would become more animated once the bedroom door was shut for the night and the sheets pulled back and the wife splayed across the mattress, her knees raised, making an easy target for a lazy man demanding one more bit of business before allowing his darling wife to sleep.

In a matter of months, Jane had mastered the fine art of drudgery, and while Sally Roy, her fingers a more nimble army, was kept indoors and taught how to press the fine linens these mothers took in to make ends meet, Jane was given the job of caring for the children she'd so recently played with. Jane was grateful to be outdoors again, away from the busy women working with the shutters pulled tight, moving about in near darkness, their senses sharp as moles. But she knew her world had changed forever. She was supposed to not only mind the children but also wash the East River muck from their faces and the shit from their drawers. She became expert at twisting ears to break up fights, at kicking the shins of boys who dared to wipe bloody noses on their shirtsleeves, and she was soon shouting orders loud enough to make any mother proud. Even Mickey avoided her, scattering with the others whenever her shadow crossed their makeshift field of play. A young harridan in the making, she hated herself for it and went to bed exhausted, moaning with nightmares of her aging self: her breasts hanging down to her belly and her backside wide as a doorway, and a dirty man plowing through her pillows of flesh. From such dreams she would awake with a start, brown curls sweat-plastered to her cheeks and neck, and vow to herself that she would never live such a life.

Jane was fifteen and Mickey thirteen when their uncle came to his senses and took them away—an act of kindness not so much for their sakes as for his own. After six years, Joe knew he would never marry in Dutch Hill, the clannishness of the settlement no better than the one he'd fled from in Ireland. Although he was easy to look at, with a handsome grin, neatly combed hair and a chin free of stubble, all the young women on Dutch Hill were aware of his "Dublin indiscretion." It was a single night of mistaken dalliance with an unclean girl that sent him off on the *Virginus*, young Joe stumbling drunkenly from the gloomy whorehouse off the quay, his pecker shined for the first time, cheered on by the men who had paid for his enlightenment and would later spread the tale of his misfortune. Jane could remember hearing him crying himself to sleep many evenings behind his closed door, the shame of his condition more painful than the discharge that stained his sheets. And because of this affliction and his own natural shyness, he took to drinking too much. He was a sorrowful drunk, and men of good cheer soon found his company unbearable, while women of good quality found him despicable. So Joe worked hard all day and went to the saloons at night, living in the shadow that he himself had unwittingly cast, awkward in his own stinging skin, unloved and unwanted by anyone other than Mickey and Jane.

Equipped with an imagination as distinctive as any Irishman before him, he found multiple justifications to leave his first American home. It was the food they served, he grumbled, too peppery for his tender Irish guts, and the lager they poured too tame even for a man of common thirst. Manhattan itself was a smoldering pit, he liked to complain, the stink of it an affront to his sensitive rural nose. And the people who lived there baffled him. The Jews and Germans had accents so different from the honeyed tones of Irish speech that he was confounded by even their simplest use of language. "Every time they open their mouths, it's as if a curse is being issued," he'd say. And the fast-talking Negroes he worked with in the quarry left him stunned. "I can no more understand them than I would cats and dogs." Joe Devlin never suffered for a lack of excuses, real and whimsical, and his compilation of them was enough finally to force him out the door.

But he was good to Jane and Mickey. He kept his promise to his dead sister and shepherded her children to the new country, where he made sure they were as well fed and healthy as a man who himself was barely beyond childhood could be expected to. He told great jokes and gave then the loose pennies that collected in his pockets, and he never asked questions about their daily whereabouts or made them go to

Sunday services unless he was sober enough to accompany them. On good nights he told them stories of their mother and father, hoping to keep the flicker of memory alive.

"She was a pretty one, my sister Aggie. You look like her, you know. When she was a girl," he would say, and Jane would close her eyes and imagine just that: her mother's smile and the dimples that punctuated it. This was easier than remembering the wisp of life they'd visited in the fever ward at Beaumont Hospital, when their mother's beautiful white teeth were mostly gone and her skin as gray as the sheet that covered her.

"And your father, Michael, was a handsome boy. It was shameful how good they looked together, like a king and his queen. They were born three days apart, Aggie being the older, on neighboring farms that shared a stone wall, their own mothers and fathers already best friends. The babies were rocked to sleep in the same crib and napped in the sunshine with their arms around each other, breathing the same breath like a tiny husband and wife. They spent their whole lives together, except for those first three days when Aggie was alone on this earth and Michael was pounding on his own mother's belly, waiting to join her. And once he did, you couldn't pry them apart."

Joe paused to sip the rum and warm milk he drank before bedtime. "Sure they fought, sometimes yelling themselves red in the face like the married couple they'd become, but it never lasted long, 'cause Michael was smart enough to apologize with a bouquet of sheep's bit that he picked from the rocks below Blackstairs Mountain, the flowers the same blue as Aggie's eyes, and your mother would accept the flowers and bake him a basket of sweet cakes, and the next day they'd be arm in arm again and the clouds would disappear and the birds would chirp and all would be right with the world. It was love all right, and I don't think a day passed that you couldn't see it in their faces."

Jane loved these stories and slept well on the nights she heard them, glad in her heart that her parents had known some happiness in their short lives. She was a young girl during the years of famine, and the dreams she had of their courting helped to allay the suffering of what she remembered most.

They left Dutch Hill in the fall of 1855 and took a packet boat up the Hudson, searching for a town with enough Irishmen and saloons to satisfy Joe's simple needs. It was a bright September day and Joe shared the railing with other itinerants, passing around a flask and treating the voyage as if it were a holiday. Jane and Mickey stayed on the bow of the ship and raised their faces to the cold autumn wind. Looking down the wide corridor of the river, Jane imagined she was entering a jewel box. Coming through the Highlands below Newburgh, Mickey pointed out the flight of an eagle sweeping along the eastern shore, and when the great bird lifted its wings and alighted on the uppermost branch of a bright-leaved maple, the leaves shook and fluttered to the water like flakes of gold.

The packet boat, a filthy livestock vessel inappropriately named *Apple Blossom*, stopped at the river towns of Fishkill and Beacon, but Joe stayed on board and drank with his new friends instead of exploring prospects for employment. He discovered that these men were heading upriver to work in the new glass factory being built outside Rensselaer, and he agreed to join them. He swallowed his rum and determined there were worse occupations than making windowpanes, and although the village had a Dutch-sounding name, he was certain there would be enough countrymen lurking about to keep him company. When the *Apple Blossom* docked in Rondout to pick up a dozen crates of live chickens, he decided it was time to stretch his legs and refill his flask. With Jane and Mickey at his side, he strode into town and made it as far as Brian Kelly's saloon. He stayed long enough for the stinkboat to sail out of the harbor without them and long enough to see sunrise the next morning. Kelly's wife made up burlap pallets for Mickey and Jane in a back room that smelled of lye soap, while Joe continued to enjoy the good graces of his host, joining him beer for beer and splitting the cost. At daybreak he stepped outside to clear his head, and on wobbly legs he walked up Division Street. At this early hour, harried wives opened their windows to throw last night's cooking grease into narrow alleys already running with swine eager to gorge on the leftover gristle and congealed fat, desperate as opium eaters. He could hear the grumblings of husbands as they rolled over in their beds and poked blackened fingertips into their ears to quell the morning disturbance, begging for one more minute of sleep. Wagons loaded with bluestone clattered down to the docks, their drivers bleary-eyed and barely awake. He stood in the middle of the wide street and looked up the length of it, squinting into the morning light, almost blinded by the dew shining on rooftops and window glass, and saw a tavern on every corner. He walked back to Kelly's, sobered by all this beauty, and paused in the doorway for a moment, glancing down at the ships and coal barges that crowded the wharves in Rondout Creek. He sucked deeply of the air that smelled of dead fish and human waste, and he knew that he would never leave.

By noon he had found them lodging in two small rooms on the top floor of a boardinghouse on Mill Street. By evening he had taken a job as a night watchman on the coal docks, responsible for checking the moorings on the barges tied up there, and making sure their loads weren't tampered with. He celebrated with a few more rounds at Kelly's, content in the knowledge that the saloon was only a few paces away from his appointed rounds.

Jane went right to work for Ann Burns, the widow who owned the boardinghouse, helping to clean the rooms of the weekly boarders and prepare the meager breakfasts included in their rents. The house was always full of single men working in the Rondout brickyards, and the red dust they carried home with them every day powdered the stairs and the hallways leading to their rooms. Jane's afternoon job was to follow after them with a broom, her own eyes itchy and red from the grit she swept off the floor. The men woke her every morning with their persistent coughs and the stamping of their bare feet, and she would jump out of bed and race downstairs before them, helping Mrs. Burns set the big dining room table with bread and butter and boiled coffee.

Ann was good to Jane and let her use the parlor while her uncle slept away the long afternoons. Some days she read one of the Charlotte Brontë novels that Mrs. Burns favored, and on others she curled up on the roughly upholstered sofa to catch up on her sleep.

She awoke one Friday afternoon about a year after they arrived in Rondout to find Dan Casey, a brickyard foreman, bending over her. He had a room on the second floor, and every morning Jane would catch him peeking out his door as she raced to the kitchen, greeting her with a smile and a wink. Unlike most of the other men in the house, he kept his fingernails clean, and when he sneezed, he didn't erupt like a windblown dandelion. He was almost thirty, a handsome man with his cap on, but when he doffed it, you could see that his blond hair had already receded to the back of his skull, the exposed freckles on his scalp as dull as gravy stains. He was well mannered and drank whiskey only on Saturday nights, and Mrs. Burns told Jane that he sent most of his paycheck to his wife and two little girls in Cornwall, Connecticut. Still, the morning wink bothered Jane, and the eyes following the whirl of her skirt as she grabbed the wobbly post and ran downstairs, so she kept her guard up and paid as little attention to him as she did to the rest.

Napping that Friday afternoon, she felt something brush against her foot and opened her eyes to see him staring down at her legs with so much concentration that it was as if he were trying to lift the hem of her skirt with his eyeballs. Before she could move, he put a hand on her bare ankle and started using his fingers to achieve what his will couldn't. He had his cap in the other hand, pressed against his heart, and the sweat on his face ran like tears. She could feel the tips of his fingers following the blue veins under her skin, moving up her calf, and in that moment she blinked and pulled her leg away. She was bracing herself against the armrest, getting ready to kick him, when a shadow passed over his head and took the shape of the broken chair leg Mrs. Burns had put out with the firewood just that morning, the thick end of it smacking down on the top of Dan Casey's head.

Mickey stood there clutching his weapon and staring down at Casey, now limp as a dead cat. Blood seeped onto the wood floor from the blow he'd landed, and with the toe of his boot he nudged the Persian runner to the side so it wouldn't get ruined. Then he looked up at Jane and smiled. "You can still kick him if you want to."

Mickey was fourteen, tall for his age, and had been taller than Jane since he turned twelve. He was lean through the body but strong in the shoulders and arms, the muscles rangy and defined from all his years of swimming.

Jane leapt off the sofa and stood next to him, looking down at Dan Casey, his chest now heaving as if he were having a nightmare, the blood stippling his chin. She pulled his cap over the bloody wound, her fingers accidentally brushing his clammy skin, and stumbled backward, sick to her stomach. She forced herself to take one of Casey's legs while Mickey grinned and grabbed the other. They dragged him out of the parlor and down the narrow hallway to the back door, where they dumped his moaning carcass in the yard, amid the skittering, squawking chickens, which flew into bushes and their shed as Casey rolled in their fresh white droppings.

Ann Burns made little fuss when she heard the story from Jane, just went up to Dan Casey's room and packed his belongings into the woolen valise she retrieved from under his bed. Then she dropped it out the window, where it landed with a splat next to where he still whimpered and squirmed. She didn't inform the constable, but she did write a short letter to Casey's wife, apprising her of his misdeeds. She sent Mickey to the post office with it and went to work in the kitchen with Jane, making supper for the men coming home from the brickyards, and frying Mickey an extra pork chop. She left the back door open throughout the meal, Casey still lolling there in the chickenshit, and let the boarders draw their own conclusions. Joe Devlin slept through the whole ruckus, and when he stopped in the kitchen for a cup of coffee before leaving for work that evening, he didn't even notice the lump of Dan Casey in the yard.

Casey was gone by daybreak, and by noon Mrs. Burns had rented his room to another boarder. The chickens didn't lay for the next three days, but all was right in the house.

The story spread quickly through Rondout, and Joe must've caught part of it at Kelly's when he stopped in for his usual rum and conversation, because when he came back the next morning, he was mostly sober. Instead of going directly to bed—where his snores would purr so gently through the house that Mrs. Burns would sometimes hum along as she put out her laundry—he kept an eye on Jane as she went about her chores, as if seeing for the first time the points where her dress filled out and her waist tapered, and this made him blush with stupidity. She was no longer the orphaned niece who clutched his hand so tightly that the tips of his fingers went numb, and he moped around her with such a sorrowful mug that she had to beg him to stop. That afternoon he moved Mickey's things into his room, giving Jane the privacy she'd so convincingly grown into.

Joe's fresh sensitivity was courtesy of Glenna Owens, a young woman he'd been seeing for the past year. She lived in the house across the alley on Mill Street and worked afternoons at Kelly's saloon, boiling eggs and slicing ham and onions for the men who needed nourishment with their beer. Joe wasn't much of an eater when he drank, but he always ordered one of her thick sandwiches just to watch her thin little arm work the knife. Glenna would bring him his sandwich with a shy smile, and when she lowered her eyes, a loose curl would fall across her forehead, and he'd reach across the table and hook it back behind her ear with a nubby finger. He soon made it a habit of stopping by Kelly's before going to work on the docks, and returning a few hours later for an evening rum and the chance to walk Glenna home. He stood close to her and held her delicate elbow in his hand as she talked about the men who'd come in that day and the gossip she'd heard, and all Joe would have to do was listen. She was a pretty girl, not much older than Jane, with a lively spirit that complemented his own good nature. When he left her at her door, she liked to reach up and grab his ears as if she were raising a jug to a high shelf, giggling at the face he'd make just to get her to smile. She knew nothing of Dutch Hill or his amorous mistake on the Dublin quay, and Joe made certain it stayed that way, at least for now. Ann Burns put in a good word and Brian Kelly vouched for him, telling stories of his great character that made Joe wish he inhabited such fabulous skin. On the evenings he walked her home, Glenna would let him kiss her, and in the shadows of the alley he would let his cheek linger against hers, breathing deeply of his own good fortune. Her hair was the color of whiskey and smelled of spilt beer, and he was in love.

Joe proposed marriage on a snowy evening in February 1860. Glenna said yes without hesitation, and he kissed her red and running nose and spun her around in the alley between their houses. He went immediately back to Kelly's for a celebratory rum and ale, accepting another round or two from the whiskey-happy backslappers inside. He was drunk and merry when he left, stepping into a sudden gust of flurries that enveloped him like a halo of goodwill. He jumped over the slushy curb and marched down to the coal docks, raising each leg as if keeping time to a military drummer. It was a bitter night, but he charged right into it, his head down and his cap tight, the tips of his ears scarlet but warmed by the rum flowing through him. Glenna's name sang in his head and he tried to whistle to it, but the frigid wind hurt his teeth, so he hummed instead. He was possessed by grand feelings he hadn't experienced since his mother's own love, his life's course on a straight path to happiness.

The wind blew fiercely off the Hudson, and by the time he finished his rounds the flurries had turned to steady snow, appearing like angry sparks out of the black sky. There was no one else so foolish as to be out that night, the coal tenders either hunkered down in their barges or keeping warm in one of the Division Street saloons. Joe decided to check in with Rodney Hill at the company office—show his red and runny nose and complain just enough about the cold to prove he was on the job—and then stomp through the snowdrifts back to Kelly's to raise another glass and continue the celebration of himself he'd instigated less than an hour before. But first he'd have to empty his bladder, so he stepped over to the edge of the dock, across from McMillan's block shop, where he was protected from the wind by crates full of hand spikes and jib hanks, and used his numb fingers to fumble through his coat and unbutton his pants. He chose Oliver Taggert's coal barge to piss on, only for convenience, the boat rocking in the wind-kicked waves as Joe set his feet and reached inside his pants for the flesh that was already shrinking from the cold. The thought of hosing down Oliver's stinkpot made him laugh so hard that he almost lost his balance, and when he was finally able to take aim, he misfired, sprinkling his own boots instead. He hastily raised the arc of his piss and at the same time shook his foot, awkward as an ostrich, and slipped on the thin sheet of ice that coated the dock. He twirled his free arm as he went feet first into the black creek, splashing into the narrow space between Taggert's barge and the dock. The shock of the frigid water froze the scream that rose in his throat, and the weight of his woolen coat encased him like cement. He grabbed a loose rope hanging from the barge and was able to wrap it around his arm to keep from sinking. He was resting when the first wave rolled in and slammed him against the pier. He felt the air gush from his collapsed lungs and a gentle pressure as the wave receded and held him in its tarry swells. The rope had tightened around his arm, as if stitched into the heavy folds of his coat, and kept his chin above water. He was strangely warm, and the blood that rose in his mouth tasted thick and sweet as syrup. His body was growing numb when the second wave came in and lifted him, crushing his chest between the barge's wooden side and the ice-slicked pier. When the surge released him, he was surprised to be alive, and he spit out the water that lapped softly at his lips. He smelled fish and tar and then smelled nothing at all. He floated there with his one arm raised high, grateful for the lack of sensation. He thought of Glenna when she'd said "Yes" that evening, smiling and lifting his face to the dark sky. Snow fell on his eyes and eased them shut as a third wave heaved into the harbor and pounded his skull against the piling. When they pulled him out of Rondout Creek in the morning and laid him out on the dock, he was more a stain than a corpse.

With Joe's last pay from the Canal Company and a few extra dollars Kelly chipped in, Jane and Mickey were able to bury their uncle in a crowded corner of Montrepose Cemetery. The tearful graveside ceremony was attended by Ann Burns and the Mill Street boarders, the brotherhood of saloon regulars and Glenna Owens, who cried and whimpered as if they'd been married for fifty years. Brian Kelly's beery eulogy made little sense, but Jane and Mickey were thankful Joe got the send-off he deserved and that he would be forever interred under the graceful maple trees above Rondout Creek.

Jane had loved her uncle and mourned his passing, but by the next morning Kelly had offered her a job at the saloon and she accepted without hesitation, since the money meant that she and Mickey could still keep their separate rooms at Mrs. Burns's house. She'd give Mickey the room with the view of the harbor, where he could sit in the window and watch the big schooners as they made the turn around Sleightsburg. Jane would take the slightly larger room with a sloping ceiling and narrow window facing the alley, a dismal place of criss-crossing lines slung with gray laundry and slaughtered chickens, and gutters bubbling with human filth that steamed and ran even in the dead of winter. But it was quiet at this end of the house and at least the room was her own. She was twenty, and though it was a comfort having Mickey on the other side of the door, it was the door itself that comforted her more.

Jane still helped Ann in the mornings, making coffee and sweeping up brick dust, and was behind the bar at Kelly's before the midday crowd arrived. At first the men treated her with the solemn respect and kindness that the niece of their dear dead friend was due, and they cooed their drink orders and followed her with eyes puffed up in sadness. Tom Mardy, who'd given Joe his job, would start to blubber every time he saw her, and if Jane hadn't known he was already drunk, she'd have thought him simple. Feeling like an actor on a stage these men had set, she played the part of the brokenhearted waif to satisfy their dramatic impulses, dropping her gaze as she handed them platters of meat or refilled their glasses, gladly taking the extra coins they left so as not to offend their gentlemanly pride. They behaved with proper deference throughout the short days of winter, but the sad fact of Joe's demise soon faded away, and by the time the roads were churned with springtime mud, he was all but forgotten. Jane had enjoyed those quiet months and was smart enough to know that change would come, but she didn't think that Tom Mardy would introduce it.

Mardy was a young man of twenty-five, with thinning hair that he parted in the middle to frame his round and boyish face. Able to read and manage a ledger, he held a good job with the Canal Company, but his life had spoiled when his young wife died of consumption in September. Kelly said he'd cried so much that he lost fifty pounds and broke blood vessels in both his eyes. He was a sensitive young man to begin with—fond of reciting Tennyson's "Locksley Hall" with ease, complete with oratory flourish—but poetry now eluded him, two beers made him melancholic and the distant hoot of an owl might set him weeping inconsolably.

But with the advent of spring, Mardy's more physical senses became aroused. It was if he was coming out of a long hibernation, and when the sleep was rubbed from his eyes, the first thing he saw was Jane. As the days warmed, he began going to Kelly's earlier and staying longer, claiming a table where she was the bright center in his field of vision. At first he was shy and full of smiles, and Jane didn't mind the attention. But with this reawakening came a steady thirst, and soon he was drinking a half dozen beers and performing Tennyson again, his eyes fixed on her as he trilled his favorite verse:

> *When I dipt into the future as far as human eye could see;*
> *Saw the Vision of the world and all the wonder that would be.—*
> *In the Spring a fuller crimson comes upon the robin's breast;*
> *In the Spring the wanton lapwing gets himself another crest;*
> *In the Spring a livelier iris changes on the burnish'd dove;*
> *In the Spring a young man's fancy lightly turns to thoughts of love.*

As Mardy's feelings became more expressive, other patrons began to imitate his urges, as if a collective ardor had seized the room. They raised their noses at her every movement, sniffing the air like a pack of hounds. Jane was no longer Joe's poor niece, just a pretty young girl who walked among them unattached. Having grown up with drunks, she understood how their minds worked and made the necessary adjustments, meeting their eyes directly, no longer lingering as they repeated jokes as old as their underwear.

On the night of her twenty-first birthday, Mardy entered Kelly's before dusk and took his usual table, where Jane brought him five pints of ale before the sun went down and Kelly had to turn up his gas lamps. He was in good spirits, watching Jane as he always did, and she carried him a new drink every time he beckoned, but something about his fine humor made her apprehensive. Still, as Kelly's became more crowded, she was too busy even to notice when he switched to rum, spinning as she was from table to table. The hectic pace allowed her mind to go elsewhere, and she imagined the white-frosted cake she would share with Mickey and Ann when she got home, and the toast of port wine to celebrate her birthday. These pleasant thoughts carried her through the evening rush and made her routine tolerable. She was used to the stink of men's clothes and the sharp scrape of their grimy fingernails as they handed her change to pay for drinks, and to their dumb flattery and woozy admiration as she picked up their empty glasses and pointed them toward the door. But she was hardly used to being grabbed from behind and pulled off her feet.

She first felt his fingers tighten on her waist and then loosen as he worked his arm around her and pulled her toward him. She almost stumbled and had no choice but to grab his shoulders as he yanked her to his chest. He placed his free hand on her breast and kissed her gaping mouth, his lips and teeth dazzling with rum. When she tried to pull away he squeezed her tighter, pushing his tongue so deep in her mouth that she gagged. She scratched the side of his face and beat the back of his head, and not a single man in the saloon moved to help her. It wasn't until she grabbed Mardy's ear and twisted it that he let her go, then stood there in front of her and threw his head back in laughter, the sound of it sharp in her ears. Staring at that great red hole in his face and the bloated tongue, she hawked up the rummy saliva he'd left in her mouth and spit it back in his face. The room went quiet, and Mardy blinked at her with watery eyes and pushed her nose in with the flat of his hand. She landed hard on her backside, skittering across the filthy floor on her elbows and heels, but then his face rose over a table, furious with rage, and as he raised his arm to strike her, another hand seized him by the wrist.

It was Frank Quinn. "That's enough, Tom," he said gently, and when Mardy tried to break away, he gripped him tighter still. "That's enough."

Jane already knew of Frank's reputation on the Rondout docks, and suddenly she felt sorry for Tom. He was just a wifeless drunk, carried away by his own disastrous infatuation, and didn't deserve the beating that the evening now promised. She looked away, anticipating the blows and gasps, but when Mardy didn't come crashing down on the floor next to her, she looked up again.

Frank had calmly forced Tom's arm back to his side and rested a hand on his shoulder. Tom was still staring at her, his red-rimmed eyes already blinking with remorse, tears running down his cheeks. "Now say you're sorry, Tom, and help the girl up."

He nodded in a rummy haze, ashamed enough to cast his eyes to the ground. "I'm sorry, Miss Blessing," he mumbled, and offered his hand. Jane accepted and, once she was back on her feet, watched in surprise as Frank Quinn, instead of balling his hands into fists, used his thumbs to gently wipe the tears from Mardy's eyes.

"Enough of that, Tom. Now come to the bar and buy me a drink," he said, squeezing his shoulder and turning him away. Then he looked back at Jane for the first time, smiling broadly, as kind a man as she'd ever met.

. . .

It was still warm when Jane left the house that July morning in 1864. She crossed the street at the first corner and stayed in the shade of the First Baptist Church, where the fragrance of honeysuckle was strong enough to dispel the foul aroma wafting up from Rondout Creek.

Jane turned on Division Street but didn't glance at the Grieves building. The sidewalk in front of Van Buren's grocery store was crowded with women watching Dora Seitz argue with Van Buren about the four cracked duck eggs she'd found in the basket of a dozen she'd bought from him the day before. Her accent was so thick that it sounded as if she were gargling with stones, and the grocer just stood there scratching his head and pretending to listen. Jane sidled past just as Dora pulled one of the cracked eggs out of her basket and smashed it on the stoop between Van Buren's boots. He did a little jig while the other women roared in laughter and Dora reached into her basket for another.

When Jane arrived at the post office, she noticed a small crowd had gathered in front of the *Courier* office across the street, looking at the yellow broadsheet taped in the window. Jane knew what it was, of course, and paused in the doorway for the few seconds it took her to find the courage to walk over and read the list of war dead. She knew Mrs. Rangel and Mrs. Koch, both of whom had sons in the regiment, but they didn't acknowledge her as she moved between them and scanned the names of casualties from Spotsylvania and Yellow Tavern and the Confederate victory at Trevilian Station, stopping only when she reached a longer list under the black heading of COLD HARBOR. She found Ulster County and didn't blink as she read the entry for the 120th Regiment. There were three dead, but no Frank Quinn.

She took a deep breath, which felt like her first in two weeks, and looked on the right of the sheet, where the missing were listed. Near the top was "Frank Quinn, 120th Regiment, New York Volunteers." For a moment she felt like smiling, overcome by a strange exhilaration. Frank wasn't dead, only missing, and would survive because he'd promised her he would. That thought made her want to cry, but she knew if she started now, she might not be able to stop.

COLEY WOKE up twice that morning. The first time was in the front room of Hackett's whorehouse, slumped in a green velvet divan, his bare feet splayed over one overstuffed arm and his face mashed against the other. He didn't remember getting there, or the walk over from Natterjack's, where he'd shared glasses of whiskey with Charlie O'Fay. He sat up slowly and kept his eyes closed, waiting for the tingling to pass through his legs. The house was quiet and smelled of lavender. He glanced out the window and saw clouds over the harbor, fat and green-bellied with rain. He was tempted to take a swig from the brandy decanter on the oval table next to him, but the thought of it made his stomach roll. He found his boots in the corner by the door, but when he crouched down to lace them, his head throbbed, so he slumped to his knees, grim as a supplicant, and waited until it stopped. When he looked up, a young woman was walking down the staircase, her long brown hair tied loosely at the top of her head and her nightgown of a light material rising from her limbs as delicately as smoke. She paused to yawn, and Coley stayed perfectly still while her jaws and pretty lips worked open and shut and she took her final steps down the stairs, his eyes bouncing along with the fleshy sway of her backside as she entered the opposite parlor. He breathed again only after the door clicked shut behind her, then shook his head, finished tying his boots and walked to the window, his footfalls hushed by the floral runner. Without looking behind him, he dropped into the garden and ran back to Shapiro's.

Unfortunately, Shapiro was already up when Coley arrived at the stable. He'd been checking on the big bay, Soldier, who'd come up lame the day before, and was carrying a bucket of pine tar out of the dark barn when he saw Coley sneaking around the side of the house.

"Coley!" he hissed. "Is that you?"

Coley stopped. He knew Shapiro would be standing there with a hand on his hip, rolling his big head back and forth, and he could already hear the breath snorting out of his nose and his tongue clicking against the back of his teeth. It wasn't the first time he'd been caught like this, but he couldn't bear to look Shapiro in the eye. He felt guilty enough just listening to him.

"You'll change Soldier's dressing in an hour," Shapiro grumbled, putting the bucket of tar down and walking into the house.

Coley waited until he could hear Shapiro's footsteps in the hallway before retreating downstairs to his own room, cursing Shapiro for his goodness and lamenting his own bad timing.

The second time he woke up, the little squirrel was squatting on his chest, clicking his nails and staring at Coley with his bulging black eyes. Coley knew Pinch was hungry, but his head ached too much to do anything about it, so he shifted his weight and pulled his blanket tight. He had just turned over again, taking that deep breath that would put him back to sleep, when Shapiro's fist boomed against the wall and called him to work.

After Coley changed Soldier's dressing and painted his hooves with pine tar, Shapiro made him do the job he dreaded most—cleaning bird nests and ratshit from the rafters. But he refused to whine or complain and climbed up to the top rung of the wooden ladder, reaching above his head with the broom to swat at the cobwebs hanging from the roof beams like tinsel. He was still woozy, and the old ladder shimmied as if it were constructed of sticks and paste, but he'd rather have fallen off and broken his neck than let Shapiro think he was too sick to work. He stood there beneath Coley, chin up and belly pushed forward, pointing at an old hornet's nest Coley had missed. He kept grunting until he was either bored or satisfied, then shuffled back to his office.

Throughout the morning, Coley did whatever was asked of him. He was sitting on a short three-legged stool and rolling fresh bandages for Soldier's sore hock when the stable doors opened. The sudden burst of sunlight stung his eyes and he looked away, aware only of boots thudding across the dirt. On another morning he would've jumped right up, but he was still mad at Shapiro and didn't give a damn about his customer.

"I want my horse," the familiar voice announced, and when Coley looked up, Mickey was grinning at him. His black twill pants were tucked into his stovepipe boots, and he'd rolled the sleeves of his blue tick shirt up past the elbows. His face as pink and bright as a pasture rose, he leaned on a post and flipped a coin expertly off his thumb, letting it spin in a blur until Coley dropped the bandages and snatched it out of the dusty air.

Shapiro came out and greeted Mickey with a deferential nod. Although the disdain was evident on his open face, he turned to Coley and clapped his hands. "Get his horse!"

Mickey was still grinning when Coley headed to the back of the stable. "I want the boy, too," he added.

Coley stopped and turned around.

Shapiro just looked at him. "The boy? I need him here."

"I need him more."

"He works for me."

"Not today." Mickey was almost laughing when he said it, a convivial man in good spirits. He took another coin out of his pocket and flipped it sharply at Shapiro, pinging it off his forehead.

Shapiro didn't look at the coin at his feet or touch the pink welt above his eye, just turned toward Coley with his gaze averted. "Go." The word seemed to die in the still air, and he went back to his office as Mickey just leaned there, grinning as if he ruled the day.

HE ROLLED onto his back, woke abruptly and blinked, forgetting where he was for a moment. It was a bright morning, and the sunlight streaming through the window opposite him was jittery with leaf shadows. The bed he slept in had a long-ago familiarity, and as he raised himself on his elbows and breathed deeply, it all came back to him, and he smiled. He had an erection, as he often did in the early morning, and even though he couldn't remember his dream, he imagined it had been a fine one.

Arthur rose and walked to the chair his pants were draped over. He dressed, slipping the wide suspenders over his shoulders, and found his boots under the desk. He pulled them on and walked into the kitchen, fiddling with the loose button on his sleeve. "Will?" he called, but the room was empty. The fire in the hearth was smoldering and a pot of coffee steamed gently on a grate over the ashes. He saw an empty cup on the table, and the bottle of whiskey. He stepped onto the porch, put his hands flat on the railing and stretched his back.

He'd ridden back to the Clove the night before, planning to stay as long as he could. He didn't have to be back in Rondout until the end of the week, when Francis Horn and his new bride were coming in from Samsonville for a formal portrait. He'd tried to convince them to have the portrait taken "in the natural," offering to load his camera and equipment onto a wagon and drive out to their farm at no extra charge, but the Horns preferred the artificial accoutrements of his studio and the glamour of faux scenery, which was so popular with their class.

Looking toward the Shawangunk Ridge that jutted outward as if emerging from a shadowed plane, he relished the morning light, the mysterious trick of it, and wished he'd brought a camera along. He heard the rumble of galloping horses and turned to the barn, where he saw four of them running into the fenced pasture, and Will stepping through the open doors to watch them settle into the tall grass.

And then he heard the barking dog.

Will heard it, too. He turned from the field and saw the wagon coming through the break in the trees below the farm. The dog was out in front, racing through the culvert alongside the road, jumping in and out of the yellow tickseed that grew along the edge of the meadow.

By the time Will joined Arthur at the house, the wagon had pulled up to the porch. Joop House was driving the team of mules and two Jug Hill boys rode side by side in the back. It wasn't until he got closer that Will saw the other man sprawled out in the bed, his legs covered in a blood-soaked canvas tarp, his hands tight on both rails.

"What happened, Joop?" Will asked.

"Mr. Vandeman got gored."

"What gored him?"

"The damndest thing I ever saw," Joop replied.

Will hoisted himself into the back of the wagon and stood over Vandeman, who was grimacing in pain, the tendons raised in his thin neck. "What happened, Mr. Vandeman?"

"Got my goddamn leg skewered."

"How?"

"Pulling goddamn stumps!" he screeched.

Will carefully pulled the canvas off his legs. A white shirt had been wrapped around his upper right thigh, but blood had still pooled in the crotch of his pants and spread across the boards beneath him. Will unwound the shirt, looked at the black wound through the tear in his trousers and turned to the Smitty brothers. "Get his pants off."

"I can get my own goddamn pants off!" Vandeman screamed, the pitch of his voice unnaturally high, and both Smittys had to turn away to keep from giggling.

Will glanced at Arthur as Vandemann began to loosen his belt. "Get me a bottle of whiskey, Arthur. And a clean sheet."

Arthur nodded and went into the house.

Vandeman scowled and swore as he eased his trousers down his legs, careful to cover himself with the front flap of his long shirt. The dog was still barking in the distance, his yips sharp in the quiet morning. "Useless sonofabitch," he muttered as he stretched out his punctured leg.

Will knelt down to examine the four-inch gash in his thigh, running his thumb along the blood-crusted edge, ignoring the gasps that Vandeman emitted through his clenched teeth. He reached around the back of the leg and felt the exit wound, not as large as the front but the flesh still ripped and puckered.

Arthur stepped back onto the porch with a bundled-up sheet and a whiskey bottle and handed them to Will. Vandeman's mouth was contorted into a rictus of true misery, and every ligament in his body was stretched tight on the bone. Will had seen this same communion with pain after battles in the western campaign, the wounded soldiers submitting to some unheralded agony. He felt sorry for Vandeman because there was no glory in his injury, only anger.

He remembered what his father had written to him several years ago:

Oliver Bogardus finally got free of that property he owned alongside our place, two hundred acres of bog and stone that's pricked him for a decade. Sold it to a fellow named Vandeman, who must've had the sun in his eyes when he surveyed the property, because that land isn't good for anything but heartache and Indian corn. They say God loves a fool, and for Vandeman's sake I hope it's true.

Will gently lifted Vandeman's leg and bent it at the knee. Vandeman turned his face away and squeezed his eyes shut, the tears squirting down his cheeks. Will quickly reexamined the wound from both sides and used the end of the sheet to wipe away the bright freshness of blood that began to seep out of the hole.

"It went all the way through, Mr. Vandeman. It's deep and ugly, but it's only flesh that's been damaged."

"It hurts like hell." He winced.

"It'll hurt for a long while, but it will heal," Will told him as he nodded to the Smitty brothers. "Grab his arms, boys." They hesitated. "Quickly now."

Joop nodded, and they jumped up on either side of Vandeman and held each arm tightly. Before he could wiggle free, Will sat on his good leg and used his teeth to pull the cork out of the bottle, then poured whiskey over his thigh. Vandeman screamed and convulsed, but the Smittys held him fast until his body collapsed in exhaustion.

Will eased up and started ripping the sheet into strips. "That's the worst of it, Mr. Vandeman. I'll put some stitches in it, but you'll need to see a doctor in a week's time."

Vandeman opened a bloodshot eye. "Ain't you a doctor?"

Will paused as if to think about it. "Yes, I am." Again he turned to Arthur. "I left a brown bag in my father's study. Could you bring it out here, Arthur?"

"Sure, Will."

"Hey, Doc," Vandeman called out hoarsely, and waited for Will to look at him. "Get these niggers off my goddamn arms."

Will nodded to the Smittys, who let go, and Vandeman slowly sat up. He pulled the front of his shirt between his naked legs and looked down at the hole in his thigh, poking his fingers at his purple skin. When it started bleeding again, Will tossed him another piece of torn sheet. "That's a mean steer you've got there, Mr. Vandeman."

"Wasn't no damn steer," Vandeman snorted, and stuck his good leg straight out, his dirty boot brushing the solid lump covered by ripped feed sacks in the far corner of the wagon. Will noticed it before but hadn't paid much attention to what he'd thought was an uncut gravestone or boundary marker. Now that he looked closer, he saw the dried mud underneath the sacks and the smooth curve of what looked like bronzed rock weighing down the wagon bed. He moved to Vandeman's feet and in the same motion pulled the sacks away. Leaning in front of him was a thing of primordial beauty, rounded and thick and rising as high as Will's chest. There were deep cavities on both sides, and Will realized it was a fossilized skull. When he knelt down and reached his hand behind the point where it narrowed, he felt a short row of thick teeth and two empty sockets as big as platters.

"A tusk," Will whispered before turning to Vandeman. "It was a tusk."

"Huh?"

"It was a tusk that gored you. Where is it?"

"That horn?"

"Where is it?" Will pressed.

"It broke off and sunk to the bottom of the goddamn swamp," Vandeman replied stubbornly.

"Did you see another?"

"Only saw the one."

"Was it long?"

"Long as I am. Longer maybe."

Will slowly stood up and admired the great skull in front of him. "It must be enormous."

Vandeman ignored him, glaring down at his naked limbs. "Bad hip. Bad leg. Jesus Christ, it's a mess I am." He grimaced and shifted his weight. "Should've sold the goddamn land to Grieves when I had the chance."

"How much do you want for the land?" Will asked without turning around.

Vandeman swallowed his next moan and glanced at Will, pausing long enough to think straight for the first time that day. "You interested?"

"How much do you want?"

A smile crossed Vandeman's lips. "Grieves offered me almost two thousand dollars."

"I'll give you two thousand plus a hundred more," Will countered.

Vandeman blinked twice and was glad to see that Will was still there, not some figment conjured up by the pain. "That don't include the stock," he said warily.

"I don't want your stock." He placed a hand on top of the skull. "I want this."

Vandeman sputtered in laughter. "It's yours, all of it. Every rock and flower and goddamn horn." He cackled as if he'd gone mad. "The day ain't turned out half bad, has it, Dr. Harp?"

COLEY RODE an old horse Shapiro had taken in trade earlier that year, a potbellied mare with a fierce temper, just as likely to bolt at the wrong touch of a heel or stop to eat daisies on the roadside. She was too ornery for ladies and too stubborn for most men, but she was the perfect fit for Coley. She minded him because he held his reins still and his legs were light on her barrel, but she was still quick to buck if the flies grew thick around her ears. He'd learned to gentle her by stroking her withers, a trick he kept to himself. He called her Melon because she was fat as one, but it didn't matter what you called her, because she came only for buttered bread, another trick he'd kept to himself.

The fifth stop they made since leaving Rondout was the Damon farm on the turnpike above High Falls. Coley sat atop Melon and waited for Mickey, with nothing to do but lean back with his face in the sun, his head filled with fresh air. He was grateful to be out of the stable and tried not to think about Shapiro's expression when they'd ridden out of town that morning. He'd stood there in the shadows with his arms crossed, glum in the knowledge that his authority had been compromised in his own domain. It was shame that Coley saw in

Shapiro's face, and shame he felt himself, but he allowed himself to forget about it and think instead of the man whose company he now kept.

Melon had her head down by the fence, chewing the yellow cone-flowers and whatever other green stalks she could stuff into her mouth. Mickey's horse was tethered beside her and doing the same. Dutch Eddy was a small Morgan with a broad back, and Coley was surprised that a man of Mickey's abilities would claim such a spiritless gelding, deemed passive enough for children, and built low enough to the ground that anyone with moderate physical skills could mount her with the slightest hop. He was smaller than Melon, and as Coley and Mickey rode together along the plank road, they appeared almost equal in stature. Coley thought it must've been a comical sight, but no one they passed dared to laugh.

Coley knew it was a privilege he was being given, and he was obliged to Mickey for singling him out. He looked forward to telling the Magruders and Al Deyo about his adventure over warm beer that night, enjoying the rapid blinking of their eyes and their green envy as they battered him with questions. He was Mickey Blessing's charge now, an apprenticeship any of them would covet.

They hadn't spoken much those first few hours on the road, no words of wisdom imparted nor instructions given. Mickey seemed perfectly content to trot along in the early-morning silence, punctuating it only with an occasional yawn or the murmured greeting to the driver of a hay wagon they'd passed in Hurley. Coley, hoping this countryside venture would involve some grand retribution like the one given Duncan Fisher on the Rondout wharf, grew fidgety in his saddle. And he was disappointed that no pistol bulged in Mickey's wide belt and no knife was stuck in his boot. There was only the single-shot Kentucky rifle in a scabbard on his saddle, as dusty as the rig it was attached to.

Mickey, never less than mirthful that morning, sensed the boy's impatience. "It's a quiet day we'll be having, Coley Hinds," he said. "A reward after the vigors of the last week." He then reached into his saddlebag and tossed him a black leather-bound book.

Coley turned it over and saw the name *GRIEVES* embossed in gold leaf on the cover. "What am I supposed to do with this?" he asked.

"That's the riddle of the day." Mickey grinned as they picked up the old mine road outside of Marbletown.

The first of Grieves's properties they'd stopped at was a small farm Cecil Geddes rented on a wide bend of the Esopus Creek south of High

Falls, the land arable enough for him to pasture a dozen cows and plant enough corn to turn a profit. It was a neatly kept spread, with a fine timber-built farmhouse and outbuildings that didn't sag or bow. As they rode through the gate, Coley saw three children watching them from the dirt yard in front of the chicken coop. When they recognized Mickey, they ran toward the house, whooping like Indians. Mickey laughed, and he was still smiling when Geddes came onto the porch carrying a burlap sack in his hand. He was a dour man, and his long black beard held two patches of gray that hung from his bottom lip like fangs. He tossed Mickey the sack even before he'd had a chance to get off his horse. "No need to stop," Geddes told him.

Mickey hefted the sack in his hand. "You make my job too easy, Cecil, but I'm still going to have to count it, make sure the figures match. You wouldn't want me to make another visit like I did last month, would you?"

Geddes blinked but stood by the rail. Coley noticed his worn overalls, the patched knees caked with fresh mud and the hems shredded around his boots, the black dirt limning his fingernails and streaking his damp hair. He'd already put in a full morning's work, but the tremor Coley saw in his hand was not from exhaustion.

Mickey handed Coley the sack. "Count it and square it in the ledger. Let's make sure Mr. Geddes is an honest man."

He carefully counted the money and pulled the leather book from his saddlebag, found Geddes's name and matched today's sum against the notations in the column below it. "It's the same as last month," he said.

Mickey nodded and tossed him a pencil from the pocket of his shirt. "Then enter it and we'll be on our way."

Coley wrote down the figure and glanced up.

Mickey gripped his reins and touched his heel to Dutch Eddy's side. "Back to work, Cecil," he said as he turned his horse in the front yard. "Everybody's got a job to do."

Coley quickly shut the book and followed Mickey onto the road leading toward the Clove, where they continued their rounds.

Coley sat up in the saddle when Mickey came out of the Damon front door, the jingle of the coins a warning bell. He had his hands ready to catch the money pouch, and the black ledger was already propped up against the pommel of his saddle. As he poured the coins into his hand, Mickey surveyed the horse-damaged garden along the fence line. "The horses certainly enjoyed Mrs. Damon's flowers."

"Don't worry," Coley said after he'd wet the tip of the pencil with his tongue. "It won't make them sick."

"It's not the horses I suspect will be ailing," Mickey said, laughing as he mounted up. "It's not them at all."

"Let's get something to eat," he said when they approached Rickert's Tavern. They'd been smelling the grease smoke ever since they'd turned the bend, a hint of sweetness from the bacon Rickert cured himself. He'd wisely built his tavern at the junction of two valley roads, and the field next door was always ajumble with horses and wagons parked there by thirsty farmers coming back from New Paltz and the canal landing at High Falls.

Mickey found them a small table by the open door and treated the boy to a plate of ham and eggs. Coley ate quickly and thoroughly, wiping his bread over his plate to pick up every drop of grease, and drank three cups of Rickert's foul coffee as easily as if he'd been weaned on it.

The men inside gave Mickey a wide berth. It wasn't as rough a crowd as those found in Rondout saloons, but they still knew who he was and watched him as they would a dog prone to fits. Coley watched him, too, which Mickey expected and desired. It was all part of his plan to give the boy a broader and necessary view of the world he inhabited. He sat loose-limbed in his chair and enjoyed his breakfast, ignoring the discomfort his presence unleashed in the room. He ate slowly, and the moment he pushed his plate away, Rickert's Jug Hill girl appeared to clear the table. Only then did he ease back his chair and encourage the men to come to him, farmers paying rent or locals just stopping by to acknowledge his presence among them. As the money piled up on the table, Coley counted it and entered the figures into the black book, and they both accepted the glasses of beer Rickert sent over without charge. In an hour, the tavern was almost empty and their business was done. Coley fed both horses thick pieces of buttered bread that he paid for himself, and with the sun high they got back on the road to visit the last farmhouse of the day.

Coley had done a good job, and Mickey was glad to have him along. He knew the boy was still running on the vapors of the week before, but the roar in his ears would soon diminish, and he'd have to learn to trust the echoes that remained. A bruise or broken bone always provided a certain persuasion, but it left behind only temporary impressions. If impact was to have influence, it had to linger in both flesh and memory. This was a lesson Mickey had learned early on, and one he wanted to share with Coley. The boy would someday be grateful for the knowledge, as grateful he'd been to the men who years ago had plucked him from the pack of young wolves that roamed the Rondout docks.

Mickey's initiation had started with Patrick Fallon, who'd made his mark lending money to canal workers, glad to be of service when they needed a loan, happier still when it was time to collect. His office was the wharf itself, and he carried out his transactions with the pomp of a Wall Street banker, meeting clients in the snug alleys of stacked crates and barrels. He covered dogfights and saloon debts and whores, whatever the need, and the interest he collected, though exorbitant, was the unfortunate price a poor man paid to keep his transgressions to himself.

From the morning Mickey first sailed into Rondout, he'd spent most of his time down at the wharf. He'd been Coley's age when he started running errands for the men who worked there, fetching tobacco or newspapers or carrying messages from home, pocketing the pennies they tossed him and keeping a wary eye on the dockside hierarchy. He learned whose whistles to heed and whose to ignore, and which other boys he needed to whip in order to leave the sidelines and work his way into the center. He hadn't been much of a fighter until then, but he quickly learned how a well-placed elbow in the ribs would slow a boy down, and that rapping a knuckle to the back of his head hurt more than a solid punch in the eye. And he got good at it. Soon he had the attention of the men who mattered, who'd call him by name from the dozen of other boys loitering around the docks. His worth established, he could strut among his peers without fear of a nail pushed into the small of his back or a rock smashed against his ear.

And when he felt the calling, he would take to the water. The men on the docks called him a "river rat," but he didn't mind. From late April, when the turtles emerged from their muddy sleep, until the end of October, when the chill breezes coming down off the Catskills brought the first frost, Mickey swam. He'd launch himself off the highest piers on Rondout Creek and enter the water without a splash, using long, fluid strokes to carry himself out to the schooners anchored in deeper water. He'd flip onto his back and watch where the sailors pointed and then dive deep to untangle lines, accepting the coins thrown to him even though he dove for the thrill of it, savoring the pressure of the water as he spiraled deeper, letting it clutch at him and fill his ears and strain his lungs. It always reminded him of the day his father first tossed him into the River Slaney. A child then, naked and afraid, he'd clawed at his father's arms and then the air, trying to avoid the cold slap of his flesh as he hit the water. "Breathe!" he heard his father shout as the river exploded against his spine, sending up curtains of silver around him. He held there a moment in that liquid concavity before it washed over his arms and legs and carried him under. He could hear his father laughing and then the hum of water as it cupped his ears, but he kept his eyes open and relaxed and settled into the rocking motion of it, letting himself drift downward through the shallows. He came to rest in the silky mud of the river bottom and looked around, the sunlight from the world above turning the water bronze. He stayed there until his lungs hurt, and only then dug his bare toes into the jammy muck to push himself toward the surface, his arms extended in his very first stroke.

Now he swam in Rondout Harbor for the pure pleasure of it. He dove deeper than the other boys could, and while they hung on to the mossy ropes of the pier, holding their breath and scissoring their legs and watching him, he swam down into the blackness, out of sight, and retrieved the lost watches and Spanish coins that studded the creek bottom. He gave the useless trinkets to his young admirers, kept a few coins for himself, and handed off anything of value to his new mentor, Patrick Fallon.

Fallon was easy to pick out in a crowd, strutting down the Strand with his red satin cravat tied wide and loose around his neck, his frock coat pinched at the waist and a brown bowler hat pulled down over his dark curls and cocked over his left eye. He was of medium height and build but swaggered like a prizefighter. The Bucklin brothers usually accompanied him, rough Galway men who'd emigrated to America on his coattails. They were taller than Fallon and less well dressed, their thick arms heavily tattooed with serpents and dragons, mementos from their years of service in the Chinese navy. They claimed to be married to Samoan princesses, and to have drowned a British seaman in Galway Bay before Fallon booked their passage across the Atlantic. They repaid his largesse by becoming indentured enforcers whose silent menace and mythic history precluded the use of fist or blade.

It was at about that time, when Mickey was fourteen, that the big German, August Heber, came to Rondout with his family. He had a wife equal in stature and two married daughters with husbands, all of them generously proportioned. They'd left the house they shared in Harlem and ventured up the Hudson to buy a saloon on Ravine Street from the widow of August's second cousin, who'd died of cholera the year before. Though the price was fair, it consumed all the money August Heber had in the world, and he requested a loan from Fallon, who hesitated at first—distrustful as he was of foreigners—but in the end decided it was a fine opportunity to make inroads with the German community. The Bucklin brothers were at his side as he handed Heber two hundred dollars in gold coins, and compared to the bulky German, they looked as harmless as ordinary men. Heber accepted the money and didn't flinch when he heard the interest rate, just counted the coins placed in his paw and walked back to Ravine Street.

A month later, the *Rondout Courier* announced the opening of Heber's Tavern, and Fallon went to collect his debt. It was early in the evening, and Mickey and some other boys were already lurking outside, waiting to follow home the drunken canal men who'd eventually exit the bar and stumble back down the alleys to the coal docks. It was just getting dark when Fallon came up the middle of the road with the Bucklin brothers, thumbs in the pockets of his tight trousers, and stopped to inspect the high caliber of his investment. The woodwork was freshly painted in shades of dark green, and the lintels redone in cast iron. Three burnished-copper gas lamps were fixed over the front window to illuminate Heber's elaborate hand–painted sign, the large black letters trimmed in gold:

HEBER'S TAVERN
FINE GERMAN CUISINE
SAUSAGES AND BEER

Fallon stood there, his chest puffed out, and admired the craftsmanship. The lamplight shone on his face, his red cravat bright as a beating heart. Mickey sat in the back of a brick wagon with the other Rondout boys and waited. As soon as Fallon stepped to the front door, he sprang out of the wagon and rushed to open it for him. "Evening, Mr. Fallon," he said.

"Evening to you, Mickey boy," Fallon said as he briskly stepped inside.

Mickey stood at the door and watched him and the Bucklins make their grand entrance. Men were lined elbow-to-elbow at the polished bar, where August Heber smiled widely. When he saw Fallon, he motioned him forward with a broad wave, making room for him at the walnut counter. Before Fallon could even squeeze into position, one of the sons-in-law had placed a glass of whiskey in front of him and poured a pint of lager for each of his companions. Fallon acknowledged the proprietor's generosity, then touched the rim of his glass against Heber's. "To your success!"

"To more success!" Heber replied, and each downed his whiskey in a single gulp.

Mickey watched from the door as Heber poured them both another drink from an amber bottle that looked no bigger than a baby's rattle in his oversized hand. Then he reached below the bar and dropped a fat white canvas sack in front of his patron. "For you, sir," he announced.

Fallon looked at the sack of coins and beamed in pleasure. He then untied the cord and his eyes took quick measure of the twenty double eagles inside. "There's only two hundred dollars here," Mickey heard him say.

Heber shrugged magnificently and fixed him with a smirk. "That's all you loaned me."

"There was interest to be paid."

"I will not pay robbers," the German told him.

"What?" Fallon asked, his ears ringing with the noise around him.

"Shyster!" Heber shouted, his breath hot and his words like punches. "Thief!"

"We had a deal!" Fallon shouted back.

"I don't deal with you, thief!"

"You owe me fifty dollars!"

"Irish thief!"

Mickey leaned farther inside and watched Fallon clutch the canvas sack and rise to his feet, the Bucklins getting up with him.

"Take your money, thief, and get out!" Heber bellowed, pointing a massive arm toward the door.

Mickey watched the Bucklin brothers reach into their pockets for their saps, and Heber's sons-in-law come in from either side of the bar, the bats in their hands held high as torches. Men in the tavern clustered around, bobbing up and down to get a better look, but Mickey lost sight of the Bucklins until the door banged open and they were tossed into the street, tumbling arm in arm like wrestlers. The next minute, Patrick Fallon himself walked outside, the laughter thrusting him through the door. Holding the sack of coins as if it held nothing more than hard candy or chocolates, he stopped in the middle of the street, where the brothers writhed at his feet.

Mickey looked at Fallon's wretched face and then back at the tavern, where Heber stood in his big front window, the reflected lamplight shining above his head like a corona of stars. His thick arms were crossed and his body shook with the roar of his merriment, loud as a tuba, and his sons-in-law and daughters and all the Germans crowded around. Keeping an eye on him, Mickey backed up to the wagon, grabbed one of the bricks, and ran to the front of the tavern. He waited for Heber to spot him, then he took aim at that great laughing maw and let the brick fly. The huge window shattered like a crash of cymbals and showered the street with a jeweled rain. Everyone ducked but Heber, who took the brick directly in the face, and Mickey saw the blood erupt from his mouth and nose, hoping he'd choke on the teeth he swallowed. Then he ran, and as he jumped the white picket fence on the corner, he heard Fallon break into laughter behind him. He ran as fast as he could, fast enough to escape the clutches of Heber's sons-in-law, but not Constable Sirrine, who found him hiding in Turck's lumberyard, boxed his ears and almost broke his arm when he yanked it behind his back and dragged him to the county jail in Kingston.

Mickey was charged with assault and served 120 days. It was his first time in jail, and he celebrated his fifteenth birthday in the small cell he shared with John Hodges, a Rondout man convicted of murdering his wife. He'd taken a shine to Mickey, showing him how to fashion a knife from a shoe last and read to him from his copy of *David Copperfield* before being transferred to the penitentiary in Auburn. Mickey enjoyed the story immensely and would ask Jane to finish reading the book to him when he got back home. Jane visited him every Saturday, passing on the gossip she'd overheard at Kelly's and telling him that Patrick Fallon had given her fifty gold dollars the day he'd gone to jail.

On the October morning of his release, Mickey went straight to Rondout Creek. He walked by way of Ravine Street, where a new glass window announced DICKEY'S SALOON where Heber's had been. Along the coal dock, men greeted him by name and boys he once ran with shied away; he knew his mark had been made. He also knew that Jane was waiting for him at home and that Patrick Fallon would be expecting him, but for now that could wait. He walked briskly to the wharf and stripped off his shoes and shirt and dove into the creek, swimming out past the schooners into the wide expanse of the Hudson, taking long, clean strokes until his muscles burned from the effort. He swam for an hour, glad to be home, and let himself drift back to shore on the strong current, smiling, his eyes closed, as a cold rain began to pock the water around him.

Now it was Mickey doing the initiating, and Coley the new recruit. He led the boy along a well-used logging trail that branched off the Clove road and led onto the broad ridge above the Millen farm. He reined in his horse and waited for Coley to catch up, looking down to where a weak spire of white smoke rose from the kitchen chimney, and Millen's gray gelding raced in nervous circles in the corral next to the barn.

"Something's itching that horse," Coley said as he rode up alongside, the gelding now rearing up to kick the boards of the enclosure, each bang loud as a guncrack.

"Must've stepped in a nest of snakes," Mickey said.

Coley shook his head. The horse was lathered from rump to neck, and he could hear the panicky snorts. "He's gonna bust out of there."

"He won't get far," Mickey replied, easing Dutch Eddy down the trail and smiling at the pleasure of seeing Hannah again. He would let the boy water their horses and tend to the gelding while he went inside, his first visit in a month, and he looked forward to running his hand across her naked belly to feel the changes inside her. He still loved looking at her—the constellation of freckles that stretched across her shoulder blades, the dimples at the base of her spine, the paleness of her skin and hair. And if the boy happened to peek through the window and see them, he wouldn't mind; it was just another lesson to be learned.

As they rode up to the farmhouse, the gelding saw them and began to whinny and buck. Even Mickey could see the terror in his eyes. Then he heard a crash in the kitchen, and scuffling, and his hand searched for the Kentucky rifle scabbarded to his saddle. He pulled it loose as Dutch Eddy snorted and pawed the ground, and when he looked up, he saw a mountain lion leap out the side window of the farmhouse, ears cocked back and front legs fully extended. It landed without a sound and kicked off with its powerful hind legs, its elongated body seeming to explode as it bounded toward the stream. Mickey raised his rifle and fired, the bullet sailing high before chipping bark off a beech tree twenty feet beyond his target. The lion's pace remained fluid as it ran, big paws sending up sprays of dirt, its thick tail whipping behind. It jumped over the stream with little effort, the sunlight picking up the red in its coat, and when it moved through the pasture only the tall grass shimmered, the cat out of sight until it broke onto the rocky slope below the Shawangunk Ridge, gaining speed as it headed to the freedom of higher ground.

Mickey jumped off his horse and ran to the farmhouse. There was blood on the porch and the front door was open. He barged inside, almost tripping over the chair that had been knocked to the floor, then caught himself when he saw Hannah lying curled up near the hearth. He recognized her only by her yellow hair. Her face was gone below her eye sockets, her neck chewed through to ligament and bone. Her chest and stomach had been ripped open so the cat could feed on the muscles and organs within, her arms and legs torn deeply by claw and tooth. The whiteness of the exposed bone was startling. Only one foot, untouched, lay outside the shadow of blood that pooled beneath her. She had been dragged and nudged across the floor, and Mickey realized he was standing in a smear of blood that ran from the threshold to where she lay.

He heard Coley come in behind him, breathing heavily before falling silent, as if he'd suddenly disappeared. Then he turned and ran, retching over the porch rail.

Mickey walked to the open window. He could smell the feral scent in the room, and the spray of urine where the cat had marked the wall. He could smell the end of Hannah's life. He put his hand down on the windowsill and touched the stain left there by a bloody hind paw. He looked to the ridge and tried to track the lion's climb into the dense pine forest that ran along the summit.

Then he closed his eyes and tried not to think about what it had done to Hannah and his unborn child.

∽◉◡

LOOKS LIKE a little Dutchman," one of the women said.

"He's purely pink," another chimed in.

"Ain't born on this side of the hill," clucked a third.

Pearl held the baby in her arms, its body swaddled in white home-spun. He was asleep now, his fat cheeks full, his eyes and nose crusted with tears. The scant hair on his head was faded and soft, not yet any color. The little cord at his belly button was dry as a dead twig, and he looked as serious as any baby Pearl had ever seen.

Things had calmed down now, but when she'd first carried the baby home a few hours before, it was as if she were bringing malaria into their midst. Both Tally and her mother screamed, and all the shouting woke the baby again and he started to wail, too. Pearl held him to her chest the whole time and waited patiently for the lungs around her to deflate and her mother to utter simple words of common sense. "Baby needs a tit."

Sallie then braved the task of fetching Dorrie Smitty, who'd been married to Elton for eighteen years, and they had almost as many children to show for it. Although the phases of her maternal obligations made her shout curses at the moon, she couldn't resist the soft pull of a baby's lips at her own well-used nipple. She changed into the worn gingham dress she wore as a nursing frock, the blouse stained with the butter she used to lubricate her sore breasts, and followed Sallie back to the House farm. She sat down at their kitchen table and took the baby in the crook of her arm, lifting it to the same breast she used to suckle her youngest daughter, Lorette, who now sat wide-eyed on Tally's knee.

Pearl thought Dorrie looked much older than forty, the wrinkles on her dry and sallow skin as deep as engravings, but the breast Pearl saw that morning was as fresh and plump as a young girl's. Pearl grinned as the baby butted the breast with his head until Dorrie aimed the nipple into his mouth. Sallie sat beside her, her anxious knees jiggling back and forth. "What were you thinking?" she whispered to her daughter.

"Not much time to think," Pearl snapped.

"You should've been minding your own business."

"I was minding my traps."

Sallie pulled her chair closer to her daughter. "This isn't a stray kitten you can raise in a box under your bed."

"I know that."

"And he wasn't left out there for you to find."

"Was he left out there for the buzzards?"

Sallie bit her lower lip in frustration. "Somebody didn't want that baby."

"Doesn't make it right to turn him into birdfeed."

Pearl heard heavy footsteps on the porch and turned to see her father and Sam enter the cabin, their sleeves rolled up and their shirts yoked with sweat. Joop stood between his wife and daughter and looked at the baby at Dorrie's breast. "Who was carrying?"

Sallie and Dorrie both shook their heads. "Nobody up here," Sallie replied.

"Looks like a town baby to me," Sam said.

"Looks like he could be anybody's old baby right now," Tally said, smiling at him.

"The more people I know, the less I understand them." Joop put his hand on Sallie's shoulder. "I'll get word down to the sheriff."

"What's he going to do?" Pearl asked.

"Nothing, I suppose."

"Wish somebody else would've thought to do the same," Sallie said flatly, eyes fixed on her daughter. But Pearl ignored her, proud of her discovery. She watched the little baby's fingers trace the blue veins along Dorrie's fattened breast, his eyes closed and his lips pumping as though they'd never stop. She'd saved him, and for now that was enough. He was one day old and certain to live another.

THE BIG PORTFOLIO was on Grieves's desk when he arrived at his office that morning. Simpson must have put it there before he left for the bank in Kingston, since the room was still redolent of the camphor and skunk-oil liniment he constantly rubbed on his aching neck.

He opened the portfolio, and inside were the hotel drawings that he'd been expecting for a month. He'd hired the young architect John Wood almost two years before, because his vision was capacious and his office was in Manhattan, away from the prying eyes of local businessmen and politicians who might catch wind of his project and beg to invest. He took the steamship to New York every few months and met Wood at a Chambers Street restaurant for lunch, where he described his plans in great detail. Over time it became more of a soliloquy than a conversation, and Grieves was grateful that Wood absorbed it as easily as the Château Climens he liked to drink at Grieves's expense.

"I want a graceful and noble structure of stone and timber built on the highest point on the land," Grieves remembered telling him. "When you approach it from the road below, I want your first response to be one of wonder, so as you draw nearer you are forced to tip your head back in admiration. I want the lobby to reflect the elegance of a great European lodge, and the rooms themselves to be well appointed, each with a view that will give one pause. I want a stone terrace along the back, accessible in fine weather by huge French doors in the lobby and ballroom, with parapets overlooking the lake. I want tall windows throughout the building, from floor to ceiling beams, so the guest never forgets his nearness to the wild, sees it wherever his eye falls, keeping him in mind that the beautiful nature of the mountains is as inspiring as it is tangible."

Wood had jotted down copious notes while Grieves expounded, asking only questions of scale and expense. At one of their first meetings, he had requested a map of the area in question, to highlight the land Grieves already owned or was in the process of acquiring. He drank his sauterne and teased his client with florid sketches of his vision, rendered in ink on white linen napkins that Grieves would stuff into his pockets and study on the bow of the steamboat as it plowed back to Rondout.

He leaned on his desk and spread out the drawings, the great hotel now gloriously manifest. Wood had captured all the singular details Grieves had suggested and contributed embellishments of his own, extending the vast parlor and dining room along the top of the summit, letting it cantilever beyond the stone precipice overlooking the lake. The sensibility was dramatic and modern, all the while retaining the exquisite traditions of civilized comfort. It was precisely what Grieves had seen when he first narrowed his eyes on Isaac Stokes's property high above the Clove.

He carefully put the drawings back in the portfolio and walked to the window, excited but constrained, as if he were being clasped from behind, his head lost in smoke. He didn't need to be clairvoyant to know the war would be over soon and the railroad would come. Over seven thousand had been killed at Gettysburg, another two thousand at Cold Harbor. There couldn't be many left to feed to the cannon. Afterward would come a boil of good fortune, and Grieves was preparing himself for it as he stood at the window watching the bright morning sunlight bring clarity to his kingdom.

~⊙~

WILL STOOD over the desk and drew the picture from memory. He used the pencil quickly, the sudden movements of his arm causing the lamplight to flicker across the paper. Arthur stood at his left shoulder and poured two glasses of whiskey, pushing one toward his friend.

"I saw my first one at Peale's Museum in Philadelphia about twenty years ago," Will told him. "I was lucky enough to visit before the fossils were sold to a collection in Europe. They were found in New York, on a farm outside Newburgh, about twenty-five miles from here. George Washington himself once visited the site, but the first complete skeleton wasn't excavated until the turn of this century."

Will continued to sketch, and to Arthur, the bones in the monster's feet seemed to spread like the roots of a tree trunk.

"Their bones have been discovered from Mexico to the Atlantic coast. In a Boston museum a man by the name of Warren has a complete specimen that was unearthed not far from Newburgh. Haven't seen it, but I did see some bones in St. Louis when I went through there about ten years ago. Those came out of the Great Plains. Good bones, a complete rib cage, but no tusk. Especially not a tusk like the one that got Vandeman."

Arthur glanced out to the porch, where the five-foot skull was leaning against the railing. It was almost full dark now, and moonlight cast a silver glow along the shield of its gigantic brow. "How tall will the beast stand?" he asked.

"Twelve or fifteen feet at the shoulder."

Arthur turned back to the desk and watched Will finish sketching the rib cage, leaning closer as he shaded in the huge plates of the shoulder blades and the eye sockets in the skull. "It looks like an elephant."

"We didn't have elephants in the Americas." Will smiled. "We had mastodons." He gestured at the completed drawing. "We had these." He stepped back and lifted his glass of whiskey for the first time. "We have one here."

Arthur hovered over the sketch. With its massive head and tusks curving outward as dangerous as scimitars, the whole skeleton was both unsettling and grotesque. "And what will you do now?"

"First I'll dredge the swamp for the rest of its bones."

"And then what?"

"I'll put them together."

"Where?"

"Right here."

In the lamplight, Will's expression was animated, and Arthur liked seeing him like this. He raised his glass in a toast and both men drank.

"The intact skull is already a great find. To have both tusks would make it a treasure, and chances are good that we'll find the rest."

"And if you don't?"

Will grinned and poured himself more whiskey. "Then I spent almost two thousand dollars on property that isn't worth half that. And men will be amused and make a good story of it, and for a long time the name Harp won't be mentioned without a laugh. But even if I'm wrong, I'll have the pleasure of digging and discovery—on my own land. And that alone makes it worthwhile."

He lay awake and thought about the day to come. At first light he would get up and do a refined sketch of the skull and start a detailed journal recounting his meeting with Vandeman and the acquisition of his property. Then he'd ride to the swamp and see what he'd need to proceed with the recovery. He would hire Joop House and some other Jug Hill men to assist him, and ask Arthur to photograph the exhumation. He would draw a new map to designate boundaries, and go to the bank in Kingston to withdraw funds before Vandeman had a chance to reconsider. He had to smile at that notion, because he could imagine Vandeman, in his own bed, worrying that Will might do the same.

As a boy, he'd collected the skulls of muskrat and pine marten and fox, learning to identify them by the scat or fur that was left behind. When he was nine, he found the carcass of a blue heron near the swamp, leaving it there to let the insects finish their job, and a month later he went back and retrieved the skull and beak and first seven vertebrae of the neck. He boiled the bones in a soup kettle without his mother's permission, then reassembled them and mounted the skeleton on a block with a thin rod to hold up the jaw, looping the brittle pieces with a wire thread to secure them. It was still in this room, on a shelf his father had built for his first specimen.

He breathed deeply, knowing he would never sleep. When he reached for the whiskey glass on the table next to him, he heard a low growl outside his open window. He sat up as it continued and slipped quietly out of bed. He walked barefoot to the window and saw Vandeman's stout little dog crouched on the porch, growling at the darkness.

Will walked into the parlor, where moonlight fell in blue shafts through the twelve-paned windows, and took down the large-caliber Hawken rifle his father had kept on a rack above the mantel. It had been his hunting gun, the only one in the house he'd kept loaded. He gently pushed the front door open and stepped outside. The little dog growled louder, but Will knelt down and put a hand on his neck. The fur was coarse as he ran his fingers along the dog's spine to his stump of a tail. He never stopped growling, and Will felt the unease in his trembling skin. The crescent moon was hooked in a clear sky and everything stood in sharp relief, the silhouettes of pine trees on either side of the Clove road as chiseled as spear points. Will kept stroking the dog, who gradually eased his snarling. He laid the rifle across his knees and listened. The air was still and he quieted his own breathing. He heard a deer racing through the woods on the western slope below the Shawangunks, careening through laurel and sumac. Squinting, he thought he could see the brush shiver with its flight. Then he heard the doe's scream, unmistakable as a baby's cry, and the sound of scuffling as the animal was brought down. The little dog tensed under his fingers, his ears tipped to the racket, and Will bore down on his back to keep him still.

Arthur stumbled onto the porch from his own bedroom, half-asleep. He buttoned his pants and stood beside Will, blinking into the night. "What is it?" he asked softly.

"A lion."

Arthur yawned and smirked. "I see. Elephants *and* lions."

And in the crackling darkness the crying ceased and the cat roared, the sound guttural, raw and victorious.

JANE WAS ALREADY asleep when Mickey came in that night. His clomping around woke her, and when she came out of her room she found him hunched over the table, slathering apple butter on a thick slice of bread. He was quiet, which surprised her, but what surprised her more was the fact that he was here instead of at Hackett's or with one of his other women. If he'd heard the news that Frank was missing, he didn't say. And when she came out in the morning and saw that his door was still shut, she let him sleep.

She restarted the fire that smoldered in the hearth and put the pot on the grate above the flames. It would be another warm day, as it had been all week. She opened the windows and looked out onto the street, empty except for the Witherses' mule, loose again and munching on the Feeneys' roses, calmly biting off the flowers as if they were fancy cakes. She walked into the parlor, where the cat was curled up on Frank's chair. Jane had awoken with the intention of working on the quilt that the cat was now sitting on, but instead she took the chair on the other side of the room and picked up the oval frame that held a portrait of Frank taken the day before he left with the Ulster Volunteers. Arthur Dowd had photographed him, and many other local men, for a minimal charge. Frank's uniform was government-issue, but he'd had a Rondout tailor alter it to his own specifications. He was not only the most handsome man she'd ever met, but also the vainest, and he indulged this narcissism. "Can I still pray to a God who has cursed me with such good looks?" he once asked her, gazing upon himself in a mirror. "Why, yes I can," he replied before she could, both of them laughing.

In the photograph he was standing in front of a plain white wall, holding the barrel of his musket in his left hand, his right hand planted on his outthrust hip. His wool trousers were draped perfectly over his tall boots, and his new Hardee hat was tilted to the right and adorned with a turkey feather. He was wearing a long, high-collared frock coat, the sleeves and shoulders trimmed with sky-blue piping. Frank was staring at the camera, straight at Jane, with his chin held high, his eyes clear and the trace of a crooked smile on his face. He looked like a man blessed with confidence and eager to fight.

Jane had picked up the photograph from Dowd's studio five days after Frank left Rondout with the troops. When she saw it for the first time, she laughed out loud with joy: How could a man with so much life in him not persevere?

From the moment he'd picked her off Kelly's floor to the morning he'd left, hardly a day had ended without Frank calling her his "pretty girl." She might have been only twenty-one when it started, but wise enough to know that he'd probably used the phrase on most young ladies in Rondout with the frequency of a trained parrot. She'd noticed him, of course, before that night at Kelly's, but until that evening he was just something attractive to look at. He was seven years older, bred Irish but native-born and willing to fight anyone who doubted it. He had a scar over his left eye that was visible only when he wrinkled his brow—from a knife wielded by a boy who went home with a broken arm. When he was twenty, his nose got broken, giving it a bump and angle that added character to his too-perfect face and made him look fierce as a Mongol warrior. He fought often as a young man and rarely lost, earning a reputation without the need of pomp or fabrication, the black eyes and broken teeth of his opponents the proof of his skill.

Frank's mother and father had died during the cholera epidemic that raged through the waterfront two years before Jane and Mickey arrived. Frank had stayed in Rondout during the initial outbreak, when the victims tended to be reverends and the poor they administered to, but when the disease took a more democratic turn, his parents sent him to work on a farm in the country. He came back in the fall, when the ravages had subsided, and found their graves among the hundred others in the common burial ground behind St. Mary's Church.

He was going on twenty, already a young man. He took a room above Sweeney's cigar shop on Union Street and found jobs on the wharf, cutting ice in the winter and bluestone in the spring. He preferred working outdoors, and the repetitiveness of his labors made him strong. He caroused with the men he worked with and learned to defend his reputation only when pushed. He drank and whored in moderation, neither saint nor sinner, and there wasn't an unattached girl in town who didn't stop to daydream every time he crossed her path.

Jane was used to seeing Frank at the saloon, but she treated him no differently than she did the others who came in for beer or sandwiches. She saw him often on the street, because the room he kept was only a block away from her own, and at times found herself staring, if only because he provided a bit of freshness in her otherwise dreary days. The only future she had was tomorrow, and to look beyond that was too much to bear. Ever since her Dutch Hill years, when she'd witnessed the domestic meanness of married life, she had vowed never to seek a lover or a husband—a promise she kept until the night Frank Quinn gentled Tom Mardy in Kelly's saloon.

He picked her up at Mrs. Burns's house the next morning, driving a carriage he'd hired for the day. He was shyer than she expected, not the bold Frank Quinn who commanded the attention of men and boys and stole away a woman's breath as surely as a common thief. They spoke little as they went up Chestnut Hill, taking the rutted road until it ended in a half circle of spruce trees, where Frank stopped the carriage in the shade and helped her to the ground. They tethered the horse and walked up the narrow path to a clearing on the top of the hill. Jane felt a mild dizziness as she turned and gazed down at the waterfront. It was a late spring day, the Hudson as deep blue as the ocean. She counted three dozen sloops on the water, sails swelled with the wind that pushed them southward. She could identify each neighborhood by the church spire that rose above it, and make out the wagons going up and down the Strand. Smoke still pumped into the air from waterfront industry, but the distant plumes were as white as the clouds drifting in the sky. This view of Rondout astonished her. It looked picturesque, almost beautiful, and when she turned to Frank, he was smiling at her.

"Pretty, isn't it, Jane?" he said. "Hard to believe it's home."

They spent the whole afternoon on Chestnut Hill. She'd prepared a chicken, and he'd brought apple cider for her and a bottle of porter for himself. She noticed his chafed knuckles and the hooked scar over his left eye, which became pronounced whenever he laughed, and she tried to make him laugh often. His fingernails were clean, but his cuffs weren't, and she was glad of that, since it meant there were some improvements to be made. He became easier with her as the day went on, self-assured, but not bragging like most of the young men who tried to impress her. He didn't talk about the fights he'd been in, though she already knew he liked a good brawl, or about the hardships of his circumstances. There were few complaints in his vocabulary, that day or any after, and his outlook made her forget or regret her own niggling preoccupations.

As the sun began to set, Jane gathered their things together, and he presented her with a small box of chocolates, which they shared as the shadows deepened. Walking back down the path, Frank took her hand for the first time, and before helping her into the carriage, he kissed her so lightly that she barely felt his lips. He held her hand on the way into town, and she insisted on accompanying him to Shapiro's to return the rig. He agreed, as long as he could walk her home, which had been her intent all along.

She put the photograph back on the table and looked out the window. Ann Feeney was by her fence, trying to chase the Witherses' mule away from her roses. Jane smiled, but it was the photograph that had lightened her spirits. She was grateful for the memories it evoked, but she wanted more than that. She wanted Frank home.

~◦⊙◦~

MICKEY HAD SLEPT poorly all night. Every time he closed his eyes, he saw Hannah's face, or what was left of it, and when he opened them, the same image was still visible in the darkness of his room.

He had the boy wait outside while he wrapped her body in a blanket he'd taken from the foot of the bed, careful to cover her completely, folding the corners around her feet and arms, making sure every loose strand of hair was gently tucked within the rough wool. He carried her remains to a small clearing just inside the woods behind the farmhouse, Coley following with two shovels he'd found in the barn. They dug the grave together, setting a rhythm to the crunch of the iron blades in the stony soil, and neither said a word.

Now he lay on his bed thinking about the baby he would never see.

He didn't feel the shame that Hannah had endured these past months, and never considered the life she would've led after the child was born. He thought only of lying naked beside her, stroking the roundness of her belly, tracing the heaviness of her breasts, resting his head against her skin so he could feel the push of the baby within. He wondered then if he'd fathered a boy or a girl.

He still did.

GRIEVES TOOK his usual table by the window. It was still early, and though the Mansion House Hotel's restaurant hadn't opened yet, the manager was always happy to set him a table. Waiters in short vests were polishing the silver service, and through a side door he saw the chef carrying a leg of lamb over his shoulder like a war club and, behind him, a parade of suppliers with baskets of eggs and tomatoes and greens and carrots with the field dirt still clinging to them. For breakfast, Grieves would have his usual fried rainbow trout and bacon, followed by a baked apple and coffee. But he'd wait until his guest arrived and use this quiet time to contemplate the early-morning stirrings.

His table offered unobstructed views of both Division Street and the Strand. Thomas Cornell was being driven to his steamboat dock in an open-sided Rockaway coach, looking up from bank reports to dole out limp waves like a munificent prince. J. P. Hageman, publisher of the *Courier*, pulled a hair from his nostril as he walked to his office, puzzling over the day's editorial. Florence Laughton, president of the Female Gospel Society, had her mouth screwed into a sour pinch as she looked in every saloon for her husband, Edward, president of the Men's Gospel Society, who'd failed to come home last night after an alleged evening of "scriptural study and reflection."

Grieves then saw his guest, Isaac Stokes, sauntering down the opposite sidewalk with an Irish wolfhound on either side, the giant dogs timing their steps to his. Handsome and well trained, they pranced along like mindful heirs. Stokes himself walked with a grace unusual for a man his size, his short arms pumping up and down and his belly working as ballast. It was a real achievement, and he carried himself along as if he were a golden egg.

Stokes dressed with more flair than most Rondout men, and Grieves attributed that to his wife, who shopped in Boston and Manhattan before each new season. Today he wore a black frock coat over a notch-collared vest and fashionable high-waisted pants. Black brogans gleamed on his tiny feet. He was bald on top and the hair that fringed his ears was chestnut brown, treated monthly with the same dye and restorative used by his wife. He entered the Mansion House Hotel with a jolly step, and with a snap of his fingers he sat the dogs down.

Stokes had made his fortune in bluestone, his quarries producing upward of thirty wagonloads a day, his three sloops making deliveries from New York to Philadelphia. He also invested well in local businesses and real estate, showed cunning in his political backings and was a director of the First National Bank and a proud member of Masonic Lodge Number 343. Grieves neither despised nor respected him; he was simply one of the twelve men in Rondout who needed to be reckoned with.

"It's good to see you, Harry," Stokes said as he pulled out his chair and sat down as delicately as if he were straddling a commode. "But I still won't sell you Butterfields."

Stokes was always direct, which Grieves appreciated, but he was mistaken if he thought it gave him the upper hand. "You don't appear entirely convinced of that, Isaac," he replied, returning his smile. "You're here."

"I'm here to repeat my rejection of your offer," Stokes said as he wiped his pink forehead with a napkin. "Again. For the third time, is it? I've lost count."

"It's a fair offer."

"It's more than fair, Harry. It's extraordinarily generous. But I'm afraid I can't return the gesture, because a gesture's all it is. I'm delighted you think my property is so valuable, but it's not for sale today or tomorrow or anytime in between."

"I'm persistent, Isaac."

"As am I. Butterfields belonged to my father. I was born in the house he built, and intend to die there as well."

"You've been very square with me. Straight as a pistol shot," Grieves responded. "But perhaps you should take a broader view and consider selling the family property in order to make a mark of your own."

"Perhaps you should consider making your own mark instead of trying to usurp mine," Stokes responded testily.

"But that's how I intend to make my mark." He watched the anger flush across Stokes's cheeks. "I don't mean to offend you, Isaac, and if I have, I apologize. I just want to make sure that you appreciate the seriousness of my proposal. You're a creature of free will and have every right to refuse it, just as I have every right to keep coming at you like a freight train. And I will. You know me well enough to be sure of that."

Stokes slowly eased back in his chair, which creaked and wobbled beneath him. He took a deep breath, letting out a faint whiff of the mint and cloves he chewed on. "You won't change my mind, Harry."

"But it's a challenge I enjoy, much as I enjoy a few pleasurable minutes of your company."

"It's always good to see you, too, Harry," Stokes said as he put his hands on his thighs and stood up. "But I must be going."

"You won't join me for breakfast?"

"Not this morning. I have too much to do." He sighed. "With this war dragging on and the train service so often interrupted, it's hard to do business west of Cincinnati. I've got ten tons of bluestone sitting on a wharf in New York, waiting to be shipped to destinations impossible to reach. Now I've got to figure out another way to sell it."

"You'll manage, Isaac. There's always need for good stone."

"I'm certain of that, though these past three years have been difficult. Sometimes I wonder if Lincoln has figured out how to untie this knot."

"The South is finished, Isaac."

"Really? I think Cold Harbor and Petersburg prove otherwise."

"That's just a death rattle. The war's coming to an end."

"Not soon enough for me," Stokes said as he smoothed his vest.

"I'll bring you another offer in September, Isaac."

Stokes laughed. "I can't stop you from wasting your time." He walked away from the table, but halfway across the room he looked back at Grieves, a mischievous grin on his face. "Did you hear, Harry?"

"Hear what?"

"About my neighbor, Peter Vandeman."

"What about him?"

"He sold his property."

Grieves blinked but betrayed no other emotion.

Stokes watched him with enjoyment, his sharp laugh like the twisting of a knife. "Yes. For a tidy little profit, I'm told."

"And who bought it?" Grieves asked, his voice sounding strained even to himself.

When Stokes reached the threshold, he snapped his fingers and the wolfhounds rose to their full, enormous height and fell in at his side. "I hear it was Will Harp," he said as he left the room. "The major's son is back in town."

THE SOGGY GROUND radiated outward from the swamp, a helical buzz of gnats and mosquitoes rising with each brown suck and squirt of his boot. He saw the deep ruts Vandeman's wagon had made and the muddy grass where his mules had kicked and struggled, and he scanned the oily water where the skull had been raised. Years ago he'd come to this same swamp, hunting for spotted turtles and frogs so plentiful that the water would pop and boil when they burst from the mucky shore. One bright afternoon, when he and Charlie Brodhead were young boys, they spotted a large bullfrog basking on a log. Pushing carefully through the gummy water, cunning as little Indians, they approached from either side. From the size, probably eight inches long and weighing at least a pound, Will guessed it was a female. He'd seen bigger, but not that summer. It would jump, he was sure of it, but he intended to jump faster and have its two back legs pumping uselessly in his closed fist. Except for the relentless hum of skimmers flying low over the water, it was perfectly quiet. When Will was close enough to see the frog's yellow throat gulp and quiver, he nodded to Charlie and they crept forward. They were only six feet away when a shotgun blast obliterated the frog, the lead shot riffling the surface like a sudden burst of wind. Will and Charlie flattened out in the putrid water and didn't move until they heard laughter echoing above them. When Will finally angled his face upward, sputtering out the gritty brown muck, he saw Bogardus astride his big horse, resting an old musket against his thigh.

"Get out of my pond, you dirty brats," he shouted, "before I shoot again!"

The boys raced to shore, the water churning to coffee behind them. Charlie lost a boot and hopped awkwardly along as Bogardus's laughter faded to a caw behind them. They followed a dry streambed that cut through laurel thickets, finding trails used only by fox and deer. Finally clearing the ridge, they ran all the way back to the Harp farm, where Will's mother laid out dry clothes and tended to Charlie's bloody foot. The major, his face shaded by the crimped brim of his hat, sat on the porch and listened to the boys' tale, never once interrupting. When they were finished, he stood up and walked briskly to the barn. "Will," he called over his shoulder, "get Beechnut out of the pasture."

By the time he rode her bareback through the gate, his father had saddled his own horse and was waiting for him. When they reached the Clove road, the sun was already low in the sky, and without a word they turned onto the old Indian trail that led to the Bogardus farm. Will, knowing better than to voice his misgivings, stayed close and glanced down at the swamp as they passed it, the sun casting one last spear of yellow light across the center.

It was suppertime when they reached the Bogardus farmhouse. Smoke coughed from a chipped chimney and the slate roof sagged in the middle like a swaybacked nag. "Stay here," his father told him, then dismounted and walked up the porch steps. The front door was open to let in the cool of dusk, and he walked in without announcing himself. Oliver Bogardus and his wife looked up from the kitchen table, where they'd just sat down to a cold supper of venison back straps and garden tomatoes. The major ignored them, walking directly to the hearth, where Bogardus kept his musket in a wooden barrel next to his muddy boots and long coat. He lifted it by the muzzle and swung it over his head, shattering the stock on the hearthstone. Bogardus watched with his fork poised, ducking when a piece of the metal lock broke the windowpane above his head. When the major had rendered the weapon useless, he tossed the splinters into the fire and threw the barrel out the door. Then he nodded politely to Mrs. Bogardus and turned to her husband. "The next time you want to teach my son a lesson, you'll ask my permission first," he said. "You won't receive it, but you'll spare your rifle."

Bogardus never uttered a word, and from that day on the men were cordial as neighbors when they passed on the road or met by chance in town. But it was the last time Will had been on the property until today.

He waded into the swamp until it reached above his knees, his feet sinking into the soft, sticky bottom. They would have to trench the bog and construct a waterwheel to make the work go faster, then build platforms on which to dry whatever bones they uncovered. He'd need draft horses and a sturdy wagon to haul the bones to his barn, and metal rods he could have fabricated at the Rondout Foundry, and he'd write to the Academy of Natural Sciences in Philadelphia and ask for the notes on Peale's excavation sixty years ago.

The water was up to his waist when he saw the tusk sticking above the surface in front of him, the tip looking as common as a willow branch or the head of a water moccasin. It was splintered and sharp where it had pierced Vandeman's skin, and there were stress lines running along the shaft. Will bent down until his arms were fully submerged and his chin rested on the water, then ran his hand along the tusk. It was smoother than he'd imagined and seemed to be intact. He was able to haul about three feet of it above the waterline, where he cradled it to his chest as he would a sleeping child, realizing it had been in the swamp for ten thousand years.

Vandeman's little mutt paddled out to where he stood, the sunlight fragmenting in his wake. He circled Will once before climbing up on a log, shook off the mud, barked at a dragonfly and jumped back in again, lapping at the water as he swam back to shore, where Arthur sat casually on his horse, fanning a shadow of blackflies away with his hat.

"Arthur!" he called. "Would you give me a hand with this?"

"Will you give me the loan of some dry boots if I do?"

"I'll buy you all the dry boots you need."

Arthur swung off his horse and waded in, stepping over hummocks of sedge and milkweed that set off whiffs of musk. Rolling up his sleeves, he mulled over each footstep before committing to it, and his white shirt was splattered with mud. "This stench is worse than Rondout on the hottest day in July," he said as he joined Will in the middle of the swamp.

"That's the smell of history, Arthur," Will replied, "and it's lovely." He bent at the knees, took a deep breath and ducked his head underwater. Eyes closed, he wrapped both arms around the thick end of the tusk and pried it from the mud, bringing it to the surface. The buoyancy of the water relieved much of the weight, and the men were able to hoist their prize and struggle to shore.

Laid out on the grass, the tusk was eight feet long and weighed over 150 pounds. Will knelt down, soaking wet, and ran his hand along the shaft. It was mostly smooth, and aside from the brown stain, it showed little sign of being submerged for centuries. The curvature was almost perfect, bowing outward as it rose to the tip.

"Will you find the other?" Arthur asked.

"I think we will."

"It's extraordinary."

Will nodded and smiled, then stood up and studied the wide expanse of the swamp before him. He could see the stumps of cedar trees Vandeman had cut over the years, and the dams he'd destroyed and the new ones beavers had built close to the opposite shore. He imagined the lake once cupped in this valley, knowing that these dregs were all that remained.

They left the tusk to dry in the grass and mounted up. As they set off along the trail, the runty dog burst from the goldenrod and pranced ahead of Will's horse, his tail held high and only inches from the falling hooves.

"It looks like you've got yourself a dog, Will," Arthur called.

"If you can call that rag a dog."

"What do you think you'll call him?"

Will thought for a moment and smiled. "Rump!" he shouted.

The little dog glanced up at him, and with his tongue hanging from his open mouth he looked as if he were grinning, getting the joke.

JOOP STOOD BEHIND his daughter as she strung up the two raccoons by their feet. She took the short-bladed knife out of her dress pocket, pulled it free of the sheath and sharpened it four times on the stone she held in her other hand. She made circular cuts around both ankles and vertical incisions down their hind legs, never once looking at her father.

"You got to find something to do, Pearl," Joop told her.

"I am doing something," she said, cutting the small ligaments by the first coon's feet and peeling the skin from its legs.

"Something else I mean."

She dug her fingers between the pelt and the darkly meated carcass and loosened the skin around the hips and tail. Joop watched her pull a green stick out of the canvas bag by her side and slip it over the coon's tailbone.

"I want you to help Dr. Harp."

"Help him what?" she asked as she pinched her hand over the fur and yanked it down, stripping the skin with one fluid movement.

Her actions were so brisk that Joop knew she was getting angry. "You're going to cook for him and keep his house and be of use."

Pearl poked her fingernails into the thin muscles that fixed the skin to the shoulder blades and tore them loose. "What about my traps?"

"You can set them when you come home and check 'em in the morning like you always do."

"What about Tally?" she said through closed teeth as she stripped the skin from the front legs and started working on the head.

"Tally can help you down there till she goes home."

Pearl pulled her knife out again and carefully sliced the raccoon's ears off and cut the skin around its eyes. "What about the baby?"

She couldn't stop thinking about the baby. She had helped Dorrie rock him to sleep just the night before and would've stayed by the crib until morning if Elton hadn't sent her home. She heard the baby's screams from the hill above their farm and smiled at his belligerence. She wondered if those were the same frantic cries his mother had heard when abandoning him to the wild, and what terrible misfortune had given her the coldness to run from such a desperate noise. And she wondered who would raise the baby now, and what they would call him. She'd already picked out a name but dared not speak it, not just yet.

"You already done enough about that baby." Joop shook his head at his daughter's back. "Nothing more you can do for it now."

Pearl gripped the knife tightly and cut the skin away from the coon's mouth and nose, flattening the blade slightly so she could keep the snout intact. "Baby's my responsibility."

"It sure ain't," Joop snapped. "That'll come when you have your own."

"But I found him!"

"Yeah, and I ain't taking the chance of you finding another. You'll help Dr. Harp."

Knowing better than to argue, she grabbed the loosened hide with both hands and pulled it cleanly off the carcass, which swayed from its roped feet while she set the fresh pelt over the railing.

"I'll take you over next time I go," Joop said firmly.

Pearl never once turned to face him. She gutted the raccoon down the middle and pulled the innards out with two simple swipes of her knife, then cut off the thick pockets of fat. Joop looked on approvingly, knowing Sallie would cube the meat and fry it up with potatoes and carrots.

"I'll do it," Pearl said softly, turning to the second raccoon.

"Good," Joop replied, thinking about his supper.

"But I ain't gonna be happy about it."

August 1864

AMERICAN MONSTER FOUND IN CLOVE

The skull of a mastodon was found last month in the Clove. The massive fossil was uncovered while Peter Vandeman was pulling stumps from the swamp on the back portion of his land. Mr. Vandeman was unfortunately injured during the discovery of this important specimen, and his neighbor, Dr. William Harp, has purchased the property and will continue the excavation.

Dr. Harp has recently returned to Ulster County after ten years of service as a medical officer on scientific surveys of the American West. A resident of Los Angeles, California, Dr. Harp was a captain during the Indian wars and, like the illustrious Harps before him, served his country with great honor. It is reported that Dr. Harp has already reclaimed one of the ancient beast's tusks, and we can only wonder what other marvels the glorious earth will reveal.

Rondout Courier, August 10, 1864

WILL STOOD in front of a photograph of a bluestone cutter on the Rondout wharf. It must have been a warm summer day: The man's sleeves were rolled above his biceps and sweat darkened the front of his shirt. Sitting on top of an enormous rectangular slab of stone with his legs splayed in front of him, he had his chisel angled between his legs and his hammer raised above it, ready to strike. All activity behind him was a racing blur, but his image was so sharp you could see the holes in his shoes.

The photograph next to it depicted another young workman at the coal dock, perching on a tall barrel near his boat, his feet dangling high off the ground. The cuffs of his pants stopped inches above his ankle-high boots, and his hands rested between his knees. His shirt was buttoned at the neck, his cap was pushed back on his head and his broad smile revealed two missing front teeth.

The third picture on the wall showed a stern older man sitting on a big black gelding in the woods, both man and horse caught in a soft ray of light that fell through the boughs of the oak trees all around them. A long rifle rested across his knee, and three dead pheasants were tied by their feet to the pommel of his saddle. Wearing a canvas coat and canvas pants tucked into high riding boots, he was hatless, and a shock of gray hair was combed back from his forehead. He was clean-shaven, and light filled the deep hollows of his cheekbones and sculpted the bony fingers knotted with arthritis. He sat tall and straight, with a slightly impatient look. It was a portrait of Major Harp taken the year before he died.

Will stared at the photograph and smiled. His father had aged in the ten years Will had been gone, and it must've pained him to have his once-strong body fail before his eyes. He never wrote about getting old, his mind too sharp to dwell on that. By the time Will learned of the cancer, his father was already dead.

"He was a good subject, but not very cooperative," Arthur said, coming up behind him. "I followed him around for three days while he hunted pheasant in the Clove. He'd disappear into the woods, and when I heard a shot, I'd set up my camera in anticipation, then he'd take another trail home and leave me standing in my own shadow. By the time I got back to the house, the birds would be dressed and your father would be sitting on the porch, enjoying the afternoon. He'd apologize, of course, blaming it on the excitement of the hunt, but I'm sure he had a good chuckle over it after he went to bed. I never met a man more averse to having his portrait made."

Will laughed softly. There was only one other photograph of his father that he knew of. The summer before Will left for Albany, they'd been visiting Elizabeth's family in Saratoga Springs, and over the course of a week the major had successfully ducked any attempt to photograph him. On the day they were to leave, he was finally waylaid by his wife and the photographer on the veranda of their hotel. She looked very beautiful in a sleek white day dress and leghorn hat, and he appeared dignified in a cream-colored suit. At the photographer's urging, he gently took his wife's elbow, but as she smiled at the camera, he reflexively turned his head, leaving only his blurred profile.

When Will once asked his father why he hated being photographed, he said, "I think an image held in memory is much kinder than one held in your hand."

"On the third day I watched him ride off," Arthur continued, "and once he was out of sight, I put my camera back in the wagon and drove the team down to the farm. I set up my equipment on the trail he'd use to return, and while waiting for the gunshots I knew would come, I enjoyed a meal of cheese and bread and even squeezed in a nap. Two hours later your father emerged from the woods. I had set up the camera in the middle of the path, so he had to stop, and as he sat there scowling, I got my picture and the last laugh."

They were standing in the front parlor of Arthur's studio, and Will kept studying the dozens of photographs on the wall while his friend poured them each a glass of whiskey from a decanter on the sideboard.

"I don't think he would've let me get away with it if it weren't for our friendship," Arthur said as he handed him his drink.

"I'm sure this is a likeness even he would've admired."

"It's a shame he never saw it."

They'd ridden back from the Clove earlier that day to pick up supplies. They stopped first at Bowen's carriage shop in Kingston, where Will was lucky enough to find a sturdy brewery wagon for sale. He found the small hand drills and bits he needed at Dodge's Hardware, and placed an order for narrow-gauge steel pipe at the Rondout Foundry. In the morning he'd take care of business at the bank, then load up the wagon with provisions and get back to the Clove by nightfall.

But they would spend the night in Rondout, and Will was already restless, anxious for the first time in a long while for one day to be over and the next to begin. He finished his whiskey and poured himself another.

An hour later, he was lying in bed thinking about the photograph he'd sent to his father from Los Angeles. He'd had it made just a week before he left to join the army in Stockton, wearing his regulation uniform, tall Jefferson boots and carrying his old Texas musketoon. On the back of the picture he'd written, "Keeping up the family tradition. Yours, Will."

The war was already a year old when Will joined the California Volunteers at Camp Halleck. He enjoyed his work there, treating soldiers for the usual maladies, from broken bones incurred during fights at local saloons to venereal disease picked up from the Portuguese whores who worked the port alleys along the San Joaquin River. He trained with the men and dined with the officers. In his free time he explored the pine-spotted Sierra foothills, and spent a few days riding through the dead river valleys near Murphys, filling his journals with notes and sketches. And he enjoyed the company of the post's commander, Col. Patrick Connor, the two of them often talking of the homes they'd left behind in New York. A brash Irishman who'd already served in the Seminole and Mexican wars, Connor invited Will and some of the other officers over for brandy before they left California to establish Camp Douglas in the Utah Territory. As the sun burned out over the distant mountains, they gathered on his porch and talked about their mission.

"Hunting Indians is no more a challenge than hunting deer or elk," Major McGarry carped when the brandy went to his head. "There's satisfaction in the kill, but it's just sport."

"There's no sport in killing a man," Connor said.

"I'm not talking about a man; I'm talking about an Indian," McGarry bellowed. "It lives by wits, not common sense, and ruts and howls through every phase of the moon. Though it can be as irascible as a wild boar, it's just as easily tamed by a well-placed bullet. Now, you put me face-to-face with a rebel across a field in Virginia, that's a fight worth honoring."

"You'll honor this one, too, Major," Connor told him, "because it's the fight we've been given."

"I'll honor it and fight like hell," McGarry allowed, settling back in his chair to wait for the bottle to come his way again.

Connor held the same desire to take his regiment east, into the real war, but he accepted his command on the Mormon frontier with a professional soldier's stoic resolve. "We'll go where we're kicked, gentlemen, and if we can't win the war on Virginia soil, we'll damn sure keep California in the Union," he declared, and the officers raised their glasses to the cause.

Will knew from the start that Edward McGarry was a man to watch out for. He'd made his reputation in Los Angeles, where he owned a dry goods store and served in a local militia called the Mounted Rifles. In the first year of the war, he'd helped round up a dozen Confederate sympathizers who'd tried to sabotage the final mile of telegraph line that was coming down from San Jose. After some of them escaped from the Spring Street jail, it was rumored that McGarry had orchestrated their flight just so he could hunt them down again, killing all but the two he'd grievously wounded. Will had been introduced to him upon arriving in Stockton. McGarry was just a few years older, his hair and beard a rich, oily black that set off dark eyes pushed deep in his wind-burned face. He kept gripping Will's hand long after they shook, and his gaze was unbending. "Have you saved many lives, Dr. Harp?"

"A few," Will replied.

"And have you taken them, as well?" McGarry asked, the right side of his face hooking into a smile.

"No, I haven't."

"Then I suggest you stand to the side when that time comes."

"I'll stand with my men, Major," Will responded without pause.

McGarry grunted through his smile and pumped Will's fingers one last time before walking away.

Even then Will could smell the liquor on him, and he soon discovered that it was a rare hour when McGarry wasn't drunk or trying to get there. But he still managed to carry out his duties with a brutal simplicity, and Connor trusted him and wielded him like a vicious dog.

Will witnessed this firsthand when the California Volunteers arrived at Fort Churchill, Nevada Territory, in early August. It had taken them only two weeks to cross the High Sierras, and in that short time a few of the less dedicated soldiers decided that the stringent demands of military life didn't suit them. In a flurry of dust and confusion outside of Carson City, they stole horses and weapons and headed for home. It was McGarry whom Connor sent after them. He took Billy Motes and Eli Birdslee with him—two privates who gladly followed his lead—and was back in Carson City in three days. They had easily captured all six deserters in a saloon in Genoa, where they'd stopped to drink with the local farmers, assuming they wouldn't be missed. McGarry and his men tied the deserters to wagon wheels and beat them beyond recognition, then leisurely drank to their success with the same valley farmers. When they returned the prisoners to Fort Churchill, Will and Eli tended to their fractured bones and missing teeth, and also treated Billy's broken finger. Motes, a young man whose bad complexion wasn't concealed by his pale beard, had run cockfights behind the barracks at Camp Halleck, diligently sharpening the spurs on his champion Red Quills, his passion for violence ratcheted by his delight in inflicting pain. Will had once stitched the boy's lip after a Stockton whore tried to bite it off, then treated the lip of the same whore, victim of Billy's reciprocation.

"I busted it on Gannon's head," Billy said, holding out his bent and swollen finger. "I was trying to poke him in the fucking eye, but the sonofabitch turned away."

"Gannon put up some fight, did he?" Will asked, tying on a splint.

"Gannon?" Billy replied with a wide-eyed blink. "Gannon didn't fight a'tall." Then he laughed, and Eli Birdslee, in on the joke, joined him.

Will sat up, drained the glass of whiskey on the side table and listened to the sound of distant voices through the open window. He stood and got dressed, careful not to wake Arthur on the other side of the bed. He decided to walk the few blocks down to the docks, where he'd breathe the fresh air and get another whiskey, perhaps enough to help him truly sleep.

~⊚~

EVEN AFTER MORE than a week, Coley still couldn't put it out of his mind or accept that the thing he'd seen had once been a woman. Now he sat at Natterjack's and tried to drink his beer, but it had a metallic odor, like the spilled blood he'd slipped on when he ran through that farmhouse door. He held his breath and gulped it anyway, hoping it might wash away the dark images that stayed with him.

Mickey had told him to keep the woman's death a secret, and though he didn't understand why, he knew enough simply to nod his head. After they'd buried her, Mickey cleaned the blood from floor, and together they tidied the room and righted the furniture, making it look like the farmhouse had been abandoned. Mickey reloaded his rifle and scanned the ridge before they mounted their horses and headed back to Rondout in silence, both of them brooding over the unexpected end of the day.

They arrived on Division Street long after dark, and Coley couldn't even enjoy the envy of his friends when they gathered behind the Fitch Brothers' stone yard. They peppered him with questions, especially Danny Magruder, who'd always thought he'd be the one to catch Mickey Blessing's eye. Coley told them the stories they wanted to hear, about the humiliation of Fish on the coal dock and how farmers shriveled up like cold peckers when he and Mickey rode in to collect the rent, but his words didn't sound very convincing, and the others accused him of acting like he'd already outgrown his hat. Coley only shrugged. They could think what they wanted, because he had a hard time thinking about anything at all.

When he got back to the stable after midnight, Shapiro came out and helped him stable Melon and Dutch Eddy, making his usual grunts and clicks, and blew out the lamp when they'd finished. As they walked out of the barn, he rested his hand on Coley's shoulder and kept it there until they came to the gate, where he went to the front of the house while Coley headed to the back.

When he blinked awake the next morning, images of the woman torn to pieces fluttered through his mind like a shuffled deck of cards. It was still dark, but he saw no sense in closing his eyes again, so he shared a slice of buttered bread with Pinch and went to do his chores. He'd cleaned out all the stalls and was done with the feeding before Shapiro had finished his own breakfast.

Charlie O'Fay showed up to collect him at noon, and Coley wasn't surprised. He glanced at Shapiro as he followed Charlie outside, but Shapiro just turned and rolled his giant shoulders and let his broad back fill the doorway.

Whether he was drunk or sober, Charlie O'Fay's lips never stopped moving. It was as if the words gathered in his mouth like a swarm of bees and he had to spit them out before they stung him. When Coley fell in at his side, he was babbling about a bookkeeper who'd started a fire at the bank on Ferry Street, but he was too distracted even to try to follow along.

"And that bookkeeper's got a good-looking daughter, too, your age or thereabouts, and I don't mind admitting I'd gladly raise her skirt given the chance. I imagine she's as blond on the bottom as she is on top, and many nights I've drifted to sleep gazing up between her legs, eyes smiling on that golden pocket."

Charlie was the ugliest man Coley had ever laid eyes on, with a huge head and a nose broken so many times that it resembled a mushroom. O'Fay slowed down to pick up a rock, then flung it at a crow picking at the remains of a dead cat in the gutter.

"I ate a crow once," he continued. "Shot him myself behind Dick Harmon's barn after Dick got tired of the birds bothering his sick cow. Shot his black brother, too, when he come back to swoop at my head, and me and Dick plucked 'em both and put 'em in a pot of boiling water. Birds had breasts big as ducks and meat dark as beef. Tough, though, and strong-flavored, and I ain't saying that's good or bad, but the taste stayed with me as long as wild onions."

Some thought O'Fay was slow-witted, but Coley knew he was smart enough to appreciate whose shadow he stood in. He was a loyal friend and would take a knife for Mickey Blessing, and that's what counted most.

"Did you hear about Wilbur Jones?" O'Fay was asking as they turned the corner. "Wounded in the arm at Chancellorsville, shot in the belly at Gettysburg, comes home a hero to his wife and child, gets a good job with the gaslight company, gets his wife pregnant again and now his basket's full. So last week he decides to teach his little boy to swim in the creek, catches a cold and dies in his bed Saturday night. A damn cold. Where's the glory in that? Makes you wonder why God didn't put him out of his misery when he had the chance."

When they got to Natterjack's, Charlie banged through the door and paused long enough to whisper, "Watch out for Mickey today. He's riding a bear."

Mickey was sitting alone at his usual table in the middle of the saloon, rolling a hard-boiled egg across the wooden plank and flicking the shell off with his thumbnail. Other men were standing at the bar or crowding around tables in the back, shying away from him. Tim Rooney stood behind the bar, adding fresh pickles to the jars that sat on the counter, and the morning girl, Annie Gump, was wiping down tabletops with a damp rag she kept in her apron pocket.

O'Fay dropped into the chair across from Mickey, the first sentence already half out of his mouth. "I was telling the boy about Wilbur Jones. You remember him, Mickey?"

"No."

"Wilbur Jones? Lived over on Ponckhockie Street?"

"Don't know him," Mickey said, picking up a knife. "Don't care."

Coley saw Charlie bite his lip as he tried to keep himself from speaking again. Mickey calmly sliced his egg in quarters, sprinkling the first piece with salt and pepper and chewing it slowly. Then he looked at Coley. "I want you to go to Harry Grieves's office and get his carriage and bring it here."

"Sure, Mickey."

As Mickey seasoned another slice of egg, Annie came up to the table and began sweeping the mess of shells into her apron. When she accidentally tipped over the saltcellar, he grabbed the hand that clutched the broken shell, banged it hard on the table and closed his fist around it. Rooney's niece was eighteen years old and had been working at the saloon for the past year. She was a thin girl, pale as a freshwater oyster, and her uncle Tim was ready with a cudgel for any man who raised an eyebrow in her direction. Now he could only stand there and watch her lips disappear as she sucked them in.

Mickey looked up at her, ignoring the thin stream of blood that trickled between both their fingers. "I'm not finished," he said calmly before letting her go, and to the girl's credit, she nodded her head and slowly walked away, cradling her hand in the sling of her apron.

Mickey righted the saltcellar and turned back to Coley. "Go on," he said, "get the carriage."

But Coley wasn't fooled by how smooth his voice sounded. He left Natterjack's and ran the whole way.

They were waiting out front when he returned. Mickey had changed into a tight black suit of light wool, and he wore a smart black derby pushed back on his head. Charlie had simply buttoned his vest and donned his wrinkled frock coat, and they climbed up and sat down beside him without a word.

It was a warm afternoon, and for a while Coley forgot his worries and let himself enjoy the day. Grieves's horses were well behaved and needed little guidance, and although the open-air carriage was simply appointed, the horsehair seat was more comfortable than any in Shapiro's yard.

It had been almost two years since Coley had traveled the three miles into Kingston, and he was grateful for the outing. The wide, well-maintained road led past the small farms that separated the two villages, the air flavored with the scent of fresh-cut hay and the sweet musk of cattle tramping along a muddy creek. As they climbed the last hill into Kingston, he saw handsome houses behind whitewashed fences, and detected a more genteel bustle than what he was used to in Rondout. The commercial buildings in the heart of town were just as tightly packed, the street just as crowded with wagons, but the stench of industry wasn't nearly as lively.

Coley headed the team toward the stockade district, where they were delivering papers to Erastus Cook's law office on Fair Street. He'd become the Grieves's family attorney decades ago, and Harry retained the old man's services because they shared a mutual disdain for fiscal timidity. As Coley started to turn onto St. James Street, Mickey directed him to keep going.

"But Cook's office is on the corner."

"Go down to Main."

"That's the long way around," Coley protested.

"Just do it."

Coley nodded, and it wasn't until he turned on Main that he knew what Mickey was after. On the corner was Fireman's Hall, a fine two-story brick building, its wide wooden doors open front and back to allow a breeze to circulate during the heat of the day. Some of the men of Engine Company Number 3 were standing on the sidewalk, throwing a baseball back and forth, while others were inside polishing the huge boiler on their Silsby steam engine. Sitting in the shade of the doorway, with his chair tipped back, his eyes closed and a cigar in his mouth, was Jesse Gray. Coley remembered him from the night on the coal docks. He recognized the other two Bumble Bee Boys, as well, and he hoped Gray would keep his eyes shut until their carriage had passed.

But that wouldn't happen.

"Afternoon, Jesse!" Mickey called out.

Gray lazily opened one eye and squinted in the wavering smoke of his cigar, his hand automatically going up to wave until he realized who'd hailed him.

Mickey smiled as if they were brothers. "Hell of a day, isn't it?" he hollered over Coley's head.

Gray stared at him and blinked twice, as if to make sure he was really there.

Mickey laughed. "Ain't you got a hello for your old pal?"

Jesse tipped his chair upright, stood up, and walked into the fire-house.

Mickey grinned and patted Coley on the back. "Now we can go see lawyer Cook."

Ten minutes had passed since he stopped the carriage in front of the office on Fair Street, and while he waited there for Mickey and Charlie, even the sound of chipmunks playing in the leaves was enough to make him jump. Certain there'd be a charge of Bumble Bees, he scanned the street again but saw only a group of boys taking turns leaping over the wrought-iron fence in front of the Old Dutch Church. The next buggy that went by also seemed harmless, but he couldn't resist double-checking anyway, and that's when the men came out of the alley behind him and yanked him from the carriage.

He was turned upside down, his feet flying in the air above him before he landed flat on his back in the dust of Fair Street, a boot heel on his chest and the point of Jesse Gray's knife blade tickling his neck.

Bob Baggs, king of the Bumble Bees, stood over him with his hands on his hips and the long row of brass buttons open on the dark blue fireman's coat that he wore as proudly as an officer in General Grant's army. No taller than anyone else in his crowd, he was broad at the hips and shoulders, proud of his small potbelly and vain about the thick wavy hair he gummed up with pomade. From a distance he was just one in a million, but as you drew closer, the features on his face stopped you cold: eyes as black and small and fierce as a wild dog's, and a sneer that lifted only the right side of his mouth, giving a glimpse of sharp and very crooked teeth.

Coley tried to move, but Baggs leaned forward and pushed down with his boot. "If you move again, you Irish prick," he purred, "I'll have you nailed to the fucking dirt."

Gray twisted his knife and Coley didn't feel a thing as his skin burst and a thin line of blood dribbled down his neck.

"Let him up, Bob," Mickey said as he stepped onto the sidewalk.

Baggs turned and glowered at him. He took his foot off Coley's chest, but Gray still squatted over him, the edge of his blade now held in a straight line across his throat. When he lost his balance and shuffled backward on his heels, Coley quickly angled his head and stared at Mickey.

Baggs took a step closer. "You laid Fish up real good," he said to Mickey.

"That was my intent, Bob."

"You knocked out every goddamn tooth."

I was hoping he'd choke on them."

Baggs squared his legs and let a thick metal wrench slip down his sleeve and into his hand. "I ought to break your fucking face."

Standing there with Charlie O'Fay at his elbow, Mickey seemed genuinely pleased with himself, and the lilt in his voice carried like a song in the air. "You move one more inch and I'll take that wrench and break your arm. And while you're on your knees screaming and begging me to walk away, I'll bring it down between your fucking eyes and you'll spend the rest of your life staring at nothing in particular and shitting your pants."

Baggs blinked once and held steady, gripping the big wrench. "You must be crazy, Blessing."

"Oh, Bob, I do wish you possessed the spine to find out for certain," Mickey replied. "I do wish that, oh, yes."

Baggs just stood there and shook his head.

Mickey never stopped smiling. "Now let up on the boy," he said.

Baggs kept his eye on him and nudged Gray with his boot, and when Gray folded his knife, Coley rolled away until his back slammed against the front carriage wheel. He took in a breath and felt a sting in his neck, and when he touched it, the blood was sticky on his fingers.

"Fucking Irish," Baggs mumbled as he turned and strode back toward Fireman's Hall, the other Bumble Bees trailing behind.

"Good-bye to you, Bob!" Mickey shouted. "Will you take my best to Fish?"

Coley finished his second beer and contemplated a third. His shift at Von Beck's was supposed to have started an hour ago, but he was sure Dickie Flanagan would already be fast asleep, and the barley vats could boil down a few hours more without his attention. And he knew Mickey most likely would spend the rest of the night over at Hackett's. He'd come back from Kingston in high spirits and was anxious to focus what was left of them on his pretty Hungarian whore. Charlie O'Fay was sprawled across a table in the back, his face mirrored in a cool puddle of beer, and would probably end up sleeping there at Natterjack's like he did almost every night. Coley was on his own for as long as he pleased. He was neither tired nor drunk, and a third beer would suit him fine.

He walked to the bar, sat his empty glass on the counter and waited to catch Rooney's eye, but a man at the far end of the bar laid a stack of coins on the plank and got his attention first.

"Whiskey," he said.

Coley frowned. When Rooney reached back for the bottle, Coley glanced at the man, hoping the stranger would register his irritation. But he wasn't a stranger, and Coley's annoyance evaporated in the short moment it took to recognize him. "Mr. Harp!" he called out, raising his empty glass as the man looked at him and smiled.

Will followed him through the loose weave of streets on the tattered edge of Rondout, ducking his head as they took the stairs down to the cellar below Shapiro's house. He waited in the doorway while the boy moved through the darkness and lit the lamp on the table. When the flame rose through the glass, he saw a squirrel sitting on a stool and gnawing at an apple core.

"Pinch!" Coley yelled, and the squirrel darted across the hard-packed floor and leapt onto the narrow windowsill above the boy's bed, where he sat licking his paws and lips.

Coley picked up the lamp and led Will to the back of the room, where rows of shelves were built into the corner. He hooked the lamp to a post and stepped back so his guest could view the items on display.

The four shelves were crammed so full of objects that Will had to move closer to see them all. Animal bones were scattered everywhere, grouped like a thicket around the skulls Coley had collected. In addition to the usual deer skulls, Will found an immature bear skull, a beaver skull and a small phalanx of rodent skulls, ranging in size from mole to muskrat. There was a board with three desiccated bats pinned to it, alongside the stretched skin of a large rat snake. There were rocks bearing trace fossils and fifty different arrowheads, and an old Lenape stone pipe and Esopus pottery shards and what might have been a tomahawk blade, Indian wampum and porcupine quills and turkey feathers and old French coins, bird nests made with horsehair and mud, a dish brimming with a variety of loose teeth and fangs.

Will picked up pieces of the pottery and spread them out in his hand. "Where did you find these?"

"On the Hasbrouck farm. I go there every fall when he plows under the summer corn, and every spring when he gets ready to plant again."

"And what about the pipe?"

"In the roots of a blown-down oak near the Esopus meadow."

Nodding in admiration, Will put down the pottery and picked up the bear skull. "You've got a regular King's Cabinet," he said, then caught Coley's curious look and went on. "A long time ago, a Frenchman named Buffon was asked by King Louis the Fifteenth to oversee his Royal Garden. Buffon was an ambitious man, and he took it upon himself to identify every plant and animal on earth. Over the years he amassed hundreds of specimens from around the world, enough to turn the King's Cabinet of curiosities into one of the great museums in Europe."

"I bet he didn't have a mastodon skull," Coley said.

"No, but he had a tusk, a tooth and an assortment of bones that were collected for him." He held the bear skull up to the light. "You've got a good eye."

"I like looking for things."

Will glanced around the sparely furnished room, taking in the tall stack of bundled magazines under the table and the *Courier* article about the mastodon pinned to the door, the water bucket on the narrow table against the wall and the amber whiskey bottles piled beneath it. He saw half a dozen apples and a loaf of hard bread on the lopsided pantry shelf, and a small pile of neatly folded clothes on the wooden box at the end of the bed.

"Do you think you'll find all the bones you're looking for, Dr. Harp?"

"I think we might."

"Have you ever seen one before?" Coley asked. "I mean the whole skeleton."

"Yes."

"That must be something," Coley mused.

"It is."

"I sure would like to see one."

"Then come out to the farm," Will said. "You're welcome any time."

∾⟨૭⟩∾

LATER THAT NIGHT, Will sat in Arthur's parlor, thinking again about his former medical assistant. Eli Birdslee was only seventeen when he joined the California Volunteers at Camp Halleck, having been given permission by his father, a physician in Santa Barbara. Dr. Birdslee, who'd served with Colonel Connor during the siege of Vera Cruz, had sent a letter along with his son: "I do not expect Eli to be pampered or shown any privileges. This is the fight he chose, the good and the bad of it. All I ask is that you keep an eye out for him, just as we did for each other in '48." Connor honored his old friend's request, and made Will the young man's guardian.

Eli was a gangly boy, thin as a flute, with a hairline that was already receding. He did whatever was asked of him and didn't shirk his responsibilities, often volunteering for patrols nobody else wanted. "He's his father's son," Connor once said, and Will took to him immediately.

Camp Halleck was on the grounds of the old racetrack, on a dusty plain much trampled by horses and marching troops, and the winds that came every afternoon churned the yellow dirt into a milky haze. The infirmary was set up in two small rooms at the back of an old barn that reeked of horse piss and manure, and the cloth that covered the windows filled like sails when the strong gusts rolled in off the Sierra foothills. The heat that summer was oppressive, and Will and Eli mostly treated the men for dehydration and sunburn. They kept vinegar compresses and buckets of cool water on hand, and it seemed as if a fresh rotation of patients passed through every few hours. They also attended to the broken bones and hangovers of soldiers waiting for assignment, the hapless victims of boredom and horseplay. Eli was a good assistant, having learned the basic skills at his father's elbow. He could stitch a gash with assurance, was neither queasy nor dismayed at the sight of blood and was always anxious to learn something new. On a hot morning in June, a private by the name of Stouffer was carried in with a knife wound between his ribs, received the night before in a drunken scuffle with a man he couldn't remember. Certain the blade had nicked his lung, Will quickly cleaned and dried the edges of the wound before applying a cloth saturated with collodion. Eli hovered over Will's shoulder and gladly helped seal the wound with adhesive straps and roller bandages. Within minutes, Stouffer's cheeks turned ruddy and he was breathing freely again as his lung inflated, soon asking for something stronger than water to sip. Eli, having never seen a chest wound before, asked Will to explain the procedure and took comprehensive notes.

Eli was born in California, and like most westerners Will had met, he was patient and open-minded. He said he wanted to study medicine in Philadelphia as his father had, and would've done so when he turned eighteen if war hadn't been declared. "My mother's family's from Georgia, but my father comes from a long line of New Hampshire farmers," Eli told Will one afternoon. "I love my mother, but it's the rebels I choose to fight."

In their free time, they rode into the hills above the Calaveras River to hunt mountain quail in the scrub-oak chaparral. Eli was an excellent marksman, having grown up shooting wild turkey in the dry creekbeds behind the Santa Barbara Mission. Although Will was more than ten years older, he found the boy well read and curious, and they shared similar childhood experiences: Will searching for Esopus Indian tools along the creeks below the Shawangunk Range, and Eli searching for Chumash pottery shards on ranchland near the Goleta Slough. On those afternoon rides they talked about the writings of Darwin and James Hall's early work on paleontology in New York, and Eli had endless questions about life back east.

"The cities must be full of clamor."

"You get used to it," Will told him. "After awhile, it draws you in."

"The biggest city I've ever seen is San Francisco, and even there I couldn't sleep at night with all the rumpus."

"New York and Philadelphia make San Francisco seem like a sleepy village."

Eli grinned at the notion. "I imagine I'll be wide-eyed all day long."

"There's a lot to catch your attention."

"Like pretty women."

"That's a start."

"I hear the prettiest girls live back there."

"There are pretty girls everywhere."

"Maybe so, but the odds say there's more to choose from in the East. Maybe I'll find a wife in one of those cities and bring her back to California with me," Eli mused. "As soon as this war's over, I'll be on my way. Heck, I would've been there by now, if they'd the sense to send me."

As Camp Halleck came into view, he turned to Will. "How could you stand to leave it?"

"Leave what?"

"New York."

Will shrugged. "It's where I grew up. I guess I just wanted to see something new."

Eli nodded. "Yeah, me too."

Once they were back in camp, Eli would wander back to the enlisted men's barracks and Will would retire to his quarters on the other side of the racetrack. First thing in the morning, Eli would be back at the infirmary, checking on the men already there, ready to start the day.

Will sat in Arthur's parlor and smiled. In those early days, Eli had reminded him of his old friend, both of them slightly uncomfortable in their baggy skin, gregarious and confident only in intimate company. Arthur had never mixed easily with boys their own age, and Will had seen the same tendency in Eli, who kept apart from the other soldiers in camp. Will sometimes watched him drill in the scorched ring of the racetrack, the boy noticeable only by his height in the stampede of dusty blue uniforms, and he had seemed shy even then, careful not to tread on the shadow of the soldier in front of him. He never joined in their pranks or whored with them in Stockton, perfectly content to spend his time in the infirmary with Will. It wasn't that he acted aloof or superior; he just lacked the bravado and carelessness that carried most of the others through their tumultuous youth.

But toward the end of July, a few weeks before they were to leave for the Nevada Territory, Will heard loud cheers. He left the infirmary and walked through the camp gates, following the noise to the crowd gathered at the far end of the abandoned cornfield used for target practice. It was a hot afternoon, the air heavy and streaked yellow with sand. At least three dozen California Volunteers were horseshoed around two soldiers loading their Sharps rifles. One was Billy Motes, the other Eli.

Will moved into the scrum and stood by Major McGarry. Two scarecrows were set up about thirty yards away, dressed in buckskins and each topped with a pumpkin decorated with a bandanna and turkey feathers, the ground at their feet heaped with the mess of pumpkins the soldiers had already blown to pieces. Motes raised his rifle first, aiming at the scarecrow on the right, and Eli drew a bead on the other. They both fired together, and the pumpkins exploded in chunks of orange rind and meat. The soldiers let out a unified shout, and McGarry's voice boomed above them all. "You've got a steady hand, Mr. Birdslee," he said. "It will give me pleasure to see an Indian jump from the sting of your bullet."

Like most young men, Eli was easily flattered, and Will saw him blush. When Eli noticed Will, the blush rose higher on his face. And though Will was smiling, Eli quickly turned away, as if suddenly embarrassed by the attention.

Even Will wasn't impervious to the heat that radiated around men like McGarry, but he knew the damage that it could do. Eli might not have been looking for the camaraderie peculiar to soldiering, but it found him nonetheless. He still came to the infirmary every morning, but was anxious for his hours there to be over. A week before they began the march to Nevada, he stopped coming at all.

JANE TOOK HER daily walk to the post office, hoping for a letter from Frank, and left empty-handed. It was hot when she crossed the Strand, the clouds above her rumpling the sky like an unmade bed, so she stepped into the breeze, squared her shoulders and headed down for a stroll along the harbor.

The wharf was already crowded with the first boats coming up from Manhattan, their colorful flags waving from the tallest spars. Jane let herself be drawn deeper into the clamor of activity along the Strand, the sound percussive enough to drown her own stray thoughts of dread.

She stopped to buy a bag of lemons from an olive-skinned boy selling fruit from burlap sacks at his bare feet. He spoke little English but knew the value of every coin and dispensed change with the fluidity of a cardsharp. After Jane counted out her money, she saw Mary Knetch standing at the end of the dock, watching passengers disembark from the *Reindeer*. Her bonnet matched her pale blue dress, the pretty effect marred only by the apron still tied around her waist, and Jane imagined that her hands and hair were still flour-dusted from the bakery. She smiled at the notion and was about to greet her friend, when she noticed Mary's husband, Alfons Knetch, walking down the steamer ramp. He still wore the uniform of the 120th Regiment, baggier now on his shrunken frame, and kept his hand on the rail as he took slow, deliberate steps. A broad patch was tied over his left eye, and his stiff brush of reddish hair was shaved close over what remained of his left ear, a florid, scarred mass that resembled a baby's fist. Mary rushed up as his feet touched the dock and flung her arms around his neck, and he smiled for the first time and hugged her back with the arm that still worked, burying his face in his wife's neck. They stood like that for a long time, keyed into the familiar curves of their bodies. And when Mary pulled away, flour clung to Alfons's uniform jacket like a ghost, and then they laughed and brushed it off.

"Lemons, lady," the boy said in his lilting accent.

Jane took the bag and watched as Mary began to pace herself to her husband's unsteady gait. He was damaged goods but had been delivered back to her nonetheless. She gripped his dead arm as they made their way through the crowd and back to the bakery that bore his name, smiling shyly, as if she were a bride walking down the aisle for the first time.

When distant thunder clapped, Jane turned toward home. She was glad for the Knetches and truly wished the same war's end for herself and every other wife and mother. In the last year it was wishes she had come to rely on, having given up on prayers. It wasn't her faith she'd lost, only the ability to embrace it completely. And so it would be until Frank's face was before her once again.

At the corner of Union Street, she stopped and waited for a wagon to pass. It moved slowly, trailing two handsome horses tethered to the back gate, and she was suddenly anxious to flee this commotion and get home.

"Good morning, Miss Blessing."

Jane looked up and saw Arthur Dowd sitting on the wagon bench. He tipped his hat in greeting and she instinctively nodded back. The man next to Arthur looked at her and smiled. She recognized him from the stable, and while she didn't recall his name, she did remember something more important, that he knew Frank.

Their eyes held until the first drops of rain began to fall. Jane blinked, and when she looked back, the wagon had passed and the man had turned away.

✺

DON'T I ALREADY have enough to occupy my time?" Pearl asked as she grabbed hold of a beech branch to gain leverage on the muddy trail.

"You sure do know how to fill a day," Tally replied as she carefully followed her up the hill.

"They act like I'd done something wrong."

"It is peculiar."

"It's like they're punishing me."

"It does feel like that."

"Was I supposed to let that baby die?"

"Not unless you're as chickenhearted as his mother."

"Well, I ain't," Pearl said as she grabbed another branch and pulled herself along. "Now, instead of minding a baby, I'm minding an old man. Where's the sense in that?"

"Nowhere I can see it."

"That's right. It's not to be found." Pearl raised the hem of her dress and climbed up on a rock, teetering there to avoid the squishy muck that sluiced down the path. "It's not to be found."

The rain had started the day before and fallen throughout the evening, gaining strength as the wind whipped and the sky turned smoky. Pearl hadn't even bothered setting her traps. After supper, when her father and Sam came in from checking the animals, they stood in the doorway soaked to the bone, shivering as though it were deep winter instead of the middle of August.

The storm ended near midnight, and Pearl had lain awake and listened to the final waves of it tap against the roof. It took all her strength to stay in bed and not run to the Smittys' for a peek at her baby. She lay on her back next to Tally until the sky lightened, then quietly went outside to help her father and Sam dig trenches to drain the standing water from the pasture. It was warm again, and a fine mist rose from the ground and tree limbs. She enjoyed working alongside her father and brother, though she was still mad and spoke not a word to either of them. She was still digging when the sun showed along the treetops, glowing whitely through a scrim of clouds, and they got ready to leave. She didn't even look up until her father stopped the wagon in the slick road across from her.

"You come down to Dr. Harp's as soon as you can," he said.

"I'll be there when Tally wakes up."

Sam smirked. "Girl's on princess hours. You go by her clock, you won't be down till Sunday."

"I'll expect you before supper," Joop told her. "And bring enough for the Smittys, too."

Pearl had turned her back on him, a slight rudeness all she dared. Now she struggled with the basket of chicken and bread she'd prepared at home, her boots sliding in the mud as she and Tally fought their way to the top of the ridge. Sweat ran down from her shoulder blades, and she could feel it on the small of her back where her belt cinched her tight. She glanced down at Tally, who had her legs spread wide over rivulets of mud, balanced on two rocks, trying to figure out where to move next. She clutched the other food basket to her chest and held her gray skirt high in an effort to keep it clean, her bare legs splotched to the calves with mud.

Looking down at her cousin, Pearl had her first laugh of the day. "I wish Sam could get an eyeful of you now. I swear he'd marry you where you stand."

Tally glowered at her. "If you don't help me, I ain't gonna be standing for long."

Pearl put her basket on a dry hump of bunchberry and eased back down the path, grabbing the trunk of a young sycamore, which bent with her weight and lowered her far enough to grab Tally's hand. Then, branch by branch, they made their way to the top of the hill, both of them dripping as if they'd been caught in another downpour. As she put her hands on her knees to catch her breath, Pearl glanced down at the strange tracks in the soft mud. These weren't the telltale prints of a fox or a dog, and they were twice the size of those of the bobcats that sometimes came down from the high Catskills. The big animal had loped easily over the path, neither hurried nor scared. She knelt down to get a closer look, and she was hovering over the pawprint, running her fingers through the indentations in the mud, when she heard the men's voices rising from the swamp on the other side of the ridge.

∾☙∾

WILL WALKED to the wagon for more nails and stopped to admire the tusk they'd pulled out of the swamp earlier that morning. It was in better condition than the first, having laid in a rich decomposition of shells and soil, cushioned on a bed of marl. It was now propped in the back of the wagon, where the little dog slept in its warped shadow.

Will slapped at the mosquitoes that skimmed his neck and turned back to the swamp, which during yesterday's rain had erupted into a brown boil that now filled every depression it could find. They would have to drain the bog and keep the excavation area clear, but he knew that seepage would persist and every hard rain would put it back underwater. He'd need to bring out a windlass later in the week and construct a pump and sluice like the ones the miners had used to control the streambeds outside of Sacramento.

He had come out at daybreak, Rump weaving expertly between his horse's hooves, occasionally veering off to chase butterflies through the open meadow. Will had enjoyed those hours alone, walking the perimeter of the bog and making sketches of the wide valley, trying to square what he saw in front of him with what had been here ten thousand years before. He could imagine the ancient forests of the Hudson Highlands before geography shifted and the skies convulsed with thunder and burned with fire, and he wondered what earliest man thought when he saw the scorched and barren earth he had inherited. Was it then that they had conjured up a deity to allay their fears and fuel their hopes? Will had read Darwin four years ago, when the book first reached him in Los Angeles, and was drawn to the tangible evidence of a new social order. And though he still believed, as William Paley did, that God had a place in nature, he also reasoned that nature had been in place first. It was a conflict he wished he could've discussed with his father—this crossroads of faith and the natural world. Will knew the major had read Darwin, but he also was certain his father would've found many of his theories as fanciful as Bible stories.

Musing as he walked the edge of the swamp, Will hoped that he might soon uncover his own piece of the historical puzzle and add another challenge to popular opinion. And just then, Joop and the Jug

Hill men descended on him, Arthur arriving not long afterward to set up his small orange tent on the cusp of activity.

∼◦❧◦∼

HE HUNCHED low under the canvas and poured sulfate over the exposed glass plate. Sweat dripped off his nose and chin, the sharp vinegary smell of the chemicals irritating his eyes, but he concentrated on the plate held carefully in his hands, and in ten seconds the image began to appear. He washed the plate with water and laid it in a hypo bath, tilting the tray back and forth, and in a few minutes the negative became sharper. His eyes having already adjusted to the darkness inside, he could make out Will and Joop House standing up to their waists in the swamp, a femur bone held up in their arms. He put the exposed plate in a rack to dry, along with the others he'd made earlier that morning, then quickly pushed through the tent flaps, sucking in the fresh air.

He grabbed a small towel off the wagon before dousing his head with handfuls of water from the bucket beside him, then dried his face and rested his eyes. When he opened them again, his focus was more reliable, so he turned back to the activity in the swamp, standing on the back of the wagon for a better view and using his fingers to frame his next angle of opportunity. When he saw the two girls walking down the hill in their long skirts and aprons, he ran back into his tent to prepare another plate.

∼◦❧◦∼

IT WAS the stranger Pearl noticed first, the man responsible for her being here. He was banging together a large wooden stand with Earl Smitty, their arms swinging rhythmically as they nailed boards to the frame. His hair was long, like that of an Italian prince she'd once seen in a picture book, but he was strong and graceful when he reached for a fresh board and knocked it into position with the head of his hammer. When Earl saw Pearl coming toward them, his face froze in the helpless expression Pearl had seen a hundred times before. She knew he was trying to smile at her, but halfway there he just got stuck. He'd been shy as a lynx ever since they first played together as children, splashing in the same mud puddle. She had been convinced he was simple, until Sam assured her he had as much brains as any other Smitty.

"I guess you just bring out the stupid in him," he said.

"It doesn't take much," she replied. She knew Earl was in love with her, but her own feelings didn't run in the same direction.

"Hey, Pearl," Earl called out, keeping it brief.

"Hello, Earl."

"Hey, Pearl", he said again, unable to stop himself.

The stranger never turned around. It wasn't until her father stepped up and guided her forward that he finally paused in his work.

"Dr. Harp," Joop said. "This is my girl, Pearl."

He wiped the sweat from his eyes and stood. He was taller than her father, though not as wide or as strongly built, with a ranginess that came with hard work.

"She's gonna help out at the farm," Joop continued. "She and her cousin Tally. Keep things tidy. Cook if you want her to."

Will glanced at her, but she could tell he was distracted. "That'll be fine."

Pearl felt the swish of Tally's skirt as she came up alongside her. "I'm Tally," she said lightly.

"I remember you," Will said. "I saw you weeks ago on the boat from Manhattan."

"I saw you, too."

Knowing that Tally was smiling, Pearl wanted to kick her shins and yank the hair from her scalp, but instead she stood there fuming in silence. Another man she'd never seen before was walking toward them from a funny little tent at the edge of the swamp. He was dripping wet and carrying what looked like a book in his arms. "Ladies!" he called. "Would you mind posing for a portrait?"

Tally was the first to move, using the same coy sashay she used around Sam. "Sure, mister. We'll pose."

"Good." He nodded. "Come with me, then. To the wagon. And bring your baskets."

Pearl, flustered by the intrusion, gripped her basket to her chest. "But we got supper here," she said. "Aren't you hungry, Dr. Harp?"

"Yes, but we have plenty to do," he replied, still dangling the hammer. "You go with Mr. Dowd. We can eat when you're done." He knelt back down by the frame but suddenly swiveled on his knees and looked up at her. "Thank you, Miss House," he said, then turned away again and raised his hammer and brought it down on a nail already in place.

Pearl nodded at him, relaxed her grip and smiled for the first time that day, without meanness or regret.

GRIEVES WAS no longer angry, but the conversation with Stokes that had upset him at breakfast the morning they met at the Mansion House Hotel continued to spoil his usually healthy appetite for days. In his house on Chestnut Street, he sat ruminating over the recent turn of events, mostly keeping to himself in his spacious office on the second floor, a corner suite with a ship's bow of windows that looked over the wild back garden his mother had planted so many years ago. The quarter-acre front property, open to public view, was more refined, a formal parterre garden complete with boxwood arabesques designed as a walkway to show off his mother's many roses, particularly the delicate Alfred de Dalmas she favored, so creamy white they seemed to have been whipped on the stem. The rear garden, screened from the street by forsythia and pine trees, though equally well groomed, was contrived to mimic the rugged English countryside. A mature row of cedars followed a serpentine path that led through shrub thickets and spruce trees, ending at a cast-iron pavilion overgrown with Russian vine. Absent of the vivid colors so evident out front, the view allowed the mind to relax and was the one that Grieves preferred to contemplate in those long hours he spent alone.

He had pulled his father's favorite mahogany recliner in front of the window, its cracked leather and humped seat feeling snug to him. As a boy, he'd spent many afternoons playing on the Turkish rug with his marbles or tin soldiers while his father sat bent over his books, a map of Rondout hanging like a coat of arms on the wall behind his desk. And he remembered the year he put his toys away and sat across the desk to receive his first lessons in commerce. He was twelve years old, and his father groomed him for the family business as assiduously as his mother tended her roses.

"The first choice you make is the one that will stick" was one of Abraham's lessons. "Be gracious to the men in your circle and indulge them their opinions" began another, "but remember that their clucking is only the noise that accompanies whiskey and cigars. If a man hesitates, be aggressive. Go after him like a dog to an ankle. If necessary, nip to the bone and draw blood."

Grieves was certain his wife and sons weren't happy having him around. His mood had been so dark that the boys quickly learned to retreat at the sound of his advancing footfalls, and poor Albertina was made to feel unwanted in her own house. He had extended no civil word or husbandly affection, treating her much like the girl who came to hang their laundry.

On the third day, a storm arrived. Grieves remained in his study all afternoon as the rain pelted the windowpanes and wind tore at the spruce trees. He sat there in the reclining chair, pondering why he'd paid so little attention to Major Harp's property. Once he'd died, with his son somewhere out west, to acquire the land quietly through the bank had seemed a simple matter of shuffling papers and transferring deeds. It was essential for his mountain hotel, and he'd always imagined it would be the easiest piece to gain. It hadn't occurred to him that the major's son would ever return; in fact, he neglected to think about the son at all. It was a rare lapse in judgment, and one that needed immediate rectification.

When lightning began to glint in the distance, accompanied by bass notes of thunder, he focused his attention on Will Harp. He'd left the area over a decade ago, leaving behind neither mark nor permanent record. Grieves vaguely remembered the boy riding by the major's side on his business trips to Rondout, as indistinct a presence as any other child. But now he was back, and Grieves needed to move quickly.

That night he visited Albertina in her bedroom. Despite the storm, he opened the windows, and the room filled with the scent of rain and devastated roses. She made no fuss and sat up as he undid her robe and drew the nightgown from her shoulders.

Now he was back in the Mansion House Hotel's dining room, and when the waiter placed his trout and bacon in front of him, he tucked his napkin into his vest and reached for his knife, careful not to rip the crispy skin of the fish. He was very hungry, having already spent three hours at his office, taking care of paperwork that had accumulated in his absence. He was cutting the last of his trout when he glanced up and saw Mickey walking down the Strand like a man who owned the world. He was as clever as he was handsome, and Grieves was glad of his services. By now he had little hope that Frank Quinn had survived the debacle of Cold Harbor, and if Jane was unwilling to accept the fact, he couldn't afford to. It was her brother he would rely on now.

He watched Mickey navigate the deep puddles outside the hotel and come up the stairs two at a time. He entered the dining room without pause, removing his derby as he smiled at Grieves and glided across the room without waiting to be summoned.

He swung into the chair across from Grieves and sat there with his legs apart, thumbs notched in his waistband. "How are you, Mr. Grieves?"

"I'm fine, Mickey, just fine." And that's how he truly felt.

∿◎∿

COLEY WENT directly to Natterjack's after he left the brewery, and it was two in the morning when he cautiously stuck his head in the open door. A few bargemen stood at the bar, wringing out every drinking minute they had left. Coley lingered on the threshold and scanned the room, but neither Mickey nor Charlie O'Fay was in sight. He ducked away, glad he'd be of no use that evening, and ran down to the Strand to rustle up his friends. But he walked from the Fitch Brothers' stone yard to the end of the coal dock without raising a shout, and finally settled himself at the end of Cornell's pier, drinking two bottles of Von Beck's porter and watching the schooners roll in the Rondout current. Then he tossed the empty bottles in the creek, walked back up the hill to Shapiro's house, and was in bed before three for the first time that week.

He slept soundly until the screaming woke him. Opening his eyes, he saw a cloud of dirt filtering down from the floorboards above. He jumped up and raced barefoot out of the room. His pants were still on, but his belt was loose, and he clinched the front in his fist as he bounded up the stairs and barged into the kitchen, where Esther was standing on a chair, one hand gripping the hem of her nightgown and the other an iron ladle. Her eyes were fixed on the high shelf across the room, where Pinch's tail was hanging down by the sugar tin. Then she turned on Coley. "I'll put that squirrel in the soup pot if you don't keep him out of my kitchen."

Coley spotted the tray of overturned biscuits on the floor, collected a handful of crumbs and held them out to his pet. "Here, Pinch. Come on, boy." He threw some crumbs in his own mouth, and Pinch jumped from the shelf to the table and onto his shoulder, where he sat nibbling from his palm.

Coley smiled and looked at Esther. "Don't you feel foolish?"

She was still standing on the chair, her thick hair loose and wild around her shoulders, and he couldn't help staring at the pale flesh of her bare legs showing beneath her bunched-up nightgown. He ignored Pinch, who chirped in his ear and sprayed crumbs on his shirt, riveted as he was by a glimpse of flesh. Seeing this, Esther gave him a hard look, jumped off the chair and smoothed out her nightgown before picking up the tray of broken biscuits. "I'll kill that squirrel next time."

Passing Coley, she stopped for a moment, standing only inches from his face. It was just light enough for him to see wrinkles burst around her eyes as she smiled at him, and as he smiled back, she slapped him sharply across the face. Only the squirrel flinched.

"Don't you feel foolish?" she whispered in his ear, walking around him.

Coley couldn't stop grinning, feeling very foolish indeed.

SITTING ON the top step of the Smittys' porch, Pearl held the baby in her arms. It was early morning, and Dorrie was sprawled on the rocking chair near the railing, loose-limbed as a rag doll. She'd been up most of the night trying to comfort the crying baby, who'd spit out her nipple and sobbed with such operatic abandon that her husband had ordered them both out of the room so he could get some sleep. And that's how Pearl found them in the morning: Dorrie slumped in the rocker and the baby clinging to her like the love of his life, each finally exhausted.

Pearl gently extricated the baby from Dorrie's arm and carried him along the main road through Jug Hill. Joe Ogden was up already, feeding the pigs he'd named after his grandchildren, and Pearl waved at him and yawned at the same time. She, too, had been up most of the night. The sheriff had come by the previous afternoon, when she was still down at the swamp, and Sallie was furious about it.

"Sheriff took up all my time," she complained. "Only thing he didn't take was that baby."

Sheriff Davis Winnie was blade-thin, with lank hair so greasy that it looked as if he'd just stepped out of a rainstorm. Almost sixty, he had a maddening habit of speaking very slowly, as if each word had been invented on the spot.

"He chews on every last thought like it had some flavor to it," Sallie went on. "Took him nearly an hour just to say hello."

She'd led Winnie down to the Smitty farm, where he'd picked the chubby baby up by his armpits and held him to the light.

"You should've seen it, the two of 'em eyeballing each other. If I hadn't been so mad, I might've laughed out loud."

When the baby started crying, the sheriff handed him back to Dorrie, and then, in his unhurried, deliberate way, told the women that there was nothing he could do. "Unless somebody steps up to claim him, he's better off here."

"But the child's white," Dorrie said.

He shrugged. "Might be, but not much whiter than your Pearl. All I can see for certain is that he's got the particulars of a boy. What he turns into tomorrow or the day after, I don't got a notion."

"But he wasn't born on Jug Hill!" Sallie exclaimed.

At that, Winnie smiled, and in the time it took him to form a sentence, Sallie frowned and bit her tongue, because she knew what was coming.

"Oh, yes he was," he said, with drawn-out satisfaction. "He most certainly was."

"And that was that," Sallie told Joop and Pearl when they got back from the swamp. She was still riled, her every move tense and jerky. When Joop put his arms around her, she grew stiff as a broom handle.

"Sheriff will find something out. And if he don't, it's just another baby on the hill," he told her.

Sallie pulled away. "But it ain't a Jug Hill baby, no matter what he says. And it ain't like a puppy gonna go off and fend for itself when it's whelped and ready to play. That baby's gonna be here a long time, and it's a boy baby, meaning he's gonna stay a baby least half his life!"

When Sallie stormed toward the door, Pearl made the mistake of speaking up. "I'll help," she said.

"You're damn right you will!" Sallie said as she turned on her. "And you'll stay close to home when you're doin' it. I don't want you goin' off to those woods trying to find another!"

They didn't speak again the rest of the night.

Tally made things worse by teasing Pearl about Dr. Harp. "You should've seen your face when you first got a look at him. Went soft as pudding."

"It did not."

They were lying on top of the sheets because of the heat. Pearl had her hands under her head and was staring up at the twists of paint peeling off the ceiling while Tally leaned on an elbow and faced her in the speckled darkness.

"And you got all cow-eyed," Tally went on. "Like he was the first and last man on earth."

"Stop it."

Tally ignored her and snuggled up close. "You can't fool me. I saw you. Earl Smitty saw it, too, and a dumber look's never been seen. But Dr. Harp, he's too busy carrying bones and stinking of mud to pay you any attention. But you put some effort into it, I'll give you that. I never saw a girl do as much as—"

"Shut up!" Pearl hissed. "Just shut up right now!" She knew Tally was grinning in satisfaction, so she refused to face her.

"My goodness. Love sure does make you cross," Tally said as she settled into the thin mattress. "Good thing it don't happen every day."

Now Pearl yawned again as she took a second walk through the hamlet, the baby napping in her arms, then carried him back to Dorrie, who was still sleeping on the porch. Pearl kicked off her shoes, tiptoed up the steps, and eased the baby onto Dorrie's chest.

She left them that way, grabbed her shoes and headed back across Jug Hill, toward the Clove.

⟨୨⟩

WILL KNEW HE'D worked too hard that day, straining the muscles in his ravaged shoulder, and was paying for it now. He hoped the long hours would grant him the deep sleep that had eluded him for a full year, but it still came fitfully, no matter how much he drank. Whenever he lay down and closed his eyes, the bloodletting of the Utah campaign flared red in the darkness.

Col. Connor had led the California Volunteers into the Nevada Territory in August 1862, and in early October, Will and Eli rode out with Major McGarry and his cavalry unit to investigate the murder of immigrants along the Humboldt River. McGarry's orders were to hang any Indian involved in the killings, and leave the bodies as an example of what the Shoshone could expect from the new command.

McGarry rode the men hard to the site of the Gravelly Ford attacks. The soldiers were keen after weeks of hard labor in the sagebrush flats around their fort in the Ruby Valley, where they'd collected stone and cedar to build barracks and storerooms and corrals, all this in a hot wind that blew freely and stung with grit. Even Will was grateful to leave the drudgery behind, and he kept his eyes on the green mountains to the north, where the Humboldt flowed.

Five days later, in a piñon-covered canyon just west of Gravelly

Ford, they found a small band of Shoshone camped near a stream, resting while their stolen cattle grazed on bullberry bushes growing close to the banks. McGarry's scout led them to the top of the canyon, where they found cover in a fringe of cottonwood trees. As they rode through the sparse tree line, Will could see the anticipation in the men's faces. They sat lightly, leaning forward in their saddles and gripping their rifles across their chests.

They'd gone almost fifty yards when a corporal's horse dislodged a shelf of loose rocks, sending them tumbling down the canyon. The Indians looked up, everything at a sudden standstill until Will glanced behind him and saw McGarry raise his rifle to his shoulder, shouting out a command as he fired.

The air erupted with gunshots as the major led the charge, the men urging their horses over the rim, whooping and hollering as the canyon wall slid beneath them, flailing their arms and firing wildly into the greasewood as they were caught by the momentum of the crumbling scree. Three soldiers were sent airborne, and two horses' legs snapped as they were forced into this vertical descent, Will watching them roll on their necks and backs as they plummeted into the swirl of raised dust.

He pulled out his Colt revolver and looked down at the Shoshone scrambling to their picketed horses, grabbing their guns and racing through the sparse brush, their backs to the bullets that pinged around them. One was spun by a bullet to the shoulder, and as he turned, another bullet caught him in his open mouth and scattered his brain against the cedar stump behind him. The others had already disappeared into the buffalo brush, fleeing the salvos all around them.

Will eased his horse down the slope, cutting back and forth through the dust storm of those who'd galloped ahead. He saw thrown men holding on to the shards of white bone that had burst through their skin. A horse with his leg twisted behind him whinnied in agony until a bullet silenced him. Once on the canyon floor, Will galloped toward the river, through the red haw and sage, passing four more Indians dead in the brush, their bodies torn by bullets and hooves, their long hair slick with blood. When he got to the Humboldt, two Shoshone on horseback were racing across and two others were running through the knee-deep water while McGarry and a dozen soldiers, sitting their mounts on the muddy bank, took lazy shots at them. Eli was among them, and although his rifle was resting against the pommel of his saddle, he laughed along with the others. Will watched Billy Motes, easily the best marksman in the company, raise his Henry breechloader, first taking down the two horses and then the Indians who'd catapulted over their heads once they bobbed up again in the current. Pivoting slowly in his saddle, one eye nipped shut, he let the two Shoshone on foot get closer to the opposite shore before firing, shooting them in the legs, and then waited until their heads broke the surface and shot again as if it were muskrats he was obliterating. He rested the rifle on his knee while the other soldiers shot at the floating corpses, yelping with glee every time a bullet hit, shooting until the Indians were long out of sight.

That evening, Will asked Eli if shooting those men had bothered him.

"Course not," he scoffed. "They were already dead."

Over the next few days, they found and executed fifteen more Shoshone, following Connor's orders. Will didn't challenge them, nor did he participate. He tended to the men who were wounded that day on Gravelly Ford. Eli assisted him in the makeshift hospital tent, stitching up the less severely injured and helping him reset broken bones, but at the end of the day he was quick to join his young friends, who gathered outside McGarry's tent as if he were an oracle and passed around a flask as the major regaled them with heroic elocution.

Will knew from his own family history that wars were inevitable, that obedience to leadership was mandatory and death often a possibility, that it took courage to survive with your hope and honor intact. Anything beyond that was a question without answers.

Riding back to the Ruby Valley, and finding himself alongside Major McGarry, Will asked, "Do you think we accomplished anything, Major?"

"Only what we were sent to do."

"But will it stop anything?"

McGarry grinned. "It stopped a couple dozen Indians, didn't it?"

Will dropped back, and as they came out of the cottonwood forest, he saw that Eli and Billy Motes had formed a perfect chevron behind McGarry, and he knew then that the boy was lost to him.

Will awoke to the clatter of pots in the kitchen. He sat up fast, blinded by sunlight bright in every window, and cursed himself for oversleeping. He pulled on his boots and strode into the kitchen, where he was brought up short by the sight of the girl standing at the cooking stove.

She turned to him and smiled. "Got some coffee, Dr. Harp."

He relaxed and studied her. She was very young and very beautiful, and her long ropes of black hair were tied back, revealing a slender neck as light in color as those of her Dutch ancestors.

When he smiled back, she could tell he didn't remember her name. "It's Pearl," she said.

"I could use some coffee, Pearl."

When she handed him a cup, he was staring at the pair of rabbits, trussed by their hind feet, that were hanging from the doorknob. "I trapped them last night. Thought they'd make a nice supper."

"They will." He glanced at her, and she looked away. "You do a lot of trapping, Pearl?"

"Every day."

"And what do you trap?"

"Whatever animal makes up its mind to come across Jug Hill. Raccoons mostly. Skunks, rabbits, fox. A beaver once or twice."

"You sell the skins?"

"A man in Rondout buys everything I bring him."

He nodded and drank some coffee. "You can set some traps here, if you'd like. And down by the swamp if you want more beaver."

"I will, then."

"But be careful," he told her. "There's a mountain lion in the Clove."

"I know. I saw his tracks."

"Where?"

She raised her chin toward the western window. "He came across the ridge above."

"Did you tell your father?"

She nodded. "Everybody knows. They're looking out for him."

Will stood at the window and finished his coffee.

"I can make you some eggs," she said. "Fry 'em up with some tomatoes."

He shook his head. " I should've been out of here an hour ago."

"At least let me wrap you up some bread and ham."

"Just bring some extra for supper." He was halfway to the door when he stopped and looked back at her. "I think we're going to get along just fine, Pearl."

He'd been a father of sorts, something he hadn't considered when Hannah was still alive. Now he couldn't stop thinking about it, and he felt the ache in his hands as he balled them into fists and did everything he could to keep them still.

"Be careful, Mickey."

He didn't know that Hannah was childing until he'd undressed her in the new year, seeing how soft and round she'd become. He was used to the fact that she'd grown quiet since her husband had died, and it didn't bother him that she mourned that way. It was regretful that a Confederate bullet had found Joe at Gettysburg, but it was a fight he'd raced to. The scope of the war frightened Mickey, though he admitted that to no one.

"You're hurting me."

He hadn't told anybody about the baby, neither his sister nor Charlie O'Fay. And he'd known Hannah would tell no one; she was too ashamed.

"Goddammit it, Mickey!"

He blinked, looking down at Gitta's face beneath him, her long hair braided between his fists and her head pinned to the pillow. He let go when he saw the tears streaming down her cheeks, staring at the strands of blond hair still twisted between his fingers.

The morning had not gone well. It was rent day, and it seemed she was forced to stand her ground at every stop she made. When she'd entered Jim Conklin's tobacco shop, he just rolled his eyes, and she watched his head tick-tock back and forth as he walked to his safe with all the emotive sway of a Shakespearean actor. Returning with the coins, he confronted her with one last dramatic wheeze.

"If you don't stop that snorting right now, I'm going to stick my fingers up your nose and stop you myself!" she'd told him, and snatched the money sack out of his hand before he had a chance to reply.

Now she waited impatiently in front of Grieves's desk as he counted the money she had handed him. Then he looked up at her and smiled.

"Of course you can stay in the house as long as you wish, Miss Blessing," he said.

"What do you mean?" she asked, genuinely bewildered.

"Considering the circumstances, you may keep the house as long as you work for me," he told her, standing up to look at the large map behind his desk.

"The house?"

"Yes."

"Frank's house?"

"Yes."

"As if there was any doubt about that," she said, unable to hide her irritation. "There never was any doubt, was there, Mr. Grieves?"

"No," he said, his tone more cautious. "Of course not."

"Then I don't know why you bring it up. I don't know what you mean."

"I simply mean you may keep—"

"Of course I'll keep it!" Jane snapped. "Because it's Frank's house and he'll expect me to be there when he comes home. And if that's what you're worried about, Mr. Grieves, Frank *is* coming home." When he stared at her without answering, the lingering silence almost drove her mad. "And I'll thank you now for your generosity and good-will, and I'm sure that when Frank's done with this war, he'll extend his hand in person and thank you, as well. And I'll stand there smiling when you tell him face-to-face what a fine and good man you are!"

And she slammed the door behind her so hard that she was surprised the knob didn't come off in her hand.

Too furious to go back to the house Grieves seemed to consider more a favor than her right, she walked down to the Strand, determined to speak to no one until she calmed down. Then she saw the crowd gathered in front of Arthur Dowd's display window, men and women alike. Her first instinct was to cross the street, but her natural curiosity kept her walking straight ahead. She slowed down long enough to peek in the window, then came to an unexpected stop. Leaning over the shoulder of Oscar Kleinhardt, the diminutive porter at Metzger's Hotel, she put her hand over her eyes, blocking the glare, and saw half a dozen framed photographs suspended from wires in front of a black velvet drop. The one in the center was of a giant skull propped against a porch railing, its sheer bulk causing Jane to doubt her eyes. The other pictures were of men working in a swamp, up to their knees in muck. Jug Hill men smiled for the camera as they hoisted up a bone as long as a wagon tongue. But the photograph she found herself staring at was of a man she recognized; he was standing next to a wagon, with one hand on the tip of a great tusk, the other on his hip. His smile was broad and genuine, and as Jane bent in closer, resting a hand on Oscar's girlish shoulder, his gaze seemed focused directly on her.

* * *

IT WASN'T LONG before they began appearing on the ridge above the swamp. At first it was just Jug Hill people coming through the trees after their morning chores were done, arriving by foot or wagon or blue-nosed mule. They'd started coming out after the first few days, and by now Will was used to seeing them sitting on their buckboards and eating hard-boiled eggs as they watched the men wading through the bog. They were silent observers until the wind shifted and blew the noxious stink in their direction, and then they'd cover their noses with sleeves or handkerchiefs and go home. But they'd be back again the next day, and soon they were joined by other Clove farmers and locals who'd heard about the digging.

Will ignored them, glad when Al Shirley finally arrived with his wagon and the windlass he'd ordered in Rondout two weeks before. It was the largest he could find, shipped up from the Morgan Iron Works on the East River, with handles on both sides so two men could work the crank. He'd also hired Jonas Andersen, a wheelwright in High Falls, to construct a ten-foot wheel, and Jonas, inspired by the challenge, worked day and night and delivered the wheel on the morning of the third day. In the meantime, Joop and the Smitty brothers built a trough fifty feet long, running the cedar planks from the edge of the swamp into a stagnant hollow overgrown with skunk cabbage and wild grape. Will rolled Jonas Andersen's wheel down the hill like a giant hoop, nailed eight wooden buckets to its rails, then rigged it to the shaft of the windlass. Sam House helped him build a wooden frame around this odd-looking fandangle, held rigid by fence posts they had to sink eight feet deep to find firmer ground beneath the muck. It was late in the afternoon when they were ready to test the waterwheel, the sky white with heat and the air perfectly still. Will let the Smitty brothers operate the windlass, and as they turned the cranks, the wheel slowly revolved and dipped each bucket into the swamp and arced it around to spill into the trough, where the nut-brown water gurgled and splashed and ran along the length of the planks, leaking a little as it flowed down to the hollow. They kept at it until the sky darkened, taking turns at the windlass and watching the swamp drain just enough to reveal branches that hadn't been evident an hour before. Will knew that it was only a temporary solution, but it would ease their plunder of the mastodon's grave.

He got in the habit of arriving at the swamp well before the others came off Jug Hill. He'd wade into the water with a long iron rod, gripping the cross handles and poking around until he hit something solid, patiently twisting the rod in his fingers as he prodded the thick mud, ignoring the mosquitoes and concentrating on that moment when the tip quivered with resistance. The excitement of discovery thrilled him, as it had when he was a child, and he gladly sank up to his shoulders or chin for the smallest segment of toe or vertebra. In the beginning his rod deceived him more than it proved accurate, and he pulled out almost as many turtles and rotten willow sticks as he did bones. But the bones did come, and as he became more practiced, they came with greater frequency.

Joop or Sam would wade into the swamp whenever he needed help. A majority of the bones were fragile, and he was pained to have broken two of the fourteen ribs already recovered. He preferred Sam's help because he had the most delicate touch and wasn't afraid to bend deep into the brown surge. Even so, when the two of them uncovered the left scapula, squatting in the mud and digging carefully with their sore fingers, the three-foot bone split along its fragile spine.

At the end of the second week, a wagon came down to the swamp from the Clove road, driven by a tiny old man wearing a slouch hat. Will left Earl Smitty to work the windlass and walked up to greet his visitor, who was dressed in a shirt as white as his beard and a worn canvas coat that came down to his knees. He had a long, narrow nose and translucent skin that clung to his high cheekbones as if it had been tanned and dried there.

"Will Harp?" he asked in a deep cackle that Will had never forgotten.

He smiled and held out his hand. "How are you, Mr. Quick?"

Jacob Quick, his father's oldest friend, was born three weeks before the country declared its independence, in a farmhouse not more than ten miles from the one he now owned in the Clove. He, too, had fought in the War of 1812, serving under William Henry Harrison in the Northwest frontier when they chased Tecumseh into the wilds of Canada, and he saw firsthand the mortal chest wound the great Shawnee chief suffered on the banks of the Thames. He had lost three fingers to frostbite during the winter campaign at Raisin River, and when Will first shook his hand, only a boy at the time, it felt as if he were tussling with a claw. It still did, and though Quick was nearing ninety, those two remaining fingers were as strong as steel.

He grinned. "The last time I saw you, you were playing in a mud hole. Not much has changed, has it, Will Harp?"

"No," Will replied with a smile. "But the hole's gotten a little bigger."

The old man laughed. "They said Peter Vandeman must've been struck stupid when he bought this sorry land from Bogardus all those years ago. I wonder what they have to say about you?"

"Whatever it is, it hasn't been repeated to my face."

"Nor mine, for they know I'd use both fist and boot to make the fool regret it!" Quick made a knuckly fist with the arthritic fingers of his good hand.

Will smiled warmly. "Let them enjoy a laugh. It hurts no one."

"If a man laughs in my presence, he'll do it through broken teeth," the old man snapped. "You're still your father's son, and don't you forget it."

Will never doubted Quick's spunk. When he was ten, he'd seen the man come to the aid of Aardt Van Wagenenen's daughter when she was surrounded by three drunk Pennsylvania canawalers outside Heller's market at the landing in High Falls. The boys meant no real harm, but he thrashed them with a hickory knob until they ran off, then offered the fourteen-year-old his arm and escorted her to his wagon and a ride back to her father's farm. He'd married four times but had no children. "Other than his wives," as Will's mother liked to say. He always married younger women, and Will hadn't been surprised when his father wrote him five years ago in Los Angeles to say that he'd got married once again, to Alice Nelson, the sister of one of Will's schoolmates at the Kingston Academy. She was only a few years older than Will, and he could imagine his father chortling as he conveyed the news. But in the very next letter, he learned that Alice Quick had been stung in the neck by a honeybee—her allergy unknown—and by the time Jacob found her, her eyes had rolled back in her head, white as opals, and she was gone. Will's father also wrote about the conversation they'd had the evening after they buried Alice in the cemetery behind the Clove Church.

It was just the two of us on that slanted porch of his, which you needed sea legs to navigate. We sat side by side like the old men we are, and Jacob held out his whiskey glass and turned to me, wondering about the women he'd married and lost. "Is it their youth I'm chasing, or my own?" he asked. "I don't know, Jacob," I replied. "What difference does it make?" He thought about this as he drank deeply, and smiled for the first time that day. "It makes no difference at all, Daniel. It's paradise I'm after, not a legacy." And I thought then, as I think now, that Jacob had a pretty smart idea.

"It's good to see you, Mr. Quick," Will told the old man.

"I'll say it for your father, and I'll say it for myself," Quick said. "It's good to have you home."

~⊘~

THE CLOVE MASTODON

Dr. Will Harp continues to excavate the old Vandeman swamp, and the mysterious earth continues to reveal her riches. Dr. Harp hopes to uncover a complete mastodon skeleton, one of only a few ever to be found on the American continent, and he is confident of his success. The giant's bones are being unearthed on a daily basis, and as they are laid out on the grass at the water's edge, even the least scientifically keen observer would be able to discern the approximate appearance of a most unusual beast. The many ribs themselves define a mammal of tremendous size and appetite, and the dimensions of the right femur, which Dr. Harp and his assistants brought to the surface just last week, promise a Goliath of extraordinary proportions. Thus far, the bog water and its organic components have been kind to the natural scaffolding of this ancient monster, and Dr. Harp predicts that by summer's end the bones he has raised from the swamp will be ready for mounting.

That is truly a sight we are all anxious to behold.

Rondout Courier, August 20, 1864

~⊘~

HE LEANED FORWARD on the bench in front of the stable and read the article over and over again until it was committed to memory.

Shapiro sat next to him, eyes closed, his head tilted back to catch the full sun. Coley knew he wasn't asleep, only resting and waiting to ambush the next man who strolled by with a barrage of conversation. But it had been a quiet morning, and his nose was already badly burned, as sure a sign of summer as the tart strawberries Joe Fraser sold on the Strand.

Coley was about to turn the page when he heard a sharp whistle. He looked up and saw Charlie O'Fay standing on the opposite corner, two fingers of one hand hooked into his mouth and the other raised to hail him over. He frowned, knowing the easy part of his day was done, and lowered the newspaper.

Shapiro's eyes opened as the whistling continued, and he tilted his head to the boy at his side and sighed. "I can't stop you," he said, eyes closing again in surrender.

Coley knew it was true, though he wished it weren't. "You ought to wear a hat," he told Shapiro, then dropped the newspaper to the ground.

"Herm Walker bought himself a new horse last week," Charlie told him. "He knows nothing about horses, except that you feed them from one end and they feed your garden patch from the other. Herm just buys 'em and rides 'em till they get sick or old and die, then barters for another and hops on its back like it's a fancy carriage he's taking to and fro."

They were heading down Division Street toward the docks, and Coley had to walk quickly to keep up.

"Doesn't matter if it's bay or chestnut, 'cause being pretty don't mean a thing to Herm Walker. Just look at the woman he married, or don't if you're wise, 'cause she's just some other kind of female for him to jump up on and ride to and fro."

Charlie glanced over his shoulder to make sure Coley was still there. "Story goes he traveled all the way up to Callicoon, 'cause you get more horse for the dollar there. So he finds a slab-sided mare with big withers in a barn by the Delaware River, and if it wasn't love at first sight, no matter, for the deal was done. Herm boosted his saddle on top of that horse, hoisted himself up on it, got comfortable, pointed the animal toward home and promptly fell asleep. People from North Branch to Loomis looked up and saw him passing through, saying to themselves, 'There goes Herm Walker on his new horse.' He never woke up, slept right through Sundown and Samsonville, the horse stopping to shit, maybe chew on some fence-post weeds or drink some ditch water, but staying on the right road like she'd been down it a hundred times before. Walked right into Rondout around sunup the next day, straight down the plank road to Meadow Street, turned left on Union and right on Hone. Herm woke up in his own front yard, the horse eating the hollyhocks his wife'd planted along the porch. He was too confounded by his whereabouts to say a word, or even think up a sensible one, but the wife did when she stepped outside and saw that horse making breakfast of the flowers she tended more lovingly than the children she never had. I heard her face screwed up ugly, and when she started screaming at the horse, it looked up and bolted at the sight of her, stuck a hoof in a gopher hole, threw Herm into his ivy hedge and come up lame. Constable Sirrine was called to the scene and he shot the horse in the head not ten minutes later, then Herm tried wrestling the gun away so he could shoot his wife in the exact same place. It was a sight for those fortunate enough to see it."

"You didn't?" Coley asked him.

Charlie shook his head. "I was asleep in bed, but I heard the shot— the first, not the other—because Sirrine popped Herm in the forehead with the butt of his Colt Walker before Herm could put his woman out of her misery. Herm woke up on the settee in their parlor and didn't remember a thing about his ugly wife or his ugly horse, and when he was told the story, he didn't believe it himself."

"But you do, Charlie?"

"I seen John O'Neill using his deep-sided wagon to haul a dead ugly horse off Herm Walker's front yard. I seen his ugly wife enough times to know to look the other way. That's enough believing for me."

They turned the corner on Catherine Street and saw Mickey walking toward them from Rondout Creek, his hair soaking wet from swimming, his look so ferocious that Coley thought about turning around and running in the other direction. But then his eyes brightened and he fell in between the two of them, one hand resting on Coley's shoulder while the other reached into his pocket. "Get our horses," he said. "Meet me at Natterjack's in an hour."

"Where we going, Mickey?"

Mickey just shoved some coins in Coley's hand and gave him a push. "Go."

⟳⟲

IT WAS ALREADY past dark when they came through High Falls and rode past Terwilliger's boardinghouse. Coley, having missed his supper and feeling pukish with hunger, looked longingly through the amber glass of the dining room windows, where canal workers were sitting down to plates of fried chicken and corn. But Mickey kept going, sitting straight on the back of his dainty horse, staying in the shadows on the far side of the road. When Coley looked over his shoulder, the kerosene lamps in the houses behind them burned dim as church candles. They kept traveling south, riding parallel to the Shawangunk cliffs until they reached a sheep-grazed hill above the Snyder farm. Mickey stopped and looked around, the road in front of them stretching straight as a board through a colonnade of bent and spindly trees. "Let's eat," he said.

Coley watched him lift a burlap sack from the back of his saddle; then they both dismounted and tied their horses to the post-and-rail fence that ran along the road. He sat on a rotting tree stump as Mickey unfolded the greasy paper that held slabs of fatty beef and bread the girl at Natterjack's must have prepared that afternoon.

He handed Coley a thick sandwich and tossed him a black bottle of beer that had been wrapped in muslin to keep it from breaking. He drank nothing himself, just chewed slowly as he gazed up at the spray of stars above them. "The outdoors is a wonder," he said. "When I was a boy, I thought the evening sky in Ireland was the finest anywhere, but it remained a spectacle over the ocean and stayed so over New York, the blackness of it stretching farther than my tiny brain could tumble."

Coley pulled the cork with his teeth and drank half the warm beer before stopping to breathe. It was the strong porter he favored, and he felt the alcohol coursing from his cheeks to his fingertips.

"The river and the sky, Coley boy," Mickey continued, "that's what we've got."

Coley took another large swallow of beer, thinking he wasn't as fond of the night as Mickey was. He reached for the second sack of meat, but Mickey yanked it away from him.

"That's for later," he said, brushing the crumbs from his pants. "Let's go."

❧

WILL SAT ON the porch and listened for the big cat. Though he'd heard it only once, Jacob Quick had told him it had taken one of his goats, and that he'd seen it himself in his far pasture, early one morning. "It was moving along the outside of the fence line like a ripple on the water. My old rifle weighs more than I do, but I got a shot at him anyway and did nothing but ruin a good board and waste a shell. Cat was gone like that, and I haven't seen him since." But Will knew the lion would stay in the valley until it was dead or scared off by some vigilant farmer.

It was a clear night and, after the heat of the day, had a fresh bite. He and Arthur had finished the supper Pearl left for them, and Will sat now with a glass of whiskey, exhausted but eager about returning to the swamp in the morning. Before the sun had gone down, he'd walked to the barn to survey the first pile of bones. He laid out the seven cervical and fifteen thoracic vertebrae, placing them in the same articulation he imagined running the length of the mastodon's spine. Larger bones rested against the wall, each tagged and numbered. They'd made splendid progress.

When Arthur appeared, he was topping his glass from the bottle at his feet. Rump was sitting there with his chin on the floor, his ears twitching at every new sound, and didn't bother to look up when Arthur settled in the hickory-backed chair next to Will's and poured himself a short whiskey.

"I never thought the day would come when we'd be sitting on this porch like two old bachelors, gazing at the stars and brooding over the same riddles as when we were boys."

At this, Will grinned.

"I would've thought you'd be married by now," Arthur went on. "A pretty wife at your side, a child on each knee and more Harps waiting in the future."

"I've thought about it often. But mostly while riding across the plains or exploring the coast of California or lying in a bedroll on top of some mesa in Arizona."

"There must've been women, Will," Arthur insisted. "Someone in Los Angeles, perhaps. Surely you settled down long enough to kindle a spark."

"Yes, but not long enough for it to catch. And I certainly won't find a wife in a stinking swamp." He turned to Arthur with a smile. "And you, Arthur? Why did you never marry?"

"It never occurred to me."

"But you're settled. Prosperous. Young enough to attract attention. I imagine the girls come at you with a fury."

"If they do, I haven't noticed."

"You always were modest."

"I've been many things, but never modest."

Will sipped his whiskey, enjoying himself. "The women must've found you a real puzzle."

"They've never said a word about it to me."

"And was there none you thought a proposal might entice?"

Arthur smiled. "I never felt the inclination."

AS THEY RODE deeper into the woods, Coley recognized some of the farms he and Mickey had visited a few weeks before, but even this familiarity gave him no comfort. When they passed the Millen place, he looked down from the ridge and saw it standing empty, the rectangular windows darker than the house itself. The gray gelding was gone from the pasture, and Coley didn't want to imagine what might've happened to him. Every time the wind shook the trees, he thought it was the big cat slithering through the dark, getting ready to pounce. He wished Mickey had given him a gun to carry, something more practical than the useless old Kentucky rifle he still had strapped to his saddle. He'd drunk a second bottle of beer as they rode slowly through the Clove, but it had exacerbated his fears instead of taming them.

And all the while, Mickey stayed quiet, sometimes humming softly as if a midnight ride in the woods was just part of his daily routine. A mile past the Millen farm, he led them back onto the main road, the dark forest suddenly opening up to a wide expanse of pasture that almost glowed in the moonlight.

Relaxing for the first time in an hour, Coley found himself staring up a rounded hill at a grand two-story clapboard house with a long, deep porch that wrapped around the front and both sides. Even from a distance, he could see fruit orchards on the gentle slopes, and a big barn along the gravel drive leading up the hill. He was surprised when Mickey nudged Dutch Eddy through the gate, but Coley followed him dutifully, the night's brightness a comfort after the smoky gloom of the woods.

Mickey gestured for him to slow down. "Quiet now, Coley boy," he said without turning around, "and just do as you're told." A hundred yards short of the house, he pulled his horse to the side, dismounted and nodded at Coley, who did the same. Mickey grabbed the burlap sack off his saddle and, staying under the red spruce that lined the drive, led Coley closer.

"What are we doing here?" Coley whispered.

Mickey hushed him and moved forward, Coley craning his neck and looking over his shoulders. Fancy lace curtains fluttered in the open windows upstairs, and a pair of young squirrels scampered on the roof, their nails plinking along the cedar shakes. Then an animal raised its head on the dark porch, and his feet and breath froze. But in the very next second he swallowed his panic and knew exactly where they were.

Butterfields, he thought.

He'd seen the giant dog many times before, one of the black-and-tan wolfhounds that belonged to Isaac Stokes. Women on the Strand were known to scream at the sight of them, and he'd heard that one of Stokes's dogs had outrun Peter Durant's fastest colt on the quarter-mile track near Kingston, then jumped the six-foot fence with a single bound to chase down a rabbit in a neighboring field, trotting back with Stokes's supper in the slobber of his soft mouth. Coley had always admired the dogs, if only at a distance. They seemed smarter than most men he knew, which was enough to make him turn away.

When Mickey got down on one knee and held up his burlap bag, the wolfhound leapt off the porch and came galloping down the driveway, followed by two puppies blundering after him, loopy as bear cubs. Not knowing what to do, Coley stood with his arms pressed to his sides and watched the three dogs skid to a graceful stop right in front of Mickey. He smiled at the bitch and scratched her head as the two wheaten puppies nuzzled in under his arms, almost knocking him over.

Coley knelt down and let one of the puppies jump up and put its big tufted paws on his shoulders and lick his chin. It took all of his concentration to keep from laughing as they wrestled back and forth. Then he saw Mickey take two hunks of meat from the bag, tossing one to the bitch and the other to the pups, who tugged at it until it tore in half. Then they trotted to the far side of the drive and lay down with the prize between their front paws, chewing lustily with their long tails beating the ground behind them.

Mickey sat back on his elbows in the grass, the wolfhound bitch eating obediently at his feet. He reached into the burlap bag, pulled out the last bottle of beer and tossed it to Coley, who caught it and rested back against the fence post to drink.

Watching the puppies eat and frisk about, he turned to Mickey with a lightness he hadn't felt all day. "What do we do now?" he whispered.

"Drink your beer," Mickey replied. "Rest awhile."

"For how long?"

"Not long."

"Are there any sandwiches left?"

Mickey only smiled and shut his eyes.

Coley sat up and finished his beer, the two puppies quiet now and watching him from the other side of the drive. He shut his eyes, too, but twenty minutes later the mother wolfhound's leg shot out and kicked him in the knee, waking him with a start. He watched her try to stand, but she only stumbled into him and then collapsed. He scrambled to his knees, swiveled around and saw the puppies sprawled where they'd been but now gasping like old men, their legs gone stiff.

"What happened?" Coley murmured to Mickey, who was leaning over the bitch, scratching one of her ears.

"Strychnine."

"What?"

"It was in the meat."

"You poisoned them?"

Mickey just caressed the big dog's neck, and Coley could see it tremble under his touch. "Won't it kill them?" Coley asked.

"Yeah, if I let it."

Mickey reached into his pocket and pulled out two Barlow folding knives, tossing one to Coley. "You take care of the pups."

Clutching the knife, Coley looked across the drive, where one puppy had gone rigid and the other was convulsing so violently that the nubs of his shoulders rose like wings. Then he jumped to his feet, swallowing hard to keep the beer from bubbling back up his throat, and threw the knife as far as he could before running to Melon, his head roaring and eyes blind with grief.

"Coley!" Mickey hissed, running quickly after him.

He jumped on Melon's back and dug his heels into her sides to turn her toward Mickey.

"Coley, goddammit!"

Coley felt the brush of Mickey's fingers, but he ducked low and shook him off, galloping away from Butterfields and into the black night.

IT WAS PAST midnight when Will heard the little dog barking at the window, his paws up on the wall and his nose barely reaching the sill. He sat up quickly and listened for the cat, but instead he heard a horse coming down the road.

Rump ran to the front door and Will followed him through the dark house, grabbing the rifle from the rack above the fireplace. The dog was already scratching at the door, and when Will opened it, he jumped onto the porch and yapped even more furiously as the boy galloped right up to the steps. He looked at Will with wide eyes, breathing heavily, as if he'd run all the way from Rondout, and was close enough that Will could smell the beer on his breath. Rump kept barking until Will nudged the dog silent with his bare foot.

"I come like you said," the boy told him.

～◯～

HEADING DOWN TO take care of her morning chores, Pearl walked through the opaline dawn with the rifle her father had given her the night before, an old flintlock blunderbuss her great-grandfather had taken from a British soldier at the battle of Crown Point in 1758. It was a short-barreled gun, heavy as a cannon. It wasn't used for much anymore, except to prop open a door or window, and she'd never seen it fired. After supper, her father had filled it with a charge of powder and a half pint of nails while her brother stood behind her and shook his head.

"Gun ain't good for nothing," Sam said, "except shooting a big hole in the sky."

"It'll shoot a hundred holes in a panther if it gets too close," Joop replied, then showed Pearl how to unlock the folding bayonet and told her not to worry too much about her aim.

Now she switched the gun from one numb arm to the other, even though the mountain lion hadn't been seen near Jug Hill in more than ten days. "You don't have to see it to know it's there," her father warned her. "And you ain't going anywhere without me or Sam or this rifle."

The night before, she and Tally had stayed out as late as they could, picking huckleberries on the highlands that surrounded Jug Hill. It was easier at dusk, when the wasps were drunk on berry juice and didn't bother them.

Tally was going back to Brooklyn in a few weeks, leaving triumphantly. All the attention she'd lavished on Sam these last few years had finally gotten through to him, and even Pearl could see the change. Her brother no longer left a room when Tally entered, and he didn't shove her away when she sat close. He began to look for her when she wasn't around, following her scent as she'd once followed his, becoming petulant and crusty when she was out of his sight. He even talked about moving to her Weeksville neighborhood in Brooklyn, where her uncle might help him find work at the orphanage or the shipyard near Fort Greene. "He says Jug Hill's too small for a man of his ambitions. Says the world is bulging all around him and he wants to see what it's all about."

"I never heard him speak such nonsense."

Tally smiled. "It's not nonsense to my ears."

"What if Sam doesn't find this bulging world to his liking? What if he wants to come home?"

"Then I'll come back with him."

"You'd come back here?" Pearl asked, surprised.

"I'd live in a beehive if that's where Sam wanted to lay his bones."

Pearl watched her as they walked through the tall grass. "Has he asked you to marry him yet?"

"Not yet, but he will."

"And you got that figured out, too."

Tally grinned.

It was his mother who'd helped tip Sam in Tally's favor. The week before, sweeping up around his bed, she found a recruitment broadside poking out from beneath his horsehair mattress:

MEN OF COLOR
To Arms! To Arms!
Battles of Liberty and the Union We Appeal to You!
Strike Now!

The bold letters scared Sallie to death. She doused Tally with Florida water, dressed her hair, equipped her with a basket of strawberries and sent her out to get him.

"That's about as slick a trick as I ever heard played!" Pearl laughed. "I ought to tell Sam you're leading him around like he was your billy goat."

"I'm just leading him to the truth," Tally told her. "To where he should be going anyway." She stopped in front of a huckleberry bush, shooting the fruit into her basket like they were marbles. "What about you, Pearl? Don't you want to find a man?"

"No sense in looking."

"Why not?"

"I won't find one on Jug Hill."

"Sure you will," Tally said, smiling. "I did."

On the path alongside the barn, the little dog ran up to her as he did every morning, sideways, bowlegged, sounding as ferocious as an army. She balanced herself on the cumbersome rifle and knelt in the dirt to greet him, but he veered around her open hand like she was an obstacle in his path to glory, and raced behind the barn.

Pearl stood up and walked to the house. When she opened the front door, Arthur Dowd was standing at the stove, cracking eggs into one cast-iron skillet while bacon crisped in another. Dr. Harp sat at the table drinking coffee, across from a boy whose back was to her as he poured sugar into his cup.

"Good morning, Pearl," Dr. Harp said with a smile.

Then the boy turned and looked at her, grinning as if this was the best day in his life.

⌒◎⌒

JANE WAS SURPRISED to see the number of wagons and horses tied to fence posts when she arrived at the top of the Clove road. Local farmers were selling salted tomatoes and slices of bread topped with honey, and George Southwick was roasting ears of corn over an open fire and handing them out at a penny apiece. She found a spot in the shade to tether Solomon, then followed the well-trampled grass to where dozens of people were standing on the hillside looking down at the swamp. She moved closer, nodding to the few she knew: Mary and Alfons Knetch; Jonah Best, with his three children clinging to his arms and shoulders like monkeys; Amos Hyde, a Kingston banker, in his freshly blocked beaver hat and linen trousers, and his wife, Faye, wearing a strict black dress more suited for a bishop's wife, her expression just as harsh.

At the bottom of the hill, Jane watched a group of boys playing baseball, the homemade ball smashed and stitched into an almost unrecognizable shape, the dark leather blackened by the sweat of their hands. And then she saw Arthur Dowd with his camera aimed at the giant waterwheel. A line of boys waited to take their turns at the handle, the younger ones splashing one another with the water they scooped out of the rotating dredge buckets. Three of the boys were posing together in front of the wheel—shirtless, wet hair plastered to their skulls, laughing. In the swamp, dark-skinned men from Jug Hill were standing up to their belt loops in a straight row, using long sticks to feel through the mud that squished beneath their feet. It took her a moment to find Will Harp, and she had to look twice to be make sure it was him. She watched him lift a wood-framed screen out of the water and sift through the ooze as though he were looking for nuggets of gold. When he looked up and saw her, his face speckled with brown water, he smiled, and she smiled back at this stranger who'd known Frank Quinn before she had.

Having greeted the woman he'd seen only twice before, Will soon was telling her how Frank first came to the farm, riding in on an old mare one summer years ago. Like many wealthy families in the Ulster hinterlands, the Harps offered summer work to a child from Rondout, providing an escape to the country and a chance to make a little money doing chores on a farm. The major had served with Frank's father in the local militia. Ethan Quinn was a stonecutter on the docks and an excellent marksman, and they'd hunted bear in the Catskills each autumn and turkey in the spring. Their sons knew each other from the annual Fourth of July party at Columbus Point, but it wasn't until the that summer that they became friends.

"Frank was thirteen when he first came to the Clove," Will told Jane as they walked along the meadow, away from all the commotion at the swamp.

"What was he like then?" she asked.

"Then?" Will smiled. "I never thought of it. I just imagined he was always the same."

Will, who was two year older, was taller, but Frank was broad-shouldered and strong from helping his father lift bluestone, and he carried himself with an air of boyish authority. While Will had spent his youthful days learning Latin and studying the histories of dead empires, Frank had been honing his social skills among the living and being instructed by expert prevaricators and barroom toughs. Confidence came naturally to him, and he was smart and had a wit quick enough to keep him out of most trouble, with his pugnacity and fast left hand backing him up when trouble refused to fall away.

They became fast friends that summer, spending most of their time tending to the southern boundary of the Harp property, where the land was overgrown and the fence neglected for decades.

"We enjoyed the work," he told her. "We were away most of the day, with no one to supervise us, out in the cool woods and setting our own pace, competing just for the fun of it, resting when we wanted to or swimming in the creek, then working some more, keeping it up until we were arm-sore or dusk settled and ended our day."

Jane smiled. She knew Frank loved outdoor work, the hot sun on his back or the cold sting of winter on his face. She could imagine him here in these fragrant woods, a handsome boy, not yet the splendid man he would become.

"Did he ever tell you the story about the bat?" Will asked as they strolled along.

"No, I don't think so."

"It was at the end of August. We'd almost finished the new fence and decided to camp out that night, as we often had that warm summer. We laid out our bedrolls under pine trees, where the ground was soft and the canopy of leaves thick enough to delay the morning sun, and built a fire from old hickory branches. I remember we had coffee and a pot my mother had given us, along with potatoes and onions and carrots from the garden and half a dozen eggs. My father had let us borrow his old Charleville rifle, a heavy gun but easy to sight, and we took turns shooting squirrels when we were tired of fence work. At the end of the day we cooked them right over the fire, laying them on the flames until they were almost charred black, then chopped them into pieces on a big rock and threw the pieces into the pot with creek water and the vegetables and cooked the stew until it was thick enough to walk across." Will smiled and shook his head. "That's one thing I remember about Frank. He liked his meat hard and his vegetables soft. My mother used to say he'd need a bucksaw to cut his steak if it was cooked the way he wanted."

He suddenly stopped, and Jane turned with him to look at the rounded hill behind them.

"It wasn't far from here, just over there to the west. The fence separated our property from Vandeman's, and it's still holding, though the field is high again, since my father took the sheep out years ago." He looked back at Jane, still smiling. "While we waited for our supper to boil away, Frank would tell stories about Rondout. He could spin them like a born showman."

"Yes," Jane said softly. She knew that if she uttered another word, she'd start to cry.

"He told me about the Portuguese sailors, wild as any men he'd ever seen, who'd strip off their clothes and bathe in Rondout Creek, then walk along the dock in full daylight, naked as heathens. And about the locust swarm the year before that laid waste to the wheat fields outside of town, and how their cast-off shells crunched under his boots. Then there was the story about the knifing of Joe McGuire at Kelly's saloon, Joe standing with his own guts in his hands, bundled there as if it were a baby he was carrying, until Doc Eckert put them back where they belonged, and how Joe loved showing off his scar, which was shaped exactly like his own first initial."

"He's always been a good talker," Jane was able to say.

Will nodded. "My father once said that Frank had a singular talent for recollection and recitation, and he used to linger in the room when Frank went off on one of his rhapsodies, enjoying it as much as I did."

"And the bat?" Jane asked.

"Yes, the bat," Will said as he picked up the pace again. "It was that same August night, with us sitting there in the woods while the stew cooked. I think when the bats came, Frank was telling me about the dancing cat that used to entertain the drunks at a saloon called Flannery's. About a dozen were fluttering through the twilight, and I realized they were starting to roost in the half-dead sugar maple I was leaning against. Did you know Frank hated bats?"

Jane nodded and smiled, remembering the time one got in the house and he broke a window trying to chase it out with a broomstick.

"He cursed every last bat he saw and swore he knew three men who'd died of their bites," Will continued. "He just couldn't stand them. On that night, he jumped up and reached for the rifle, but I laughed and told him not to waste his time. 'You'll never hit a bat,' I told him. 'It's like shooting a fly!' Frank grumbled a little but knew I was right, so he put the rifle down and picked up a rock. 'Damn bats,' he said, and threw that rock straight up in the air, flipping his wrist just as hard as he could. And I laughed some more and glanced up as that rock flew above our fire, and I saw it catch a bat right in the belly, and the little thing just spiraled down into the clearing as graceful as a leaf. Landed right at Frank's feet. It was the only time I ever saw him speechless. Then he kicked the bat into the fire and we both scrambled around the pine needles looking for more rocks, throwing them at the bats until we couldn't lift our arms anymore. Never hit another one, but it was something to see." Will looked back at the rounded hills. "It was a long time ago."

"Did you see much of Frank after that summer?"

"Frank came out to the farm and worked a couple weeks every year. I think he enjoyed it, and we certainly liked having him. Then when the cholera epidemic struck Rondout, he came here to work, but by then I had gone out west. His parents died in the epidemic, and when he returned to Rondout, he settled into his own life. He was a good friend, though, when we were boys."

"I hope you'll be friends again someday," Jane said.

"So do I." He put his hand on her elbow and started back to the swamp. "Is there any word from Cold Harbor?"

Jane shook her head. "Only that he's missing."

"Frank's a resourceful man," Will said. "That alone counts for a lot."

"I know. He's a wonder. That's the one thought I hold on to." She looked up at Will, shielding her eyes from the sun. "Did you serve in the war?"

"Yes, out west. A different kind of war."

"I imagine it was equally terrible."

"It would be best not to imagine it at all," he replied, his voice suddenly cold.

Back at the swamp, the crowd had grown in the short time they'd been gone. Women carried umbrellas to shade themselves against the midday sun, and men had their coats folded over their arms.

Jane thought the only thing needed to complete this scene of summer diversion was a brass band. "Do they come like this every day?" she asked.

"When the weather's fair. Mostly women and children. What men are still left in town come on Saturday or Sunday."

"You don't mind?"

"No," he said, smiling again. "If I were still a boy and heard about the bones, I'd be here, too."

They stopped in front of the pallet of fossilized bones, which to Jane's eye resembled nothing more than broken tree branches. "I read in the newspaper that it's going well."

"Yes. In a few weeks we should be finished in the swamp, and I'll be able to piece the beast together."

Jane couldn't help but smile at his enthusiasm. "That will be something to see."

"So you must come back to see it."

She glanced past him and into the crowd on the hillside. "Now I'd better be going."

"May I walk you?"

"No, no. I'll be fine."

As she started off, Will put his hand on her arm.

"If anyone can survive this war, it's Frank Quinn."

～◎～

SHAPIRO WAS SITTING on his chair outside the stable when he saw Blessing and his ugly chum turn the corner at Hone Street, Mickey walking as if the daylight shone for his benefit only. The short, stubby man with him had to take two steps for every one of his, and even from a distance Shapiro could see his head was greasy with sweat. When he heard them crossing the street, he sat back and shut his eyes, comfortable as an Arab in the shade, sleepy from his light lunch of smoked shad and cold beer.

"Where's the boy?"

He smacked his lips and tasted fish.

"Where's the boy, Shapiro?" Mickey asked again.

He opened one eye and then the other, slowly bringing Mickey into focus, and feigned a leisurely stretch. "The boy?"

"Coley Hinds." Mickey was standing in front of him with his arms crossed.

"He's not with you?" Shapiro replied. In an instant, Mickey leaned in very close, pressing a finger deep into Shapiro's belly.

"I won't play any Jew games today, but I'll gladly split your head open if you don't answer the question I've repeated more kindly than I intended."

Shapiro tried to move away, but Mickey pressed even harder, right up against his kidney. "I haven't seen the boy," he gasped.

"Since when?"

"Two days."

"Saturday?" Mickey asked gently, the weight of his finger like an iron poker.

"Yes, Saturday, dammit!"

Mickey eased up then, and Shapiro twisted away, clutching his side. "You see him, be sure to tell him I'm looking for him."

Shapiro thought he saw Mickey wink at him before continuing

down Hone Street, the bullfrog at his side. He stood up, rubbing his belly, and took a short, sharp breath. For two days he'd despised the boy for running off with Mickey Blessing, his mood fouled by the thought of it. He walked through the house banging cupboards and doors, cursing Coley Hinds so often that his wife clapped her hand over his mouth and made him promise to stop. "It's not a son who has abandoned you, just an ungrateful boy," she reminded him, but this gave him little solace.

The sun had shifted, and he moved his heavy chair back into the shade, glancing inside the stable. He couldn't deny the fact that Coley meant something to him—a son, no, but more than just a boy. And for the first time since Saturday, he considered this insight without anger or recrimination, and felt delighted. Coley had been safe living under his roof, and if he wasn't with Mickey Blessing, then he might be safe yet.

～ඬා～

HE HEARD THE commotion and looked up from the papers fanned across his desk. He somehow knew the racket in the hallway was an overture being played out for his attention, so he leaned back in his chair and waited for the performance to begin. He heard the outer door burst open and his assistant's muffled protests, followed by the general huffing and puffing of older men engaged in physical contact, ending with his own door crashing in under Simpson's weight.

Isaac Stokes pushed past him, his sizable girth fully puffed with anger, his usually oiled hair a swirl of discontent. He held a derringer of the sort a valiant wife or mother might carry on a train, the one-inch barrel waving wildly in Grieves's direction. "You!" he shouted. "You killed my dogs."

"Isaac, I just heard about it this very morning."

"You heard about it the moment their throats were cut!" he cried, tears leaving tracks on his pink and dusty face. "And for what? You killed my dogs for what? Land? Money? My dogs? My beautiful dogs!"

"I've killed no dogs, Isaac."

"Liar!" Stokes shouted, his spit shooting across Grieves's papers. "You sonofabitch!"

Stokes's whole body trembled with his suffering, and he bent over, hands on knees, crying and drooling on Grieves's fine carpet.

"I'm sorry about your dogs, Isaac. I truly am."

"You," was all Stokes could moan.

"It was three dogs lost, was it not, Isaac? But you have others. A half dozen, perhaps more?"

"You."

"I'll pray for their safety, Isaac."

Stokes wiped his dripping nose. "My dogs."

"Yes."

"You bastard. My beautiful dogs."

"Beautiful they are."

Stokes raised himself up with a quickness that surprised Grieves, pointing the tiny pistol at him again. "I will not lose any more dogs."

"I certainly hope not."

Stokes stared at him with his vacant, rheumy eyes, and Grieves stared back, not trying very hard to suppress the satisfaction he felt rising in his chest. Although the derringer was still pointed somewhere over his left eye, he knew that he had won.

◦◦◦

EVERY TIME HE tried to speak to her, she abruptly turned and walked away. He smiled at her whenever he had the chance, but in return she offered nothing more than a frown or a glassy stare. At suppertime she served him last, and his every thank-you and compliment went unacknowledged. She doted on Dr. Harp, and on Mr. Dowd when he visited, but treated Coley worse than the little dog that growled impatiently for his scraps.

"Morning, Pearl," he said now when he found her alone in the kitchen. She was using a fingernail to scrape chickenshit off the eggs she'd collected, placing each one in an ironstone soup bowl. She didn't turn around but merely shrugged, which Coley took as a good sign. "Want some help with those eggs?"

"I'm done with the eggs."

"Can I do anything for you?"

She shrugged again and flipped her long braid over her shoulder, then finally looked up. "You can go to the smokehouse and bring me a ham so I can make some breakfast."

"Sure, Pearl." He almost tripped over his feet as he hurried to the door, but as he reached for the handle, something on the plank table caught his eye. Sitting in a woven basket was a small fox skull, bleached white by the summer sun. And when he looked back at Pearl, she was smiling at him.

She wasn't mad at him anymore, and didn't think she ever really had been. When she first saw him in Dr. Harp's kitchen, she thought it spoiled what she'd stumbled across, or been forced into when her father made her take this job. Once he arrived, it felt as if the newness of her experience had been tarnished, even if the boy had nothing to do with it, and it wasn't even tarnish, just a minor irritation, no worse than the smear of blood from a slapped mosquito.

She enjoyed tending to these men. They ate everything she cooked, even though her biscuits were too crumbly to sop up her thick gravy, and she usually burned the meat until it shriveled into shapes unknown. When she put fresh bedding on their thin mattresses, they sniffed the air as if the blankets had been strewn with rose petals. Dr. Harp sometimes acted so distracted that she wondered if his digging for bones in the hot sun had made him simpleminded, but then he'd look at her and ask questions about Jug Hill and tell her stories about her father and all the other men he knew there. And Mr. Dowd was just as kind, complimenting her on her excellent posture and beautiful expression and the exquisite tones of her perfect skin. He took count- less photographs of her at the swamp or pulling rabbits from her traps or just sitting on the porch. The men focused so much attention on her that she spent half her day in embarrassed bliss, enjoying every moment of it. And that's what made it different. Over the years she'd grown used to the esteem of the Jug Hill boys. They engaged in every trick possible to catch sight of what flesh they imagined filled her dresses, and she often heard them lurking around behind the outhouse, the slow crush of leaves under their bare feet so different from the sounds of a romping squirrel.

But she was older now, and these were grown men she worked for. They treated her well and often asked her to join them for meals. Although shy in their presence, she did so with pleasure, always taking the chair closest to Dr. Harp, looking at him as often as she could, mar- veling at how his hair, as long as an Indian's, framed his handsome fea- tures. The men drank wine and drew her into their conversations, and Pearl realized that she much preferred to be respected than adored, though she hoped that would come later.

THE FOUR LANTERNS on the corner beams threw a weak light into the center of the barn where they worked. The doors on either side of the threshing floor were thrown open, and the night breeze picked up the decades' old hay dust caught in the grooves of the floorboards, making them sneeze.

Will crouched in front of the bones collected from the mastodon's right hind foot, scattered around his knees like rubble. He picked up a handful of the pea-size pieces, shook them and ran his index finger over the small twiglike phalanxes and the longer metacarpals, then laid them out in an almost perfect sketch of their future assembly. Next to them were broken pieces he hadn't figured out yet, as were a few nuggets of cuneiform bones.

The boy sat cross-legged on the other side of the barn, laying out the dorsal vertebrae. Earlier that morning, Will had numbered them with India ink, and now Coley was placing them in corresponding rows, checking off each on a chart and adding them to the wide boards they'd use to stage the eventual rearticulation of the complete skeleton.

"Would you like me to start on the ribs now, Dr. Harp?" he called as he flexed his legs and stood up.

"Yes, go ahead." Will watched him walk across the barn to the platform that held the rib bones. He got down on his knees and laid the chart alongside, put his pencil behind his ear and turned over the first piece to expose its number.

Will had never pressed the boy about his midnight arrival. He'd seemed wild those early hours, his eyes cutting in every direction, and had asked for a glass of the brandy he spotted on the sideboard. Will had never shared a drink with a thirteen-year-old, but he obliged and joined him, then poured them each another while Coley asked anxious questions about the excavation. Later, after Will thought he'd finally settled him down, he heard him get up from the bed made up for him in the parlor. He opened the door a crack and watched Coley walk to the window and peer into the darkness, his skinny back tilted behind the curtain. Coley offered no explanation that night, or anytime since, and Will could only assume there had been trouble he'd managed to avoid. It was shelter he was after, and Will could certainly provide it, at least for now.

Coley was eager to work and had already taken care of all the horses before Will awoke that first morning. Then he came along to the swamp and was waist-deep in the bog without having to be asked. By the end of the afternoon, he'd found and unearthed the humerus of the mastodon's left foreleg, a bone Will had been hoping to find all week. He took his turn on the waterwheel without complaint and shoveled mud alongside the Smitty brothers. When they broke to eat the sandwiches and drink the beer that the girls had brought, he fell silent and followed Pearl's every movement with the most intense gaze Will had ever seen. And once she was out of sight, he changed completely, happy to stalk through the cattails for bullfrogs and snapping turtles.

Will knew the boy was smart. He could read and write and possessed a curious mind, a trait that would help him to keep his chin above the deepest waters.

They worked through the night with little discussion, each of them concentrating on the job at hand. Rump slept in the corner, his legs pumping with running dreams. Picking up his small brush and a can of paint, Will started marking where the larger bones would need to be drilled. Tomorrow they'd ride into Rondout for supplies and pick up Arthur and his new camera, and maybe he'd call on Jane Blessing.

"Are you ever going back, Dr. Harp?"

When Will looked up, Coley was leaning on a femur and watching him.

"Are you going out west again?" he asked.

Will smiled. He hadn't thought about that in a long time. "Maybe."

"Then maybe I'll go with you."

~∽ල∽~

THERE WAS a new girl in the studio, and he did his best to stay patient. Her steamboat from Manhattan had docked two hours late, and she insisted on dinner when his assistant, Thomas, went to fetch her. Instantly smitten, he took her to the Mansion House Hotel, where she washed down her meal of Hudson River oysters and eel pie with four glasses of champagne. When Thomas finally escorted her to the studio, she held a hand over her mouth and hiccupped relentlessly. Her name was Violette. She was a young woman, eighteen at most, with long blond hair and crooked teeth stained the same color, although still very pretty as long as she kept her smile tight.

After sending Thomas to Natterjack's to get Mickey, Arthur watched her move around the room. "May I get you some water?" he asked.

"Water ain't the answer," Violette replied, then spasmed again. "If water cured 'em, I'd be drinking it all day long."

It was after eight o'clock when Mickey strutted into the studio with Thomas at his heels. He was tanned and handsome, and just the sight of him helped Arthur relax. Mickey looked at the new girl approvingly, and she chirped again and looked back at him, the two of them like rooster and hen. Then he broke the spell by turning to Arthur with his lovely smirk. "What am I to be this evening, Mr. Dowd?"

Arthur looked to the far end of the studio, where the stage had already been set: a large bed fitted with billowing white sheets and pillows, behind it a backdrop depicting thick clouds against a blue sky, the four bedposts draped with long scarves of white silk and muslin.

"Ah," Mickey said, exhaling, "a dream."

He undressed quickly and splayed naked across the bed while Arthur took up his position under the black cloth. Peering through the lens, he saw Mickey lean on his elbow and rest his other hand on his hip, gazing into the distance with such mooning artistry, one would've thought he had been born to the stage.

Arthur pulled his head from beneath the stifling cloth and took a deep breath. Thomas was standing behind the partition with his baths and chemicals, staring at Violette as she disrobed in plain view by the bench, forgoing the modest curtain most of the other girls used. She took a few chiffon scarves from the bench and wrapped them around her neck and waist, then walked over to the bed. She had small breasts and wide hips, and her pubic hair was as fair and light as that on her head.

She put her foot on the bed, inches from Mickey's cock, hiccupped once more and smiled at Arthur. "What would you like me to do?"

He'd never been asked that question before. The preamble to sexual encounters seemed to come instinctively to these women, and he assumed his client had selected each one for her carnal abandon. The only instructions he'd ever given were to hold a pose or turn a head; the performances themselves had always been their own creations. "I suppose anything you'd like to try would be fine," he told her.

Violette shrugged. "I don't get paid for tryin'. Just tell me what you want and I'll do it."

Mickey grinned and looked at Arthur through the girl's upraised leg, running his fingers along the underside of her thigh from knee to rump. "Come along, Mr. Dowd, show her!"

"Pardon me?"

Mickey jumped up, and in three brisk steps he grabbed Arthur by the arm and flung him on the bed. "You want her like this, Mr. Dowd?" he asked as he mischievously shoved the giggling Violette next to the photographer. Arthur tried to scurry away, but Mickey grabbed his ankles. "Or maybe like this?" he said, lifting the girl by the waist and putting her down on top of Arthur. She was laughing in his face now, and Arthur could smell the orange flower water she used on her skin. When he turned his head away, Mickey was standing there, his cock only inches from Arthur's face. "Is that better?" he continued. "Or how about this?" He grabbed the girl again and scooted her up Arthur's chest until his chin was in her crotch and her smooth thighs had boxed his ears. "Or maybe you'd like her with her head between your legs and her bum in your whiskers. Is this the picture you're looking for?"

Violette laughed outrageously, hiccupped again and wriggled free, giving Arthur the chance to roll off the bed and resume his position on the other side of the camera.

"I think anything we just discussed would be sufficient," he said, ducking under the cloth.

"That's what we needed to hear!" Mickey roared. "Just a bit of instruction to get things started." Then, while Arthur calmed his nerves and looked through the lens, Mickey flopped back on the bed, his head ringed by pillows. Violette jumped up next to him, crawling between his legs, her small bottom thrust toward his face. He kissed each round, fleshy globe, smacked it playfully and turned to the camera. "Ready when you are, Mr. Dowd!"

Arthur blinked, astonished by the theatricality of the scene. The glow washing down from the skylight gave the bed an aura of softness, and the sharper light cast by the gas lamps elongated the players' limbs and shadowed the rumpled sheets. The girl seemed both exhausted and jubilant, her hair a mess and her eyes wild, while Mickey leaned back with his hands on her thighs, grinning like an absolute beast. It was perfect.

"Thomas!" he shouted, eager for the first plate.

He was sitting at his desk in the front room of his studio when Mickey sauntered in from the back. He was dressed again, with the top buttons open at his collar and his jacket over his left shoulder. Arthur turned back to his paperwork, scratching orders with the worn nib of his pen.

"She's a good one, that girl," Mickey said, strolling around the room. "Game for anything and limber as a licorice twist."

Arthur put his pen down and pushed the envelope that held Mickey's payment across the desk. "I'm glad you enjoyed yourself."

"When a man enjoys his work, it makes his life all the better, doesn't it, Mr. Dowd?" he said as he turned around, his smile so great-hearted that Arthur couldn't help but return it. "And we're both men with a brimful of joy." He slipped the envelope into his trouser pocket. "I'll keep the girl company till the morning steamship arrives, make sure she looks forward to coming back."

Walking toward the door, he paused in front of the new photographs on the wall, leaned forward with a slight squint and whistled through his two front teeth. "There's a pretty one."

Arthur swiveled in his chair and saw that it was a picture of Pearl that had caught his eye. Standing at the back of a wagon filled with rib bones, she was smiling at the camera, her light skin a fine contrast to her dark dress, her arms folded under her small breasts. She looked like a young girl who knew her worth.

"Jug Hill girl, ain't she?" Mickey asked.

"Yes."

"The mongrel doesn't show much, does it?" he said, mostly to himself. "Not much at all."

SHE WAS STILL raging in her head as she came to the tree-twisted path that ran along the bottom of Jug Hill. Dorrie Smitty had no right naming that baby.

She'd found out the night before when she came home from the Harp farm. Her mother and Tally were sitting on the front porch to escape the heat of the kitchen, where chicken and corn were stewing in a big pot over the fire. Her mother was shucking late-season peas while Tally darned a dress. Pearl sat down on the step next to her cousin, squeezing into the sliver of shade that lipped off the eave. She was exhausted from walking home in the heat, and she could feel her feet tingling now that she was off them, and the dampness that began to collect along her back. "Wake me when supper's ready," she moaned, closing her eyes.

"Supper's ready," Sallie said, smiling as she shucked the last pea and threw the pods to the chickens pecking in the yard.

Tally laughed. "You look about as done in as baby Moses."

"Baby who?" Pearl asked, sitting up again to kick off her shoes.

"Moses," Tally said. "That's what Dorrie Smitty named that white baby."

"What?" Pearl snapped.

Tally just put her lips together and looked back down at her dress.

"What did you say, Tally?"

"Calm down, Pearl," her mother said. "Had to name the boy something. Can't just whistle at it to get its attention."

"When did she name the baby?"

Sallie shrugged. "Last night, this morning. Just heard it myself when she come by for some peppers."

Pearl could feel the blood rushing through her cheeks as she threw her shoes in the dirt, scattering dust and chickens. "She had no right to name that baby!"

"Yes she did."

"But I found him!"

"So?"

"So I should be able to give him his name."

"First one you find in your own belly, that's the one you can name. Baby's called Moses and that's the way it is," her mother said.

Pearl stomped off the porch in her bare feet and stormed across the yard, mad not only because Dorrie had named the baby but also because Moses was the name she herself had picked out and kept her own secret. That she hadn't spoken up right away made her madder still. It still rankled when she woke up the next morning and started down from Jug Hill.

She saw the mountain lion in the clearing just before the Harp farm. It was strafed by shadows and color-blended into the elder bush at the edge of the field three hundred feet in front of her, nothing but a breeze between them. A small fawn was clamped between its jaws, a large flap of skin already torn from her side, exposing the red meat of her left flank. The black tip of the cat's thick tail swished through the leaf litter as its teeth gnawed sinew and bone. It raised its head to find a fresh strip of meat, ears tilting forward as it surveyed the open grassland.

Pearl slowly raised the short-barreled gun and anchored it to her shoulder as her father had taught her. She squinted into the rising sun and settled herself, aiming at the elder shrub and trying her best to steady the barrel's sway. As she cocked the hammer and the tumbler clicked, the cat looked up. She could see its shoulders rise, the animal already in flight before she even pulled the trigger.

The kick of the shot and the weight of the rifle sent her sprawling. She dropped the gun and scuttled to her feet fast enough to see the blasted elder bush still shaking. The cat was long gone.

THEY BOTH KNEW who'd fired the shot. Will was already at the door when Coley reached it, picking up the rifle leaning against the jamb, and they jumped down the porch steps together, racing toward where the echo of the gunshot still reverberated in the hushed morning air. They ran to the pasture where Pearl was standing, circling around from either side, looking in every direction for any sight of the lion. It was quieter than church; even the birdsong had ceased.

The three stood together by the elder bush, where Will gently pried the flintlock from Pearl's hand.

"I missed," she said, and Coley flinched at the suddenness of her voice. "It was beautiful."

He saw Will put his hand on her shoulder, and Pearl tilt her head to rest her cheek there for a moment, and he'd had enough. "Fawn ain't beautiful," Coley grunted. "Fawn's just dead."

HE'D SLEPT THROUGH the early morning on the buckboard seat, waking up only when the Ellenville stage clattered by as they approached Rondout. His head had been resting on Will's shoulder, and he quickly sat up straight and pretended he'd dozed off for only a minute. Then, at the top of Division Street, he bolted over the side without warning. "I'll see you in the morning!" he shouted over his shoulder.

"We'll be leaving from Arthur's studio!" Will shouted back as Coley vaulted over a short privet hedge and disappeared.

Will wasn't surprised; the boy had been in a peculiar mood since they found Pearl in the field at daybreak, the incident turning him sober as a judge. He knew Coley was lovestruck—he practically levitated in her presence—but his brooding had lingered even after they harnessed the horses to the wagon, and Will was glad when he fell asleep just as they left the Clove road.

He eased his wagon behind the line of carriages on the long hill leading down to the harbor. The cobbled street shined with horseshit, and every alley reeked of garbage. Children ran naked as savages down the sidewalk toward the creek, leaping curbs and dodging the mothers who gave chase and picked up the clothes the children had discarded in their rush to cool water. Men sat on stoops and fanned themselves, while dogs and cats shared the same shade.

Tilting his hat low over his eyes, he thought about the letter John Dillon had sent from the Rondout Foundry a few days before. The frames and braces he ordered were now complete, and he was anxious to see them. He'd given Dillon specifications based on the notes he received from the Academy of Natural Sciences in Philadelphia, a relatively simple structure of Y mounts and small-gauge iron bars that he could cut to length himself, making it easier to translate the skeleton's basic outline into something as rudimentary as a child's stick drawing. They had amassed over 250 bones from the swamp, fortunate far beyond his expectations. In a few weeks he would leave just the Smitty brothers to poke through the muddy brown water while he and Coley began the process of making the mastodon stand as tall as it had ten thousand years ago.

Passing through the intersection at Union Street, Will felt the first whisper of a Hudson breeze, and he sat up straight and took off his hat, letting it find him. He knew it would be cooler on the Strand, and he'd have time to stop for a cold beer at a Ferry Street saloon before heading to Dillon's. And then Jane came into view.

❧

SHE WAS JUST about to enter Flynn's Groceries, hoping to find a few pints of blueberries, when she saw Harry Grieves walking toward her. He wore a black suit despite the heat and strolled down the middle of the sidewalk as if it were a red carpet.

He smiled as he blocked her path. "Good afternoon, Miss Blessing."

"Hello, Mr. Grieves."

He stood in the blazing sun and looked down to the waterfront—where, no doubt, he had a ship coming in—while Jane tried to fit herself into the shade provided by Flynn's storefront.

"It's a fine afternoon for a walk," he said as two older women had to step in the gutter in order to get around him. "It's summer at its best and we should all take advantage of it, because from this day forward it will be a crisp march into fall."

"Some would hope so," she replied, feeling perspiration trickle down her spine. She thought back to their ghastly conversation, when he'd written Frank off as dead, and could barely bring herself to look at him.

Grieves smiled into the sunshine. "Take advantage of what you've got, Miss Blessing. Life is so much better that way." Then he turned to her. "Have you seen your brother lately?"

"No, I haven't."

'He's been a phantom this past week."

"He has."

"I've sent Simpson to every known saloon and whorehouse in Rondout, and Mickey seems to have left a warm pint or a warm bed just minutes before my assistant's arrival."

"My brother enjoys both."

"Yes, but not as much as his ability to turn into smoke."

Jane felt the sweat following the tight seam from her armpit to her waist. "We agree that Mickey is a singular individual," she told him curtly. "Is there anything else we need to discuss, Mr. Grieves?"

Grieves raised his eyes and smiled at her. "You Blessings have a knack for charm, though I much prefer Mickey's blarney." He paused a moment to nod at a passerby before turning back to Jane. "Is it the afternoon sun that irritates you, Miss Blessing, or is it me?"

"Miss Blessing!" another voice shouted out from the street, and she was grateful for the distraction but surprised to see it was Will Harp. He'd stopped his team of horses on Division Street, and she stepped around Harry Grieves to go greet him. Will was smiling broadly, and she couldn't help but smile back.

"I was going to call on you today," he said, "but this is even better."

"I didn't expect to see you this soon."

A wagon came to a stop behind Will, the driver's impatience heard as he taunted his mules. "Hold up, you dirty bitches! Stand still, damn you!"

Jane lowered her eyes and smiled. "Jack Mahon will serenade you, too, Dr. Harp, if you don't get moving."

"I'm in Rondout until tomorrow morning. Would you have dinner with me tonight?"

Jane hesitated.

"Please join me."

Then Mahon stood up and raised his frayed whip. "Will you move your fucking wagon, sir, so I can fucking move mine?"

"All right, Dr. Harp," Jane said quietly. "Just go."

Will let loose his reins. "I'll meet you at the Mansion House Hotel. Seven o'clock."

She nodded and watched him drive off, Mahon's mules just inches from his back gate. When she turned to move out of the hot sun, Grieves was standing right behind her, staring over her head at Will's wagon, his hands pressed together behind his back.

~⊙~

COLEY RAN straight down Livingston Street and cut through Edward Gill's backyard before heading west on Murray and south on Ann, where he passed the home of Apollos Fink, a young veteran of the Ulster Guard who'd lost both legs on the Gainesville Pike in 1862. One of the first to be shipped back to Rondout from the war, he was greeted as a hero, serenaded by bugles and pitied by crying girls. He now spent his days sitting on the porch in his uniform, pressed fresh daily by his mother, the legs pinned up right below his knees. He'd creak back and forth on his rocker, using the power of his strong hands and shoulders, daring the neighborhood children to touch his mottled stumps.

"Hey you!" Apollos cried out. "Coley Hinds!"

Coley had already touched the hammy flesh, so he waved without breaking stride and ran right through the New Dublin shantytown until he got to Deyo's Market, down by the docks. He went to the back of the store, spit on the palm of his hand and wiped clean the fouled and pebbly glass. Peering inside, he saw Al stumbling into the storeroom with a forty-pound sack of dried beans over his shoulder. When Coley tapped lightly on the window, his friend jumped, saw who it was, tossed the beans to the floor and darted into the alley.

"Jesus, Coley," he hissed. "Where the hell you been?"

Coley dragged him behind the beer kegs, and they crouched there with their backs against the wall.

"We thought maybe you'd drowned in the river or run off with the old Jew's daughter," Al said. "Not a word from you in all this time. Nothing. Even Shapiro just clamped his mouth shut when I mentioned your name and chased me out of the goddamn stable with a broom."

"And Mickey?" Coley asked.

Al snorted. "He comes in here every fucking day asking for you, and my father ain't too happy about it. Scares off customers, he says. Mickey offered the Magruders a dollar each if they'd tell him where you were, and when Danny made up a tale about you being press-ganged by Spanish pirates, Mickey boxed his ears and threw him in the creek."

"He already come around today?"

"Yeah, and you can be sure he'll be here tomorrow. What happened, Coley?"

"Nothing."

"You do something bad?"

"I just need to stay here till it gets dark."

"Sure, Coley."

"And can you get me something to eat? Some beef and bread, maybe, and a couple of those peaches you got in the back."

"Sure."

Al started to get up, and Coley yanked him back down to the ground. "And you'll keep your mouth shut?"

He pulled his skinny arm free and punched Coley on the shoulder. "I ain't gonna say a word, goddammit!"

"Not even for a dollar?"

"I'll bounce that dollar off your thick fucking head."

Coley smiled. "Go on. Get me something to eat."

Al jumped to his feet, and before he shut the storeroom door behind him, Coley said, "And, Al, can you find me a pint of gin?"

HE SAT BACK in his chair, finished the whiskey still in his glass and reflected on how nervous he'd been when this evening began. He had arrived at the Mansion House Hotel almost an hour early and ordered a drink while he waited at his table in the front of the almost empty dining room. He came early for just that reason, to drink in peace and collect his thoughts and watch traffic slow down along the Strand. He didn't regret the invitation he'd extended that afternoon, but he was more skittish than he realized, and ordered a second drink. Other diners began to fill the tables around him, and he nodded to the men and smiled at their wives, who gave him sidelong glances as they assessed his hair and attire with the same exacting eye they turned to the canapés, creamed asparagus and veal chops that soon arrived at their tables. He sat more erect than was his habit, feeling confined by the tight-fitting cashmere jacket that Arthur had bought years ago in Paris and lent him for the occasion. He was about to order yet another whiskey when he glanced out the window and saw Jane walking up the steps in a mauve dress, her brown hair held back by a tortoiseshell comb. He relaxed then, and stood up when she stepped into the room, thinking how fine she looked, and how bright her smile when she'd spotted him from the open doorway.

He ordered a bottle of German Riesling to accompany the stuffed brook trout they'd both selected, and then watched Jane reach for the beaded bag at her side.

"I have something to show you," she said.

While the waiter poured their wine, she handed Will the photograph she'd pulled from her purse. It was of Frank in his tailored uniform, rifle in hand, looking as if he owed the world nothing more than the gift of his charm. It had been many years, but Will would've recognized him anywhere. "What an expression he wore," he said with a smile.

"Yes, he could peacock with the best of them."

Will propped up the photograph on the wine bottle. The candlelight flickered across it, and Jane's smile turned wistful as she tilted the glass in her hand.

"Still, I wonder if a look alone could've carried him through Cold Harbor." She turned to Will. "Did you see many battles?"

"Not many," he replied, unable to avoid her gaze. "It was another war we fought in the West. Different enemies, different goals."

"But you participated?"

"Yes."

"And you fired a weapon and had weapons fired back at you?"

"Yes."

"You saw men die?"

He nodded.

"And you were hurt, weren't you?"

Will just looked at her.

"You were hurt badly, weren't you?" she continued.

"I was shot."

"That's not what I mean," Jane said, her voice soft but insistent. "But you survived it and walked away, and resumed the life you led before the war."

He looked at her but couldn't answer.

"Tell me that's so, because it's the slenderest of threads I'm clinging to."

Will could have taken her hand in the crowded dining room, ignoring the subtle looks that such a display would've incurred, and told her the truth, but a shadow passed over their table and he looked up to see Harry Grieves standing above them.

"Good evening, Miss Blessing," he said before turning to face Will. "And to you, Dr. Harp."

Will glanced at Jane, whose eyes, quick as those of a cornered cat, darted back and forth between them.

Grieves waited for an introduction she didn't offer, then said, "I'm Harry Grieves. I knew your father well, and I can tell you without compunction that I admired him greatly."

"As did I," Will replied, and shook his hand.

"I remember many years ago having the pleasure of watching the two of you ride into town when you were still a boy and the major was making one of his quarterly visits to the bankers and lawyers who oversaw his business interests. Always on those handsome saddlebreds your father raised. And I remember telling myself that I was bearing witness to four of the proudest and most excellent beings in the county."

Will smiled. "My father loved his horses."

A waiter approached the table with a small silver platter and handed Grieves a glass of wine. "To Major Harp," he toasted, then settled himself at the table as if he were the tardy guest they'd been waiting for.

Will sipped his wine and looked at Jane over the rim of the glass. Her face was pale, and a tempest was rising in her deep blue eyes.

"I was curious, Dr. Harp, as to what your intentions are for your father's property."

"I have no intentions, Mr. Grieves."

"Then I would propose to purchase it from you."

Will almost laughed, but he caught himself when he saw Grieves's expression.

"Your father's property, as well as the Vandeman land that you so recently acquired," he added.

"I have no interest in selling any property, Mr. Grieves."

"Even if I told you that your father and I were having the same discussion not a month before he died?"

"That I find difficult to believe, but if you did, I imagine you received the same answer I'm giving you now."

Grieves neither flinched nor contradicted. "You've been away for a long time, Dr. Harp."

"I'm home now."

"Yes, but for how long?"

Will bristled and drank more wine. "You must have more important concerns than the length of my stay."

Grieves chuckled. "Of course I do, Dr. Harp, of course. But for me, the acquisition of Clove property is the most pressing matter at hand."

"Whether I remain in the Clove or not, the Harp farm isn't for sale."

Grieves raised his glass without taking a sip. "I've been following the story of your behemoth with great interest. It must be satisfying to find such a treasure so close to home."

He stood up then, but Will didn't respond.

"But it must've been a rather stupid animal," Grieves mused, his eyes still focused on Will. "If not, he might've survived into another age." He turned and walked away from the table, jostling it with his hip, leaving his untouched wine trembling in the glass.

~⊙~

HE WENT BACK to the stable after midnight, lurking on the corner until the light in the Shapiros' upstairs window went out. He waited another ten minutes before creeping down the alley, rising quietly on the toes of his boots. He paused outside the stable, then pushed the upper door open to look inside, lingering there a moment to savor the smell of the horses standing in their stalls with their heads down, one letting go a great roar of piss.

Slipping through the warped door into his room, he heard the little squirrel scurrying around. He'd been worried about Pinch, even imagining him dead in the time he'd been gone. He'd feared that maybe Esther had drowned him in a bucket, or Shapiro himself had stomped him to death in a rage, or the little animal had just died of hunger after scouring the four corners for every last dusty crumb. But he looked as healthy as a house cat, and Coley saw crusts of bread and old fruit that Esther must have left out for him, tossed through the barely opened door before she slammed it shut behind her.

He whistled through his front teeth and whispered, "Here, Pinch!" and watched him climb down the wall and up the table leg to sniff at the small piece of cheese in his open hand. Coley felt the rasp of the squirrel's tongue on his finger, stroked his small red head and whispered, "Good boy."

He left the cheese on the table and looked around his small room. Over the years he'd worked for Shapiro, he hadn't collected much of value. His old magazines were just a pile of brittle paper, and his few articles of clothing could be stuffed into a satchel that would rouse pity from even the poorest beggar. But none of that mattered. It was time to move on, Coley knew that, and the only things he'd miss would be his bones and trinkets.

He knelt by the foot of his bed and brushed the dirt away from a concealed board near the wall. He pulled up the board, reached into the hole he'd picked out of the hard dirt, and snaked out his woolen money sack. It was heavy with coins, every penny he'd saved from his long hours working in the stable and at the brewery. Over eighty-five dollars, it would take him a long way from the Clove when he was ready to set out and begin his adventures in the faraway West.

For now, he stuffed it, along with all his clothes, into a burlap bag, propped the bag up behind his pillow and drew the guttering candle closer to his narrow bed. Then he picked up the *New York Weekly* that was still on his table, took a sip from his half-empty pint of gin and lay down to begin the third chapter all over again. He'd left off at the part where Diamond Jack Barkley was bucking the Missouri rapids on a raft riding low with the fortune in gold he was transporting to the bank at Fort Pierre, when Chief Dogface and his Sioux warriors attacked from their camp below Potato Creek. With magnificent skill, Diamond Jack swung the raft between boulders and swirling eddies until a tree limb caught him and swept him into the treacherous currents of the boiling river. Jack broke the surface as arrows sliced into the water like a violent rain, his pistol clenched between his teeth. . . .

He didn't make it to the bottom of the first page before he fell fast asleep.

A bear was looming over him when he opened his eyes, and he scooted back until his head banged against the wall and knocked him fully awake. When his senses cleared, he saw it was just the bulk of Shapiro, made significant in the glum light of dawn, and was amazed how a man of that size could enter a room with no more noise than a whispering breeze.

Coley grabbed his burlap bag and drew it in front of him as he would a cloak. "I didn't mean to run off," he said. "I was gonna come back."

Shapiro just made a low rumbling noise in his throat.

"I was gonna pay you for Melon."

"Keep the horse," Shapiro finally said. "Keep the horse and go."

Although Shapiro had never struck him or yelled at him any louder than he would at an obstinate nag, Coley still expected the usual mumbled curses in a language he didn't understand. But Shapiro, hulking over him, his shoulders rising with each deep breath, only said, "Just go."

Coley sat up and retied the boots he hadn't bothered taking off before he fell asleep, then glanced into the sack containing his belongings, threw the unfinished story of Diamond Jack Barkley on top and cinched it closed with a piece of rope, Shapiro watching his every move. He grabbed his canvas coat off a peg, slipped into it, hefted the bag to his shoulder and coaxed Pinch into his deep front pocket.

He could barely face the man who'd looked out for him this past year, and when he did force himself to look up, all he could think of to offer was a shrug. He flinched when Shapiro raised his hand and brought it toward him, but the stable master just laid it gently on his neck, gave him one last squeeze with his rough, warm fingers and pushed him out the door.

◦⟋ℚ⟍◦

MICKEY WALKED through the cattails along Rondout Creek. It was just after dawn, the sun already humped low in the sky. He dove in once the water surged over his knees and stayed under as long as he could, gliding through it with his body fully extended until he lost speed and was buoyed upward, his hands pressing together to break the surface. He swam past the breakwater and into the Hudson itself, letting the falling tide pull him along. He swam hard like this for ten minutes, straight out into the middle of the river, where he flipped onto his back and let the water carry him, the river waves lapping over his chest, and massaged the knuckles he'd split open on John Grindle's teeth the night before.

The cartman had been delivering beer kegs to Von Beck's Brewery when his little donkey balked in front of Natterjack's saloon around midnight. In his younger days, Grindle had worked in Manhattan, hauling firewood and furniture to homes and businesses in the Bowery, but when better organized delivery services began to take over ten years ago, he grudgingly loaded up his modest cart and drove it north to Rondout, where he found only miserable jobs for meager pay. Bitter about the displacement, he took to muttering to himself all day long—his mind more bent than his aging body—as he ran his penny errands.

The night before, in front of Natterjack's, his donkey had come up lame, having caught a rusted nail in his overgrown hoof. Grindle was yelling at both the animal and himself, heedless of the small crowd that had come out of the saloon to watch the spectacle. Mickey and Charlie O'Fay were among those laughing as Grindle stood on the seat of his cart and whipped the donkey from head to tail, cursing violently as it pawed the street and refused to budge. Then the cartman jumped down, kicked at the donkey and pulled out clumps of its shaggy coat, and in a sudden burst of fury, jabbed the blunt handle of his whip in the donkey's eye. Silence held long enough for the men to gasp, and when the donkey brayed in pain, bucking at the small cart it was tethered to, shaking his head wildly and spraying blood from his gouged eye, Mickey stepped into the street and punched Grindle in the mouth, slashing his knuckles on broken teeth.

He floated on his back a few minutes more, then turned over and dove as deep as he could, to a point where the river grew green-black around him, hanging there a moment under the weight of the water, looking up at the pale underbelly of the river, then closed his eyes and rose to the surface, opening them only when his head burst into the cool air. He swam almost a mile to Hemlock Point before turning to fight the current, following the long bank of the Esopus Meadow back to the Rondout docks.

And now he walked down the Strand toward Division Street, in as fine a mood as he'd known all week. He had his shoes, tied together by the laces, looped over his shoulder as he had when he was a boy, his bare toes kicking up soft dirt from the sidewalk. A feeling of generosity swept him along, and he decided to invite his sister to dinner that night, buy some frilly garment for Gitta and maybe a maple-handled knife for Charlie O'Fay. When he stopped in front of the butcher shop to button his shirt and tuck it neatly into his trousers, he saw Arthur Dowd riding up the street in a wagon, sitting beside a long-haired stranger who was holding the reins. But his eyes were fixed on the boy riding in the back, a squirrel perched on his shoulder. When Arthur laughed at something the stranger had said, Mickey could tell they were in high spirits. They didn't notice him as the wagon headed up the hill that led out of Rondout, but Mickey had seen them, and in the brief instant it took them to pass from view, everything good in him was gone again.

⚬

SHE AWOKE WHEN the first hint of sunlight fell across her bedroom sill, pulled on the striped dress she'd laid out the night before and went out to feed Solomon his alfalfa and oats. In the garden she picked a green pepper and tomato, fried them up with some eggs for breakfast, then worked on the endless quilt until her fingers were sore. At ten minutes to eight, when she knew Mr. Acly would be opening the post office, she took off her glasses, grabbed her bag and walked into town.

It was a perfect morning, and when she passed the churches that stood on opposite corners of Spring Street, the shadows of their spires crossed like swords in the middle of the street. When she turned onto Division Street, she waved to Mary and Alfons Knetch as she walked by the bakery, and stepped away from the open door of Hauptman's Grocery, where the scent of smoked fish was strong enough to bowl her over. It was all such an unwavering routine that she could've walked to the post office with her eyes closed, where everything was always the same when she stepped through the door and walked to the counter: Mr. Acly would lower his eyes and shake his head, and she'd smile at him and turn around, hardly slowing her pace at all. But this morning he was waiting for her, holding an envelope in his left hand.

"Good morning, Miss Blessing," he said in a high, cheerful voice she hadn't heard in months.

"Good morning, Mr. Acly," she responded, then took the letter and turned it in her hands. Addressed to her in an unfamiliar handwriting, it had been sent from Armory Square Hospital in Washington. She opened it immediately, unfolding the two sheets inside, wishing she had her glasses with her as she hurried to the front window. As she stood there, holding the letter up to the light, the first words swam across the page: "Dear Miss Blessing, I hope it will be a comfort to you to know that Frank Quinn did not suffer . . ." And that is as far as she got before the rest of the words fell off the page.

She slipped the letter into her bag, but she didn't remember leaving the post office or walking through town, and she didn't become aware of herself until she was back on Spring Street. She measured her strength and felt nothing. Three boys raced by, late for class at the academy, and Ann Feeney was bent over her roses, plucking aphids one by one. She walked on, invisible, passed through her gate and entered the house, where she closed herself in and the world out.

She picked up her glasses from the side table, pulled out the letter and carried it to the window. She read the opening sentence three more times before she could go on:

Dear Miss Blessing,

I hope it will be a comfort to you to know that Frank Quinn did not suffer, and he fought the fever as bravely as he did the rebel traitors. He came to us just a few weeks after the terrible battles waged those first days of June, and the surgeons here did all they could to save him, and the hundreds of other soldiers who came each day from the battlefields of Cold Harbor. I know nothing of your Frank, other than his name and the note he left behind for you, found in his hand the morning he succumbed to the fever. God makes brave soldiers, and God bless Frank Quinn.

Lorraine Hartley, United States Sanitary Commission volunteer,
Armory Square Hospital, Washington

She let this letter drop to the floor and held up the note. Her name was written in Frank's own hand, though the letters were cramped and seemed weighted by his effort. She unfolded the single sheet and read the words:

I see you I see you I see you

"You see me?" she cried, then wrenched the curtains closed and plunged the room into shadows. Her rage was so strong that it threw her to the floor, where she cried out between gasps of the dusty air that was choking her, the waves of sorrow so great that she clutched her stomach and forced herself to breathe. "You see me?" she cried again, rolling on the carpet and cursing Frank and God and herself in a raw, strangled voice, then repeating herself, rising to her knees and falling back again. She beat her fists on the floor until her hands were numb. The heat of her anger grew suffocating, and she threw off her clothing until she stood shaking in her chemise, then got down on her knees and ripped the discarded skirt apart. "You see me?" she screamed out, undone. She pulled her sewing basket to the floor and rummaged through the spilled ribbons and spools for her heavy brass shears. She attacked the dainty beaded pillows and the cushions on the settee, the sharp edge of the shears bringing up a hiss that sliced through her brain. The room was dim, but her blindness was deep. She grabbed the quilt off the chair and took the shears to it, too, cutting every triangle, breaking every stitch, destroying it with her own hands before crawling onto the ravaged settee and pulling a fringed Spanish shawl over herself. Subsiding into moans, exhausted by her fury, she closed her eyes. Her helplessness was hateful to her, and she trembled with loathing and rage for both of them and kept her eyes shut. And then she saw Frank, his skinned body hanging like a side of beef from a butcher's hook, dripping, swaying, swarmed by flies. She was disgusted and furious because she had trusted him to protect her and now she was deserted and alone, with the full consciousness that men were nothing but meat. She opened her eyes and screamed his name but then pinched them shut again as the sound echoed in her ears, and she saw him lying in a field, his empty skull a cup for maggots. Then she slapped her own face, over and over, for there were maggots there, too. "I see you?" she cried, her body a confusion of heat and cold, her clothes on and off, her voice switching between a croak and a wail. A scrap of light had foiled the heavy curtains and moved halfway across the room, but she never once wondered at the hour. Pain was an opaque shroud with no future. It pressed into her eyes and ears and throat, and she wished for death. But she felt the tears on her face and knew the dying didn't weep. Sobs racked her body and hate rushed in to fill the void, and if Frank had walked through the door that very instant and stood before her, she would've killed him with her bare hands. "I see you!" she screamed, and found the shears again and pushed back the hair from her damp face, her hands merely collaborating. When they rejoined in her lap, one held her hair, the other the shears, and all energy was dissipated. The last scrap of evening light found her, and she recoiled from it. What a waste to have a body. She waited for her heart to stop, and when it didn't, she closed her eyes again and he found her. He came to her without speaking, sweeping the shorn hair from her face and putting his lips to hers. She turned into his kisses and he cupped her face and wiped her tears with his thumbs. Slowly, they removed each other's clothing. He had never before laid a hand beneath her clothes. He had never seen her naked body, nor she his. With all the eagerness of perfect innocence, she accepted the pressures and strokes of his caress, and instinctively returned their meaning. She did not shy away as he led her to the bed, didn't curl her body or cover herself.

Instead, she extended herself, stretching her long legs and opening her arms to him. Not a single impulse was checked, and she held him between her thighs with a confounding of senses. Then she looked up at his face. He had a fresh tan across his nose and at the top of his cheeks. His hair was a thicket of russet curls. That smile, those shining eyes, alive. "I see you," Frank said to her. "I see you," Jane replied, gazing at him until she was pushed under by the dead hand of sleep.

◦⟨e⟩◦

WHEN HE CAME home from the swamp that night and changed his shirt, he looked down at the old wound and massaged the puckered skin, thinking he could feel the slivers of bone and metal still lodged inside him, the shattered junk scraping together beneath his flesh. He poured himself some whiskey and sat on the porch, watching the horses and the thin spiral of clouds blowing in from the north.

It had been the same most nights the past two weeks, and he was no longer surprised when he heard shuffling behind him and the creak of the door as Coley stepped outside with an empty glass. The boy helped himself to some whiskey, like it was the most natural thing in the world, and sat in the other chair, his bare feet on the rail and his eyes looking up where the chiseled treetops cut into the black sky. "So what happened with Iron Bull?" he asked.

And Will picked up the story where he'd left off the night before, as if these midnight conversations, too, were natural as could be. "We'd been days in that rough country, coming west through the canyons around the Tongue River. There was scant grass for the mules and horses, and we found water only by chance. Dry riverbeds were filled with sage, and the hills were bare except for a few cottonwood trees. It was a hundred degrees most days, and the nights cold enough that you'd shiver yourself awake." He paused to sip his drink. "But Captain Raynolds kept us moving, and at week's end we came to the bluffs overlooking the fertile plains along the Yellowstone and saw thousands of buffalo, the rangeland black with their woolly backs, as far as you could see."

The boy leaned back in his chair, his eyes closed, glass balanced on his belly. "What about Iron Bull?" he asked again.

"We camped that night not far from Emmel's Fork," Will continued, "where the mules were hobbled along the muddy banks, filling up on salt grass that the buffalo wouldn't touch. A patrol had gone out that afternoon, and the men came back with three enormous elk, so for the first time that month we had meat and water and enough wood to cook a decent meal. At night we could see fires burning in the foothills of the Wolf Mountains just five miles away, and knew the Indians were watching us."

Coley sipped his whiskey but kept his eyes closed.

"The next morning, Iron Bull and forty others rode into our camp. The Crow were known for the horses they raised or stole from other tribes, and each man was well mounted. They were armed with bows and rifles, and though not as vicious as the Sioux, they were formidable warriors."

"Did you have to fight them?" Coley asked.

"Not all Indians came to fight."

"But they had guns."

"Yes."

"Why?"

"To show us they'd fight if they had to."

Coley sighed in acceptance, and Will went on. "Chief Iron Bull was about as fierce-looking as any man I'd ever seen, with long hair that ran down to the back of his knees, the length of it thick and shiny with gum. He wore moccasins made from grizzly bear paws and was draped in a buffalo cloak trimmed with ermine and decorated with dyed blue and yellow porcupine quills. Two lines of crimson war paint ran down his cheek like bloody tears."

"If he wasn't going to fight, how come he had on war paint?"

"To make an impression."

"And he didn't want to fight at all?"

"Not that day."

"And you weren't there to fight Indians?"

"Not that day."

Coley pushed his chair back in frustration. "Then what were you sent to do?"

"We were looking for wagon routes through the Yellowstone Valley."

"But you were traveling with the army."

"The Topographical Corps. I accompanied them as a field surgeon."

"But you had a rifle, right?"

"I did."

"And you were ready to fight Indians if you had to, right?"

"Yes, but we tried to avoid it."

"But you would've if you'd had to."

"If we had to, yes," Will replied, turning to face him directly. "Provocation's the worst enemy in Indian territory. There are problems enough without compounding them."

Coley frowned and settled in his chair, his knees wobbling back and forth. "That's fine by me. But when I go west, I'm gonna fight Indians."

"When you go west, I hope the Indian wars are over."

"Not me," Coley said before he finished the whiskey in his glass. "I'm going all the way to California, and if an Indian gets in my way, I'll shoot him where he stands."

Will sipped his drink. "Then I hope you never get west of the Missouri," he said softly. "They're too many like-minded men in the territory already."

Coley snorted and wiped his nose. "You're just saying that because you got shot by an Indian."

Will watched the boy stand up and grab the whiskey bottle that stood between them on the porch floor. He filled his glass to the brim and took a good swallow, staring out at the Shawangunk Ridge.

"You drink too much," Will said.

"So do you," Coley replied, and filled Will's glass before he set the bottle down and lowered himself into his chair again, tipping it backward, eyes raised to the black sweep of sky as his naked toes found a foothold on the railing.

As Will studied the boy in the darkness, he allowed his mind to go back to Utah. The trouble had started with the deaths of George Clayton and Henry Bean on the Montana Trail in January 1863. Until then, the Shoshone had been mostly content with nicking horses or supplies from the wagons on the freight route between Salt Lake City and the gold mines near Grasshopper Creek. But as winter came on, they grew more desperate. Clayton and Bean, carrying rifles and flour to Bannock, were ambushed near the Idaho line, where twenty of Bear Hunter's warriors materialized out of the gray snow that had just begun to fall.

The California Volunteers were now outside of Salt Lake City at Camp Douglas, hunkering down until spring. When the bodies of Clayton and Bean were brought in, they clamored to avenge the killings and put an end to the Shoshone raids that had been flaring ever since McGarry's rampage on the Gravelly Ford. The soldiers were restless, tired of the bitter cold and the sanctimonious posturing of the local

Mormons, who allowed brothers to marry sisters but inhabited a city where a decent whorehouse was hard to find and willing daughters even harder.

Colonel Connor had already begun to make preparations when word came in a week later that a band of Shoshone had attacked a group of miners at the Bear River, near Franklin. He called his officers together on the morning of January 21, all of them bundled in long coats against the cold wind that whistled through the plank walls, their wool scarves wrapped tightly around their necks and ears, even though a fire blazed in the corner. The colonel stood behind his desk and said the California Volunteers would march north the next evening and engage the enemy at their winter camp on the Bear River. Will watched McGarry nod when Connor added that "any Indian who participated in these present hostilities will be shot or hanged on the spot."

Upon hearing the news, the soldiers cheered Colonel Connor's wisdom. This would be the first battle for most of them, and they readied themselves diligently. They buffed their boots and sewed new buttons on their tunics, and all were clean-shaven for the first time since Christmas. Will watched them oil their Burnside carbines, fill their haversacks with ammunition and write letters home as they prepared for the coming crusade.

Battle fever soon infected Eli Birdslee, who questioned Will as he hadn't for many weeks. "Do you think the Indians are expecting us?" he asked.

"I don't imagine they'll be expecting anybody in the middle of January."

"And how many do you think they'll have at their winter camp?"

"I don't know."

"But we'll outnumber them?"

"I have no idea."

Eli just nodded his head and looked over Will's shoulder, staring out a window rimed with ice. "We'll teach 'em," he said.

"What will we teach them, Eli?"

"That the world's a changing place, and there's only room for those willing to change with it."

Will could hear McGarry's ruthless inflection in the boy's voice. "And if they're not willing?"

"Then the change will roll right over them," he said, and then drifted away, eager to rejoin his pal Billy Motes and ready to march.

Will rode with McGarry and the Second Cavalry, armed with a government-issue Sharps rifle and the 1847 Colt Walker pistol that his father had given him before he left New York. Connor rode alongside him for a while and admired the pistol, having used one during the Mexican War. "It sits heavy in the hand," he said, "but the damn thing shoots straighter than a Mississippi rifle."

It was a clear night when they came to the hills above Salt Lake City, the snow no deeper than the cuff on a man's pants. The infantry marched with a quick step, as anxious to keep warm as they were for battle. They headed north on the smooth bore of the Cache Valley Road and made good time in the blueing night, arriving on the outskirts of Brigham City at dawn. They lit huge bonfires on the grounds of the old courthouse, fortifying themselves with hot coffee and frozen and dried beef they had to hold in their mouths until it thawed enough to chew. By late afternoon, the sky had turned to hammered pewter and heavy snow began to blow in off the Wasatch Range. When darkness fell and Connor led the soldiers away on their nighttime march—designed to throw off any Shoshone scouts—the temperature had dropped twenty degrees and the snow was coming down thick and wet. At Wellsville, about ten miles north, they were fighting through five-foot drifts, and Connor had McGarry send his men door-to-door to roust the Mormons from their beds to help dig out the sunken howitzers.

Will had never seen a storm so horrific, and even McGarry complained when the whiskey nearly froze in his canteen. Will's own gloved hands were frozen around his reins, but he knew he was lucky to be mounted and it was the infantrymen who suffered most. When they arrived in the settlement at Mendon an hour before daybreak, Connor ordered them to break into the post office and sawmill so his soldiers could get out of the bitter, brutal cold. Will set up an infirmary in the schoolhouse, and over the course of the day examined almost a hundred men for frostbite. He'd built fires and warmed the room as best he could, and he had the men put their frozen hands in their armpits, their bare feet under their backsides, and sit side by side under blankets, quiet as punished children. Some developed blisters, a few had toes turn gray and black, and Eli helped him shave away the damaged flesh. When the sun went down and it was time to march again, seventy-five men stayed behind, unable to take the first step.

The temperature hovered right below zero when they set out, but the snow had stopped and Connor sent the wagons ahead, allowing the infantry to walk two abreast in the deep wheel ruts. When they reached Franklin, every building was commandeered, and soon the men crowded around their fires, letting the ice melt from their beards and eyebrows, the air soon reeking of singed hair as they leaned into the flames.

Will had supper with Connor and the other officers in the courthouse, where a fire blazed and they drank brandy from the bottles McGarry pulled from each of his deep pockets. "And how is the disposition of our troops?" the colonel asked them.

"They're disposed to kill Indians," McGarry grumbled. "Have been for months."

"And their general health?" Connor asked, turning to Will.

"I don't think that concerns them much at the moment," he replied.

"That's right, Dr. Harp," McGarry added. "They don't give a damn about their health. They came here to take care of the Shoshone, and that's what they're going to do. The cold won't kill them, and sure as hell neither will a frozen toe."

Connor picked up his brandy and swirled it in his cup. "We leave for Bear River at midnight."

Finishing the whiskey he still held in his hand, Will glanced over at Coley. The boy was fast asleep with his feet on the rail, no doubt dreaming of Indian battles that, for Eli Birdslee, were all too real.

◦⊚◦

IT WAS ALMOST dawn when she found herself awake in bed, her eyes wide open, her body motionless under the sheet, arms at her sides, toes pointing upward. It felt as if she'd been in this position all night long, paralyzed between dread and slumber, numb except for a heartbeat she could feel as well as hear.

There was a story Frank had told her about his grandfather that she now couldn't put out of her mind. Andrew Quinn had come to this country with his wife and son early in the century, glad to sell the small fishing boat he kept in the mirrored calm of Dingle Bay to take a job on a bluff-bowed whaling ship out of Hudson, New York. He went on a dozen consecutive two-year voyages to the heart of the North Atlantic and the waters off the Cape Verde Islands, learning enough Portuguese to keep mistresses in the busy ports of São Jorge and Pico.

When those boom days came to an end, he moved his family to Rond-out and captained a sixty-foot sloop carrying bluestone to Manhattan. But the placid river tides seemed tame compared to the rogue waves he'd crashed through off the coast of Morocco, and within a year, he gave up his life on the water. It was 1846, and he was an old man of sixty, his back as bowed as his legs from his decades at sea.

Frank was only a young boy at the time, but he remembered his grandfather well. The old man would accept the small glasses of beer he brought him throughout the day, telling him stories of hunting sperm whales off the rugged coast of Boa Vista and showing him the ancient tattoos of bare-breasted mermaids that ran down both arms, their breasts now sagging on his baggy skin.

Jane loved these stories, especially the last one Frank ever told her. "My grandfather kept a little room in the back of my parents' house," he said, "and had enough money of his own for beer and cigars. And every other evening I'd walk him down to Kelly's and stick around while he drank with the other old sailors. I'd listen to the stories that passed back and forth between them, their voices rough as stones, each taking his turn as politely as ladies in a parlor. They talked about their sailing days and women, just bantering about whatever crossed their minds. One night, while I tried to cadge a whiskey out of Kelly himself, I heard one old-timer turn to my grandfather and ask, 'Andrew Quinn, if your house was on fire and you could take only one thing away, what would that be?' And my grandfather, feeble only in body, paused just long enough to drain a pint before firing back, 'I'd take the fire.' And I sat there, with my mouth hanging open like every man at that table, and thought it was the wisest thing I'd ever heard. And if given the choice, that's what I'd do. Take the fire."

Jane opened her eyes, her body outlined by a ghost of sweat, and understood with a certainty that the fire had taken him.

September 1864

COLEY WAS ALREADY in the barn, cleaning the mud and grime off bones, when Will awoke that morning. He sat up in bed, looked out the window and saw the boy through the open barn doors. He was sitting cross-legged on the threshing floor in a quadrant of sunlight, running a dry brush over the mastodon's lower jaw as if putting a shine to a boot. Arthur was up, too, clattering around in the makeshift studio he'd set up in the small room Will's mother had used as a pantry. It was a narrow space with a wooden counter on both sides, where Arthur could organize his photographic plates and baths of nitrates and sulfates and cyanide. Though there was barely enough room for him to turn around, the pantry was dark as a root cellar and stayed cool even in the heat of the day, when the awful fumes of his chemicals lingered in the hallway. But Will didn't mind, because it saved his friend trips back and forth to town, and he was glad to have him around.

He picked up the shirt he'd worn the night before and opened his bedroom door. Looking down the hallway, he could see Pearl busy in the kitchen, swatting at the smoke that rose from the butter burning in the cast-iron pan on the stove. In the weeks that the girl had been coming to the farm, she'd tried in vain to conquer this monstrous oven that crouched in the corner like a squat black dragon. All day long she would load armfuls of wood into its belly and check its cooking surfaces with a licked fingertip, but whatever cut of meat she attempted to fry was still burned beyond taste or recognition, and Arthur joked behind her back about his fondness for "salted embers." Her grace was the perfect shortcakes she served in the morning, crusted golden on top and bottom; she made them by the dozen, and they went down well with the coffee she boiled, filling their bellies with enough fuel to get them through the day. But only Coley would gladly consume the murdered bacon and black-eyed eggs, which even the dog wouldn't touch, smiling at Pearl with brave resolve.

Will stood there in the doorway and watched as the smoke rose around her like a dark mist, smiling at the thought of the strange little family he'd acquired.

SIMPSON TRIED to stop her, but she ignored his useless chirps and barged through Grieves's door without bothering to knock. She was surprised to see her brother sitting opposite him, his legs stretched out, the two men loose as lizards and most likely pondering some odious scheme. They stared at Jane, who was glad to hold their attention. She reached into her bag, took out the black rental ledger and slammed it down on the desk. "I won't be needing this anymore, Mr. Grieves. I no longer work for you."

The two looked up at her, unblinking, as dumbfounded as if she'd just announced the war was over.

"I'm sorry about Frank, Miss Blessing," Grieves said.

"Me, too, sister," Mickey added.

She paid them no attention. "And I will keep the house—Frank's house."

"Of course," Grieves responded.

"And I'll pay you rent, the same as you charge anyone else on the street."

He just stared at her and nodded.

Jane nodded back and walked out of the office, surprised at the ease of their exchange, free of haggle or recrimination. It wasn't until she was down the stairs and back on Division Street that she realized why they'd been so gape-mouthed in her presence: It was the haircut she'd given herself after receiving Frank's letter. The next morning, she'd gotten up, wrapped herself in one of Frank's shirts and surveyed the wreckage in the parlor, then grabbed her broom and swept up all the shredded remains of her torment before she had the nerve to look at her shorn head in the mirror. Her hair, which for over twenty years she'd worn long and full, now sprang up around her scalp more like Frank's wavy locks. And she laughed at herself and wiped the tears from her cheeks. She'd gone mad, just slightly and very secretly, and she was grateful for that. A little madness made living possible.

Jane kept her laughter in abeyance as she continued down Division Street to Knetch's Bakery. Mary was at the counter arranging berry pies in the glass display. She straightened up and wiped the flour from her

hands when Jane approached, both engaged in the silent commisera-
tion they'd developed when Frank and Alfons were gone from them.

"I'm not much of a baker, and the bread I make at home isn't
fancy," Jane announced. "But I'm willing to learn, and I learn quickly,
and I'd like a job if you'll have me."

❧

HE WANDERED through the large crowd that gathered on the slope
above the swamp, carrying his heavy camera and tripod like a tramp's
bindle. One of the Smitty brothers—he didn't know which—was
pulling a small cart that held his folding tent and chemicals. He paused
a moment on a rutted cattle trace and gazed around him, overwhelmed. It seemed the whole of Ulster County had descended on
Will's property at the same time, still dressed in their Sunday best and
ready to enjoy an outing on this warm fall day. The women remained
bonneted and the men were just starting to loosen their collars, but
their children were already running wild and barefoot at the edges of
the swamp, skirt hems and pant legs splattered with mud. Picnics were
being laid out on the flattened grass, and chickens roasted over modest
fires. John Brunner, from High Falls, had tapped a keg of ale out on one
side of his wagon, while his wife ladled cider from a barrel on the other.
Two boys ran down the hill, their kites catching a burst of wind that
quickly tangled them up like fighting hawks. Arthur's eyes went everywhere at once, and he had to shut them for a moment to find his bearings.

The week before, he'd written another letter to Jean-Yves, telling
him of his definitive plans to return to Paris in the spring. They had
corresponded over the years, perhaps a long letter every four months or
so, in which they wrote about whatever seemed important or relevant
at the time. Arthur relished each humorous anecdote and mundane
fact of Jean-Yves's daily life, the personal history that made his friend
more real, and in every letter they would acknowledge in language
both unequivocal and private the brief, happy time they'd spent
together almost a decade ago. Soon after Arthur left Paris, Jean-Yves set
up his own photography studio in Montmartre and became famous for
the series of portraits he'd made of Courbet. It wasn't long before other
European artists and writers, fascinated by photography and prey to
vanity, gladly sat in his basement studio to achieve the same glorious
renown. Over the years Jean-Yves had sent Arthur copies of his photo-

graphs of Bouguereau and Manet, a young Zola and the whiskery Flaubert. Arthur's favorite was one of Nathaniel Hawthorne looking old and gray and somewhat lost when he visited Paris just a few years before. At the end of every letter, Jean-Yves always asked when he'd be returning to Paris, and now that Arthur had an answer, he hoped his friend would be as delighted by it as he was.

He'd been in great spirits since posting the letter, and he was glad to be back at the swamp. It had been a fruitful morning, and he'd already photographed Isaac Stokes and three of his wolfhounds as they walked across the ridge for their daily exercise. Arthur had caught up to him as he rested at the base of a thick oak tree, quartering apples for himself and his dogs. In shiny leather boots that laced up to his knees, a buff-colored coat with a wide belt around his thick middle and a soft felt hat expensively collapsed on his head, he was as ludicrously costumed as a Tyrolean mountaineer, and Arthur couldn't resist the urge to photograph him, just as Stokes couldn't resist the invitation to pose. He sat under the magnificent tree, rotund pasha that he was, with his silver knife in one hand and an apple in the other, the giant dogs at his side like loyal retainers.

An hour later, Arthur came across old Jacob Quick riding to the swamp on his one-eared sorrel mule. The westerly breeze had pushed his long white beard toward his left shoulder, and the long nose in the center of his face was as sharp as a baling hook. He sat the mule straight as a youngster, guiding it along with a willow stick he held in his two-fingered hand. Arthur convinced him to pause for a moment, and the old man frowned down at him with all the gravity of Elijah, not allowing the slightest twitch as Arthur made his exposure.

Now Arthur walked toward the Jug Hill families, the men as shy as the women as they picked out a patch of trampled earth away from everyone else, as exiled here as they were on the hill. They were a handsome group, some of them as dark as southern slaves and others white enough to pass as his own family, and he waited, as patiently as he could, for whichever Smitty it was to catch up so he could take advantage of the afternoon sunshine and use every last plate he carried on the wagon.

❧

HE WALKED BEHIND her as they headed across the open pasture to the swamp. She had a woven basket full of food slung over her shoulder and held another in her hand, and he enjoyed seeing her narrow waist twist as she stepped around rocks or branches in the thick grass. He was cradling Dr. Harp's cumbersome Hawken rifle in both arms; it grew heavier with each step, and he'd rather have left it in the bushes, but he'd promised both Dr. Harp and Joop House that he'd carry it with him whenever he walked Pearl back and forth. It was a small price to pay for the pleasure of her company, and he would've gladly toted a twelve-pound field gun on his back if that's what it took to be by her side. As he shifted the weight of the rifle, he had to blame somebody, and it was John Frost who bore the brunt of his bad feelings. The farmer claimed he'd glimpsed the mountain lion five days ago, and though he was half-blind from childhood measles, people in the Clove still heeded his alarm. Coley scoffed at him, praying the cat was long gone or shot dead on Overlook Mountain, because he never again wanted to see a sight as grim as the woman he'd found with Mickey. So he struggled with the rifle and scanned the trees when he wasn't scanning Pearl, because even if he didn't trust Frost's eyes, he did his own.

Pearl stopped abruptly, put down the baskets, grabbed her long black hair and pulled it tight behind her head. Coley watched her retie it with the yellow ribbon that had loosened there, then shuffled sideways on the path so he could better see the beautiful sharp angles of her profile.

"You keep staring at me like that," she said, "I'll poke your eyes out."

"You don't like being looked at?" Coley asked without turning away.

"I don't mind the looking," she said, fiddling with her bow. "It's what you're thinking about that raises the hair on my arms." She hoisted the baskets again and walked on.

Coley gripped the rifle and took off after her, marching through the tall grass until they were elbow-to-elbow. "You don't think much of me, do you, Pearl?"

"I don't think of you hardly at all."

"But you think about Dr. Harp, I bet." She didn't answer, but he could see her doing just that. And he could feel the color rising to his face as he stomped alongside her. "He's an old man."

"Not that old."

"Old enough to be your father."

"I already have a father. Ain't looking for another."

Coley shook his head, confounded by her mulishness. "You're wasting your time," he told her. "Will's got his head stuck in the mud."

"Will, is it?" she said haughtily. "What happened to Dr. Harp?"

"The hell with Dr. Harp!" he blustered. "I can take care of you better than he could."

Pearl glanced at his blotchy face and couldn't help but smile.
"You're a boy."

"Not for long I'm not! And you'll be sorry when that day comes,
'cause I'll be in California with some other girl while you're stuck here
on Jug Hill waiting for Dr. Harp to come out of that swamp!"

She shifted the food basket on her shoulder and looked up at the
ridge where the sightseers had left their wagons. She knew she had a
gift for riling boys, and sometimes she regretted it. Coley meant her no
harm. He was more considerate than most of them, and though he lavished her with attention like the rest, she couldn't hold it against him.
She reached into the basket with her free hand and pulled out an apple.
He was close enough so that she could nudge him, and when he
glanced up, she tossed it to him. "So you're going to California?" she
asked.

"That's right," he said, his tone still rough. "As soon as we get this
mastodon built and done, I'm heading west."

"What are you going to do?"

He took a bite of his apple and thought about it as he chewed and
swallowed. "First I'm going to see the cities of Chicago and St. Louis,
'cause it might be the only chance I get; then I'll take a train as far as I
can and cross the Missouri River up by Omaha. I figure I'll buy a horse
there and ride out along the Platte, through the Dakota Territory and
out to Fort Bridger, where the Bannock and Shoshone Indians live.
There's fur traders and hunters there, too, and I'll travel with them
over the mountains into Utah and then into the Sierras, where I might
stake a claim and look for gold. After that I'll make my way to San
Francisco and Los Angeles and settle down for a time in whichever one
suits me better."

"But what will you do?"

Coley's voice grew husky as he contemplated his future. "I'll get a
job on a horse ranch or run cattle or join the army and chase Indians.
Maybe after that I'll go work for a newspaper or join a survey expedition or travel into Mexico and send letters to the girl I got in San Francisco or Los Angeles, telling her all about it. And then when I get back
home, maybe I'll write a book that folks back east like you can read

and wonder about. There's plenty I can do, and I figure to take my time doing it."

"You got big plans," Pearl told him.

"I've been thinking about it."

"Sounds like you got no room for a girl anywhere."

He looked at her indignantly. "I got room. That's one thing I always got room for." Then he took one of her baskets, hefted the rifle over his shoulder and escorted her to the swamp.

HER DAYS SEEMED different now that she no longer started them at the post office. She still visited every few days, in the afternoons, when she was done at the bakery. From the very beginning it was Mr. Acly who'd seemed more distressed by the breaking of her routine, but now he said nothing and just craned his neck as he looked at her, perplexed as a baby bird.

She resumed the normal pattern of her life, though the change was hardly noticeable, and she soon realized that life continued in its awkward jolt, sunrise to sunset and back again, and that all around her wives worried, lovers mooned and mothers lamented, all the women of the town and countryside with weeping hearts and far away from the battles that seemed a continent apart from the America they inhabited: husbandless, childless and bereft.

On her days off, she rode Solomon. She'd cut back on his hay, and though he kicked the stall and snuffed the dirt floor looking for scraps, in two weeks she could see the difference in his appearance, and she started cinching the girth tighter around his shrinking belly. On warm days they headed out past the brickyards, where a few farms remained and fertile land ran down to the banks of the Hudson. They'd canter through the river shoals, scattering the wood ducks and canvasbacks that dabbled the surface, until Solomon's strong chest was lathered and her hands were sore from gripping the reins. Then she'd walk him farther into the river, up to his withers, and they'd cool off as the water lapped up around them. As she became more confident, their journeys stretched into hours. She gave up on conformity and bought a pair of boy's boots from Bill Welch's shop on Garden Street, took in a pair of Frank's old canvas pants and rode astride, ignoring the clucking and muffled oaths of proper men and women who thought this improper. When they were brave enough to face her, she held their gaze and defied their contempt, because the horse she rode had once belonged to someone better than they were and now belonged to her. If they perceived her as slightly lunatic, she didn't care.

One afternoon, the clouds that rolled in off the Catskills suddenly massed and curdled above them. Within minutes the wind shook the treetops, carrying with it buckshot rain that was cold as ice. The thunder spooked Solomon, and she let him gallop home along the road, which turned to mud beneath his hooves. They raced through the storm and then ahead of it, and by the time they got to Rondout it was only drizzling, and east of Chestnut Street it hadn't rained at all, the sky blue and unbothered.

Back home, she brushed Solomon until the mud flaked off and his coat shone, then fed him early, adding a few crab apples to the hay she forked into his stall. She was tired and filthy, thinking only of the long bath she'd take that evening, staying submerged in the tub long enough for the hot water to cool and muddy around her. When she walked into the kitchen to light a fire, she was surprised to find Mickey sitting at the table with Charlie O'Fay, eating the cold chicken she'd cooked the day before.

"Hello, sister," he said, a drumstick in his hand.

"What are you doing here?" she asked.

"I've come to have supper with you."

"If there's anything left, I'd be pleased to share it," she replied, unable to keep the brass out of her voice.

Mickey smiled and took another bite. "I'll spend the night, too, if you don't mind."

"You're always welcome," she said. "You know that."

"And I thank you for your hospitality."

"And your chicken," O'Fay piped in, chewing with his mouth open.

"Thank you, Mr. O'Fay."

He nodded vigorously. "Good, good chicken. But if you don't mind my saying so, you look a mess, Miss Blessing."

"Yes I do," she said, running a hand through her storm-battled hair, now short as a boy's, and thinking again of her bath. "And I thank you for that observation, as well."

O'Fay gave her a wink, pulled a wing off the half-devoured carcass and stood. "I'll bring the horses in the morning, Mickey."

"First light, Charlie boy."

"First light," he said as he pushed through the door with his greasy fingers.

She knelt before the hearth and lit the kindling under the kettle. "Where are you going so early in the morning?"

"I thought I'd take a ride out to see the elephant bones."

"What?"

"The bones that doctor dug up in Vandeman's swamp."

"The mastodon?"

"If that's the monster's name, yeah."

She rose to her feet and faced him. "And what's your sudden interest in those bones?"

"It's the blather on every lip and tongue," he said. "You can't step into a tavern or stop on a street corner without hearing comment on those damn bones. I just want to see what all the fuss is about."

"Since when are you interested in anybody else's fuss?"

"I've got the curiosity of a common man, Jane, nothing more."

When he turned his head away, she moved with him. "It's Grieves who's sending you, isn't it?"

"He's got no command over my personal urges."

"It's trouble he wants, isn't it?"

"If he wants anything, I ain't privy to his wishes."

"I'm going with you," she told him.

"You're welcome to."

"Welcome or not, I'm going."

BY NOW HE was used to the crowds and didn't even look up as they swarmed around him, treating his property like a great amphitheater while he knelt in the swamp below them, an actor in a Greek drama. The weekends were always the most celebratory, when bystanders came countywide to gawk at the bones being dredged from the swamp, then stayed on to eat a meal and drink a draft of beer or a dram of rum as they chatted with neighbors and friends.

The swamp became his haven. The tall boots he used that summer were now permanently warped and stained, and all his shirts carried a faintly gray watermark that ran under his arms and across his sleeves. Joop House and the Smitty brothers still came down from Jug Hill every morning, but mostly they ran the waterwheel for the children and shuttled the last of the bones back to the farm, where Coley sorted through them and numbered each one according to his chart. Will still entered the water every morning, moving inch by inch, carefully poking his iron pole into the mud, almost in a trance, while the crowds murmured around him and the waterwheel squeaked in its endless rotations. For hours at a time he could ignore the distractions, and even on this Sunday when the work was all but done, he still enjoyed the quiet hum of concentration as he made one last pass through the brown ooze that bubbled around his boots.

That morning, Arthur had called him out of the swamp to meet with Jerrold Hazelhurst from *Harper's Weekly*. It was the reporter's third visit, and he was making notes for an article to be published the following month.

"And does the antiquity of the great beast correspond with the antiquity of man?" he asked in a voice that boomed from the pit of his stomach.

"Yes, it's possible that early man and the mastodon coexisted."

"Coexisted, you say?" Hazelhurst barked. "How many savages do you think your mastodon plucked up with his tusks and gnashed with his teeth?"

"Judging from the teeth we've uncovered," Will told him, "it's more likely the mastodon gnashed on leaves and bark."

"A creature of such immensity certainly couldn't survive on simple vegetation, Dr. Harp. Bones and flesh are what it craved, I'm sure of it, and I pity the poor Indian who hunted it alone with bow and spear."

"It was a slow-footed mammal, Mr. Hazelhurst. I doubt it could've outrun an Indian."

Hazelhurst ignored him, lost in his own thoughts. He was a tall man, with great waves of curly brown hair and wild eyebrows to match. "The giant must've had quite a presence, wouldn't you say, Dr. Harp?"

"Yes, I'm sure it was quite impressive."

"And those tusks. Sharp enough to breach a man from breastbone to coccyx. Fiercer than an African tiger, I'd say."

Will glanced at Arthur as the journalist took another deep breath, ready to expound again.

"Can you not hear the roar of it, Dr. Harp? Strong enough to scare jays from the trees! And to think it roamed our own continent, this very bit of soil we stand upon now."

"Yes," Will replied. "And I thank you for that last observation. It's the one thing you've said this morning that has a ring of truth."

Arthur grinned, and Hazelhurst looked at the two men solemnly.

"They might stretch the truth, Dr. Harp, but I wouldn't call my ruminations entirely fictitious, would you?"

"They teeter on the brink of possibility, Mr. Hazelhurst, I'll give you that. Still, every theory is valid until it's proven false. I have strong doubts about the viciousness of your mastodon, but there's much we don't know about him."

"Then you'll allow me a certain latitude in my depiction of your discovery?"

"As long as you include the basic facts of its existence and quote only yourself, you can make all the suppositions you'd like."

"So with your permission, I'll address this article with a flourish." He acknowledged the swamp with a great contented sigh, then turned to Arthur. "Have you the photographs I requested, Mr. Dowd?"

"Yes. I had them sent to your hotel in Kingston."

"Splendid!" Hazelhurst said. "They'll make fine engravings to display in the *Weekly*." He folded his notebook, shoved it into the outside pocket of his jacket and held out his hand.

Will shook it. "You have a fine imagination, Mr. Hazelhurst."

"The imagination of my readers is the only thing that concerns me," he countered.

Now Will looked up at the men and women gathered on the grassy slope above him. This was a diversion that took their thoughts away from the war and allowed them to marvel at a strange long-dead creature that had trampled this valley ten thousand years ago, a brute so beyond the reach of their ordinary lives that they couldn't truly grasp its existence until they saw for themselves the bones that he'd salvaged from the muck. So he continued to trudge through the brown mire, shutting out the sibilation of dragonflies and mosquitoes, leaning on his iron pole as rigorously as Thoreau on his walking stick, and contemplated the swamp as if it were his own Walden Pond.

◦◦◦

THEY LEFT THEIR horses with Abbot Barnes at his makeshift corral on top of the ridge, each paying the little man a three-cent piece for the service. Barnes, a feisty old Jug Hill farmer bowlegged with arthritis, couldn't finish a sentence without hawking up a long squirt of tobacco that left his mouth like some crazy insect. "Thank ye," he said, as if his blood was more Dutch than colored. "Horses will be standin' ready when you are." Mickey could barely understand a word, and he looked away as if the man's yellow-eyed gaze might be contagious.

They followed Jane down to the swamp, and Mickey was surprised by how many men he recognized. When they saw John Brunner dispensing beer from the keg on his wagon, Charlie stopped as if dumbfounded by his good luck. "I'll be along, Mickey," he said. "My mouth's a bit dry from the ride, and I just need to fill it with a little sputter."

Mickey frowned, losing sight of his sister for a moment before glimpsing her at the edge of the swamp. She was standing next to Arthur Dowd and waving to a man in the water. And when the man looked up, Mickey noticed his sudden smile and the widening of his eyes. Jane's presence seemed to breathe life into him, and he stepped briskly from the muck. Then Mickey glanced at his sister, her face bathed in warmth, and realized he hadn't seen her like that in a year.

He came up behind her, catching the man's attention first. Only when Jane saw it register in Will's eyes did she turn to face him.

"Will, this is my brother, Mickey," she said. "And this—"

"Good morning, Dr. Harp," Mickey jumped in. "It's a pleasure to meet you. I've heard all—"

"He works for Harry Grieves," Jane said, interrupting him.

Mickey ignored his sister and just stared at Will. Will stared back, his expression unruffled. "Are you working for Grieves today?"

"I'm a man on my own," he replied lightly. "Just out for a Sunday in the country, like my sister and Charlie O'Fay and most everyone else I know. All of us gathered around your little swamp, Dr. Harp."

When Mickey let loose a companionable laugh, Will saw the apprehension on Jane's face.

Mickey turned to Arthur, who was standing to the side, nervous as a hen. "And how are you, Mr. Dowd?"

"Fine, Mickey."

"Taking your photographs, are you?"

"That's right."

"Little different from your work in the studio, eh, Mr. Dowd? How'd you like me to pose with one of them big bones? Perhaps with my lovely sister, Jane. I'm sure you can give us some direction." His eyes were keen and merciless, and Will watched Arthur flinch as Mickey turned back to him. "Speaking of giant bones, are there any lying about, Dr. Harp?"

Will lifted his chin toward the north end of the swamp. "There are some by the wagon."

"Then perhaps I'll go see what all the excitement is about." He nodded at Will and started off, but after ten steps he turned around and held out both hands. "I'm here because I want to be, Dr. Harp, make no mistake about that, but Mr. Grieves does send along his good wishes," he said, his eyes sparking. "He and I both believe that goodwill can be spread on almost any occasion. Don't you think so, Dr. Harp?"

The smile never left his face as he spun around without waiting for an answer, walking jauntily toward the wagon.

Bob Baggs spotted Mickey from high on the hill. He was sitting in the old ladder wagon from Engine Company Number 3 that Foreman Hamblin had allowed him to purchase the year before. Baggs kept it painted the same color gold as the brass on his buttons, and he left the city seal on the sideboards, though the wagon no longer carried fire-fighting apparatus. Its long bed was filled with Bumble Bees dressed in half boots and slim-cut trousers, jackets and pants buttoned tight as those of boulevard swells, felt hats brushed and cocked low on their foreheads.

Baggs was already sweating in his dark herringbone town coat, his face as slick as if he'd dunked it in a bowl of water. His boots were on the footrest and his knees up around his chest as he leaned forward to watch Mickey.

Jesse Gray sat at his side, spitting out the seeds of an orange he was eating, the juice dripping down his waistcoat. He followed Baggs' gaze and squinted. "Ain't it the prick Mickey Blessing?"

"It is," Baggs replied. "It is."

He slowed down, trailing Pearl up the slope. He'd never seen so many Jug Hill people in one place before, and it made him skittish. Of course he knew Joop and the Smitty brothers and some of the other farmers who came down to Rondout to buy horses from Shapiro and have drinks at the one saloon they were allowed to visit, a place the locals called Nigger Bob's. But those men were as black as most of the Negroes who lived in shanties along German Street, and it startled him that Pearl came from the same stock.

He saw Tally and Sam House sitting together as they always did, knees touching as if fused that way. Joop was squatting by the side of a wagon with a darker woman, who was cutting slices of pie. She glanced up as he and Pearl trudged along the side of the hill. "What are you doing here?"

"I come to see the baby."

"Don't you see enough of that baby morning and night?" she asked her daughter before looking at Coley. "And who you dragging up here with you?"

"This is Coley Hinds," she said without slowing down. "He works for Dr. Harp."

"Boy works with you, Joop?" Sallie asked her husband.

"Yes, he does."

Sallie went back to slicing her pie. "Coley Hinds," she grumbled, as if his name was something you'd find stuck to the bottom of your shoe.

Pearl walked quickly past her mother and knelt down next to a woman leaning against a wagon wheel. She carefully lifted a thick bundle out of the woman's arms and was bringing it to her chest when Coley caught up with her. The smile on her face was genuine and pure and made her more beautiful than ever. Then she showed him the baby, who was fast asleep, swaddled in white-and-blue muslin. His little pink fingers were curled into fists, and there was a crust around his lips from his last feeding. And Coley could see curlicues of blond hair on the pale scalp that showed from under the blanket.

"This is him," Pearl whispered, "the baby I found."

Coley nodded, almost afraid to breathe as she held it up for his inspection. It was the whitest thing he'd ever seen.

"They look like cow bones to me. Big cow."

"It's no cow."

"Horse, maybe. Big horse."

"No horse, either, Charlie."

They stood on the edge of the swamp, looking down at the mastodon bones laid out in the grass. They were stained brown as old wood, like something bronzed for immortality and carrying ancient secrets. They reminded Mickey of a story his uncle had told him when he was a boy, about a huge creature that roamed the woods of Ballinderreen. "It was only seen in the midnight shadows—a big black beast that stood tall as the rooftops, with sharp claws that stripped the bark from trees and left ruts in the roadway, its moan as chilling as a thousand banshees," Joe told him and Jane as they sat on their porch on Dutch Hill. "Loud enough to put a crack in the moon. They say it preyed on crying babies, snatching them from their cradles while their parents slept, and one night on the road to Galway City, I swear I saw the thing myself spitting out bonnets and pieces of lace. Big as a church, it was, and grown fat on little boys and girls who couldn't keep their yaps shut," he went on, staring at Mickey, who was still young enough to wail at night for his dead parents. "They say the creature left Ballinderreen when the famine came and took away his nourishment. Dove straight into the Galway Bay and swam the ocean to Manhattan Island, where it lives today, still feeding on plump Irish children who thought they'd got away." The story had so frightened Mickey that for months he'd stuffed socks in his mouth to stop from crying in bed.

"It's not of this earth, then, whatever it is," Charlie muttered.

Mickey could smell the beer stink rising off Charlie's skin, and it made him sick to his stomach. "Not anymore, it ain't," he said. "Let's go."

They walked along the path that bordered the far side of the swamp, through a thicket of huckleberry bushes that had been picked clean by scavenging turkeys. Even at this distance they could hear the crowd on the hillside across from them.

"And that's the thing I can't shake when I close my eyes at night," she told him as they came around and took the path back to the wagon. "Was he frightened? Was he in terrible pain? Or did it happen so quickly that he felt nothing at all?"

"Some things are best left unknown."

Jane shook her head. "I can't do that. I want to know everything. I want to know what he saw and what he shut his eyes to. What he was thinking of as he took his very last breath." She glanced at Will and tried to smile. "I'm selfish enough to wonder if he thought of me, and I hope that he did, because there would've been comfort there, because he knew I loved him, and I have no doubt at all that he loved me. That's the good of it. We had that at least."

"You did."

"But I can't kneel at his grave and ask, because there's no grave to visit."

Nearing the wagon, they saw Pearl and Coley coming down the hillside, the girl carrying something in her arms, the long hem of her dress lost in the short grass, which made her seem to float. Coley walked alongside, his arms swinging back and forth with all the wildness of youth.

"I'll never know what happened."

"It's enough to know that Frank was a brave man."

"There are tens of thousands of brave men. And just as many women." At the wagon, she stopped and turned to him. "You saw men die."

"Yes."

"And you heard their cries."

Will could barely look at her. "Yes."

"I hear them, too, and it's a sound I can't abide."

"Frank wouldn't want you to suffer."

"But he knew I would," she said, wiping the tears from her face. "It was his choice to go." She looked over the swamp. "You're lucky. You have something to occupy your mind. You have this to come to every day."

"Yes."

She turned back to him. "But what will you do when your mastodon's done? What will fill your time then?"

Before he could answer, Pearl and Coley came around the wagon. Jane turned away as Pearl grinned and held up a baby sleeping in a blanket. "Here he is," she said. "Moses is what we call him."

Will admired the baby. "He's a handsome boy."

"Yes, he is," Pearl said proudly, gently rocking the child in her arms.

"And no one's claimed him?"

"Sheriff Winnie checked every town from Ellenville to Kripplebush, and no one's looking for a baby. I guess he just belongs to Jug Hill now."

"Coley boy!"

He jumped when he heard the loud voice behind him and turned to see Mickey, all teeth and guff, grinning as if Coley was an old friend raised from the ashes. Mickey was a great mimic of cheeriness and goodwill, but Coley didn't trust him for a second.

"Getting your hands dirty, are you, working for Dr. Harp?" he went on, winking at the boy. "It's a fine effort you're making, but I must say it's lonely on the Strand without you running about. Isn't that so, Charlie?"

"Yes, it's true," O'Fay said, scratching the hump of his broken nose. "Watching you boys work the docks was one of the great pleasures of my day."

"And then the fog lifts and you're gone."

"Not a word for your old pals."

"When I saw the old Jew, he said you left the stable quick as a ghost," Mickey added. "Not even a hair left on your pillow."

"Sorry, Mickey" was all Coley could stutter.

"Nothing to be sorry about, Coley boy!" Mickey thundered, his smile razor-sharp. "As long as you weren't dragged off by murdering Indians, my heart's appeased." And then his eyes drifted over to Pearl, who stood at Coley's side with her lips drawn tight and her eyes narrowed. She was a beautiful girl, and the sight of her smoothed his temper. Recognizing her from the wall of photographs at Dowd's studio, he let his gaze linger on her fine-looking face and saw her cheeks flush.

"You look like you're about to spit nails," he said to her, almost laughing, and then noticed the baby in her arms, who was poking out his head and yawning, eyes pinched and small fists boxing the air. He was as unexceptional as most babies, pink and fussy, and Mickey wouldn't have given him a second glance if not for the blond frizz on top of his head. He looked more closely, studying his pug nose and the faint yellow down of his eyebrows, and when the baby opened his eyes and looked right at him, Mickey stood up so straight, it was as if a knife was being drawn up his spine. "Whose baby is it?" he asked so forcefully that Pearl pulled the child away. "Where did he come from?"

"He's a Jug Hill baby," Coley replied quickly, stepping closer to Pearl.

"That's no Jug Hill child," Mickey said. "Where did you get him?"

"He's mine," Pearl snapped.

"That's one thing he's not," Mickey snapped back. "Where did you get him?"

"Mickey," Jane said softly, putting a hand on his shoulder.

Mickey flung it off, staring at the baby. "Give him here, girl!"

When he reached for the baby, Coley jumped between them, smashing his full weight into Mickey and wrenching his arm, but Mickey spun around and elbowed Coley on the chin. When the boy started to fall, Mickey held him up and twisted the front of his shirt in his hand and raised his other fist to break the boy's nose. Coley looked up at him with dazed eyes, his lip already split and bleeding.

Will stepped up and seized Mickey's arm. "That's enough."

His fist still cocked, his knuckles white as granite, Mickey stood there blind with rage, the shouts of Charlie and his sister a dull hum, as if heard from underwater. Then his head cleared, and it was Will Harp he was looking at, not the baby. He breathed again and felt the stiffness leave his body, easing his grip on Coley and letting him fall to the ground. He looked over Will's shoulder at the people eyeing him furtively, and the dozens more on the hillside above the swamp, oblivious to everything but the beauty of the afternoon. Then he turned around and walked off, knowing he could claim his son another day.

***

"WHAT'S WRONG WITH you?" Charlie asked as they rode back down the Clove road. "It was only a baby, for Christsakes. Girls on Jug Hill pluck 'em out of their wombs as easily as they do potatoes from the fertile ground."

Mickey ignored him, thinking of how much Hannah had changed that morning he first pulled the dress from her shoulders. He'd made her pregnant and, in the act of filling her with child, hollowed out her soul. Her heart still beat, but she was as dead to the world as her husband.

"It's just another Jug Hill nigger," Charlie continued. "Don't matter what color it is, it's always gonna have that taint."

From the beginning he'd hoped it was a boy she carried, cherishing the pregnancy and what was to come. Hannah soon stopped caring about anything, drifting vacantly through each day and night. And that's what he saw in the baby's eyes when they had opened and looked at him: that same blue stare, lost and woebegone.

"Mickey," Charlie said.

And now he would make things right, bide his time, take the baby away and raise him as his own.

"Mickey," Charlie hissed.

He looked up and saw the fire wagon blocking the road in front of them. Bob Baggs sat on the rail in the center, knees splayed and hands on hips. Jesse Gray and three other Bumble Bees stood in the bed behind him, armed with thick wooden clubs and iron shovels and long-shafted hammers. Mickey brought Dutch Eddy to a halt next to Charlie's horse and looked around him, the sun bright in a clear sky and the maples just starting to burn with fall color, and he couldn't help but admire the striking beauty of the world.

"Hello, Bob Baggs!" he shouted. "You're a long way from home."

"So are you, you Irish fuck," Baggs replied without moving an inch.

"Oh, Bob, that's no language for a Sunday."

"Get off your fucking pony."

"Now why would I do that, Bob?"

"So that no harm will come to the animal when I beat you to a bloody pulp."

"You don't want to fight me, Bob, not today. No good will come of it."

"The good will be the blood on my knuckles and the toe of my boots. Now get off that fucking horse or we'll drag you off."

Mickey glanced at Charlie and shrugged. Charlie didn't say a word, but when he lifted his foot in his stirrup, Mickey saw the outline of the short knife he carried in his boot. He climbed off Dutch Eddy and handed the reins to his friend. "Will it be just you and me, Bob, or will I be wrestling your dancing bears, as well?"

A smile creased Baggs's shiny face when he pushed himself off the wagon, trailing behind a long chain, the big links thick and rusted. "First whacks are mine, you prick."

Mickey's expression never changed as he watched the chain snake across the dirt. Baggs stopped twenty feet in front of him and started to collect it in his hands. "Ah, Bob, are you sure you want to do this?"

Baggs only grinned and raised the chain.

Mickey nodded and walked quickly toward him. Baggs, startled by the unexpected movement, scrambled backward and lifted the chain above his head, swinging it awkwardly, trying to pick up speed. Mickey heard the whoosh of the metal links being whipped through the air and watched them blur at eye level, and he timed the last swing and rushed forward to wrap his arms around Baggs as the chain came down and sizzled across his back, which arched with the shock of it. He used the pain to hoist Baggs into the air and spin him around, pulling the chain loose and wrapping the end that dragged in the road around Baggs's arm, twisting and yanking it tight; then he kicked him to the ground and faced the other Bumble Bees, who still stood in the wagon, stunned by the suddenness of it.

"Drop your playthings, boys, or I'll break his arm."

Jesse Gray jumped off the wagon with a hammer held high and took two steps before Mickey put his boot on Baggs's neck, jerked the chain and broke his arm at the shoulder. He howled in agony and tried to crawl away, but Mickey stalled him with a kick. "Be a good girl, Bob," he cooed, wrapping the chain around Baggs's other arm and glancing back at Gray. "Take one more step and I'll break this one, too."

Gray stopped and looked down at Baggs crying in the dirt, blood and snot smeared across his face and shirt, and when he dropped his hammer, the other men in the wagon did the same.

"Grab their toys, will you, Charlie?" Mickey yelled over his shoulder, then turned back to Gray. "Now untie your horses and send 'em home."

Gray hesitated until Mickey put pressure on the chain and Baggs moaned, then did as he was told.

Feeling the blood trickling down his spine, Mickey watched Charlie collect the weapons as Gray unhitched the horses from the wagon. "Toss 'em to the sparrows, Charlie." Charlie laughed as he flung the hammers and shovels and clubs into the trees. And when the horses were galloping off, Mickey scanned the Bumble Bees' faces. "Now push that wagon out of my way."

Gray paused for a moment, looking at the high slope above the road and the deep gully below it. "Goddamn you, Blessing," he whimpered, then grabbed the wagon's long tongue with the three other Kingston men. They heaved with all their might, sending it plunging end over end into the thicket at the bottom of the ditch.

Mickey bent over to look Baggs in his scarlet face, ropy blood hanging from his mouth and nose, his broken arm bent upward at his side. "How're you feeling, Bob?"

"Fuck you, you Irish cunt," he spit out. Mickey just smiled, put a boot on his back and snatched the chain again, pulling until his other arm snapped like a tree limb.

~⊙~

HE WAS FINE, just a little dazed, when they took him back to the farmhouse. Jane tied Solomon to the back of the wagon and rode up front with Will and Arthur while Pearl ministered to the boy in back. She sprinkled a little sugar on a piece of bread and made Coley hold it to his broken lip to stop the bleeding. Numb with her attention, he tried to sound brave as he mumbled "Thank you" around his swollen tongue.

He fell asleep soon after dark, calmed by the whiskey he'd taken for medicinal purposes. Later, Will poured himself a drink, took the lantern off the porch rail and walked to the barn, Rump racing ahead to bark at raccoons that might be hiding in the hay bales. Leaving the doors open to let in the sharp moonlight, he looked at the array of bones laid out on the platforms in front of him. Coley had done a fine job of cataloging them, and tomorrow they'd begin putting the skeleton together.

Before Arthur escorted Jane back to Rondout, Will had asked how he knew Mickey Blessing.

His friend flushed. "He sometimes poses for me in the studio with the young ladies a client sends up from New York. It's not work I'm particularly proud of, but it's a profitable assignment I accepted a few years ago and find myself too greedy to sever," Arthur said as he cinched his saddle tighter. "Mickey can be a charming fellow, but don't take him for a fool."

"I won't, Arthur."

"Do not take him lightly. Neither him nor Harry Grieves."

"I understand."

Standing in his barn and looking at the bones, he didn't give a damn about Grieves or Mickey Blessing or anything beyond the work at hand. He'd stay on the farm for as long as it took him to resurrect his mastodon, or as long as he wanted to, and Grieves would have to live with it.

Back in the house, he checked on Coley. The boy slept fully dressed on top of his bed, snoring gently, his bottom lip purple and swollen into a pout. Next to his outstretched hand was a copy of Edward Bonney's *The Banditti of the Prairies*, a lurid account of thieves and murderers along the Mississippi River. The red squirrel sat on top of the headboard, hovering over him like a proper nurse. Will shut the door before the little dog could get inside, poured himself another drink and went back outside to sit on the porch. His body was tired but his mind fully awake, and he hoped that the whiskey would let the two have a proper squaring off. He gazed into the warm, lambent night, sipping his drink and thinking about the boy and what Jane had asked him earlier.

The quarter moon had been bright in the southeast sky when the California Volunteers left Franklin and marched through the deep snowdrifts rolling like a blue ocean through the Utah Territory. Will rode behind McGarry, and behind him were Eli Birdslee and Billy Motes, the boys wrapped in heavy blankets against the cold. Fortified by the whiskey he nipped, McGarry seemed unaffected by the weather, his big horse stepping sprightly through snow that plowed back from his knees. They didn't talk much, each man occupied with his own misery.

It was daybreak when the troops arrived on the bluffs overlooking the Bear River, and Will rode up to get a better view of the Shoshone encampment below. It was a mile away on the flat plain across from the wide, rushing river. Behind the camp was a deep ravine tangled with willow and scrub, which formed a natural barrier to the west. Higher bluffs flanked the north and south sides of the village, protecting it from the harsh winter winds. Will counted over seventy lodges grouped tightly together, each wrapped with buffalo hides and built on foundations of packed dirt and stone. Greasy threads of black smoke spiraled up from each lodge, dirtying the pristine sky. A couple hundred horses stomped in the snowy pastures, and Will imagined in the spring this was good grazing land. He took out his Tumelle field glasses and scanned the dozen warriors standing in front of the village and watching the soldiers line up on the ridge high above. Two of them hoisted their old Whitney rifles as they paraded in the trampled snow, and when their long robes fell open, he could see that each man had pistols tucked into his belt.

"They've been expecting us," he told McGarry.

"Of course they have. They've known of our intent ever since we left Mendon." He borrowed the binoculars, and as he studied the Indians, Will saw little daggers of ice on the ends of his frozen mustache. "I'd say there are four or five hundred, half children and squaws, the rest fair game."

"They'll make a stand."

"Oh, yes. We'll give them no choice."

In the next hour, Colonel Connor and the infantry joined them on the bluff. The artillery pieces were still a quarter mile behind them, buried in snowbanks, which held them fast as concrete. Will knew this was foolishness, that no good would come of it, but the colonel, so eager to engage the enemy, ordered McGarry and his cavalry to cross the river and surround the village without benefit of artillery.

Forty men took the trail from the top of the bluff, their horses' hooves as slick as sleigh runners as they glided down the slope. Even from this far away, Will could hear the Shoshone's yips of laughter carrying across the valley like an insult.

The sun was up now but provided little warmth. The river was almost two hundred feet across, the steep banks crenellated with jagged stars of ice, the water like braided silver and swift with winter runoff. Two horses balked, and one of them reared and dropped Billy Motes into the frozen stream. He high-footed it out as if he were dancing through fire, then pulled his pistol; only McGarry's intervention saved the horse from being shot between the eyes.

On Connor's orders, Will stayed on the east bank and set up a field hospital. He requested that Eli assist him, but McGarry insisted the boy was needed in battle.

Will watched through the binoculars as McGarry gathered his men in front of the Indian camp and had them dismount. They moved forward, rifles in their bloodless hands, teeth chattering as they awaited orders. A young Indian, taller than the others and dressed in elk skins and bark leggings, rode out from the village on a handsome pinto. His two long braids were wrapped in otter fur, and he wore a necklace of twisted sweetgrass and porcupine quills. Both his ears were pierced, and a large cluster of hair-pipe beads hung almost to his shoulders. The rifle strapped across his back bounced as he pranced his horse back and forth in the snow, showing off for the other warriors, who laughed at his antics. He kept his back to the soldiers, taunting them, the disdain evident in his posture, and carried a long spear he poked high into the air; it wasn't until Will adjusted the focus that he saw a long scalp dangling from the end of it. McGarry saw it, too. He raised his Sharps rifle as the Indian galloped back into the village, and the first shot of the confrontation was fired. But it wasn't the major who fired it.

A small burst of musket discharge rose above the Indian camp, and Will swung his binoculars and quickly scanned the row of soldiers, stopping when one spun around, the man's eyes rolling up as if to spot the bullet lodged in his forehead. But he couldn't see it, only Will could, and he stared at the small black hole in the soldier's skull and the spidering of blood that glistened there before the man sank to his knees in the snow.

Now Will listened to Rump snoring at his feet, and the swish of the horses as they moved through the pasture. He finished his whiskey and thought about having another, but he knew it wouldn't help him sleep. Already the far reaches of the sky were showing a metallic brightness, and he was wide awake. He took the lantern from the table and, with the little dog walking smartly at his heels, went back to the barn to work on his bones.

~ↄⒺↄ~

COLEY WOKE in the middle of the night, his jaw aching and the taste of blood still in his mouth. He gently ran his tongue along the inside of his swollen lip, probing where his teeth had broken the skin, and thought about the look on Mickey's face; he could've crushed Coley if he'd wanted to, ending his days with a single punch to the head. He sat up for a moment, making sure his legs and head were no longer wobbly, and walked from his room. The front door was open, and he looked over the porch rail and saw Will working in the barn under the pallid glow of a lantern. He ducked back inside, moved quickly to the study and went directly to the gun cabinet, which had remained unlocked since the mountain lion had been sighted. Beneath the rifle rack were two drawers that contained handguns and ammunition. He opened the bottom one and pulled out an old Colt Walker pistol that must've belonged to Will's father. He spun the cylinder to make sure it was loaded, stuck the heavy gun in the waistband of his pants and went back to his room.

～◎～

HE STOOD NAKED in front of the mirror in Gitta's bedroom and looked over his shoulder at the plum-colored bruise that ran from his neck to his lower back. The blood had blistered beneath his skin, drops of it held there like little jewels. When he squinted, it looked as if he were decorated with a crimson sash.

Gitta knelt behind him with a big porcelain bowl and gently applied a poultice of mustard to the wound. The sting of it was like needles being pushed under his skin, but he relaxed his bunched muscles as her fingers pressed against him.

"I ain't trying to hurt you, Mickey," Gitta told him.

"That's already been done, girl."

He braced himself against the wall as the mustard began to draw the blood away from the bruise, the warm water running down his legs and dripping between his feet. He'd heard that Baggs was laid up in his mother's parlor with both arms in maple splints, forced to sit on a chamber pot when he needed to piss, obliged to have a strange hand wipe his ass and put food in his mouth. But he didn't give a damn about him or the Bumble Bees, thinking only about his own hard luck.

"If you'd lie down, Mickey, I could cover your whole back at once."

He pushed off the wall and walked to her bed. As he eased himself across the covers, Gitta pulled a side table close and set the porcelain bowl on top of it. She carefully climbed on the bed and straddled the back of his legs. "You'll have a pretty scar," she said as she tightened her knees around his thighs.

He could feel her flesh against his own, and hear dripping water when she wrung out a fresh cloth and stretched it out the length of his back. "Isn't that better?" she asked.

He made his body go limp as the pain spread from his neck to his toes, and thought only about his son.

~⟨Q⟩~

THE SCAFFOLDING they'd built inside the barn reached higher than the anchor beam, and Coley and the Smitty brothers liked to scramble to the top of it and race one another across the wide timbers to the sapling floor where the loose hay was stored. Will put an end to their play when Earl Smitty came crashing down, flapping his arms like a fledgling pushed from his nest, landing at Will's feet in a burst of hay dust.

They'd started the mastodon's resurrection with the long whip of vertebrae that would tie the skeleton together. The iron bar that John Dillon had fabricated at the foundry had been bent to replicate the curve of the animal's spine and was almost twenty feet long. Will had measured each bone beforehand to calculate the size of the framework he would need, and he'd bought a pair of heavy iron cutters from Dillon to make adjustments when necessary. Coley had already drilled each bone with a small hole, into which Will could insert a narrow hand-forged rod or thick piece of wire.

Will started with the cervical vertebrae at the neck, fitting the bones together as he would broken pieces of crockery. Next he attached the dorsal and lumbar vertebrae, butting them together with wire and screws, watching them rise and fall along the mastodon's back as graceful as a rooster's comb. There were missing bones, of course, especially the smallest ones in the caudal vertebrae that completed the tail, and Will made casts for each one with plaster and asbestos and rabbit-skin glue. He'd begun working on these molds in the evenings after coming home from the swamp, sitting at the desk in his father's study with hunks of clay and the syrupy bowl of plaster, forming casts of various sizes, some no bigger than hickory nuts. He let Coley help him, and the boy proved so adept at blending the plaster and glue that his casts were near-perfect imitations of the ossified matter that had crumbled with the ages. Will let the boy take over that job while he stayed in the barn with a bucket of plaster and repaired any breaks or missing sections of the ribs and hind legs, working under the dim light of half a dozen lanterns that hung from the rafters like flickering stars. When all the casts and repairs were dry and solid, Will had Coley shellac and tint them so they took on the bronzed, fossilized hue of decay, but he kept them lighter to differentiate between the real and man-made.

They started at dawn each morning, keeping the tall barn doors open to let in the light, even when the rain slashed inside and splattered the dirt on the threshing floor. By the end of the first week, they had the vertebrae and ribs in place, and the skeleton took on the shape of a giant bird in flight. Arthur came up from Rondout again, taking pictures daily to document their progress. He was in good spirits, already in touch with editors at *Scientific American* and *New York Illustrated News*, who needed images for their articles on the Clove mastodon.

Each night after supper, Pearl and Tally would go back to Jug Hill, escorted by Joop or Sam, while Coley lay in his bed with the latest *New York Weekly* he had Arthur bring him from Rondout, filling his head with cowboy malarkey as he sipped from a small flask filled with rum he kept topping off from Will's bottles. Arthur would work in his cramped studio by the kitchen, and Will would retire to his father's study to go over the notes he'd been keeping ever since Vandeman had shown up with the skull in his wagon. It was a habit he had developed ten years ago, filling field notebooks with observations of the vast desert and mountain landscapes from Missouri to the California coast, and he'd worked on them almost every evening, either by the light of a campfire or on a hard bunk in a remote prairie hotel. After returning to Los Angeles, he transcribed his notes onto bigger sheets of paper, with more refined versions of his sketches, and soon found that he enjoyed the leisurely act of re-creation almost as much as the act of discovery itself. As the pages accumulated, he had them bound into larger volumes by a German bookbinder who had a shop near city hall, amassing a small library of research and disquisition that he now wished he hadn't left sitting on a dusty shelf in his house on Olivera Street. For the first time since arriving in New York, he considered having it shipped back to the Clove, thinking he might stay awhile.

"I figure I'll be leaving soon," Coley said, holding two iron bars together while Will attached the clamp that would give them strength. "I figure when we're done here, it'll be time for me to go."

They'd been working on the reinforced brace that would hold the mastodon's skull in place. The incomplete skeleton loomed above them, and Coley still looked at it in amazement every time he entered the barn. When alone, he'd stand beneath the rib cage and imagine himself to be Jonah in the belly of the whale. Will had told him about all the fantastical creatures that once had roamed the seven continents, and the week before he'd even tried reading Cuvier's *Preliminary Discourse*, getting through enough of the dense text to understand that long ago the earth had been rocked by natural catastrophes, that new forms of life had appeared and disappeared with each violent upheaval, that the bones of strange and extinct animals lay beneath the rocks and soil of the modern world.

"You're still going out west?" Will asked.

"Yep, just like I always planned."

They fit the iron bars into the triangular base of the frame, and he gripped it while Will bolted it in place. "You've been a steady hand, Coley."

"Thanks."

"When will you leave?"

Coley shrugged. "Not until we're done. End of next month, maybe. Least before the weather changes."

"And how far will you go?"

"All the way to California," he said with a smile. "And I'll be looking under every rock I see."

Will grinned at him. "You know you have a place here. You're always welcome."

"I know."

"And I have a small house in Los Angeles. You're welcome there, too."

"Thanks, Dr. Harp," Coley said as he adjusted the bars. "And maybe you'll come visit sometime."

Will tightened the last bolt and looked at the boy. "Maybe I will."

The next morning, Coley sat at the desk in the study, dressed in a white, wide-collared shirt that had once belonged to Will and a black frock coat rescued from the same cedar box. The coat was loose at the shoulders and came almost to his knees. His hair was brushed and combed for the first time since he could remember, parted on the side and the tufts flattened behind his ears, and when he passed the mirror in the hallway, he saw a boy whose nose he'd have pushed in.

Pinch sat on the corner of the desk, playing with the loose end of the gold chain attached to the watch that Coley held in his right hand.

In front of Coley was a small glass of water. He fidgeted and sighed and scratched furiously at the stiff collar, which irritated his chin.

"Settle down, Coley," Arthur told him from across the room, where he stood by his big camera and studied the light coming through the window. He was waiting for the perfect shadow to replicate John Singleton Copley's famous painting of a boy and his squirrel.

"When are you going to be finished?" Coley asked him.

"In just a few minutes."

"It's been an hour."

"Not hardly. Just sit still and look toward the door, and in just a little while it will all be over."

"Can I have some water?"

"Yes, and if it will keep you still, you can pour in some rum."

Coley frowned, took a sip of the water in front of him and wiped his lips with the back of his sleeve.

"Why can't you be as docile as your pet?" Arthur said as he ducked beneath the cloth behind his camera.

Pinch pawed at the end of the chain that snaked along the edge of the desk, and Coley felt like choking him with it. He was just about to get up and be done with the whole thing, when Pearl passed the study door, looked at Coley and couldn't help but smile. Blushing, Coley turned his head and would've jumped out the window if she hadn't immediately spoken.

"You look very handsome," she said, and Coley watched her walk away, his lips slightly parted, the sun full on his face.

"That's it!" Arthur cried as he got his picture.

October 1864

THEY LEFT THE CLOVE before daylight, the sky dark as quarried slate. Coley reclined in the back of the wagon, his limbs jackknifed around barrels and boxes, and stared at Pearl's silhouette and the long braid of hair that ran straight down her back. She was perched in front of him on the buckboard seat, wedged between Tally and Will as the wagon dipped and rumbled over bad stretches of road. On occasion he would drift into sleep and try to linger in dreams that were always about Pearl, but when the wagon wheels jolted over the next half-buried rock, he'd bolt upright in a frenzy, his breath caught in his throat and his eyes wide open.

They were going to Rondout, Will having promised Joop he'd make sure Tally safely boarded her steamboat back to Manhattan. He was taking Pearl along to keep her cousin company, and Coley to help with the supplies they'd pick up in town. Quickly seeing the promise of such an excursion, Coley had cornered Will in the barn as he arranged the bones of the mastodon's hind foot.

"No need for you to make the trip," Coley told him. "I can take the girls to Rondout."

"That won't be necessary."

"I can handle the horses," Coley insisted. "I know them well as anybody. Didn't I pick them out of Shapiro's stable myself?"

"You did."

"And I don't need any help loading supplies, do I?"

"I imagine you don't."

"And I know the steamers coming into the harbor better than you, better than the Rondout paymaster."

"Yes, you probably do," Will muttered, pondering the metacarpals he held, the fat bones longer than his own hand.

"Then why can't I take them?"

"Because I have business of my own in town," Will replied, "and I need to take care of it."

"You don't understand," Coley said under his breath as he walked away. "It ain't business I'm talking about."

⁓◎⁓

SHE SAT ON the porch with Friday's copy of the *Rondout Courier*. It was an hour before she had to be at the bakery, and she was forcing herself to read the newspaper for the first time in weeks, the front page devoted to the Union victory at Winchester, Virginia.

GLORIOUS WAR NEWS!

The great battle of the Shenandoah Valley was fought last month by the indomitable Army of the Potomac. General Phil Sheridan and forty thousand brave Union soldiers were bloodied but unbowed when they met Jubal Early's rebels on the banks of Opequon Creek. Both forces refused to give ground, pounding each other with murderous fusillades over hill and ravine. Sheridan's brigades charged boldly into battle and exchanged volleys at arm's length, the violence intimate and horrific. Our own Rondout men of the 156th Infantry fought with valor under Colonel Jacob Sharpe, who was severely wounded in the terrible assault on Red Bud Run, where canister and shot rained down from the sky and the fighting was most fierce. Our army continued the attack under dogged return fire from the entrenched rebel troops. In the pitch of battle, a gap was found and the Union troops advanced through wrecked fields of smoke and fire. Infantry and cavalry succeeded in breaking the desperate rebel line and sent the Confederates scampering into the darkness, retreating through the streets of Winchester and along the Valley Pike all the way to Fisher's Hill. The battlefield was left an arena of ruin and blood, the loss of life astounding on both sides. The gentleman warrior Phil Sheridan never gave up hope or lowered his fist. His brilliant maneuvers broke the Confederacy's dubious heart. It is reported that every house in Winchester has been captured and turned into a hospital to treat the innumerable casualties. We pray for them and for Lincoln's quick victory. Our hats are off to our Ulster County boys, may God and good luck be with them.

Jane let the newspaper drop to the porch, hating the way it instilled conflicting passions of patriotism and despair, its inflammatory rhetoric and breakneck summary of the facts. Such accounts stepped lightly over the men lying dead or wounded and heralded only the spectacular, embellishing it with literary flourishes.

She hated the newspaper for being so necessary and skillful and cruel.

She stood and walked to the porch railing. The sky was rucked with clouds coming in from the north, light and harmless as a morning fog. Ben Decker drove his team of stout horses down the middle of the street, a rickety mountain of furniture piled in the back of his wagon, his assistant, Gus Mink, sitting on a chair next to the table lashed to the top of the pile, enjoying the comedy of the scene as he teetered and used his weight to help secure the load. The new schoolteacher, William Grover, as angular and thin as a mantis, nodded to her as he walked past, his tight frock coat buttoned right up to the point of his chin. Next door, Louis Pitts chased his little sister around their yard, Olive's squeals mocking her chubby brother as he lumbered after her.

Jane would have to look hard to find variations in the daily life of Rondout. It was as if the war had never come, but it had.

Nothing had changed, and so had everything.

GRIEVES HAD little time for hobbies or leisurely pursuits. He didn't mind that Isaac Stokes, besides his business accomplishments, also maintained a dairy farm that produced a modest profit and raised dogs simply for the pleasure it gave him. Nor did it bother him that Archie Russell, president of Ulster Savings in Kingston, indulged himself and his wife with European sojourns every two years, war or no war, traveling to London or Paris or Rome and bringing back oversized furniture to fill up the already-oversized rooms of their house on Fair Street. Though he might briefly have envied these men their gentlemanly endeavors, he had no desire or inclination to mirror them. His father had taught him that he must remain focused on his vision if he wished to succeed, and he was perfectly content to remain in Rondout and amass his good fortune. "Build yourself a nice house," he'd been instructed. "Wear good clothes. Be generous to your wife and children. Let people know you have money, just not how much."

So he took his wife on trips to Manhattan and Philadelphia and even Chicago, but allowed himself enough time to conduct business between fine meals and the theater, and he made sure his sons had little to wish for that wasn't granted. To remind people of his place in the community, he dined every day at the Mansion House Hotel, supported civic functions like the Sacred Musical Union, served as president of the Kingston Literary Association and purchased a new carriage every year.

His father also noted the importance of masculine pursuit, of giving the appearance of red-blooded strength and character. Grieves heeded that advice, and on this morning in early October, he found himself walking along the banks of Rondout Creek, heading back toward town from Eddyville, where he'd been out shooting ducks a mile above the coal dock. It was a calculated excursion, as he knew he'd be seen in his new hunting jacket, carrying his Springfield musket, flush from rigorous exercise, a man already up and engaged with nature before other men had even opened their shops.

He'd stepped behind a tall screen of cattails and pickerelweed, settled himself on a log and loaded his Springfield with buckshot. He watched a canal boat hauling Pennsylvania coal come through the last Eddyville lock, his mind drifting to the dozen barges he'd purchased the year the canal opened, a wise but minor investment that kept him in league with Rondout's most viable employers. Ten minutes later a skein of black ducks glided in from the Hudson Highlands and skittered across the creek twenty yards offshore, settling in the brackish oxbow where he liked to hunt. He raised the shotgun to his shoulder, and when he fired, the boom slapped his eardrums as buckshot fanned and fizzled across the water. Ducks were plentiful this time of year, and he managed to shoot four in less than an hour, the buckshot doing much to improve his aim.

Having retrieved the ducks and stuffed them in his canvas satchel, he walked briskly back to Rondout, thinking about a noon meal of baked oysters. In half an hour he passed the coal docks and entered the Strand, where Mickey Blessing waited for him in front of Herkart's harness shop. Basking in the golden morning light reflected off the big front window, Mickey watched Grieves approach before pushing himself off the wall with his left boot and joining him mid-stride.

"It appears you've had some luck, Mr. Grieves."

"It was a good morning," he replied. "Do you hunt, Mickey?"

"Not me. I'm too lazy to hunt for meat I can just as easily find on a plate."

Grieves smiled as they walked toward Division Street. "The weather's chasing, Mickey."

"Yes, Mr. Grieves, summer's turned to fall."

"It will be cold soon."

"That is the rhythm of things, Mr. Grieves."

"I was hoping the quiet winter months would allow me to finalize my hotel plans so that I might begin construction in the spring." When Mickey nodded, Grieves knew he had his attention. "But in order to begin construction, I need Dr. Harp's cooperation."

"Yes."

"He's very resistant."

"Seems like a convincible man to me."

"Do you think so, Mickey?"

"I'm sure of it."

⌒◦⌒

THEY STOOD together on the wharf as passengers boarded the *Eagle*. Tally wore the same brown dress she'd traveled in a few months before, and carried enough roast chicken and apples in her bag to tide her over. She'd gained ten pounds that summer, and Sallie had to let the dress out, but she wore it well, and Sam didn't seem to mind the extra weight.

Pearl held her hand as they waited for the steamer's whistle to signal last call. "I wish I was going with you."

"You'll be coming soon enough," Tally told her. "April ain't that far away."

"It is to me."

"It'll go by in a blink. Then you'll have a month in Weeksville to help me plan my wedding."

Pearl smiled. It had been five years since she was last in Brooklyn, and she was finally old enough to take full advantage of the opportunity. She would save all the money she made selling pelts and take it with her to spend on elegant dresses designed in the French style. She would go out dancing every night, wearing a new outfit each time, and soon attract the attention of a wealthy young man who'd fall in love and insist that she marry him and live in his handsome Bond Street row house, forbidding her from ever stepping foot on Jug Hill again. These were the plans she'd whispered to Tally when they slept in Coley's bed the night before, both of them giggling over the sheer reach of her imagination.

Glancing around, Pearl caught sight of a short, broken-nosed man behind a wagon piled high with corn, his face the color of blood sausage, and she was certain he'd been at the swamp with Mickey Blessing the week before. Now he stood forty feet away, squinting at her like an old goat. When she stared back, he ducked behind the wagon and scuttled off, raising his shoulder blades as if to hide his ugly face. Then she heard the sharp trill of the steamer whistle and saw the captain pacing back and forth along the rail as the last passengers came onboard. She squeezed Tally's hand, missing her already. "I'll keep an eye on Sam for you," she said.

"You won't have to."

"Ain't you worried he'll stray?"

Tally hoisted the canvas bag in her arms. "Nope. Nothing to stray to."

"What if he finds himself a girl prettier than you?" Pearl teased as they started toward the steamer.

"There ain't any pretty girls on Jug Hill, except for you."

❦

HE SAT ON the back of a wagon between the Magruder brothers and watched the wounded soldiers being helped down the gangplank of the *James Madison*. They were Rondout boys, and Coley recognized all three. The first one off the boat was Bill Dietz, who'd lost an eye and an ear and half of his smile, his face wrapped in white bandages already moist and turning pink. Behind him, Ike Collins was assisted by two of the ship's stewards. He'd been bayoneted during the fighting at Second Woods, and his torso was wrapped tight as a mummy's. Finally, George Mackey gimped along on crutches, his right leg gone from above the knee. He smiled as he came off the steamboat, almost weeping at the song of tree swallows spiraling off the Hudson, so different from the cries of men, and happily walked into the circle of women who'd come from the Church of the Holy Spirit to welcome them home. He hobbled by the wagon where the boys were sitting and winked, glad to be alive. All Coley could offer in return was a brainless nod, a worthless gesture that turned his stomach.

"My father says the war's gonna be over soon," Al Deyo said, his arms crossed. "Says there aren't enough men left to fight it."

"What a waste," Tim Magruder scoffed, spitting in the dirt.

"Look at 'em," Danny added as the soldiers were led off by the churchwomen. "Coming home in bits and pieces."

"Got their wits at least," Tim offered.

"Not Ike Collins."

"Yeah, but he was fairly witless anyway." Danny laughed, and Coley leaned back in the wagon as the brothers slapped each other across his chest.

He'd been down at the wharf since he arrived in town that morning, enjoying the easy company of his friends and doing his best to stay out of sight. He was particularly alert for any sign of Mickey, but he caught sight only of Charlie O'Fay making his way to Natterjack's, his face already flushed with the first beers of the day.

"When you coming back to Rondout for good, Coley?" Al asked him.

"I'm not."

"You gonna stay in those woods sniffing out that Jug Hill girl?" Tim snickered.

"No, I'll help finish that skeleton, and then I'm going out west like I always said I would."

"You gonna ask that pretty colored girl to go with you?" Danny asked, poking him in the arm.

Coley scowled. "I ain't gonna ask her anything."

"What're you going to do about Mickey?"

"Stay out of his way."

"You hear what he did to Bob Baggs?" Danny said.

"I heard."

"Arms broke so bad, they say he can wrap them clear around his back."

"He ain't gonna do anything to me."

"You sure of that, Coley?"

"Yep."

"How come you're so sure?" Al asked him.

He pulled aside his jacket just far enough to show them the butt of the Colt revolver, then closed it up again, shifting his weight to accommodate the barrel of the gun. He sat back to watch the crowds moving along the Strand, faster now, with more purpose in their step, as they took advantage of the waning hours of the day.

⟡

THERE YOU ARE, Miss House," Hap Shay said as he handed her the coins. He was smaller than she was, with sawdust-colored hair and the complexion of a pampered woman. Pearl didn't know how old he was, but there was often a dirty little boy running around the yard who called him Grampa. But for all she knew, he lived alone in this filthy shack at the end of Catherine Street, surrounded by rickety peaked sheds full of the pelts he bought from local farmers and trappers: raccoons and rabbits, mink, fox, beaver and deer. He rolled and stored them—stretched them, if necessary—before selling them to the fur traders who regularly visited port cities from Albany to Philadelphia. He was wearing the same flannel shirt and canvas pants she'd seen him in four months ago, and they smelled as if they hadn't been washed since. The sleeves and cuffs were so frayed, they hung around his wrists and ankles soft as feathers, and she could see the homemade nails hobbed into his boots to keep the soles from flapping. Hap Shay was the most bedraggled man she'd ever met, but he was also honest and fair and had the manners of an English duke.

"Thank you, Mr. Shay," she told him, putting the coins in her purse without bothering to count them.

"Will I see you before the spring?"

"I'll be here by the end of the year."

"Excellent!" he exclaimed with a broad smile, showing crippled teeth stained by tobacco and coffee.

"Good-bye, Mr. Shay," Pearl called out as she quickly pushed open the door and escaped to the porch, breathing in air that smelled of sewage and mold but which was still fresher than the sourness of Hap Shay's little kingdom.

❧

HE SAW Isaac Stokes and two of his wolfhounds walking toward him when he turned the wagon onto Division Street. Stokes was cloaked in a burgundy shawl-collared vest whose paisley design matched the lining of his frock coat. He wore short boots with a chiseled toe, shiny as dancing pumps.

"Isaac!" he called out.

Stokes slowed his vigorous pace, smiled and whistled sharply to his dogs, who stopped at his side, as attentive as children. "How are you, Will?" he asked as he stepped over to the wagon.

"I'm fine, Isaac."

"I'm surprised to see you with your head above the muck."

"Sometimes it's necessary, even for me." Then he leaned over the wagon seat. "Isaac, have you sold Butterfields to Harry Grieves yet?"

Stokes frowned and pulled on his snug vest. "The paperwork's being readied."

"Don't do it."

"It's not that easy."

"You can refuse."

"I tried."

"I'm not selling him my father's farm."

Stokes looked up at him. "Then he'll take it from you."

"I won't let him."

"You can't stop him."

"I can," Will said as picked up the reins again. "Just hold on to your land, Isaac."

"He killed my dogs," Stokes whispered, resting a hand on the bony skull of the hound leaning against his thigh. "He killed them."

"He won't kill another."

Stokes smiled sadly. "He'll kill you."

SHE WALKED along Catherine Street, listening to the rhythmic jingle of her coin purse as it slapped against her hip, thinking about all the fine-looking hats she'd seen earlier that morning in the window of McReynolds's Emporium of Fashion. But she suppressed her natural instinct to run back and buy everything in sight, intent on returning to Jug Hill richer than poorer.

Gray clouds crowned the late-afternoon sky, butting up against one another like rolls of fat, and the air began to bristle with the prospect of a storm, bits of garbage and leaves blowing past her ankles in the crisp breeze. She was looking down as she crossed Sycamore Street and didn't notice the two saloons facing each other in the dark alley, a jaundiced light glowing through the warbled glass, or the thin dogs lying with their backs against the peeling walls of shanty houses, growling lowly as she passed, attuned to the changing weather and the strange girl in their midst. And she didn't see Mickey Blessing until he grabbed her roughly by both arms and held her tight on the empty sidewalk, smiling as if he'd just pulled her out of the path of stampeding horses.

"You should look where you're going, girl."

She tried to twist away, but he yanked her closer, his chest grazing hers. "You could walk into trouble and such, your eyes on the ground like that. This ain't Jug Hill."

"Let go of me."

"Where did you find that baby?"

"Let me go."

"That's no Jug Hill baby."

"Whoever left him there meant him to be," Pearl almost shouted. Again she tried to break away, but he pressed her arms to her sides and hoisted her just inches from his face.

"Do you know who that was?"

"I don't know anything, mister, except what I found and what I'm gonna keep."

"Does anybody know?" She squirmed, but Mickey held her fast. He looked down at the pretty girl in his arms and smiled. Her hair had fallen loose from the bright green ribbon, and her small breasts pushed against the fabric of her dress as she arched her back away from him. He squeezed her and lightly traced his fingers along her left breast, enjoying the firmness of it, and eased his grip as his other hand found the small of her back. She froze, unblinking, as the first drops of rain began to fall.

"We don't have to fight, girl," he said softly, and the suddenness of his voice broke whatever sway he'd held over her.

She jerked out of his grasp and ran.

Coley turned onto Sycamore Street when he saw Pearl racing up the alley toward him. He had intended to intercept her at Hap Shay's, but this was better—until he realized that her eyes were set and blank as stones and her skirt whipped around her legs like she was fleeing a hurricane. He glanced past her and saw Mickey walking away, and then Pearl was in front of him, blind to his presence.

"Pearl?" was all he had time to say before she spun right past him. "Pearl!"

But she disappeared before he regained his wits enough to chase after her.

The fat drops began to fall harder, splattering the sidewalk in front of him, big as tossed coins. The rain felt cool on his face, and he didn't bother to raise his collar as it picked up strength. Since it was nearly dinnertime, he decided to walk to Natterjack's for a fried lamb steak and a beer and a warm place to wait out the storm. He thought he'd made his intentions clear to the Jug Hill girl, and if she proved to be as thick as the rest of them, there'd still be time enough to turn her head. She was a pretty thing, and he was lucky his child had been delivered into her tender arms, a fact that would work to the advantage of both father and son.

A long jag of lightning silvered the sky, followed by the rumble of distant thunder. The rain was coming at an angle, slashing his face and pasting his shirt to his skin, but he strolled on without haste, ignoring the two men who ran by him, bent as beetles and cursing as if it were hot oil pouring out of the sky. He heard more footsteps coming up from behind and expected it would be another sopping merchant, not Coley Hinds, who splashed to a stop in front of him.

"Coley boy!" he declared. "I thought you were long gone, a regular country gentleman by now!"

"Leave her alone, Mickey."

"What's that?" he said, cocking his head. "You've got to speak up, son. It's hard to hear the mice through the rain."

"I said leave the girl alone!"

"The girl? That Jug Hill girl?"

"Just leave her be."

"Is she your nigger wife now, Coley? Is that why you stand on your toes and tell me what to do?"

"Don't you touch her."

Mickey grinned through the sputtering rain. "And whose master are you, then? Will you teach me a lesson, Coley boy? Strike me dead for every bad thought in my head?"

"Leave her be."

"You're a good pup, Coley Hinds, but be sure of whose stick you're chasing."

Coley could feel the pistol nestled in the belt, and his hands shook as Mickey kept smiling at him in the pounding storm.

"Now come along to Natterjack's and let me buy you a steak," Mickey said, extending his hand, but Coley jumped back and ran into the streaming rain, which fell like a curtain between them.

❧

AFTER A FEW HOURS, the wind suddenly died and the dark clouds overhead pulled apart and retreated to the far corners of the sky. Arthur and Will sat sipping whiskey on the front porch of Jane's house on Spring Street, still full from the chicken and dumplings that she and Pearl had prepared for them. The air was crisp and moonbright after the storm, rainwater still dripping off the eaves. A dog raced by them on the opposite sidewalk, more shadow than beast.

Arthur looked at Will, who drank deeply and stared out over the quiet street. He seemed content, but while he'd smiled gamely throughout dinner and joined in the conversation, Arthur knew his mind was elsewhere. "I'm going back to Europe, Will."

Will turned to him in surprise. "What?"

"I'm going back to Paris."

"When did you decide this?"

"Over the last few weeks."

"What about your life here?"

Arthur laughed softly. "I have no life here, Will."

"You have your work."

"Yes, and that's why I'm leaving," he said before taking a small sip of his drink. "The only mistake I made ten years ago was coming home. But I did, and then I fell into a routine of convenience, setting up a studio in a building my uncle once owned, surrounded by people I'd known my whole life."

"There are worse fetters than those, Arthur."

"In Paris, I spent days roaming the streets, looking for the most beautiful or honest or extraordinary stranger I could find, for a face or gesture that would stop me where I stood. It didn't matter if it was an old man with a withered leg or a young woman leading a fat goat, I was drawn to both. Those were the photographs I loved to take. That's what I started doing again on my visits to you in the Clove. And I want to do more of it."

"Can't you do it here?"

Arthur shook his head. "I lack the guts, Will. Here I have appearances to keep up, and I'm too much of a coward to go against expectations."

Will drank more whiskey and looked at his friend's sharp profile, at the lines that creased his youthful face. "Then I'm glad for you, Arthur."

Arthur smiled. "It's a good decision."

"When will you leave?"

"In the spring."

"So at least I'll have your company awhile longer."

Arthur nodded and relaxed. "Yes, you will."

"Have you thought about going out west instead? It's a land full of characters."

"I've thought about it. But I miss Paris and the time I spent there. It's what first comes to mind during those nights I lie back in regret. It's where my best memories are." He turned to Will and grinned. "But someday I'll come visit you."

"Wherever that might be."

"Wherever you are," he said, settling back in his chair. "I'll be a vagabond again. It's not such a terrible life."

"You'll be alone."

"Yes, at times, but that's not the worst thing in the world, is it?"

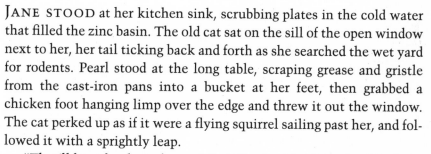

JANE STOOD at her kitchen sink, scrubbing plates in the cold water that filled the zinc basin. The old cat sat on the sill of the open window next to her, her tail ticking back and forth as she searched the wet yard for rodents. Pearl stood at the long table, scraping grease and gristle from the cast-iron pans into a bucket at her feet, then grabbed a chicken foot hanging limp over the edge and threw it out the window. The cat perked up as if it were a flying squirrel sailing past her, and followed it with a sprightly leap.

"That'll keep her busy for a while," Pearl said, wiping her hands on her apron.

Jane smiled. The girl had been good company that afternoon, and she was pleased she'd be spending the night. It had surprised her when Arthur Dowd came to her the week before with Will's request to put Pearl up, but she was glad he'd asked and glad she could oblige.

The front door opened, and Will came inside holding two empty glasses between his fingers. Pearl stopped what she was doing and watched him walk across the room. Jane saw her back straighten and her arms gently levitate from her sides as she tracked Will with her eyes. He refilled the glasses and left without even glancing at them, and Pearl did a little pirouette to keep him in view as he passed sideways through the door.

It was perfectly quiet in the kitchen, and when Pearl finally looked at Jane, she held her head high without the smallest bit of shame or fluster.

"You like him, don't you?" Jane asked.

Pearl blinked, as if that was the dumbest question ever posed. "Don't you?"

⁓◉◡

IT WAS DARK when Coley turned onto Spring Street, and he couldn't resist kicking his toes through the puddles in the cracked sidewalks in front of the Episcopal church. Maybe he was just light-headed from butting chests with Mickey Blessing, or from the bottles of beer he'd shared with the Magruders on the ferry dock. The boys had sat under a tin roof in the pouring rain, the rat-a-tat-tat louder than their laughter, all three already soaked and drunk by the time they found shelter. Or maybe he was just glad to be back in Rondout, wandering streets that his feet would know even if he were struck blind, every dead-end and alley branded in his mind like the features on a treasure map.

In his back pocket was the broadside he'd ripped off the post in front of the Mansion House Hotel. He pulled it out and carefully unfolded it, looking at it for the tenth time that evening. In the middle of the black-and-white sheet was a picture of two clowns and an elephant, and the banner over their heads read:

JOHN J. JUNE'S GREAT AMERICAN CIRCUS AND MENAGERIE
FAMOUS IN NEW YORK, PARIS AND HAVANA
Come see Elmo and Fritz, the Pugilistic Mules
Carlos, the Educated Elephant
Fancy riders and bareback girls
Guiseppe, the Italian clown
The Amazing Melville
Exotic animals and much more . . .
Saturday, October 29, at seven o'clock. Rondout, New York

He folded the sheet along its creases and put it away. He started to whistle but then stopped when he saw Will and Arthur sitting on the porch of Miss Blessing's house. He slowed down, his good temper ruined. He knew he shouldn't have let his irritation with Will turn into anger over the course of the day, but he couldn't help himself. His hands went back in his pockets and he shuffled along the sidewalk, his head hanging low when he walked up the steps to greet the men.

"You missed dinner," Will told him.

"I ate."

"How's your lip?"

"It's fine."

"Let me see."

"I said it's fine," he muttered, and walked into the house. He saw Pearl and Jane in the kitchen and acknowledged them with a cursory glance as he looked around for the whiskey bottle. He poured himself a generous glass, then sauntered back onto the porch, where he leaned against the post as if he were alone, his ankles crossed, aware of Will's eyes on his back as he took a long sip.

"Smells like you've had enough of that already," Will told him.

"How could you tell?" Coley asked, smirking.

"Coley!" Pearl chided him from the doorway.

"My lip don't hurt, and it ain't nobody's business how much whiskey I drink."

Will frowned, and didn't notice Jane coming up behind him. "You're drunk."

"So are you."

"That's enough!" Jane said.

Coley just stared at Will, the smirk still twisting on his face. "My lip don't hurt half as much as a bullet, I bet. Ain't that right, Will?"

Will looked at him and didn't answer.

"How come you don't talk about that?" he continued. "You get shot in the war and got nothing to say about it? Maybe it's because you got shot doing something else. Maybe you got shot for a reason."

"Stop it!" Pearl shouted.

"Dammit, Coley!" Arthur snapped as he got to his feet.

Coley ignored them all, his eyes fast on Will. Will stared back at him, the glass of whiskey warm in his fist. He felt calmer now than he had for a long time, then drew a deep breath and took what he hoped would be his last sip of the evening. "I had a friend," he said. "His name was Eli Birdslee." Then he had to wait a moment before he was able to go on.

I LOST SIGHT of him as soon as that first shot was fired," Will said. Ten minutes had passed since he started telling them about Bear River, and no one had interrupted him. "It escalated quickly, and the Shoshone took advantage of their position in that deep ravine. Before I put down my binoculars, I saw two more soldiers jerk backward and disappear into the deep snow like they were falling into a feather bed. The men were helpless, caught in an open field. In less than a minute five more went down. I saw one boy, Gregory Hewes, mount his horse and turn back toward the river. McGarry yelled for him to halt, but the boy was deaf in his terror and kept galloping until the major shot the horse out from under him, pitching him right into the icy current. Only after ten men were dead or screaming did McGarry call for a retreat, and they either ran or rode out of range of the Indians' bullets, their breath billowing in the searing cold, each man's face red as flannel."

He held the fresh glass of whiskey that Pearl had poured him, but hadn't touched it yet. "By that time, Connor and the infantry had started to cross the river. Some of the men pulled Hewes out and placed him on the opposite shore, his shoulder dislocated. Connor was as angry as I'd ever seen him. He quickly formed two units to box in the Indians, and another to cut off access to the river, then mounted an attack the men had been aching for.

"For the next hour I stitched and bandaged the men carried back across the river. There wasn't much I could do. The fighting was so fierce that most of the wounded had been left where they fell. The Shoshone, full of wildness over their initial victory, kept up their assault from the ravine, and the California Volunteers returned fire without caution, so weighed down with ammunition they thought it didn't matter how many rounds they wasted. But when Connor finally succeeded in flanking the Indians, the impact was sudden. We had more guns and better guns. They had no chance."

Jane and Pearl sat on the railing opposite him, and Coley still stood by the post. Arthur stared at his friend, whose face wavered in the burnished light of the lamp shining just inside the window.

"When no more soldiers were brought to the field tent, I forded the river to join the troops. Just as I reached the far side, my horse took a bullet in the neck and tossed me in the frozen mud. I recovered my rifle and fired at the Shoshone racing toward me along the high bank, and the bullet carried him away like a gust of wind. He was the first man I ever killed, but I had no time to consider it. I grabbed the extra cartridge bags off my dying horse and followed the infantry running toward the ravine. By the time I reached the village, the battle had already turned.

"The Indians ran out of ammunition first, and when they tried to flee we chased them down. When we ran out of cartridges for our rifles, we dropped them and reached for our pistols. When our pistols were empty, we fought with knives and bayonets and our bare hands. I had my father's pistol as we stormed the ravine, and I fired it often, and what seemed like minutes took more than an hour, but we flushed the Shoshone out of that gorge and back into the village, where Connor and the infantry were waiting."

He held the glass in both hands and took a drink. "I saw old men and women stripped of their clothing and thrown into the frigid water. I saw soldiers fling children against trees as if they were sacks of grain to be opened. Down by the river, I saw a few Indians floating by, holding on to branches, kicking hard with their feet as they drifted with the current, just trying to escape, but soldiers followed along on the opposite bank, firing their rifles into the churning water as if they were hunting turtles."

Will trained his eyes on Coley and left them there. "Half the lodges were already on fire when I ran through the camp looking for Eli. The sky was gray with smoke and the air stank of burning buffalo hides. A squaw staggered out of a burning lodge in front of me, her hair and back aflame as she stumbled toward the river. The gunfire was more sporadic then, like echoes in the distance, but my ears were ringing and my skin raw from the cold. When I heard a woman scream from a lodge still untouched, I ran to it with my pistol in my hand and pulled back the flap. A funnel of dim light came down from the smoke hole above, and it took a moment for my eyes to adjust.

"It was Billy Motes I saw first. He was kneeling by the cook fire, holding down a naked girl, maybe fifteen, one hand on her neck and the other on her shoulder. Her face was bruised and her eyes were open, and I couldn't tell if she was alive or dead. Billy looked up when he saw me, and I almost didn't recognize him. And then he ran. Pushed me out of the way and ran."

Will paused and rubbed his eyes.

"Where was Eli Birdslee?" Coley asked, surprised by his own voice, and waited for Will to look at him again.

Will remembered the gloom of the lodge, and the sight of Eli Birdslee, his pants down to his knees, his hands on the Indian girl's narrow hips, pulling her toward him. He blinked and looked back at Coley. "He was crouching right in front of the girl, but even in the awful light I could see the blood on his knuckles and a gash on his cheek. He was staring at me, but I don't think he saw me. Or recognized me. I yelled at him, but his eyes were empty, flat as river stones. Then he shook his head, just barely, and made a sound in his throat, and when he let go of the girl I thought it was over, that maybe he'd recovered his senses. He stood there at the back of the lodge, and I could hear him breathing, hard and raspy. He raised his hands and showed me his bloody palms, and there was blood on his pants and tunic. I kept my eyes on him, careful not to do anything to frighten him, but he moved first, fast as he could, and grabbed a Henry rifle leaning in the corner. I yelled again and held up my hands, but he shot me anyway. And even as the bullet hit me below the shoulder, I knew he could've killed me if he'd wanted to. But when the Shoshone girl dug in her elbows and tried to scurry away, something snapped in Eli again and he shot her in the back when she was not more than two feet away. And I knew it was done, that Eli wasn't coming back, so I raised my pistol and warned him to stop, I yelled it over and over, and when he swung his rifle around and took aim at my head, I shot him. I shot him three or four times, high in the chest and neck and arm, I just kept firing until he dropped that damn gun and went down himself."

He looked into the darkness and sipped his drink. "When I stepped out of that lodge, the noon sky was black from burning buffalo hides. I collapsed on the riverbank and slid down the ice until my boot caught on a body a few feet from the water. And I lay there for two hours, in my own blood, the warmth of it melting the snow around me. The gunfire eased some but never stopped. The cries of children rose above it, though that did grow fainter after a time. An Indian was shot right above me and banged into me as he rode the ice into the water, where I watched him flail until the current took him under. And I blinked away the blood, his blood, that had splattered over my face."

He looked at them with a wan smile and set his empty glass on the porch floor.

Jane stood by the railing and felt the muscles of her legs tighten as she held herself from going to his side. "You couldn't have known what would happen," she said softly.

"Yes, I could," Will replied. "I've known since I was a boy."

"You tried to stop him, Will," Arthur told him.

"That's not the point." He shook his head. He was unable to look at the four people standing there in front of him, so quiet that he could barely hear them breathe. He stood quickly and left the porch without another word, disappearing around the corner.

Pearl turned to Coley. He was staring after Will, and it took him a moment to feel the heat of her gaze. When he looked at her, he felt the sourness in his stomach and the worming in his temples from all he'd drunk, and knew it was best to keep his mouth shut. He turned away and leapt over the railing, and Pearl stood there and listened to his hobnails on the cobblestones as he ran down Spring Street.

～◊◯～

HE HADN'T thought of his father for years, but he did that night as he sat on the front stoop of Tom Moran's small house on the corner of Hone Street. Moran was a fisherman, and his yard was full of the long oak-strip eel pots he used in Rondout Creek and the Hudson. The ground crackled with the broken shells of the blue crabs he caught for bait, and every day you could find twenty to thirty stray cats prowling the yard, their muzzles greasy with eel slime, climbing in and out of the handwoven pots. They slept on Tom's porch and doorstep, and each morning a half dozen followed his cart to the Rondout docks and waited there while he fished, loyal as wives. Coley loved the taste of roasted eel, but Moran's yard had a terrible smell, and he hated it when the cats rubbed their stinking fur against him and tried to sit on his lap. Still, from here he could spy on Jane's house halfway down the block, where she and Pearl moved back and forth through the golden light of the front parlor.

He leaned back, remembering the last time he'd gone fishing with his father. It was a Sunday morning the year after his mother had died, and by then Jimmy Hinds had given up on the church, tired of the sadness he felt and the blame and anger that made his hands shake. Coley knew he'd found no comfort there, and he was glad when his father decided his spirits would be better raised on the swift currents of the Hudson.

They walked down to the end of Gill Street that morning and borrowed a skiff from Sam McGrath. Jimmy laid his old lancewood rod in the bow of the boat while Coley climbed aboard with the small bucket of bloodworms he'd dug out of the garden, and they pushed off under a beaming sun, gliding across water smooth as a storefront window. Jimmy rowed easily around the breakwater, staying close to shore, and let the boat drift while Coley baited the hook. He watched his father let out some of his horsehair line, weigh it down with two or three old keys, and cast upstream into the current, where the channel started to bend. He played his bait along the bottom, and within minutes a catfish bowed his rod until the tip touched the water. Coley carefully leaned over the side as Jimmy fought and landed the monster, grabbing it by its wide lips and cracking it between the eyes with a hammer before tossing it in the back of the skiff. In less than an hour he caught half a dozen more, slowly drifting through the small cove he always came to, and although the day was warm and sunny, he seemed to take little pleasure from his success.

As the morning came to an end, they ate slices of buttered bread, and then Jimmy handed Coley the rod while he retrieved the bottle of beer he'd been dragging behind the skiff to keep cool. Coley threw the line as far as he could and let it sink to the bottom, and on the first turn of the reel he felt a tug of resistance. "I got one!" he shouted, and his father put down his beer and scrambled over the seat to his side. "Bring him in, Coley, slow and easy," and he did, watching the rod tip quiver and hump, staring hard into the water for the first sight of his catch. But instead of a giant catfish rising from the depths, a small eel slithered at the end of his line. "Can we keep him?" he asked, swinging it into the boat, but Jimmy shook his head as he quieted the squirming eel with his boot. "Too small," he said, pulling the hook from its sharp teeth and letting the eel slip over the side. But as soon as it hit the water, a big herring gull swooped low and snatched it off the surface in its yellow bill, tilting its head back as it flew higher, swallowing hard, and Coley saw the little eel slide right down its throat. The gull spread its wings and glided toward shore, graceful and content, until it unexpectedly plummeted ten feet with a terrible high-pitched caw. Coley and his father watched as the bird careened and screamed overhead, dropping and rising in crazy flight, and all of a sudden they saw the little eel squirt right out of its backside and drop back into the water, the gull still bugling in agony as it continued its cockeyed flight toward shore.

And Jimmy began to laugh for the first time in a year, laughing until his face turned purple and tears flew from his eyes. Coley had laughed along with him, loving his father's smile and glad to see his face wide open and free of pain, if only for a few minutes.

Now he sat on Tom Moran's stoop and felt like laughing again. It had been so long since he'd thought of his father that he'd almost forgotten he ever had one.

He looked up Spring Street and saw the lamp had finally been turned off in Jane's front room. He lifted the cat sleeping in his lap and put it on the stoop, then stood up. It was after midnight, and he yawned grandly as he adjusted the gun, which had slipped in his belt. The air hummed with purring cats and the stench of eel, and he was glad to walk away.

❧

ARTHUR FOUND HIM sitting at a small table at Felix Murray's saloon, down by the canal dock. It was late and the place was quiet. He sat with his back to the big room, looking out over the creek, and didn't shift his gaze when Arthur took the chair next to him.

"My father brought me here every time we came to Rondout," Will said. "We'd order pan-roasted oysters by the dozen, or shad roe fried in butter, both of us eating as much as we could, treating it like a contest he always let me win." He stared at the canal boats tied along the dock. "I always looked forward to coming here with him. We talked about most everything, and he'd listen to whatever nonsense seemed brilliant to me at the time, no matter if I was ten or twenty."

"He was a good man."

"I wanted to come home a year ago, Arthur. I wanted to see him before he died."

"Why didn't you?"

"I was in the hospital at Fort Douglas for two months. I wrote when I was strong enough, to tell him I was all right. Then, when the thaw came, I quit the army and went back to Los Angeles. I tried to write again, but I couldn't."

"You'd done nothing wrong, Will."

"My father always told me that the greatest act of war was forgiveness. It's how enemies lived with their defeat, and how victors brought about reconciliation." He swirled his brandy and stared down into the creek. "I killed that boy. How am I to reconcile that?"

"You had no choice."

"But a choice was made."

Arthur stared at his friend. "He was your father."

"I know."

"And he loved you."

When Will didn't respond, Arthur walked out of the restaurant, leaving him alone with his view of the Rondout docks.

❧

HE WAS RESTLESS that night, thinking about the Jug Hill girl and his baby, and every time Gitta pulled him close to keep him still, he resisted. Even when she worked her hand between his legs he felt no comfort, and long after midnight he pried himself from her clinging limbs and got out of bed. He walked to the open window and thrust his head outside, the night air crisp and smelling of oil and smoke. He leaned on the sill and felt his heart racing, knowing for certain he'd get no sleep that night, so he dressed in the darkness, Gitta snoring behind him, and left the house as quickly as he could.

Starting out for the familiar sanctuary of Natterjack's, he changed his mind the moment Rondout Creek came into view. It wasn't company he was seeking, but a more elusive solace. He passed canal boats rocking in the current, their thick braided ropes sawing against the pilings, the eerie melody like badly strung fiddles, and walked to the end of Cornell's wharf, where the Hudson breeze was strongest. He took off the clothes he'd buttoned up just ten minutes before and dove into the water, slicing through the chop as straight as a knife thrown into a board.

He felt the initial embrace of cold water passing over his body like a thick coat of wax, warming with every stroke and kick he took. He broke the surface thirty feet from shore and swam hard, moving beyond the dozen schooners tied to the pier. After a few minutes he flipped onto his back and swam into the Hudson, watching the yellowing lights as they flickered over the ramshackle town. And then he turned over, annoyed by the flotsam that the evening storm had washed into the river, and filled his lungs and dove deep into true blackness, where the water turned cold as a tomb and he could remain suspended for as long as his breath would hold. And then he released himself, letting the river spin him around, arms pinned to his sides, air slowly escaping from his lungs as the water buoyed him back up.

Mickey broke the surface with a huge gulp of night air and reached out for a tree limb drifting nearby. He held on for a moment, long enough to get his bearings and look back at the masts of the tall ships drawn against the sky. He wiped the hair from his eyes and squeezed the pulpy mass in his hand, amazed how waterlogged the branch was, and when he looked, he realized it was an arm he was holding on to, horribly bloated and with skin as black as the sky. He kicked away from the body, the fingers of the dead man grazing his own, their legs tangled. And every time he pushed at the corpse it seemed to drift closer, until he could see the exposed bone on its face and smell the rot, and he panicked and yelled and clawed and splashed as if it were a living thing he was trying to scare away. Then he swam as hard as he could back to Rondout, looking over his shoulder only once to make sure that death wasn't chasing him, and pulled himself up the pilings at Cornell's wharf, lying back on the slippery boards, breathing hard, numb from head to toe, holding his knees to his chest and checking himself for damage, making sure his own skin wasn't sloughing off. When he knew he was safe and whole, he stood up, naked and shivering, and listened to the black water slurp against the pier.

～ⓔ～

SHE KNEW IT was his bed, and it was a long time before she was able to shut her eyes. She was used to the smell of men, the lingering waft of sweat and worn clothes that hung around her father and brother, but this room had no odors, no pictures on the walls, no dressertop strewn with the junk that collected in their pockets. Except for a few shirts hanging on pegs in the closet, there was no evidence the room had been occupied at all. But even if the sheets she lay on were fresh, it was still Mickey's room, and every scratch of leaves on the windowpane made her sit up to make sure the shadow she saw wasn't a hand reaching in to find her neck. It was hours before her anxiety exhausted her and allowed her to drift into a fitful sleep, tossing under the blanket, trying not to think of his hands on her body. When it was finally light enough for her to make out the door across the room, she jumped up and dressed quickly, leaving her shoes behind in her hurry to escape.

The house was quiet, and the door to Jane's bedroom was still shut. Pearl started a fire and pumped enough water to fill the kettle, smiling when the old cat weaved between her bare feet. Waiting for the water to boil, she picked up the cat and walked to the front door, looking through the window at the daylight showing pink above the trees across the street. Suddenly, the cat struggled in her arms, and when Pearl dropped her, she glanced down and saw a man sitting there on the porch. She was about to scream when she recognized the slump of his body, and she walked closer to the window above his head, her angry little snorts fogging the glass. The boy was fast asleep, with his jacket open and legs splayed, and she could see the grip of a pistol sticking out of his belt.

She opened the front door and slammed it shut behind her, roughly waking Coley from his dreams. "What are you doing here?" she snapped.

"Sleeping."

"Where'd you get that gun?"

"Borrowed it."

"What for?"

"I'm just looking out."

"Looking out for what?"

He blinked at her, his brain still moony with sleep, and she knew the answer before he was able to piece it together in his own mind. She hovered over him like an angry moth, not knowing if she should slap him or yank the gun out of his pants and hit him over the head with it. She bit her lip and glared down at his sleepy, stupid eyes, knowing he had no idea what she was contemplating. His brain was too small to consider anything beyond his own devotion, and if he was going to spend all his waking hours worrying about her, then she'd have to use the few seconds she had to spare worrying about him.

"He's not going to touch you again," Coley told her.

Pearl heard a door open across the street, where a man shambled outside, his hair sprung by sleep, holding up the pants sagging around his waist as he walked to the outhouse behind his barn.

She turned back to Coley. He'd seen the man, too, and quickly covered the gun with his jacket and squirmed in his chair as she bent over him. He was both shy and bold in her presence, and whatever anger she still felt was exhaled with her very next breath. "You just look out for yourself, Coley Hinds," she said softly. He sat there and watched her storm back into the house, oblivious to everything but the scent of rosewater that lingered behind the twirl of her skirt.

THE MORNING HAD not started out well. The previous night's storm had loosened the last of the maple leaves, and by seven o'clock the Negro boy his wife had hired was out in the back garden raking them up. It was the incessant scratching of those steel tines that woke him, and he jumped out of bed, elbowing Albertina in the process, and shouted out the window, scaring the crows from the trees. "Drop that rake, you little fool, or I'll come down there and crack it over your skull!" The frightened boy looked up and broke into a run.

"Stop it, Harry," Albertina said from underneath the covers.

"The boy's brain must be the size of a peach pit. How many times have I told him? How many times?"

"Many, Harry."

"You keep him out of my yard, Albertina, or I swear I'll empty my squirrel gun in his backside," he said as the boy scooted around the cedar trees that lined the drive. When he glanced up, he saw Ed Caldwell standing on his back steps, staring up at him through the bare trees that separated their properties, his shirt hanging loose from his suspenders, a scowl on his unpleasant face. Grieves much preferred the lushness of spring and summer, when the foliage hid his neighbors from view, and he scowled back at Ed before slamming the window shut.

He decided to forgo the Mansion House Hotel that morning and have breakfast with his sons, but one of the eggs he was served had a blood spot in the yolk and he quickly lost his appetite. His eldest boy, Daniel, sat across from him, reading aloud an article about the Union victory at Westport, Missouri, the week before. " 'General Pleasonton chased Marmaduke's rebel hordes back across the Big Blue River, where they set the prairie grass afire to hide their cowardly retreat. It was by far the largest battle fought west of the Mississippi, and with yet another triumph over the Confederate forces, Missouri is now squarely in the Union fold. It was a soaring victory for Lincoln's Army of the Potomac and a great day for all good men.' "

" 'All good men,' " his youngest son, Franklin, echoed bitterly as he spilled crumbs on his mother's fresh tablecloth. "All good men but me. The war will be over by the time I'm old enough to serve."

"You best hope so," Grieves told him.

"I'll miss the fight."

"That's what your mother and I pray for."

"It's not fair. I feel like one of Marmaduke's cowards."

"You didn't run from anything."

"I didn't run to it, either."

"No, and had you tried I would've knocked you senseless before you got beyond the front door. So blame me if it makes you feel better, because I can take the blow."

Franklin sat back, moping in the chair, until Grieves finally pushed his untouched plate aside and called for his horse. He pulled on his coat as he stepped out the door, admiring the larkspur and salvia his wife had planted along the gravel drive in front of the portico. The mounded gardens on the front lawn still flamed with the yellow-and-orange blossoms of helenium and coreopsis, and though it seemed unnatural to his more rusticated eye, he couldn't deny their visual appeal. Buttoning his coat as he continued down the path, he decided he would stop first at the Mansion House Hotel, where he'd enjoy fried trout and bacon, not bloody eggs, and be spared the sullenness of his children. The idea of a hearty breakfast brightened his mood, until he looked up and saw Will Harp on horseback at the end of his drive. He wished for a moment that he could turn around and go back to bed and wake up all over again, but then he gave in to the unrelenting fact that his morning was already under way and wasn't about to get any better.

"Good morning, Dr. Harp!" he called, his voice ringing with counterfeit cheer, and walked toward him, ignoring the stable boy who followed with his saddled horse. "What brings you here?" he asked as he opened his iron gate and stepped outside.

"I'm in town only for a short while and thought this would be the easiest way to get your attention."

"You have it," Grieves replied. He couldn't help noticing how much Will looked like his father. It didn't matter that he wore his hair as long as a Broadway flaneur; he still had the major's inscrutable reserve and a fixed expression that held little patience for equivocation.

"I'm not sure you understood me last month when I told you I wouldn't sell my land."

"Perhaps you didn't understand my determination."

"I did, Mr. Grieves. That's why I'm bringing this discussion to your doorstep so we can put an end to it."

"You've hardly given me a chance to persuade you."

"And I won't," Will said, staring down at him from the saddle. "I have neither family for you to intimidate nor dogs for you to harm. I have only my father's property, and I will not give it up."

"Be careful, Dr. Harp."

"And I have no use for Mickey Blessing. If I see him on my land again, I'll know why he's there and act accordingly."

"You're making assumptions, Dr. Harp."

"I'm just countering your own."

Grieves ignored the stable boy standing behind him and the sunlight planing across his face, causing his eyes to tear. "Some things can't be stopped, Dr. Harp."

"And other things can. This one stops today."

"You're making a mistake."

"No, Mr. Grieves," Will replied as he turned his horse in the middle of the street. "I'm preventing you from making one. Be satisfied with that."

◦◦◦

SHE SAT IN front of the bureau mirror and brushed her hair. It had grown out some since her morning of delirium, and people on the street didn't stare as much now that Mary Knetch had helped her trim it to a more even length, though it still barely reached her shoulders.

She picked up a freshly laundered collar and fastened it at her neck with a simple cameo brooch that Frank had bought her. Jane smiled when she looked at her reflection in the mirror, and remembered that she'd thought of Frank again in her sleep. The week he left for the war, they'd gone to the firemen's ball at the Eagle Hotel in Kingston. There were fifty couples dancing to the music of the Excelsior Brass Band, mingling freely in the ballroom, drinking heroes' punch that some of the men had laced with rum and eating slices of rich coconut cake and iced grapes. Toward the end of the evening he had dragged her onto the dance floor when the band started up a lively quadrille, and though Frank wasn't much of a dancer, he was sporting enough when the occasion called for it. They took to the floor with Mary and Alfons, and the men spent the first minutes of the song trying to outdo each other, prancing like trick ponies. Jane and Mary could do nothing but laugh at their antics, and as the song came to an end, Frank took Alfons by the arm and broke into an Irish jig, a romp that quickly became contagious, and as all the other men joined in, the band broke into a rousing version of "Speed the Plow," playing until everyone fell down exhausted. When they got back to Rondout after midnight, Frank was still smiling broadly, his face ruddy with the pleasure of the evening. And it was his smile that she'd awakened with this morning. And there had been no sadness this time when she opened her eyes, no regret, only the joy they shared and the memory of his beautiful face.

When she rose from the bureau and stepped into the empty parlor, she saw the mangled quilt folded over a chair in the corner. She hadn't touched it for weeks. There was still an hour before she had to be at the bakery, so she picked up her basket of cut triangles and needles and gathered the quilt in her arms. She settled herself into Frank's wide chair in front of the window, where the light fell warm and bright, put on her spectacles and started over.

ARTHUR WAS working in the back of the studio when he heard the knock on his front door. It was two hours before he was set to open, and he did his best to ignore the insistent thumping. He was in the process of tinting a series of photographs he'd taken of Frederick Godell's three daughters the month before, when they'd gathered together in the garden behind their house in Kingston to celebrate the eldest's wedding. He had his gum Arabic and pigments arranged on the table beside him, and enjoyed dabbing pink and red on the petals of the rosebuds and giving a more muted swipe of similar hues to the ripe cheeks of these beautiful girls. He'd already added a faint touch of blue to their eyes and a hint of summer cornsilk to their hair. It was delicate, exacting work, and as he used the tip of his brush to trace the cheekbone of the future bride, he steeled himself to block out the pounding that now rattled his door. And then he heard the hinges creak, damning himself for not locking it behind him. He slammed down his brush and glared behind him as Will stepped into the studio wearing the same clothes he'd had on the night before. Looking more stubborn than bedraggled, he offered a humble grin.

Arthur's irritation evaporated. "You've had a long night," he said.

"Longer than most, but I survived it." He looked at the photographs propped up on Arthur's small easel, and the wet paintbrush in his hand. "I didn't mean to interrupt. I just wanted to make sure you'll be returning to the Clove with me."

"Of course."

"Good." Will nodded and gestured toward the easel. "Then I'll leave you to your work." He took three steps toward the door before Arthur stopped him.

"Will," he said, and waited for him to turn. "Every time your father came to Rondout, he'd stop here for a visit. We'd dine together, or have a beer at Booth's, and he'd tell me about your last letter and recount for me your adventures in the southwest deserts or the mountains of California. And if he repeated a story I let him, because it meant so much to him to have those stories to tell. But when the war started and you joined the Volunteers, he spoke in more somber tones because he knew you could be killed, like the thousands of others we read about in the newspaper week after week. That possibility, however, was one thing your father never talked about. Instead, he looked forward to every single letter you sent him and crowed about your exploits, thrilled that you were alive and still having them. He was proud of you, and whatever you did, that pride never diminished. It was just that. The simplest of facts."

Will stared at him with the same humble smile. "I'll see you later."

◦◦◦

HE PUSHED and poked through the crowd that stood ten deep at the end of Cornell's pier, pausing just long enough for Al Deyo to catch up. When he got to the front of the mob, he squeezed past the Broderick brothers, middle-aged bachelors who stood in the front row like bloated cattle, and shouldered Orly's quaking guts aside so Al could pop through and join him.

People were already hooting and clapping when they arrived, and a big tent was being erected at the tip of the pier; even with its faded patches, the blue-and-white stripes of the canvas were as showy as a lady's ball gown. In front of them was a long flatbed wagon with a colorful banner flying overhead, proclaiming in red letters JOHN JUNE'S FAMOUS CIRCUS. In the center of the bed, another sign announced THE AMAZING MELVILLE, AMERICA'S GREATEST POSTURER, and in front of it stood a skinny young man wearing nothing but a pair of blue silk pants as tight as shimmering water, the fabric so delicate that it barely concealed his cock and balls. Every bone was visible on his hairless body, and his big smile was so crooked, it looked like it might fall off his face. But the most remarkable thing was that he stood there perched on one leg, the other wrapped completely behind his body and bent around his neck, where he used the toes next to his chin to wave at the riotous audience.

Al whistled through his teeth as the Amazing Melville unwound himself and turned his back, flexed his puny muscles, then crouched down and bent forward and stuck his head and shoulders up between his legs, looking back at the crowd with that same lopsided smile, his chin resting on his bony behind. Coley and Al laughed and shouted along with all the others as he straightened up again and reached behind his sign for a wooden box not much bigger than a footstool. He opened the empty box for the audience to see, then set it down in front of him with the lid raised, stepped inside and, putting one hand on top of his head, pushed himself down until he was sitting in it with his knees up around his ears. He held up his arms, each limb flexible as pulled taffy, each joint soft as butter, and folded himself into a nest of writhing snakes, cramping himself farther into that little box, until the only thing visible was a crooked little finger, which he used to pull the lid down and lock it over his head.

The crowd exploded in laughter and cheers as a huge man in a bearskin vest and leggings jumped onto the wagon and stood behind the puny box, his beefy arms crossed over his matted chest, his eyebrows almost as thick as his beard. Coley recognized Herr Baron, "the German Hercules," from the circus poster he'd seen on the door of the post office. Herr Baron reached down with one hand and lifted the box over his head as the audience roared. Then he lowered it and heaved it with both hands high into the air, where it spun crazily until Herr Baron caught it and upended it on the wagon bed, stepping back as the lid popped open and Melville tumbled out in a perfect ball that sprouted legs and arms, until the scrawny posturer was completely unfurled and took a bow.

Still clapping, Coley quickly turned to Orly Broderick, who was looming up behind him. "Have the animals come out yet?" he asked.

Orly spit a comet of brown goop over Coley's shoulder, shaking his head. "Critters ain't here yet. They're saving 'em for paying customers."

Then Coley heard the pounding of horses' hooves and turned around in time to see the Zarkova sisters riding side by side along the Strand, bareback, at top speed, only inches apart, and as they got closer they rose into standing positions, wearing identical white dresses that poofed around their knees like frilly clouds, and when they joined hands their diaphanous white scarves flew wildly behind them. They smiled gloriously as they raced by, as stunning as angels, and Coley thought it was the most beautiful thing he'd ever seen. And when he put his hands on Al's shoulders to jump up and get a last fleeting glimpse of them, he felt a hand grip the back of his neck. He clawed at it but was pulled backward past Orly's enormous thighs, unable to dig in his heels or loosen the hold on his throat. He was dragged into a narrow alley of crates and barrels and slammed against a wagon wheel, gasping for breath as he looked up into Mickey Blessing's face.

"It's good to see you, Coley boy," he said. "I thought after last night you'd be back to your muck and bones, gone for good. Just up you go like a kite in the wind and abandon Rondout and all the good friends you've made here."

Coley struggled, but Mickey held him fast to the wheel.

"Tell me it's not so, Coley boy. Tell me you've come home to stay, and that the nigger girl means nothing more to you than a romp and a fuck. Because that's all she's good for, and not hardly enough for us to be battling about."

When Coley made a fist, Mickey drove an elbow into his shoulder and pinned it there against the spokes. "It's only the baby I want," he said. "My baby."

For a moment, Coley forgot the numbing pain in his arm and stared at him. "Your baby?"

"The cat got his mother, but his little self survived. She left him on Jug Hill to die, but he's made of stronger stuff, just like his father, and so I'll claim him."

"It ain't your baby, Mickey."

"He's mine. And the next time I go to the Clove, I'll take him back. So when it's time for me to shake the trees, I need to know where you'll fall," Mickey said, easing his grip and standing back.

Coley heard cheering on the pier and the chiming hooves of the Zarkovas' horses as they made another pass along the cobbled Strand. Mickey heard it, too, and winked at Coley with an easy smile before turning lightly in the alley. Coley sat there rubbing his sore neck and watched him saunter toward the crowd.

☙❧

SHE WALKED to the front counter with a long tray of chocolate mint cookies, her apron dusted with flour, which tickled her nostrils. She quickly put the tray down and covered her face with a handkerchief just before the sneeze erupted, glad the shop was empty. Mary had baked the cookies only minutes ago, and they were still warm and moist and fragrant. The huge kitchen oven still baffled Jane, but Mary allowed her to stir the batter and consolidate ingredients, and she was teaching her the basics of the chocolate pound cakes the bakery was noted for.

Jane much preferred to work up front, away from the sugar and flour that hung in the air out back. She was good with the Rondout locals who frequented the shop, and was accurate to the dollar with the books she figured out every Saturday. If useless as a baker, she could still shave chocolate, shred coconut, stir raspberry sauce, slice apples for tortes and pies and whip bowls of thick cream until it achieved the high peaks Alfons demanded. Her lack of expertise was fine with the

Knetches, who preferred being alone with their ovens, spending all day together and baking in tandem as they'd done before the war, Alfons punching the dough while Mary sifted flour, smiling at each other like shy adolescents during courtship.

Jane made neat rows of the fresh cookies, looking up when the roar of the crowd down at the pier shook the windows. Smiling, she watched half a dozen children race past the shop on their way to see the circus. She felt herself about to sneeze again when the front door opened, and she quickly turned her back and pulled out her handkerchief just in time. Stuffing it back in her apron pocket, she looked up to see Will Harp smiling at her from the other side of the counter.

"Bless you," he said.

"Thank you," she replied, smiling back.

"I'd like to invite you to the farm tomorrow. I meant to ask you last night."

"I'm not sure—"

"The skeleton will be complete," he said, interrupting her, "and I'd like you to be there for the unveiling."

"I really don't know if I can."

"Arthur will be there as well, and it would mean a lot to me if you'd come."

Jane stared at him, and he looked back, unflinching. "I'll try," she finally said.

"Good."

❧

HE'D SET UP his camera in the middle of the barn, where he could best utilize the sheets of sunlight that streamed through the hay doors and fell across the huge skeleton. He had been taking pictures of the mastodon all afternoon, moving his camera to follow the stark shadows of the beast as the sun continued its descent.

Late in the day, he took pictures of Will and the Smittys as they assembled the metal frame that would support the massive skull and tusks. The brothers held the iron bars upright while Will knelt on the ground and secured them in their triangular footings. Arthur moved his camera closer and focused on Will as he tightened the bolts, his friend's sleeves rolled up above the elbows and his long hair dusted with bits of cobweb. The knees of his pants were stained with dirt, and there was a welt on his cheek from a horsefly bite. Arthur couldn't remember ever seeing him so happy.

He readied his camera while Will adjusted the mastodon's front foot, raising the heel slightly off the ground. "Your pet seems as if he's about to dance," he teased.

"He wasn't born flat-footed, Arthur."

"But was he born to waltz?" He waited until Will looked up with a wayward smile, then got the picture he wanted.

When the Smitty brothers left to help their father bring in the late-season corn, Arthur pitched in and held up the mastodon's lower jawbone while Will fitted it to the enormous skull that was raised on wooden blocks between them. The jawbone wasn't particularly heavy, but he was bent in an awkward position and struggled to keep his balance as Will lined up the narrow iron bar that would hold the jawbone and skull together. "I wish the boy was here to help," Arthur said.

"So do I."

"I imagine he's in Rondout cocking around with Mickey Blessing and the little troll who struts behind him."

Will took some of the weight of the jawbone as they set it on the wooden platform beneath the skull. "He has his own mind, Arthur. I can't make him stay here."

"You could, but you're both too damn willful."

Will shrugged.

"And you both drink too much."

"That's true. Which doesn't make me the best example of better living."

"Far better than Blessing, and there's the shame of it." Arthur shook his head as Will fiddled with the metal bar. "He's just a boy."

"And a good one."

"Which only makes the shame that much worse."

She sat on the porch of the farmhouse with a pair of Will's trousers across her lap, hemming the cuffs that had been torn by his boot heels. Rump was down at the bottom of the stairs, pawing at a nest of digger bees in the grass. All afternoon she'd shooed him away from the hole, but he only growled at her and stayed on point. He'd already gotten stung the week before, and his muzzle had swelled up big as a pig's snout, the dog so miserable that he'd let Pearl comfort him in her arms with a slice of raw onion held to his nose. But he was at it again, and she figured it would take another bee to teach him the lesson he was asking for.

She missed Tally and knew she'd miss her even more when the weather turned cold and she'd have to spend more time at home. And she was mad at Coley for abandoning her. She'd grown fond of him and looked forward to seeing him every morning as she came down the hill, his eyes automatically floating in her direction. Now she'd be alone, and she couldn't help but think that this might be her fate after all: taking care of an old man who didn't see her even when she was standing right in front of him, living on Jug Hill and marrying one of the Smitty boys, cooking and cleaning and calving each spring like she was just more stock.

She pulled a tight stitch and looked over as Rump raised his head from the bee hole and stood up, his legs apart and his ears tilted forward, staring off at the green slope above the cow pasture. Then he started barking, and before Pearl could shout a command, he bounded across the dirt yard and right past the barn.

Hearing the dog, Will jumped from the platform, grabbed the old Springfield rifle leaning against the barn door and burst outside. He spun around and spotted Rump running through the field, his tail raised high as he bounced over rocks and roots. He was about to call the dog back, when he glanced up and saw the mountain lion crouching low, barely visible against the rock debris along the ridge, its head stretched over its big front paws as it turned from the cows to track the dog coming toward it. Will jerked up the long-barreled rifle and aimed too quickly. He fired, and saw the bullet spark off the rocks five feet below the lion, who in an instant was gone.

Arthur ran out of the barn as the repercussion still echoed in the yard. Pearl, standing by the porch railing with the trousers in her hand, saw the big cat leap out of view. Will lowered the rifle as Rump raced back through the pasture, where the cows sat unperturbed. His ears still ringing from the wayward shot, he knew he'd soon regret his haste.

~⟨Q⟩~

HE SAT AT a table in Natterjack's, listening to O'Fay yammer on, wishing instead that he was down at the circus with the Magruder brothers, watching the boxing mules or those pretty angels on horseback. But he'd been told to wait at the saloon, and his knees knocked

impatiently as he drank his second pint of ale and tried to make sense
of the story that Charlie gobbled in his ear.

"Robbie Taft come back from the war this week, his body the same
as it was when he left two years ago, except for a scar on his cheek from
a musket ball taken at Peeble's Farm. Said he left nothing in Virginia
but a bit of skin and blood, and a gladder man coming off a boat I never
seen." Charlie's big head bobbed back and forth, his breath stinking of
rum and cheese. "Only thing that perplexed Robbie was the fact that
his wife and kids weren't at the boat to greet him, just me and Donny
Sprague and the church ladies with their scented hankies and wet eyes
and god-awful good intentions. He looked all about for the missus,
standing up on his toes to see this way and that, and when he was certain she wasn't there he just walked on home, me and Donny at his
side, telling us all about the terrible battles at Cold Harbor and Petersburg and how he'd nearly lost his life at Deep Bottom, where the heat
was so bad that the veins on his hands stood out like ribs on a stalk of
celery, and he passed out and fell face-first into a creek and would've
drowned in two inches of water if another soldier hadn't yanked him
up by his suspenders and dragged him out."

Charlie finished his rum and signaled the girl to bring him another.
"So Robbie figures he's come through the worst of it, that he'd walked
from one end of hell to the other and that life was going to be all
sparkle and bliss from here on in. And he's talking like this when we
come to his house and walk up to the third floor, where Robbie had the
same two rooms he lived in before the war. So he knocks on the door
and Ellen opens it, with his two little girls at her side and a baby in her
arms. And he's just overwhelmed to see them and hugs his wife and
picks up his kids and kisses them until their faces are shiny with his
tears of love. But then he looks back at the baby and the look on his
wife's face and starts to thinking. Now Robbie ain't no genius but he
can do simple arithmetic, and he knows for a fact that he left three people behind, where now there's four. Of course me and Donny already
knew Ellen had been keeping company with Roy Owens while Robbie
was slogging through the Virginia mud, but I was so happy to see him
that I forgot to tell him, and by the time I remembered, the door had
already opened and Robbie could see for himself that shenanigans was
underfoot. It took but two sharp slaps to get the truth from Ellen, and
off we go again."

The girl came with Charlie's rum, and he drank down half of it with
glee. Coley took a long swallow of ale, glad for the brief respite.

"By now Roy'd heard that Robbie was back in town, and he hid himself in the back room of Turck's lumberyard, where he spent his days watering down the cheap whitewash Turck sells for a dollar a bucket. He always had an eye for Ellen and figured Robbie, luckless bastard that he was, would find a Confederate bullet somewhere between Fredericksburg and Petersburg, so for two years he prayed for a painless death, or so he said. But he couldn't wait for his prayers to be answered, his and Ellen's both, and they undid each other's buttons and bows, and I figure the baby was born about the time Robbie was at the North Anna River, chasing General Lee's army up the Telegraph Road."

Coley drank some more beer and shut his eyes as Charlie finished his rum and ordered another.

"Now, Roy was cringing behind bags of unslaked lime when Robbie came into Turck's place, and me and Donny stood behind him when he jerked Roy out of his dark corner and dunked his head in a pail of whitewash. Roy squirmed but Robbie held him fast, the two of 'em sprayed and splattered, Roy twitching his arms and legs like a puppet, kicking over buckets as Robbie held him under with all the strength he's got."

Coley glanced up just as the story began to get interesting, and caught sight of Mickey as he stepped inside and looked around with his usual conceit. Coley had stayed behind in Rondout for this very reason: to keep an eye on Mickey without being watched himself, to be ready to move before he was. Now he sat up and raised his pint glass and smiled until he had his attention.

"Roy wasn't a strong man, and it didn't take but a moment for his body to go limp. Robbie snatched him by the hair and pulled his head out of the pail, and Roy sputtered and gasped as he grabbed him by the legs and hauled him through Turck's yard and into the street, leaving a smear of whitewash in his wake," Charlie went on, unaware that Mickey was coming up behind him. "And Robbie yanked him through the middle of town, past all the prying eyes of Rondout, right up to the house on Union Street. And all Roy could do was drag his fingernails in the dirt, his face white as a ghost, moaning like one, too. Robbie just ignored him and pulled him up those three flights of stairs, and I believe Roy lost a tooth on each step. Me and Donny followed the trail of paint and blood, and when we got up there Roy's face was a horrible mess, soft and juicy as a raw steak. This time Robbie didn't bother to knock, just kicked the door right in, his wife and girls screaming as he tossed all that was left of Roy Owens into the only comfortable chair in the room before storming out without a word. Donny and me followed him back to the pier and watched him board the same steamboat he came in on an hour before, taking it all the way back to Manhattan where he joined up again and got on the first train south, more willing to take his chances in a Virginia bloodbath than with a lying wife."

Mickey swung into the chair between them, followed by the bar girl, who set three drinks on the table. Charlie reached for his rum and Coley for his ale, but Mickey left his standing, waiting for the foam to disappear before he took the smallest sip.

"I was telling the boy about Robbie Taft. You heard the story, Mickey?"

"No."

"But you do know Robbie?"

"No."

"Are you sure?" Charlie asked, smacking his lips after a long swallow. "Tall, skinny fellow with eyes big and dumb as a baby's. Worked at the stoneyard, come back from the war this week."

"Don't know him," Mickey replied.

Charlie snickered, his eyes red with drink, and went on. "Well, me and Donny Sprague was down at the pier when he came in on the steamboat, grown a full two inches it seemed, his uniform up to his forearms and ankles."

"That's enough, Charlie."

Coley held his glass and watched them. He admired how Charlie never began a story the same way twice but somehow managed to find a common end. He also knew the man was drunk, and the sound of his own voice the best company he had.

"Robbie's front pocket bulged with the letters he got from his wife when he was off fighting the rebels, and he read them over and over on the voyage home, expecting her to be there and jump up in his waiting arms."

"Stop it, Charlie," Mickey said.

Coley saw the skin pull back on Mickey's cheeks and his knuckles turn white. Though he wanted to warn Charlie, he knew the inevitable was already happening.

"But nobody was on that dock but me and Donny Sprague, and poor Robbie looked so long in the face I thought he was going to—"

Mickey grabbed Charlie by the throat and lifted him off his chair gurgling and wheezing, and not one man in the saloon even glanced in their direction. Charlie stared at him the whole time, the half glass of rum still in his hand, his eyes moist with tears until Mickey let him go. He collapsed in his chair and took short, harsh breaths, ignoring the spit and phlegm that dripped from his lips.

Mickey inched his glass of beer closer and took his last sip. "Meet me back here in the morning, nine o'clock sharp," he said, and without looking at either of them, he got up and left.

"It was just a story," Charlie whimpered, reaching for Mickey's beer and chugging it down his aching throat.

Coley nodded in agreement, even though that wasn't the story he was interested in.

~∽⊚∾~

HE STOOD in his father's study and watched the fire gain strength and roar up the chimney. It was the first fire of the season, and he'd built a tall tower of logs and kindling on the grate, hoping the flames would burn out any squirrel nests that might have appeared since last spring. The smell brought back cold nights like this when he was a boy, bending over his father's shoulder as he lit the fire, the two of them sitting back on their heels in the sudden amber swell, their cheeks warmed as the darkness was sucked out of the room.

The fire took quickly, and only a little smoke shuffled over the mantel. It was after midnight and Arthur had gone to bed hours ago, having fallen asleep in the parlor chair with a copy of Dickens's *American Notes* tented over his belly. Will had sat on the porch for a while, listening for the lion, but all he could hear were the horses moving through the tall grass. He thought about Coley, wishing he'd come back with them to the Clove. He never doubted the boy's sharpness or ambition, though he wanted a little more time to drum some sense into his head before he journeyed west. He'd failed with Eli Birdslee, and it galled him.

And he thought about Jane, wishing she were there to challenge the impenetrability of his somber mood, and hoping she'd come tomorrow to see the mastodon reshaped in its entirety.

He sat down behind the desk, turned up the lamp, opened the drawer and pulled out the letter his father had left for him, holding it in his hand for a moment before pulling out the three sheets inside, looking at the familiar handwriting through the back of the thick buff-colored vellum his father always ordered from a shop in Albany. He turned the letter over, flattened it with his fingers and moved the lamp until the ink no longer melted before his eyes.

Dear Will,

It has been many months since I last heard from you, but I know the pain it causes me cannot compare to the terrible suffering that has brought you to this silence. If I had the power to take it away I would do so, but I wander in the same darkness that has swallowed you.

I have a presentiment that I will not live to see you again, so I take up this pen to give you a father's last words. How sad I am to leave you, son, but you must know there is also joy in my going. To be reunited with your mother has long been my wish. I regret only that there is so little time to pass along the lessons of a long and happy life. The years with you and your mother were just as you saw, filled with work and love in abundance. Of the preceding years, you know less. Certainly there were stories of battles and friendships that became part of your boyhood, but there were others your mother and I agreed need not be told. It is every father's wish that his son see him as a strong and honorable man. I know from your respect and affection that you have seen me in this light, but now I must hasten to tell you a fuller truth of my experience. Indeed, I'm sure Mother would not let me join her if I left this task undone.

I was still a lieutenant when we fought at Chippawa in 1814, determined to push the British from the Niagara frontier for good. The battles fought in those early days of July were vicious, neither General Scott nor his British counterpart willing to give ground, and on the fifth day we met the enemy near the Grove farm. Even now I cannot say what caused men on both sides to break rank, but such is what happened, and the horrors that ensued I will not put to paper some fifty years later. We fought at close range, more smoke than air in our lungs, then lay flat on the ground as the big guns roared from behind and shells landed all around us. When I looked up I saw a British foot soldier sprawled not more than ten feet away. He raised his head, as I did mine, and when he stood and ran, I ran after him. The battle was over, but still I chased him down.

It is no easy task to push a knife through a man's back. Bone resists the blade, which has a taste for only flesh and muscle. Such were my thoughts as I watched the young man I'd stabbed walk across the field with his retreating ranks and slowly drop down before he reached the *smoking woods, his hands folded beneath his cheek as though all he wanted in the world was a nap. Was it a terrible thing I did? Yes. Would I do it again if the circumstances repeated themselves? Of course.*

Over the years I had only to look at my hand to recall the deed, and I recalled it often. It took your mother to recognize my melancholy for the arrogance it was. It is tempting to consort with guilt, to succumb to cynicism when one's ideals enter into conflict. But I ask you, as she asked me all those years ago, is it not a gratuitous exaltation to assume for yourself your Maker's perfection? Or worse perhaps, do you covet the mantle of His son's martyrdom? I pray not, for you are merely mortal, and grief coddled and grown too large will rob you of your future. "Examine the raw fact," is what your mother told me. "A man is dead and you had a part in his killing. That is the true and horrible face of war. You must look upon your act with all the humility it deserves. If you have made a mark you think bad, then amend it."

The time has come to think of means and deeds. That you have been given a fine education has put it within your power to enrich the world with your good works. Find a woman as near to Mother's equal as you can and tell her your whole truth. Raise your children well, and when your sons come to you wishing to go to war, tell them that loyalty must be honored, but then tell them the whole truth, yours and mine.

I was as you are, and yet I go to Mother in peace, knowing now that mine has indeed been a happy life. Do you remember the story of King Croesus? Upon contemplating his great wealth, he expected to be named the happiest man on earth. He was cautioned, as I caution you, to wait and mark the end, for each life is a story and only at its end can it be judged.

Your story, as I write this, is incomplete. Grant the two who brought you to this world our greatest wish: Live a full and good life.

Only yesterday you were a babe. Mother and I placed you on the bed between us and shared an intoxication of love for you. We slept and woke to laughter.

Your loving father still

SHE HAD GOTTEN home from the bakery half an hour ago, having gone in before dawn to help Mary and Alfons bake scones, and was packing her valise when she heard a knock. She put down the dress she was folding, wiped the last vestiges of flour from the front of her blouse and walked into the parlor. Her brother was leaning on the other side of the door with the cool familiarity of a strolling peddler.

"You don't need me to open the door for you, Mickey," she told him as she went back to her packing. "You're welcome anytime."

"I figured today might be the exception."

"And why's that?"

"I've come to collect the rent."

Jane frowned and picked up the bag she'd dropped on the kitchen table when she came home, took out ten dollars in banknotes and slapped them into her brother's open hand.

"It's not me to blame, sister. I'm just doing the job you should've had yourself."

"It's no longer a job I want, Mickey."

"You're ten dollars poorer for turning your back on Mr. Grieves."

"It's worth it for the good night's sleep I get."

"Yes, I'm sure you slumber in peace," he sneered. "You're a working girl again. Must be exhausted."

"No. I'm elated."

"If Frank were here, he'd say your senses were scrambled."

"And I'd love to hear him say it, Mickey. I'd give anything to hear those words."

He followed her to her bedroom and stood in the doorway as she refolded her dress. "Are you going on a trip?"

"I'm going to Dr. Harp's this morning."

And then he stopped grinning and stared at his sister's back. "You and the doctor have become like two birds in a tree, haven't you, Jane?"

She ignored him.

"Frank's not dead but a few months and you're already jumping the moon with another."

Jane turned to her brother and scowled. "Get out."

"There's motion in this world that not even you can stop," he said before stepping back from the door. "And don't you ever fix an ugly eye on me if you're not ready to fix it on yourself."

❦

HE SAT BACK in the padded comfort of his armchair and forced himself to look at the map that bloomed above his desk like a forest of green. The pleasure he'd once derived from it was gone; all he saw there now was a free fall, and the thought of his loosening grip made his stomach burn.

His hotel plans were rolled up and stuck out of sight. He'd spent two years preparing this undertaking, quietly going about his business without raising alarm or suspicion, keeping his plans to himself, not even whispering his hopes to his wife in the evenings when he most wanted to share the brilliance of his gambit. Instead, he'd kept true to his father's dogma and neither gloated nor took public satisfaction in this most methodical and splendid of schemes. For all those many days the hotel lived in his mind only, but now it stalled and festered there like a canker, and the taste of it was rotten in his mouth.

He sat low in his chair, staring at the map, pondering his miscalculations. There were very few mistakes, but the ones he'd made were damaging. He had believed so much in the ultimate success of his hotel that he'd allowed himself to become indolent, and was paying for it now.

His father once told him there was a fine line between risk and reward, that both must be gambled with in order to achieve anything of lasting merit. Grieves was thinking about that when he heard a knock on his door, pausing to enjoy the silence that followed before asking Mickey Blessing to come in.

~∾⊘∾~

SHAPIRO BARELY looked at him when he came into the stable, his brow furrowed and his lower lip bloated with pink irritation. Coley had seen it before, when a horse turned up lame and Shapiro was forced to put a bullet between its soulful eyes, or when his wife almost died of pneumonia a few years ago and he walked around the house blind with worry.

"I need two horses, Mr. Shapiro," he said, stepping back as the big man moved past him as if carrying an anvil on his shoulders, his heavy feet shuffling out to the corral. Coley watched him from inside the door and breathed in the horseshit and sweet alfalfa, surprised by how much he missed working here. He was tempted to follow Shapiro out back, but then he saw Nathan, Shapiro's nephew, looping toward him as if he'd been born without knees. A skinny boy, barely fifteen, he'd helped out in the stable before, and Coley knew he was as skittish as an old woman, jumping at every stomped hoof, and Coley pitied his old boss for having to hire him.

"Want to help me saddle your ponies?" Nathan whined, and Coley nodded, rolled up his sleeves and followed him to the back.

Half an hour before, he'd been leaning against the lamppost outside the Grieves building, eating his third apple and watching the parade of wagons on Division Street, the yellow dust swirling ankle-high, thick as pond smoke. It was almost ten, and he was bored and hungry. When he finished his last apple, he tossed the core to a passing mule, wiped his sticky hands on his pants, then saw Mickey Blessing step out the door. There was a new bounce to his step, and he knew for certain the day was about to change.

"Get our horses from Shapiro," Mickey told him. "I'll meet you there."

Now, as he led his horse to the front of the stable, Nathan trailing Dutch Eddy behind him, he saw Mickey walking toward them from downtown, carrying his dusty rifle and a satchel over his shoulder. Then he felt Shapiro at his side, standing so close that Coley could smell the whiff of fried bacon and eggs he'd had for breakfast. "You should never have come back," he whispered in his ear.

Mickey gladly took the reins from Nathan and slipped his rifle into the sleeve on the saddle.

Coley had picked out a more spirited gelding for himself and walked up to him. "So where are we going?"

Mickey grinned as he adjusted his stirrups. "To the Clove, Coley boy," he said. "Back to the Clove."

He'd been expecting that answer, been waiting for it, and he leapt into the saddle, his horse prancing as he jiggled the reins.

Mickey grabbed him by the leg. "What's your hurry?" he asked. Coley tried to pull away, but Mickey tightened his fingers and wouldn't let go. "This is the reckoning, boy. This is when we shake the trees."

Coley glowered down at him and reached into his waistband for the pistol. He aimed it at the top of Mickey's head, pulled back the hammer with his thumb and held it there as steadily as he could, the big horse skittering beneath him. Mickey slowly lifted his hand from Coley's leg, took a step back and showed his palms as Shapiro and Nathan looked on in wonder.

Coley stuck the Colt Walker back in his belt and spun the horse with his heel, leaning low over the saddle and kicking the animal into a full gallop up Hone Street.

Shapiro and his nephew covered their eyes from the spitting stones, while Mickey just stood there and watched as the boy raced on ahead.

～◎～

THEY'D BUILT the giant sling the week before, using rope and the leather from a pair of old plow harnesses. Will had cut the straps and traces to the length he needed to make a sturdy cradle. With a couple of snaffle bits, he'd brought the ropes through a common hoop, creating a comfortable basket they could direct from either side of the scaffolding. Early on Sunday afternoon, he climbed to the top of the haymow, inched across the upper tie beam and ran the heavy rope through the pulley hanging from a track over the center of the barn, directly above the skeleton.

Joop and the Smitty brothers held the other end of the rope as he climbed back down to the scaffold. Arthur had his camera set up inside the doorway, while Pearl and Sam waited by the massive skull already in the sling. "Are you ready?" Will called down.

Joop nodded and gripped the rope, and Sam climbed up the right side of the scaffolding to stand across from Will. Between them was a Y-shaped metal frame that would hold the enormous mastodon skull in place. Once Sam was in position, Will shouted, "Okay, Joop, bring her up."

Joop and the Smittys slowly pulled on the rope, and as it squeaked through the pulley, the leather harness pulled tight as a closed fist around the skull, which swayed a moment as it inched off the ground.

"Easy," Will cautioned, and Pearl put a hand up to steady it as it rocked over her head. When it was level with the vertebrae column, he signaled Joop to tie off the rope; then he and Sam carefully guided the skull onto the brace, fitting it right above the atlas bone, the topmost vertebrae along the spine, locking it into the metal notch, the jaws slightly agape, leaving only the tusk sockets waiting to be fitted.

"Would you please stand still a moment, Will?" Arthur called, sliding another plate into his camera. Will obliged by resting his hand on the mastodon's broad parietal ridge as Arthur ducked his head beneath the black cloth and made his exposure.

The Smitty brothers carried in the first of the twelve-foot tusks, brown as hardwood and exquisitely curved. Will and Sam climbed onto the small platform they'd built below the skull and lifted the nine feet of ivory and anchored it into the right socket, the tip almost reaching to the beam. The left tusk fit just as precisely, and even Will was shocked by the primitive ferocity when he finally stepped back and gazed at the complete skeleton for the first time. It took up most of the barn, and the shadows it threw gave it an epic grandeur.

"It's wonderful," Will heard someone say, and he looked down to see Jane standing in the bright light of the doorway, smiling at him.

"Now hold it!" Arthur commanded from behind the camera.

Will did as he was told, the pleasure evident on his face.

❧

THEY CELEBRATED that afternoon with the champagne Arthur had brought with him from Rondout. Joop allowed Pearl and Sam to have a glass each, Sam swallowing just once before handing Pearl his glass. She drank it quickly, enthralled by its cool effervescence and sour taste, and gladly accepted another that Sam gave her when the others weren't looking. When she put the empty glass down, Pinch jumped off the mantel, tipped the glass over and worked his tongue around the rim.

Later in the afternoon, Joop and Sam went back to Jug Hill, while Arthur locked himself up in his darkroom in the pantry. Pearl decided to stay and help with supper, but after skinning a few rabbits, she'd fallen asleep in the parlor rocker.

Will and Jane walked to the pasture to check on the horses. The sun was low, scratched by the upper branches of the tall maple behind the barn. The leaves were still on most of the oaks above the ridge, rusted with late-fall color, and Jane enjoyed the seasonal change as well as the diffused light that fell like brushstrokes between the upper reaches of the pine trees that lined the Clove road. Will turned to her as they walked to the farmhouse. "I'm glad you decided to spend the night."

"So am I. That way, I can ride back to town with Arthur in the morning."

"You're not worried about gossip?"

Jane grinned. "If anything I do brings a bit of pleasure to Rondout tattlers, then I feel absolved."

Will smiled with her. "I thought about Frank last night."

Jane looked at him quickly. "What brought that on?"

"I imagine it was you," he said. "Would you like to hear?"

She nodded and faced him.

"In the winter, when we were still boys, Frank would come out and visit us, bringing supplies my father had ordered from town. At our insistence, he'd spend a few days, though I don't think it took much to convince him. If the snow wasn't too high, we'd take the horses up there"—he pointed to the ridge above—"and we'd follow deer trails that were the same year after year, looking for big bucks but content if we came across a good doe. Frank was the better shot and would usually take the first deer, but no matter how cold it was he'd stay out until I had my own; then we'd gut them where they fell and haul the carcasses back to hang in the barn. Sometimes, if the mornings were bright and cold, we'd wake early and ride down to High Falls, strap on our skates and race onto Rondout Creek to hunt for ducks, holding our rifles and gliding like warriors across the ice. We'd bring home half a dozen, maybe more. There was something fine about those days, and sometimes we'd skate for miles, past the quarry and the Ten Hagen farm, skate until our legs grew tired; then we'd rest and eat whatever my mother had packed for us, and skate again. Occasionally my father joined us, and that would make the day even finer." He paused a moment to look out across the pasture.

"Thank you for that," Jane told him.

"It was you who spurred the memory."

"Then I'm glad," she told him. "Perhaps you'll be here through the coming winter and hunt on the ice again."

He liked the idea and smiled. "Perhaps," he said, then handed her a folded letter and walked toward the house.

It reminded her of the letter from Frank she still carried in her bag. She unfolded the papers, took the spectacles out of her pocket and read it where she stood.

When she came back to the house, he was sitting on the porch, a rifle leaning next to him on the railing. It was full dusk and cooler now, and Jane shivered as she came up the steps. Pearl had turned on the lamps in the front rooms, and the windows glowed yellow as cat's eyes. "Are you expecting trouble?" Jane asked, looking down at the gun.

"There's a mountain lion in the Clove," he said. "I saw him again yesterday, and I don't expect him to be in much of a hurry to leave."

She sat on the railing and turned to the lush fields leading up to the Shawangunk cliffs, the sheets of rock as gray as cold water tumbling over a precipice. "It's pretty country. I can't blame the lion one bit."

Then she handed him the letter. "Your father's right," she said, laying a hand on the one that held the envelope. "It was a war and you were a soldier." She waited until he looked at her, then held his gaze. "But you're not a soldier anymore."

They sat there until the sound of hooves rumbled through the silence. They both looked toward the Clove road as a solitary rider galloped into view, hanging so low over his horse that he almost appeared headless. Rump burst through the door, barking, and Pearl followed, still half-asleep.

Will was already at the bottom of the stairs when Coley reached the porch, his hair plastered to his forehead and his horse soaped with lather.

He looked past Will and Jane and stared at Pearl.

~©~

THEY RAN through the forest at the base of the ridge, the branches of saplings whipping back and slicing their arms and legs. It was darker now, and as Pearl wove through the familiar path, Coley's footfalls were less exact. He stumbled behind her, straining to keep up as she raced through the brush. She turned to him with that fierce nerve he'd come to admire, and when they came to the steeper rise that would take them to Jug Hill, she grabbed his hand and held it tight, and he let her, digging the toes of his boots into the stone path, the pebbles crumbling beneath his feet.

She didn't slow down when they reached the summit, where the trees gradually thinned out and the path grew wider. The moon was low in a sterling sky, and he looked at the open country, which pitched slightly in every direction. Rows of corn were planted in the rocky soil, and miserable-looking cows grazed in the sparse grass that grew around tree stumps and boulders. Sheep watched them from another field, and he caught sight of a red fox slinking along the roof of a henhouse.

He'd never been to Jug Hill before, and when the hamlet finally came into view, he was as startled as Gulliver was to be washed ashore at Lilliput. Small weathered farmhouses were built wherever possible, on top of low hills or in shaded glens, and sometimes slanted to the left or right, but they were neatly kept and he could tell it was a real community assembled on the hill, not a fairy-tale one. He saw two boys leading cattle into a dilapidated barn, and an old woman sweeping the day's dust from her porch. When he slowed to watch a three-legged dog butt heads with a tethered lamb, Pearl yanked him along, and they banged up the crooked stairs of the small farmhouse in front of them. She pushed through the front door without knocking and Coley followed, surprised to see the Smitty brothers sitting at the kitchen table and scrubbing the dirt off the pile of potatoes between them.

"Evening, Pearl," Earl said, shy as always, eyes on her feet.

"Where's your ma?"

"Out visiting her sister in Springtown."

"And the baby?"

He jerked his chin to the other room. "If it ain't crying, it's sleeping."

Pearl ran to the back room while Coley stood there and looked around the room. A fire was burning under a big kettle of boiling water and dried sunflowers hung upside down in the corner.

"You want some supper, Coley?" John asked him.

Coley was hungry and tired, but before he could answer, Pearl came back with the baby, who was swathed in a blanket against her shoulder, and stormed out the door.

She walked as fast as she could, pausing only long enough to hear Coley's footsteps pounding after her. She took a different path this time, skirting the hamlet and the meddling concern of her neighbors. Moses was awake but silent, his eyes wide as he bounced in her arms, and she held him tight as she jumped over a small brook, listening to Coley splash through it a few seconds later. Seeing the roof of her own house over the next rise, she stayed to the west of Cyrus Dunn's buckwheat fields, where she couldn't be seen, and quickly found the break in his fence that led to the woods, making for the narrow road that ran down from Jug Hill and wound through the Clove and into High Falls. Not as steep or closed in as her usual route, she knew it would provide enough moonlight for her to carry the baby safely, and they ran almost a mile in the dark woods before they reached it. It was barely wide enough for a wagon, and Pearl took the rutted track to the right, worn smooth as a wooden floor. Moses stayed quiet, and she hugged him tighter. By now, Coley was running alongside her, both of them too tired to speak.

They were thirty feet from the bottom of the hill when they saw him, and they would've run right past if his horse hadn't snorted. He was sitting on top of Dutch Eddy at the edge of the tree line, sociable as a Sunday caller when he motioned the little horse forward to block their way.

"Give me the baby," he said, his voice clear and sharp in the quiet woods.

"No," Pearl told him.

"He's mine, girl. Ask Coley. He knows."

Coley never took his eyes off Mickey. "I don't think the lady in that farmhouse wanted you to have him then, and you ain't getting him now."

"It's my wants you should be worrying about, Coley boy."

"You ain't getting this baby," Coley said, drawing the Colt from his belt.

Straightening up in his saddle, Mickey seemed almost pleased with himself. "You pulled that on me once already," he said. "I'm taking my baby now."

Coley could barely see Mickey's face in the twilight, and the weight of the revolver made it difficult for him to keep his hand steady. He waited until Mickey started to dismount before he fired, the gunshot louder than anything he'd ever heard, and in the instant of muzzle flash, he saw Mickey's body lift from the saddle and fall beneath his horse. The baby started howling, but Coley could barely hear him over the ringing in his ears. He grabbed Pearl by the elbow and they ran.

⁓◎⁓

ARTHUR WAS in the yard hitching two horses to the wagon when he heard the gunshot. Will stepped onto the porch and picked up the rifle as he moved down the stairs. He had taken ten steps toward the road when he saw them break through the trees, running to the farmhouse. He could see the baby in the girl's arms, and he relaxed his grip on the gun.

"I shot him!" Coley yelled.

"Where is he?" Will asked.

"On the road."

"Is he hurt?"

"He's shot!" Coley repeated, the Colt Walker still in his hand.

Jane was carrying a canvas satchel out of the house as Coley and Pearl rushed into the yard. Will took it from her and threw it in the back of the wagon. "Take the girl and the baby and go," he said to Coley.

"What?"

"Go," Will said sharply.

Coley froze, staring at him as Pearl climbed into the wagon. Arthur came up behind him and shoved his bindle into his arms and put Pinch on his shoulder. Coley grabbed the little squirrel and stuffed him into his coat pocket, then jumped up on the seat. He glanced over his shoulder at the woods, as if expecting the trees to part with the menace they held. He took up the reins and looked at Pearl, who sat beside him and hushed the crying baby.

"Go now, Coley!" Will snapped.

Coley looked at him, trying to speak the words that were locked in his throat. He realized he still had the pistol in his free hand, and he held it out to Will.

"Take it," Will said softly. "Get them out of here."

"I didn't mean for any of this to happen."

"It's enough that you came back," Will told him as he placed his hand on the boy's knee. "Now go."

Coley lifted the reins and got the horses moving.

〜◎〜

THE BULLET HIT him beneath his bottom rib. It went right through him, and he felt blood running from the wound before the pain registered. The impact was like a cramp deep in his muscles, and he'd twisted his left ankle in the stirrup when he was blown off the saddle. He was surprised at the boom of the single gunshot, filling his ears as he lay there on his back beneath a laurel bush and watched Coley and the girl run past him. He looked up at the sky, where the stars seemed to move in wandering patterns before he closed and reopened his eyes and everything turned right again. He slowly stood and canted to the right, as if this crippled position would stem the flow of blood that was warm on his skin and annoyed him more than the hurt. He tried lifting himself into the saddle, but his ankle was too sore, so instead he unsheathed his old rifle, put the stock under his arm and started walking through the woods. He kept his hand pressed over the wound and felt the blood streaming through his fingers, sticky as tree sap, but he knew that he'd heal. He would finish Grieves's business and find his baby, then go back to Rondout and let Gitta take care of them both.

He stayed at the edge of the woods, away from the farmhouse, and came up behind the barn. The hay doors were open and he sidled inside, barely glancing at the giant skeleton that stood in the middle of the cavernous space. He thought nothing of where it had come from, or what wonders it might've seen before the swamp swallowed it whole. He thought only of the job he'd come to do, and the rewards he'd collect when it was accomplished. He heard his own rough breathing and quieted it. He felt little pain now, but the blood had dampened his trousers. He sat down on a hay bale and pulled the matches out of his pocket. Though the box was soaked with blood, enough matchsticks were still dry. He set the first bale on fire and watched the flames spread like liquid. He lit six more bales before the matches ran out, then stood back as the smoke began to curl and rise, the flames racing up the beams like twirling snakes and dancing across the rafters above the skeleton. He stayed until the heat seared his skin, then hobbled out the rear door.

"Will!" Arthur yelled when he saw black smoke erupting from the hayloft and fire creeping up the sides of the barn. They ran down together but got no closer than fifty feet before the intensity of the heat repelled them. They stood back as the flames spiraled brightly into the sky and fully engulfed the barn, and to Will it looked as if part of the sun had fallen into the yard. Jane hurried to the adjacent pasture and opened the gate for the horses, stepping back as they galloped off in panic.

By the time the barn had begun to fall into itself, Will had retrieved his gun from the porch and entered the woods.

❦

MICKEY MOVED quickly through the thick brush, but the effort exhausted him and his footsteps faltered and carried him off the path. He groped his way through a dense stand of tamarack, unsure of his direction, but as the fire grew, it irradiated the woods behind him, and he wandered through the shimmering light. Looking up ahead, he could see Dutch Eddy still standing in the middle of the road, and even if it took all his might, he'd throw himself over the horse's back. The pain was gone now, but he could feel the blood filling his boot. Stopping to rest, he took a moment to admire the sky. It seemed black and endless, each star a possibility, as if he needed only to grasp a few to make everything all right. He tipped his head back and felt a delicate bewilderment, and almost laughed out loud for the sudden thrill of it. He would have his son back and see him grow into a man. And that was the last thought he had, closing his eyes and smiling as he savored it, and he never felt the magnificent weight of the cat as it came out of the woods like a shadow and landed on his back.

When he picked up the trail of blood behind the barn, Will gripped the rifle and followed it along the path, losing sight of it once he was deeper in the woods and the path had been abandoned. He stopped to listen, and above the crackling of the fire he heard movement in the brush ahead and the moan of an animal. He raised the rifle and crept forward beneath the boughs, peering through the woods, which wavered with the light of the fire. Just before he reached the road, he saw the big cat crouching on the ground, its paws covering its prey, its mouth shiny with blood. Will raised his gun and fired, and the cat screeched and bounded twice before collapsing in the dark. He waited a moment to lower the rifle from his shoulder, not yet aware that what the lion had been gnawing was once a man.

◦◦◦

HE IGNORED the squirrel squatting on his hip, trying to pick his pocket, and the noise of clinking chains, and tried to sleep. It was after midnight when they'd finally pulled the wagon into a stand of pines just outside of High Falls, and they were exhausted. Pearl had given the baby some of the milk that Jane had packed for them, and he slurped hungrily from the glass bottle without complaint. When he was done with it, they took blankets from the back of the wagon and found a soft patch of grass where they could sleep.

Pinch continued to scratch at Coley's pocket, and the rattling chain wouldn't stop, so he rolled on his back in frustration and opened his eyes. A chimpanzee was sitting on a low branch of the tree above him, wearing red canvas pants with big gold buttons and dangling a broken chain that was attached to his ankle. It chattered at him, grinning wildly with its whiskered baby face, and swung like a little acrobat to the next branch. Coley banged an elbow into Pearl's side as he scurried to his feet. The monkey was hanging there by a long hairy arm and twirling his chain in the other hand; then he dropped from the tree and loped off over the hill.

Coley stuck Pinch in his pocket and ran after it. At the top of the hill, he stopped short and gazed down to the banks of Rondout Creek, where he thought he saw two giant mastodons stepping through the shallow water and lusterless morning fog, the beasts having come to life to follow him here from the Clove. He had to blink twice before he realized these were massive elephants in front of him, dousing their backs with their wrinkled trunks. And then Pearl was at his side with the baby on her hip, and they stood there watching with awed delight as the animals bathed and splashed and frolicked.

Seven circus wagons were pulled into a circle at the far end of the clearing. The canvas of the lead wagon was painted with red-and-yellow letters as big and bold as balloons: JOHN JUNE CIRCUS. Men and women sat by campfires drinking coffee and frying bread in butter, while others took down laundry from a line stretched between two wagons. Hobbled horses nibbled grass along the banks of the creek, and Coley recognized the trick ponies he'd seen the Zarkova sisters riding two days before.

"Wait here," he said to Pearl, and ran across the field to the nearest wagon. Three clowns were sitting on rickety chairs out front, placing thick pieces of ham on an iron griddle and rubbing at the dried daubs of greasepaint in the cracks and hollows of their faces. At the next wagon he saw the Zarkova sisters, still beautiful in white robes and hair nets held with ivory combs, eating biscuits slathered with honey. And he recognized Melville in his street clothes, strolling through the grass with a clay pipe in his mouth, the stem as bent as one of his own contortions. Coley walked past wagons painted with bright signs, one announcing trapeze acts and somersaulters, another dancing bears, and standing alone in front of the latter was a tall Chinese man with a coolie braid and silk pants, who was juggling three hatchets as easily as if they were leather balls. When he came to the lead wagon, Coley saw a bearded man with oiled hair, his suspenders hanging loose on his striped pants. He was sitting on an overturned barrel, reading the local newspaper and drinking coffee, spitting out every other sip. A pretty woman sat behind him, brushing long black hair that fell in a crinkled mass to her knees, both her arms covered with a bestiary of exotic tattoos. The vagabond monkey sat on the roof of their wagon, picking fleas from its scalp.

"Where you heading, mister?" Coley asked him.

"Two shows in Altoona and the season's over," the man said, then sipped and spat again. "After that, we're heading west."

"How far?"

"St. Louis first, then south to San Diego."

"California?"

"All the way."

"Can you use another hand?" Coley asked.

The man looked up from his newspaper and squinted at him.

"I'm good with horses, mister," Coley told him. "I can tend to them better than most."

"We already got all the horse wranglers we can use."

"Then I'll do whatever you need, or learn what needs to be done. I'll work hard and won't get underfoot. When we get to San Diego and you want to cut me loose, I'm as good as gone. And it won't cost you a penny, unless you want to pay," he added.

The man stared at him and then up at the hill. "You come committed, sonny?"

Coley turned and saw Pearl standing there with her hip cocked, the baby resting against it as she swayed back and forth. "I don't know," he said.

"Well, figure it out. We leave in an hour."

Coley grinned and ran back to Pearl, who was smiling happily, watching two men with long, thin sticks coax the elephants out of the creek. He stood in front of her and gently took her elbow. "They're going to California."

"So?"

"I'm going with them."

"What?" she said, pulling away.

"I ain't gonna stay here to find out what happened to Mickey," Coley told her as he walked back toward their wagon, Pearl hurrying along at his side. "I'm going to California like I always said, like I told you before." He glanced at her. "Come with me."

"I ain't going to California," she snorted.

"Why not?"

"I just ain't."

Coley stopped and faced her. "I'll take care of you," he said quietly. "You and the baby."

"You can hardly take care of yourself," Pearl scoffed, spinning away from him. She knew she'd hurt his feelings, but she was too angry to take it back.

Coley jumped in the wagon and grabbed his satchel. He emptied the food that Jane had packed for them, and the glass bottle of milk, and unfolded his own bindle to retrieve the money he'd saved. "Take this," he said as he folded a handful of bills into Pearl's hand. "And the wagon."

"What are you doing?"

"I'm doing what I said. I'm going to California."

"You're going to leave me?"

"Only if you don't want to come."

"I told you I ain't going anywhere. I got my family here."

"You can write them," Coley said, pressing her. "Tell them how you're doing."

"Won't need to. I ain't doing anything," she said firmly.

"And anytime you're not happy, from tomorrow to next month, I'll turn right around and bring you home."

She shook her head.

Coley hoisted his bindle and transferred Pinch to his inside pocket, then stood there waiting for Pearl to look at him. "I told you once before I'd watch out for you, and I meant it then and I mean it now. And you know I can."

She hugged Moses to her chest and rocked him.

"I got a place to stay in Los Angeles and there's nothing to stop us."

She still refused to look at him.

"This is your chance, too, Pearl," he told her. "You don't get that many of them."

"I ain't going."

"Well, I am."

"You're going to leave me?" she asked again to his back, but he didn't turn to answer.

Pearl held her ground as he walked away. She looked at the road that led back to Jug Hill, then at the circus wagons heading to a world she didn't know. She looked at the baby asleep in her arms. Finally, she looked back at Coley and shouted his name.

⌘

THE BARN WAS still smoldering at daybreak, thin traces of smoke rising into the slate sky. Only the four center posts remained standing, each thick as a ship's mast. The mastodon skeleton was intact, its bones and tusks singed a deeper bronze. Standing exposed in the open air, it seemed enormous, a beast returned to the wilderness.

Will stood on the scorched grass and looked at the rubble. His great-grandfather had raised the barn before he built the house, living with his wife and child and livestock in the first permanent Harp structure in the Clove. And it was permanence Will thought of that morning, the durability of things, the fixedness of a place alive not just in mind but in mortar and stone, constructed on a landscape that had supported his family for over a hundred years and now sheltered their bones.

He watched Arthur walk through the debris, taking in the detail of ruin, the sunlight on floating smoke, the crafted nubs of charred timber. Rump was at his heels, sniffing everything, his snout black with soot.

He glanced down at his own filth-stained clothes, his arms streaked with sweat and ash. He'd spent the last year avoiding decisions that now came easily to him. He would clean up the mastodon and rebuild the barn. He would fence off the swamp and buy more cows to graze on the land he'd bought from Vandeman. He would come home.

He turned to look at the wagon in front of the house. Jane stood beside it, and Mickey's body, shrouded in a sheet, was in the back. She'd cried when he told her what had happened, and she sat like a stone by her brother's side throughout the long night.

There was too much grieving in the world. He looked back at the mastodon standing in the wreckage of the fire, just more bones pulled from the earth, and realized that in the last three months he'd built a monster of his own. It was a formidable task and had carried him through a long, hard time, but it was over now, done.

The wind shifted and the smoke began to drift west toward the Shawangunk Range. Will turned from it and walked back to the farmhouse, to Jane.

ACKNOWLEDGMENTS

I wish to thank Gary Fisketjon, Amanda Urban, Robert Larsen, Robert Feranec and Emily Milder, all of whom were generous with their efforts to bring this work to fruition; and my parents, Abby and Norman Murkoff, for a lifetime of encouragement.

And Suzanne, whose loving support makes all things possible.

A NOTE ABOUT THE AUTHOR

Bruce Murkoff is the author of the novel *Waterborne*. He spent many years in California, and now lives in Stone Ridge, New York, with his wife, Suzanne Caporael.

A NOTE ON THE TYPE

The text of this book was composed in Trump Mediæval, designed
by Professor Georg Trump (1896–1985) in the mid-1950s.

Composed by Creative Graphics, Allentown, Pennsylvania
Printed and bound by Berryville Graphics, Berryville, Virginia
Book design by Robert C. Olsson